A Rose For Rose

By Lenny Williams

ALSO BY LENNY WILLIAMS

She's Divine

The Loner & The Goth

The Loner & The Goth: Venus Strikes Back

Asha: The Princess of Matana

DEDICATION

This book is dedicated to everyone with a passion. Never give up on your dreams.

Many people believe that true love exists, but, as far as I'm concerned, true love is nothing but a crock of shit.
                                        -Eddie Valentine

PART ONE
EVERYTHING CHANGED

CHAPTER ONE

December 1ˢᵗ

I t's a busy December night at the Blue River Mall, and I would rather be home in bed but tonight, I have a duty to fulfill. And that duty requires me to be responsible for babysitting an engagement ring. I guess this comes with the perks of being selected as the best man for your friend's future wedding, a role that I've been prepared for since freshman year of college. I'm currently at Kay Jewelers trying to focus on the conversation my friend, Xavier, and the jeweler are having. I believe they're discussing something about ring insurance . . . well at least they were a minute ago. I'm clearly distracted by the smell of cream cheese layered cinnamon rolls at the Cinnabon across the hall from us.

"Fuck yeah," Xavier exclaims, bringing my attention back to him and the jeweler. "You see this, Eddie!" Xavier is holding up a huge diamond encrusted ring he just bought for his girlfriend, Jennifer.

"Yeah, it's nice," I tell him.

Xavier has been telling me about this ring for weeks.

After finally seeing it in person, I can see what all the hype is about. The diamond is almost the size of a golf ball and it's sparkling all over the damn place.

"What! This shit is more than nice. It's magnificent! This is the ring that caught her eye last month when we were here. I'm not gonna lie, this baby right here was mad expensive, but it's about to change my life forever," he says, continuing to hold it up in the air, mesmerized by its translucent glow.

"Yeah, I bet it was expensive, man. You need to stop holding it in the air like that before we get robbed. How much did that thing cost anyway?"

Xavier shakes his head. "Five-thousand dollars," he mutters.

My eyes automatically widen after hearing that price. "Holy shit, man, five-thousand dollars. Are you crazy? Jen will kill you if she finds out you spent that much on a ring. You two are saving up for the baby on the way, remember?"

Xavier was always a short guy in height, but his confidence is bigger than Mount Everest and his persistence is stronger than gravity. Most people say he has a Napoleon complex, but I think it's determination. Once my friend has his mind set on something, there's no stopping him or changing his mind.

"Nah, I'm not crazy." He stomps his foot on the ground. "Well I might be a little crazy; but Jen better not focus on how much I spent on this ring, all that matters is that I'm proposing to her. I'm doing a monthly payment plan anyway for five-hundred a month."

"Okay, cool, do you need me to help you out with the monthly payments? Because I can if you need me to."

Xavier stomps his foot to the ground once more. It's kind of hilarious. "Nah, man, I don't need help! I'm not a little bitch. I'm a grown man. My barbershop money is doing just fine."

There's that Napoleon complex kicking in, I guess. Maybe he does have a bit of that running in his system.

"Alright, I understand, my bad, man."

"You're all good, thanks for looking out for me though, bro. Just keep promoting my barbershop page the way you always do on social media. It's really bringing in a lot of customers for me."

"No problem, and hey, when it's all said and done, I think Jen's going to love the ring. You don't even have to worry about her crying during the proposal. She's going to cry from the glowing diamond alone."

Xavier starts clapping like I just finished preaching a sermon. "That's what I'm talking about! That's exactly the reaction I'm looking for! I can't wait till Christmas eve! Jen deserves this shit. And you have to make sure you do your best to not lose this ring, bro. Please hide it somewhere safe until the 24th."

"I gotcha. Trust me."

"Okay, you gotta excuse me, I'm just excited, that's all."

"I'm excited for you too! Man, I can only imagine how the wedding is going to be. You two have been together since freshman year of college so I know you're going to go all out."

Xavier nods. "Ya damn right we are! And Eddie, don't get mad, but I just noticed something, bro."

Aw man what the fuck is he about to say.

Every time Xavier tells me, *he just noticed something,* it's always something about me that's not directed in a positive light.

"What's up?" I ask.

"I'm noticing that everybody in our crew is either married or getting married soon. Chris is married to Hannah and I'm getting married to Jen. Everyone is in a happy and committed relationship except for you, bro. You're the only single one left so we need to find you a wife ASAP."

All I can do is laugh and say, "Nah, man, fuck that shit. I'm happy doing what I do now. Why are you always trying to get me hitched up?"

Xavier shakes his head and looks at me as if I was disappointing him. "Because we're twenty-nine years old now. It's time for you to make that change in life and find a wife."

I shrug my shoulders because that didn't mean a damn thing to me. "So! What are you, my dad? Yeah I'm twenty-nine but I'm still in my prime! You guys have to get out of this societal pressure bullshit. You and Chris act like us turning thirty next year will be the death of us. Do you realize we're just getting started when it comes to life in general? Hell, now that I think about it, I'll probably settle down when I'm in my fifties. That actor, Shemar Moore, just had a kid and he's fifty-two years old...I can do the same thing."

Xavier pretty much rejects everything I explained. "Nah, that's not the look, Eddie, if you choose to have a child in your fifties, you'll be heading toward your deathbed by the time your child starts experiencing life. And honestly, bro, when it comes to life, don't you think you're being selfish?"

Holy fuck balls, man, I can't believe what I'm hearing right now. "Me....motherfucker, you're calling me selfish, when it comes to life? The same person who gives free books and toys to kids in hospitals. The same guy who donates to cancer research and the humane society," I snap back while laughing at him. And I'm not trying to sound narcissistic or anything, but I don't think I have a selfish bone in my body.

Xavier has always been like a brother to me since our undergrad days; especially since I never had a brother and only have one sister. So it's always easy for us to cuss each other out jokingly.

He holds his hands up in the air, insinuating he's done with our debate, but I know he's not.

"Okay, okay, okay, maybe selfish was the wrong word to use," he says.

"Ya damn right it was! Look man everything's fine with me. The women that satisfy me are doing a great job."

Xavier shamefully shakes his head at me and chuckles. "Seriously, Eddie, how long are you going to keep flying to Brazil and Las Vegas to have sex with hookers? You have to be tired of that shit by now. You've been doing it for three years."

I tap my chin and think about his question before finally saying, "Um, let me think...probably for the rest of my life or as long as I need to. You know what I love about hookers?"

"What?"

"They don't give me stress, they don't nag me about any and every fucking thing, they don't post about what we're going through for the whole world to see and lastly, they don't give me mixed signals. I just do my job and they do theirs! It's a fair business exchange! That's how I keep my focus and stay goal-oriented," I explain.

I guess the explanation I give Xavier doesn't help because he's looking at me like I'm psychotic.

"Of course it's a fair business exchange . . . it's prostitution you smart ass." He laughs.

I wave him off and say, "Well, I prefer to call it a *business exchange*. The women I've met at the brothels in Las Vegas and specifically in Rio de Janeiro, Brazil, have provided me with top-tier fucking. And at least I'm only doing it in those two areas. I don't do anything else but work on my craft or hang out with you guys when I'm here in Delaware."

Xavier holds his hands up once more, signaling that he's officially ending our debate. I believe him this time.

"Okay, whatever you say, bro. I'm just looking out for you for real. I know you told me before that you were using protection with these women and all, but don't call me if you end up catching aids or some shit. I'm not gonna know what to tell my kids if their Uncle Eddie suddenly drops dead one day in the middle of a tropical rainforest with exploded balls." He jokes.

Xavier and I start laughing our asses off after he says that. While I try to calm myself down from all the silliness, out of the blue, a gorgeous woman walks right past us. And I'm talking about *drop dead gorgeous,* this woman right here is fine as fuck! She's holding a few wrapped gifts in her hands that are stacked on top of each other. And she's doing her best to balance the gifts while making her way to the line at Cinnabon.

At that moment, Xavier starts tapping me on my forearm as we do our best not to obviously stare at her.

"Good God Almighty! Yo, Eddie, I know you see that sexy ass woman standing in line at the Cinnabon right now."

I shrug and say, "Yeah I see her. And yup, she's sexy alright but, hey, it's probably best if we leave it at that."

"Um nah I don't think so. That woman over there is a dime-piece who's in your proximity right now. And you're single! That means you should go over there and talk to her," Xavier insists.

"Nope, I'm good."

Xavier instantly begins speed walking in mini circles, trying not to spazz out on me. He then places his hands together and jumps right in front of me. "Oh my fucking god, bro! I swear to God, I'm about to yell at the top of my lungs. Like damn, you can at least say *something* to her. Look at her, she's clearly here at the mall by herself! You should go over there right away! It ain't nothing wrong with testing the waters."

For a moment, I think about what Xavier is saying

and take my time to look at this woman. As she waits in line, I'm able to grasp my own idea of her. She's obviously a stylish woman from what I can see. She's wearing a thin gold necklace, a black sweater, black leather knee-high boots, and a light tan peacoat that's halfway open. And goddamn, she looks good rocking that outfit too! The woman then tucks her long curly black hair behind her ear to answer the phone. As she starts talking on the phone, she instantly smiles.

Well, I think I have my answer based on that single action alone. If she's smiling like that when she's on the phone, then she's definitely taken. I may be over thinking it, but I'm definitely not risking it.

After coming up with my own conclusion, I turn to Xavier, preparing to disappoint him with my response. "Nah, man, look at her! She most likely has a boyfriend, and she probably doesn't want to be bothered. And I damn sure don't feel like wasting my time right now. I have a book and film projects to work on."

Xavier's head almost explodes. "Hold on man, I know you said you're not looking for a wife *right now,* but hear me out, that could be your wife standing right there! On top of that, if you don't say anything to her, then I'm gonna lose some respect for you, bro. And we've been boys since freshman year. So don't make me lose respect for you."

Xavier thinks his reverse psychology method is going to get me to react, but it's not working. He's not the only one who's been trying to set me up with random women recently. Chris continuously tries hooking me up with my so-called future wives. And I feel like my mother calls me just about every week to tell me she's found the perfect girl for me. I wish I could just tell her that the perfect girls for me are hookers. But she'd go fucking crazy if I said that. My whole family would.

I shrug again and say, "Oh well, man, fuck it. I guess you have to lose some respect for me then. Like I told you, I'm not wasting my time trying to get at her."

Xavier sighs. "Your name is Eddie Valentine the Fourth! That name alone can drop Meagan Good's panties. You used to take advantage of your name! Like, damn, bro, what happened to the Eddie I went to college with? You were the man on campus, always on the hunt. Now you don't even bother chasing women anymore, you just pay for the shit. Did your last relationship fuck you up that bad?"

I have no idea why Xavier just asked me that when he already knows the answer.

"Of course it did, dumbass! You already know that. I was going to marry that stupid bitch before finding out about all the shit she was doing. How many times do I have to explain this? And newsflash, you spend more money on a relationship and less money on a *business exchange.*"

Xavier laughs and puts the ring box the jeweler hands him in a mini shopping bag. "Dang, my fault, man, sometimes I forget how damaging that was for you. I'll do you a favor now and will *officially* shut up about the relationship stuff. We can talk about football or something because you wouldn't be able to get that girl over there anyway. She's probably out of your league to be honest."

Man, why did he have to go and say that shit. Hearing the words *out of my league* hit me right in the ego. Xavier knows exactly what he's doing. There's no way I'm backing down now. I have no clue if this ravishing woman standing in line is in a relationship or not, but I have enough self-confidence to approach her. Whatever happens—*happens*, all I know is that I'm up for the challenge now!

"Oh okay, you got me, bro. That one stung a little bit, now watch me go over there and get her number," I tell him.

CHAPTER TWO

After the woman receives her order from Cinnabon, she struggles to hold onto the three gifts she has while grabbing her food and drink from the cashier. At that moment, one of the gifts drops on the floor. I use that opportunity to quickly swoop in and pick up the gift for her. It's a medium-sized box wrapped in green wrapping paper, and it's a little heavy too. She greets me with a smile as I hand her the gift back. And, my God, this woman has such an enchanting smile with hypnotic round eyes. Not only do her eyes pull me in, but her sweet fragrance does as well, causing me to stand a little closer than a normal stranger would.

Damn, let me step back, I don't want to seem like a weirdo.

"Oh my god, thank you so much," she says, gently taking the gift back.

Her voice is light and pleasant, and she's looking me in the eyes with a joyful gaze. Attempting to get this woman's number won't be so bad after all. I just have to find a way to make small talk.

I finally smile back at her and say, "You're welcome,

I see you have your hands full. I haven't seen Blue River Mall this full since high school. It's normally a ghost town in here."

The woman giggles as we take a few steps away from the line so we wouldn't hold up people waiting on their orders. "Yes, that's so true. I heard there was barely anyone here last week during Black Friday. But to be honest, that's why I like coming here." She places the gifts and her food on a table we're standing near. Subsequently, she squints at me while tilting her head. I'm not quite sure why she's staring at me like this.

"Is everything alright? Do I have a pimple on my face or something?" I joke, hoping that there isn't shit on my face.

She giggles and rubs the back of her neck. "Oh no, sorry, but if I'm not mistaken, you had a book signing here last year, right? I think I saw a few posters with your face on it at the time."

"Yeah, I did, that was me," I humbly tell her. "My name is Eddie by the way." I formally introduce myself, gently shaking her soft hand.

The woman smiles at me again. Damn, that smile of hers almost causes me to melt. She's pretty and all, but I need to keep my head together and focus. All I need to do is get her number and get this challenge over with.

"Hi Eddie, I'm Rose, and that's so cool, I never met an author in person before. I'll have to get around to reading that book you released last year. It was a romance novel, right?"

"Yeah, I guess you can say it was a romance-comedy

with a lot of action. It was called, *My Girlfriend's A Vampire*."

Rose snaps her fingers. "Oh yeah, that's right, that's such an intriguing title too! And you know what? Now that I think about it, I also recognize your face from Instagram."

My heart skips a beat. "Really?"

"Yes! Are you Emma Valentine's older brother?"

Whoa! She just said my sister's name. Where does she know my sister from?

"Yeah, I am. How do you know Emma?"

"My sister, Aida, and I went to high school with her. I was a junior during their freshman year, but we used to all cheerlead together. I probably even saw you at the graduation ceremony when our sisters graduated together. Oh and can I just say that your family has the coolest last name ever! I'm so jealous, like I would die to have a last name like Valentine," Rose explains, continuing to stare me directly in the eyes with joy.

Dammit! My sister should've hooked me up with this goddess years ago.

"Yeah, I guess we got lucky to have a last name like that. And wow, you used to cheer with my sister? That means you went to Oakville High then. Emma said you guys were always served a gourmet breakfast and lunch, since you had actual chefs."

Rose smirks and strokes her long dark hair as she ponders. "She's right, we were! My favorite meal was the lemon risotto. It always came with asparagus and shrimp. My goodness, I miss it so much! I can't even find any restaurants in our area that make it. But that was one of the reasons I loved going to a private school like Oakville."

I nod, agreeing with her. "Yes indeed, you guys had it made over there."

She shrugs and grins at me before asking, "So, where did you go to high school?"

"Well, I didn't have the luxury of going to a private school like you and my sister did. I attended Bill Pickett High," I answer.

Rose covers her mouth as if she's trying to prevent herself from laughing.

Sheesh! Was my high school's reputation that bad?

Bill Pickett High wasn't as great as Oakville, but it was far from the worst high school in Delaware. We were an average mediocre school with the same pros and cons as any other school. *I thought.*

"No way," Rose finally responds. "Now I heard you guys were served McDonalds for breakfast and lunch every day. And I heard the students there used to have sex in the stairways. I could go on for days about the things I heard. There were nonstop rumors about that school."

I laugh as I palm my forehead and shake my head.

You know what, maybe Bill Pickett High was the worst high school in Delaware.

"Were most of those rumors true?"

"Yeah, the part about students having sex in the stairways is true."

"Ew," Rose grimaces. "What was up with that

place?"

"I have no idea. The students who were caught doing that were automatically expelled though. Even back then I could never imagine putting myself in that position. That's wild as fuck."

Rose beams at me. "Well, I'm glad to hear you never put yourself in that situation. That means you were one of the good ones."

"Yeah, I guess you can say that. But when it comes to that McDonalds part you mentioned, we didn't get it every day, only Thursdays and Fridays. But that contract with McDonald's was canceled by our senior year when they started implementing mandatory healthy lunches in schools," I reveal.

Rose raises her eyebrows as she smiles and says, "That means you and I are the same age because I remember that national announcement happening during my senior year too. Did you graduate in 2012?"

I nod. "Yeah, I did. I'm part of the 2012 class."

"Oh wow, so am I! I know those mandatory healthy lunches must've been a bummer for you guys at Bill Pickett."

"It was for a while but, after that, I started packing my lunch because I'll be damned if I was going to eat some shit like lettuce and carrots every day. But I understand why the healthy lunches had to happen. They couldn't have students dropping dead from heart-attacks in the middle of a school day."

Rose briefly giggles again, grinning at me as awkward silence is building up. But based on her body language, I can tell she wants our conversation to continue. Within this short time of talking to her, I notice there's something about her aura that I like. And I'm seriously not trying to put myself in a position to fall for this woman. However, it seems like she's naturally sweet and has a heart of gold. I can't allow this awkward silence to build up any longer, so I quickly say the next thing that comes to my mind.

"So...I know this is straightforward and all, but are you taken?" I ask, hoping she says no.

"No, I'm single," she answers, keeping her grin.

"Well, can I have you?"

Rose's entire face turns red, and her smile grows wider. She covers her mouth and says, "Did you just ask if you could have me?"

I nod. "Yeah, do you need me to say it again?"

She's now curling her hair with her index finger and barely looking me in the eyes. Her smile still remains though. "Oh my god, I don't even know what to say."

At least she didn't say no. Alright now let me tell her I'm just joking.

"Hey I'm kidding around. You do seem like a cool person, and since tomorrow is Saturday, I think it would be fun if I took you out, if you don't have any plans."

And just like that, my lips move faster than my brain. Do I seriously wanna take her out and throw away my fun and peace? The last time I took some random girl out, all it did was add stress to my life.

Rose snickers. "Ooo, you had me there. You're clever. And I would like that," she replies as she bites her lip and ponders. "Off the top of my head I don't know what time I'll be free, since I'll be DoorDashing for a while tomorrow."

She's probably lying, just go ahead and leave her alone.

I ignore my thoughts. I can't leave her alone, I actually like communicating with her. "That's fine, maybe next time. How is it, doing DoorDash by the way? Is it something you do full-time?"

"Oh god no. It's just something I do on the side to get extra money in my pocket. I'm a kindergarten teacher full-time and, unfortunately, with my teaching salary I wasn't able to buy all the gifts I wanted to get for my family. So now I have to try and earn more money tomorrow. Thankfully, Christmas is three and a half weeks away."

"Shoot, it's all good, I get it. You teachers deserve way more for everything you do."

"Aw, thank you." Rose takes a sip of her drink and starts to twiddle her thumbs after she puts the drink back down. "Hey, would you be okay if I called you tomorrow, while I'm out DoorDashing? I don't know what it is, but I enjoy talking to you."

I guess we're on the same page.

Rose is putting me under a spell with every gaze. Hopefully, I'm not blushing right now. "Yeah, that's fine by me. I'll give you my number and you can hit me up whenever you want tomorrow."

"Awesome, we're going to turn my boring drive into a fun one," she says.

After hearing Rose's response, all of a sudden the

word *opportunity* struck my mind again like lightning.

"Well hey, if it's okay with you, I can actually give you a hand tomorrow. That way you can earn extra money and we would be hanging out in person. Besides, I heard that having someone help you DoorDash makes the process go much smoother, rather than when you're doing it by yourself," I explain to her.

I only know that bit of information from helping Xavier DoorDash while we were in college.

Rose blushes and rubs her hands together. "Aw! You're so sweet. Would you really do that? That sounds way more fun. I've never been on a DoorDash date before."

"And neither have I, but I'll gladly do this with you. If you feel comfortable with it, I'm all in. You can even bring a friend or a relative with you if you want. I know we just met so the last thing I want to do is creep you out," I inform her.

I believe Rose wants to say *yes* right away but she's trying to play it cool and acts like she still has to think about it. She bites her lip and looks up at the mall ceiling as she briefly thinks about my offer.

After making a decision in her mind, she nods and says, "Alright then, it's a date! I guess you can meet me at the Taco Bell across the street from the mall around nine a.m."

I literally just sat here and broke all the rules I set for myself after that vicious breakup. I haven't been on a date in three years, and I haven't slept with a non-hooker in three years. I told myself to never go on a date again until my 40s, and to continue to sleep around with my Vegas and Brazilian hookers until my 50s. At that point in my life, I figured I would finally be ready to settle down. But this Rose girl has me breaking a routine I've grown accustomed to. My mind is telling me that this is a bad idea, but that doesn't stop me from smirking at her and saying, "Okay, cool, I'll meet you at the Taco Bell around nine a.m."

"Great! Oh, and Eddie?"

"Yeah."

"Thank you for offering to help me out," Rose says as she tries to pick up her gifts from the table.

"No problem." I notice she's struggling with holding her gifts and food again. "Are you going to be okay with carrying everything to your car? It looked like you were struggling earlier."

Rose grins at me and runs her fingers through her hair. "You know what, yeah, I'm going to need your help. And let me make sure I get your number, too, so I won't forget to call you." She hands me her phone.

After I type my number in her phone, she calls it so I can have her number saved as well. I then pick up the three gifts she has and walk with her toward the exit. As I use my back to hold the door for her, I randomly get a phone call from Xavier.

"Hello," I answer.

"Fuck yeah, that's my guy! I saw y'all exchanging numbers over there by Cinnabon, now you're walking her outside. That's the Eddie I know! Good shit my boy," Xavier exclaims.

I shake my head and crack the fuck up. "Man, you were watching the whole time? Go ahead somewhere! I'll hit you up later, bro."

"Hold on! You still have to come get the engagement ring so you can hide it at your house for the time being," Xavier reminds me.

"Oh shit, that's right! Look, I'll come right back in the mall and get it from you when I finish helping Rose get these things in her car."

"Aw shit, my boy, you're already at a first-name basis?"

"I'm hanging up now, man."

After hanging up the phone, I catch up with Rose and watch her open up the trunk of her silver Toyota Corolla. "You can place the gifts in here," she says.

"Gotcha." I place the gifts in the trunk of her car. "Alright, it looks like you're all set. Before you know it, you'll probably be finished Christmas shopping by next week."

She grins and shuts the trunk. "I hope so, and thanks again for your help! Have you gotten any Christmas shopping done lately?"

"Yup, I was able to get all of my shopping done in October. I'm just hanging here with my friend as he gets some shopping done for his family," I respond.

"Lucky you and, aw, you're a good friend. Well, I'm not going to hold you guys up any longer. I'll see you at nine." Rose gives me a quick hug, and I think I recognize that fragrance as Flowerbomb.

"Okay, I'll be up and ready."

"You better be." She waves goodbye to me before getting in her car and driving off.

Damn, girl, you just made my day with your sexy ass!

CHAPTER THREE

December 2ⁿᵈ

I t's nine a.m. the following morning, and I'm parked at the Taco Bell across the street from Blue River Mall. Seconds later, Rose enters the Taco Bell parking lot, pulling up in the space right beside me. As I approach her car, she grins and waves at me. Man, it's something about that stunning smile of hers that has me hooked! I barely know this woman and she already has me under a spell. I need to get it together, play it cool, and not catch feelings this damn fast. But in the back of my mind, I sense there's a strong possibility Rose may be different from the other ravishing women I've came across in the past. She doesn't seem stuck up or boujee. At the same time, I need to remind myself this most likely won't go anywhere.

"Hey, Eddie, how are you? Do you want some coffee or anything?" She asks as I open her car door to hop in.

I went from walking out into the blistering cold, to stepping inside a toaster oven.

"Hey, Rose, I'm doing good and no thanks, I'm

already energized," I say, as we hug briefly. "It's pretty warm in here I see."

"Oh sorry, is it too hot in here for you?"

"No, not at all, it feels good. Shoot, it's freezing outside and a little icy on some of the roads. I can drive us around in my car if you'd like."

Rose smirks and kindly shakes her head. "Nah, that's okay, really, I like the feeling of driving my own car during these DoorDash trips, you know what I mean? Thank you though."

"I understand. Well, I'm definitely going to make sure I'm useful to you during this trip somehow."

"Yes, you sure are, Mr. Valentine! Do you think you can do me a favor and download the DoorDash app on your phone, too, so I can sign in under my account? That way I can receive orders through your phone and my phone. You can sign out of it whenever you're prepared to call it a day."

I pull out my phone and download the app. "Sounds good to me, and I'm not calling it a day until we make sure you get all the money you need for Christmas. How much are you trying to earn today?"

"I would love to earn $350 today. If I were to earn that much then I wouldn't even have to worry about doing this next week, but I doubt we'll make that much. This food delivery service stuff is iffy," Rose explains.

During my college days, Xavier and I would rack up $400 in a day with ease doing DoorDash, so getting the amount Rose wants should be a breeze.

"Hey, guess what? We're going to get you that $350

today," I inform her.

"Ya think so?"

"I know so! I used to DoorDash in college with my friends for extra cash. This will be a piece of cake."

Rose hugs me once more, but it's much tighter this time. "Well, thank you in advance!" Her caramel eyes sparkle with bliss.

Oh for fuck sake, just turn my playboy card in now.

Man, I would gladly give Rose the $350 she needs from my own account, but I'm not dumb. That would be an automatic red flag for her and for myself on a personal level. Those are the type of actions that women call *love* bombing. And I'll be damned if I make myself look like some love bombing lunatic to this woman. It's best if I help her earn the money instead.

≈

The first two hours of Rose and I doing this DoorDash trip goes smoothly. We're making small talk about our favorite things to do and what high school and college was like for us. In between that small talk, we listen and sing along to every radio station that's playing a hit song we like, whether it's R&B, country, pop, rock, rap, or even Christmas songs. No matter what it is, we're blasting it!

During each stop, we briefly pause our mini concert so I can rush into the restaurants or diners to pick up the orders, and rush to the homes or apartments to drop the orders off. I persuade Rose to stay in the car to keep it warm and running, as she accepts multiple orders from both of our phones. Because of that, the orders were coming in nonstop.

As I hop back in the car after delivering our twentieth order, Rose's face lights up. "Wow, surprisingly we earned $250 in two hours! That's amazing, you weren't kidding when you said we could earn a lot today. Having two people really does help."

"I told you it would! We're on our way to getting this $350 for you. All we need is one more hour and we should be good."

Rose playfully taps her steering wheel with both hands and says, "That's perfect!"

As we prepare to make more money, Rose turns the music down. "Hey, I hope this isn't too personal, but how come you aren't married with kids right now? Based on your Instagram you seem put together, you have a great career, and you're not socially awkward. Are you a serial killer like that character Joe Goldberg from the show, *YOU*?" she says jokingly.

I chuckle with her and shake my head. "Oh hell no, not at all. To be honest, it was always little things that didn't work in my past relationships. The overall chemistry wouldn't be there and I don't like forcing things to work. If there's no spark, then I don't bother. And if the relationship seems like it's over, then it's *truly* over in my opinion. But the relationship I was in three years ago with this one girl, truly fucked me up. I thought I was going to marry her, and have a family with her, but it didn't work out," I reveal.

Rose rubs her hands together. "Ooo give me the details on this. I want to hear more."

"Nah, I don't know about that. I'm not a guy who gossips and it's a long story anyway and it might bore you. And furthermore, I don't like to vent. I'm not trying to sound like some punk ass dude whining about his ex."

Rose giggles in between plopping her head back onto her seat. "Oh come on, Eddie, please. What if we happen to be on the road for a couple more hours rather than one hour. I can seriously listen to you talk nonstop. I like the sound of your voice."

It felt good hearing her say that, but I still didn't want to talk about my ex.

"My ex isn't worth the two hours. Let me hear more about your job and your students." I try switching topics.

"Here's everything you need to know about my occupation. I love being a teacher and I love my students, the end," Rose says with her killer smile. "How about this, I'll tell you what happened in my last relationship first, and then you can tell me what happened in yours....do we have a deal?" She holds out her hand for me to shake.

"Wow! You really want to hear this story, huh?" I ask her.

"Yes! I'm curious to know what went down." She's now giving me puppy dog eyes and I can't resist them

"Shit...okay with your pretty ass, we have a deal." I agree, softly shaking her hand.

"Yes! Finally!"

"Alright, since you're going first, let me do the

honors of asking you what you asked me. So Rose, how come you aren't married with kids right now? You seem put together, you have a great career, and you're not socially awkward. What's going on?" I jokingly ask her, making her laugh.

Rose suddenly takes a deep breath and gathers herself to explain her story. "I was actually proposed to and happily engaged a few years ago. My ex-boyfriend, Raymond, and I were together for six years, but shortly after that proposal.... I ended up finding out that he was sleeping with a woman he worked with."

Without notice, Rose pauses, doing her best not to get choked up.

I touch her shoulder to provide her with some comfort. "Hey, you don't have to go on with this story if you don't want to."

"No, I'm fine, I wanna get this out," she insists. "He fell asleep one night, leaving his laptop lying directly on his stomach. The sounds from him getting notifications caused me to wake up. As I sat up, I noticed that the screen light was still on because he left his laptop sitting wide open; there was nothing I could miss. I was going to close it and go back to sleep, but I saw an unread email that was titled: *Our New Sex Tape*. When I opened it up, I saw that it was a video of him fucking the girl he worked with, and they had done this on multiple occasions. There was an entire thread of them having sex together."

"Jesus Christ, that's messed up."

"Right! And what makes it even more messed up is I met this woman on multiple occasions. Since she was one of his work friends, she befriended me too. I met and talked with her at their office parties and all. I still can't believe all the messages and sex tapes he made with her throughout that time we were together. During that time, he would always tell me I was his one and only, but that was a crock of shit. After discovering what he did to me, I gave him the engagement ring back and left him for good. I was so disgusted that night, I ended up vomiting a couple times. He then ended up marrying that same woman and having a baby with her too. That dickhead was the man I thought I was going to be with for the rest of my life. Six years down the drain, just like that! My trust level has never been the same since."

Tears begin to fill Rose's eyes. I can tell her emotional wounds aren't completely healed yet. It's making me wonder if she ever went to therapy for it.

"Fuck, I didn't mean to trauma-dump on you. Just so you know, I've been in therapy for the last few years due to everything that happened. And I normally won't tell all my business to a stranger, but you have this energy that makes me want to open up to you. I don't sound psychotic, do I?"

I shake my head. "No, absolutely not."

Rose doesn't seem psychotic to me at all. What she doesn't know is that this happens to me a lot. My friend, Hannah, says it's because I'm an empath, so people don't mind opening up to me even if they don't know me.

"I'm sorry to hear about what you went through, Rose. Nobody deserves to go through something like that. And you know what? Maybe I shouldn't tell my story now. It can't even compare to what you went through," I explain.

Rose wipes the tears that stream down her face and grabs tissues from the glove compartment above my lap. "Nope, we had a deal, Eddie, remember? It's your turn now," she says, doing her best to crack a smile.

I throw my hands in the air. "Alright, alright, to keep it brief I was in a long-distance relationship—"

"—Oh god they never work," Rose intervenes, giggling and drying the rest of her tears.

"Yeah, unfortunately I found that out the hard way."

"What was her name? And I'm sorry for interrupting, I'll make myself shut up now." Rose reaches into the cupholder to take a sip of her mocha latte.

"It's fine. Feel free to stop and ask me any questions you have on this topic. I still have questions about why I allowed myself to go through the bullshit I went through. Her name was Veronica. Like I was saying before, we were in a long-distance relationship. She lived in Rhode Island."

Rose looks surprised, placing her drink back in the cupholder. "Damn, that's pretty far from Delaware!"

At that moment, I have a horrible flashback about the long drives I would take to see Veronica. It makes me sick to my stomach. "Tell me about it; it was a five-hour drive for my dumb ass every weekend."

"How did you guys meet?"

"We connected with each other on Instagram first. She would randomly message me and congratulate me on the books I was publishing. But something was off."

"How so?" Rose wonders.

"Well, based on what I know now, she was actually studying my profile and studying every single one of my posts."

"Whoa! That's creepy! What made you think that?" Rose wonders.

"Because around the time she started messaging me, she would tell me she liked all the same things I liked when it came to sports teams, books, movies, food, colors, and so on. In my mind, I was like nobody has that much in common, and since her profile picture displayed an attractive woman, I thought I was being catfished. Especially since she was messaging me every day. As dudes, we're used to being the ones chasing you, not the other way around."

Rose raises her eyebrows in shock. "Really? So in your history of encounters, not one girl you found attractive messaged you first? I'm only asking because you're really handsome."

"In person they have, but not on social media."

Rose isn't buying it. "I don't know, I find that hard to believe. You're pulling my leg, aren't you?"

"I'm going to prove my point right here. Have you ever randomly messaged a guy that you were interested in, or did you throw little hints by liking his posts, hoping he would message you first?" I ask.

Rose uncontrollably smiles and says, "Okay, I have to admit you got me there. I would throw little hints instead of messaging the guy first."

"Exactly! See, and you're sexy as hell," I admit,

causing Rose to blush. "That's why Veronica seemed like a catfish to me at first, until we finally FaceTimed each other."

"Okay, so it turned out that this Veronica girl wasn't a catfish or a liar?" Rose questions me.

"She wasn't a catfish based on her looks, but she still baited me in by lying about being interested in everything I was *interested in*. I'll get to that later. The point is that, I ended up falling for her."

"Wow, so she must've been beautiful."

"Yup and after that first video chat we would FaceTime each other a couple times a week. This went on for about three months until I finally drove to Rhode Island to see her," I deeply exhale and tighten my fist since I already know how this story ends. "Fuck Veronica though, I can't stand thinking about her."

"Aw, but this story is getting interesting. You have me hooked right now. I have to hear how this played out . . . please," Rose begs.

Of course I give in. It's only right. Rose told me her story, so I don't mind telling mine. Besides, she's so entertained by our conversation, she's ignoring the order requests popping up on both our phones.

"Okay, so when I drove out to Rhode Island to meet her in person for the first time, I thought everything was perfect. Due to FaceTiming her frequently, I always thought she resembled the model, Naomi Campbell, but when I saw her in person, I thought she *really was* Naomi Campbell. That's how beautiful Veronica is. She's a beautiful conniving witch."

Rose laughs. "You're hilarious."

"Anyways, we ended up going to the beach that same day for our first date."

"Ooo did anything happen at the beach?"

I look at Rose with a straight face. "Nope, nothing happened."

Rose chuckles. "Eddie, quit playing, what happened?"

I give in again. "Alright, well we were already so comfortable with each other by then that we held hands and kissed that day. After that first date, we made it official. I was so stupid at that time."

"Aw, we've all been there before. That *stupid* phase is the worst because you're so blinded by infatuation. So, let me guess, this is when the problems start with Miss Rhode Island," Rose says with an intriguing smile.

"You somewhat got that right. Around the ten-month mark of us dating, I could no longer recognize the personality that drew me in. This new version of her would always be upset with me, and would take out all her family issues and work problems on me. She said it was easier to get mad at me for the outside things happening in her life, because she knew I would forgive her. Which still doesn't make any sense to me! But I still stuck with her. Because of all her family problems and work problems, I would drive five hours to see her and stay with her every weekend. I would take her to her favorite restaurant, the beach, buy her new clothes, buy her new books, and I would even massage her to ease her stress. I wanted her to know that I would always be there to make her days better," I explain.

"Goodness gracious! Eddie, you were a prince charming that dropped down from heaven to be there for her. And it seems like she didn't give a damn. Please tell me that she at least appreciated what you were doing for her," Rose says, eagerly waiting for my response.

"I wish I could say she appreciated these things but nope. To add fuel to the fire, one day she even said I was doing the bare minimum and that I wasn't doing extravagant things for her like the men on Instagram did for their girlfriends."

Rose's jaw drops as she suddenly grabs the steering wheel. "She said what!!! Ooo I wanna slap that bitch across the face right now. Everything you were doing for her and she called it the *bare minimum*. You were doing the absolute maximum! And who in the world truly believes those popular Instagram couples are actually happy anyway?"

"Her dumbass did," I reply.

Rose shakes her head. "What an idiot! And who compares their relationships to the relationships they see on social media."

"Her dumbass did," I say again.

Rose finally accepts an order on the DoorDash app and begins to reverse her car out of the parking space. "She was an immature brat . . . Wait, let me be fair first before I continue to insult her. Did she ever drive five hours from Rhode Island to Delaware to come see you? And did she ever treat you to anything special like you did for her?" she asks, driving out of the parking lot and onto the road.

"She was supposed to come to Delaware for my birthday. She even used my phone to call my mom and told her that she couldn't wait to meet her and the rest of my family on my birthday. But on the day of my birthday, she never showed up; even when I offered her a ride, she refused. She said she didn't like how her hair looked that day. And to answer your second question, she never treated me to anything. Apparently, I had to keep proving that I was the one for her."

"Eddie, what the fuck! Please tell me you left her after that?"

"I wish I could say that I did but, unfortunately, I stayed with her. I wanted to prove to Veronica that I was the one for her. So the following month I planned on surprising her during her birthday weekend. I was going to take her to Los Angeles since she'd never been there before and said she always wanted to go."

"Aw, that's sweet! She's a bitch but what you planned on doing was still sweet. But it sounds like that trip to LA didn't happen."

"Phew! I'm glad it didn't happen. I had the plane tickets bought and paid for on the day I arrived at her apartment. I surprised her with flowers, a pink suitcase, and the plane tickets. She was super excited and was going to pack her clothes in that pink suitcase I got her right after taking a shower. But while she was bathing her phone started buzzing nonstop. I was sitting right next to it on the couch. It was her ex-boyfriend texting her as well as some dude on snapchat messaging her."

Rose starts smacking my shoulder, while keeping one hand on the steering wheel. "No way! Your story is almost like my story with Raymond. What did the messages say? Were they sexting?"

I suddenly look at the road as a cat takes off, attempting to sprint across the street in front of the car.

"LOOK OUT!"

"SHIT!" Rose says as she swerves and slams on the brakes, trying to avoid the cat. At that moment, Rose's car begins to slide on the ice, causing her car to do doughnuts across the road.

Holy shit balls, we might crash any second now.

Luckily for us, the car doesn't hit anyone or anything. *We're safe!*

"Are you okay?" I ask, gently touching her shoulder.

Rose looks startled as she looks around. She finally gets around to looking at me and says, "Yeah, I'm okay. Are you?"

I nod. "Yeah, I'm good, I'm gonna step out the car and make sure your tires are still in good condition."

"Ok," she says in between deep breaths.

After checking each tire, I hop back in the car and say, "Your tires are fine, we should be good to drive now. I can drive us if you want to take a break."

Rose starts her car back up. "Thank you, Eddie, I'm still good to drive. So what did those messages say?"

Damn we almost died and she still wants to know about what crazy ass Veronica did to me.

"Um, we're back on that?"

Rose laughs. "Um, yes," she says. "There's a reason

you're known as a great storyteller," she adds, throwing in a compliment to keep me going.

"Well I appreciate that. Veronica's ex messaged her asking her if she was coming over to his place again like the night before. That threw me off, because that meant she was spending the night with him while I was in Delaware during the weekdays."

"No way!"

"Yeah, and the guy on snapchat was sending her dick-pics. . . only because she was sending him nudes too."

"Jeez!!! I can't imagine how you must've felt right then and there," Rose says.

"I was livid," I reply.

"What did you do?"

"When she realized she forgot her phone in the living room, she stormed out of the shower butt ass naked, looking for it. Out of anger, I flipped the couch over and immediately confronted her about the messages and pictures. But she tried to play dumb until I said I was canceling our trip to LA. All of a sudden I was called an ain't shit boyfriend."

"Wow! So the *ain't shit girlfriend* had the nerve to call you that after you caught her cheating."

"Yup and she threw the flowers I brought her that day right in my face. She then said she lied about the things we connected on, and all she wanted was my money. That's when I found out she was studying my profile just to use me. I never spoke to her again after that and I blocked her on every medium we ever communicated on."

"My god, so you were nothing but a side-piece and an ATM to her. She gave no fucks about how you would feel if you ended up getting hurt. I'm so sorry you went through that. I'm surprised you didn't go crazy."

"It's all good, that was my fault for allowing myself to be treated that way. I should've ended that relationship way before I caught her cheating. And just like you, my trust level hasn't been the same since either," I say, realizing the location of the DoorDash order Rose accepted is now a few feet away from us. "Oh look, it looks like we're supposed to head to this diner here on the right side of the road," I add, pointing toward the diner.

"Whoa! I'm so glad you caught that or I would've driven right past it," Rose admits, pulling into the diner's parking lot.

Before I get out of the car, Rose softly touches my hand and says, "Thanks for listening and venting to me. I know you didn't have to do that, but I'm glad you did."

"Oh, no problem. Thank you for doing the same. I usually don't open up to people."

Rose smiles at me and says, "I can tell."

CHAPTER FOUR

Later on, after several DoorDash pickups and deliveries, we finally come across an order that helps us reach the $350 mark.

Rose instantly accepts the order on her phone. "Yay! Eddie, we did it! Thank you so much. I owe you some money now. I wouldn't have been able to do this without you."

I shake my head and gesture to her that I'm fine. "No, you don't owe me anything. I'm just glad I was able to help you. But we have to complete this order first before they cancel it and you lose out on that $350."

"Alright, I kind of don't want this day to end."

"How about we stop and get something to eat together after we pick up and drop off this last order? How's that sound?"

Rose beams at me and says, "That sounds great!"

After picking up the order from a cheesesteak shop, we arrive in a neighborhood surrounded by woods. We're now approaching a colonial style brick house; it reminds me of my grandparents' house. With the light snow fall coming down, it makes the home look majestic.

Up ahead I notice the GPS is leading us to an extremely long driveway. Unfortunately for us, we notice the driveway is covered in ice when Rose's Toyota begins to uncontrollably hydroplane.

"Dang, you would think the people who own this house would put salt down on their driveway," Rose complains.

"Facts! Don't worry about driving more into the driveway, I don't want you to get stuck. You can stop right here. I'll walk on the snow to drop their order off on the porch," I tell her.

"Okay, good idea." Rose puts her car in park.

I grab the bag of food and exit the car, preparing to drop it off at the front porch. While stomping through the non-shoveled walkway, I suddenly hear deep breaths and repeated sounds of something crashing through the snow.

Right after that I hear, "EDDIE WATCH OUT! RUN! THERE'S A DOG!" It's Rose yelling for me to run away from a big ass German Shepherd racing toward me.

After catching a quick glimpse of the dog, I immediately start sprinting toward Rose's car in the driveway. The dog is now barking and growling while sprinting after me. I drop the bag of cheesesteaks on the snow and do my best not to fall, but my Timberland boots are no match for the black ice on the driveway. I eventually slip and fall on the ground.

"Shit, this stupid ice," I snap, trying my best to get

up.

Rose continuously honks her horn to scare the dog off, but it doesn't work. "GO AWAY," she screams, doing whatever she can to help me.

The German Shepherd ignores her cries and bites me on the back of my right thigh. I try my best to smack and kick the dog off of me, but it won't release its grip. "GET OFF OF ME!" Now I'm starting to feel its teeth rip through my thermals and boxer briefs.

I can hear Rose unlock the door and slightly open it. Even though I'm in pain, I don't want Rose to get hurt trying to save me from this crazy ass dog.

"Rose, stay in the car!"

"Okay, but what should I do?" she asks, shutting the door in panic mode.

"Call the number they left on the order. Hopefully the owners are here."

The dog digs his teeth into me some more. And that's it, I've had enough of this fucker. I use my strength to quickly turn on my back. After getting a good look of the German Shepherd, I punch him directly in the ear and kick him in the ribs. The dog releases its grip from me and cries momentarily. As I attempt to get up again, the dog tries to strike me once more. But just in the nick of time two elderly people come outside and speedwalk off their porch as fast as they can. "SEBASTIAN, GET YOUR BUTT BACK IN HERE, BOY," the old man yells.

The dog sprints away from me and runs into the house.

"Finally," I say in relief, sitting up on the ice.

After watching the dog run into the house, Rose quickly steps out of the car to check on me.

"Eddie, are you okay?" She asks me as she caresses my face. She does it so instinctively that I don't think she realizes she's caressing me. I don't mind it at all though. In fact, I like it.

My thigh is hurting like hell, but I don't want Rose to know that. "Yeah, I'm fine. It was just a small bite, nothing too bad."

Rose helps me stand to my feet. "Your wound looks pretty bad," she says, looking at the back of my thigh.

"She's right, young man," the old man says, as he and his wife finally come to my aid.

"We are truly sorry. We didn't mean for that to happen to you," the elderly woman murmurs.

"Yes, I hope there's something we can do for you," her husband adds.

As I look down at my ripped pants and boxers, I instantly want to cuss this elderly couple out. But when I look at the genuine concern on their faces, it's obvious that they're sorry about what happened.

"I appreciate your concern but, I must say, you shouldn't order from a delivery service when your dog is capable of attacking someone. It's really dangerous," I explain to them.

The old man nods and agrees with me. "I understand, young man, you're completely right about that. And again, we apologize for the mishap. Sebastian was always a nice dog but he's been a little aggressive ever since someone broke into our house and pistol whipped him when we weren't home," he reveals to us.

"Aw, I'm sorry to hear that your dog was pistol whipped, but he seems like he's more than a little aggressive," Rose chimes in.

"We're working on getting him back to his old self. And I want you both to know that Sebastian doesn't have rabies either. To show our remorse, my wife, Mildred, and I can take you to our doctor and we'll pay for everything out of pocket. That way you aren't charged," the old man explains.

"I appreciate it, sir, but no thanks. I think I'll just go put ice on it. I should be fine."

Rose taps me on my shoulder and continues to look at my wound. "No, Eddie, you should go, I'll come with you. It'll be safe to make sure no bacteria or viruses got into your system from that bite."

I'm starting to notice that Rose is very nurturing to the point where it's second nature to her. It's making me become more attracted to her by the second.

"Okay. I'll go," I give in.

"Great! I'm Claude Cooper by the way and I'm sorry we had to meet like this," the old man says.

I shake both Mr. and Mrs. Cooper's hands. "It's nice to meet you two. I'm Eddie and this is Rose."

"Hi," Rose says as she greets the couple.

"Very well then, now that we got the proper greeting out of the way, you two can follow us to Blue River Hospital," Mr. Cooper says.

Rose and I hop in the car and follow the couple to

the hospital.

"Is your butt ok?" Rose asks me.

I laugh but deep down, this shit is embarrassing. I can't believe I fell on ice and got bit by a dog on the first date. "Thankfully, my butt is okay, since the dog bit me on the thigh."

I make her laugh. "Oh okay, I don't know why I thought he bit you there. Thank God we're almost at the hospital," she says.

My knees and my back are throbbing from falling on the ice, so I begin to recline my seat back to feel a bit more comfortable. "Alright, I'll be stretched out in this seat until we get there."

CHAPTER FIVE

When we enter the hospital, Mr. Cooper introduces me to an emergency physician, he knows named Dr. Lennon. She's a nice woman who doesn't mind taking care of me right away, thanks to the old man.

"Dr. Lennon, I'm going to need your help today. Do you think you can check out my friend, Eddie's, wounds?" Mr. Cooper asks.

"Sure," Dr. Lennon replies, before turning her chair to me. "So, Eddie, what brings you in today?" she asks.

"Nothing much, I was just bit by a dog, that's all," I tell the doctor.

Mr. Cooper makes sure he does his due diligence to explain the rest. "Unfortunately, since Sebastian is still getting used to people again, he sort of went off the rails today and attacked poor Eddie here while he was delivering food to us."

Dr. Lennon displays a look of sympathy. "Aw man, where did he attack you, specifically?" she asks.

"He bit me on my upper right thigh," I disclose.

It's so weird seeing this many people in one little

hospital room because of me. I keep my hand pressed against my wound to help cover the ripped part of my jeans. And there's no way in hell I'm pulling down my pants while this elderly couple is in here.

Mr. Cooper takes his wife's hand and says, "We're going to wait out in the hall, so you guys can have some privacy. And Dr. Lennon, you can bill this doctor's visit to me too."

"Okey-Dokey, Claude, will do!" Dr. Lennon responds.

I'm still baffled about how good-natured this couple is. It's one thing to apologize for everything that happened, but to go out of their way to come to the hospital, and pay the bill, shows me how compassionate the Coopers are. "Thank you, Mr. & Mrs. Cooper. You're too kind," I tell them.

"Anytime, young man, I want to thank you and your lady friend here for being understanding," Mrs. Cooper says.

Her husband approaches me and hands me a small white envelope. "Here, take this and please keep it," he insists.

I take the envelope and place it in my coat pocket. I'm curious to know what's in it, but I'll wait till we leave the hospital to find out. "Ok," I say, watching the couple leave the room.

Rose softly taps my hand. "I guess I'll step out with them," she whispers. She sounds hesitant.

And by observing her body language, it seems like she doesn't want to wait out in the hall either. She slowly turns away from me, preparing to exit the room.

"Wait." I clutch her hand, stopping her in her tracks. "I want you to stay in here with me," I tell her, gazing into her eyes.

She grins and sits on a chair placed against the wall next to me. "Okay, I'll be right here."

Suddenly, Dr. Lennon approaches me, blocking my view from Rose. "Alright, Eddie, I'm going to need you to turn your back to me, drop your pants, and lay on the exam table," she orders.

I follow the doctor's instructions, and lie face first on the exam table. I'm kind of embarrassed to have my bare ass exposed like this. Thankfully, it's only Rose and Dr. Lennon in here.

"You have a cute butt," Rose utters randomly.

Oh wow, you're stepping it up a notch already, Rose? Hey, I'm not mad at that. Let's see where I can take this then!

I giggle at her comment. "Thanks, hopefully I can see yours soon," I reply.

Due to the longing silence, I'm starting to think I fucked up and overplayed my hand.

Damn, did I ruin the connection already?

When I turn my head to look at her, I notice she's covering her mouth, and laughing her ass off. "We'll see about that, Mr. Valentine," Rose says.

Whew! Luckily she wasn't offended by what I said.

Surprisingly, I hear Dr. Lennon laughing too. I almost forgot she was in here.

"You two are cute," Dr. Lennon says, while examining me. "Okey-Dokey, so luckily you only have a couple bite marks that will heal in a week or two. Your pants and undergarments really protected you. I'm still going to give you a tetanus shot to be on the safe side, and I'm going to clean your wounds too."

Hearing that was such a relief. "Okay, thanks Dr. Lennon."

"You're welcome. I'll be right back," she says.

"Do you want me to pull my pants back up and hop off the exam table?" I ask the doctor.

"No, not yet, just stay like that for me, please."

"Alright," I respond as I continue to lay on the exam table staring at the wall.

When Dr. Lennon exits the office, Rose takes a deep breath and runs her fingers through her hair. "My goodness, if I didn't decide to DoorDash today this would've never happened to you. My bad, Eddie, this is my fault."

I turn my head to look at Rose. "No way. Are you kidding, this isn't your fault. It's Sebastian's fault for biting the shit out of me. Nah, you know what? It's that damn burglar's fault for pistol whipping Sebastian and causing the poor dog to have PTSD in the first place. There's only one thing you're at fault for, and you know what that is?"

"What?" Rose asks.

"You're at fault for showing me a great time today. I would do this day all over again, even if it meant getting bitten by Sebastian again. I like hanging out with you."

Rose turns her face to the window and smiles. It almost looks like she's about to cry. After a few blinks, she turns back around. "I like the way you spun that. That made my day," she says. "I'm glad Mr. and Mrs. Cooper decided to help us out in this way. I rarely come across people like them," she adds.

"Same here! And did you notice that Mr. & Mrs. Cooper kind of resemble Santa Claus and Mrs. Claus, or am I fucking tripping?"

Rose smacks her lap and starts laughing. "Yeah, I did notice that! I was thinking the same thing, like are they in cosplay or something. Mr. Cooper has the white beard, big belly, and deep voice thing going on. And Mrs. Cooper has the big glasses with the grandmotherly look!"

"All they're missing now is reindeer," I jokingly put in.

≈

After Dr. Lennon gives me a tetanus shot and antibiotics ointment, Rose and I thank Mr. & Mrs. Cooper for their hospitality. On our drive back from the hospital, Rose and I listen to Christmas music and talk about how our day went until she finally pulls into the Taco Bell parking lot to drop me off.

"Aw, now I don't want you to go, I had so much fun with you today," Rose tells me.

I feel the same way.

"We did have a good time! That was one heck of a first date, huh?"

Rose laughs. "Yes! That's a first date I'll never forget. Now I'm looking forward to the second one," she adds, hinting that she wants to see me again.

I love how straightforward she is. She knows exactly what she wants and she doesn't give me mixed signals at all. This is the type of woman I've been missing out on.

"Are you free tomorrow?" I ask her.

"Yup I'm free," she responds with that glowing smile of hers.

"Okay cool, let me ask you something. Do you know how to ice-skate? Because it looks like you do."

Rose blushes and nods. "Yeah, I do! How did you know that?"

"Probably because you went to fancy ass Oakville High. So I made an estimated guess. I remember my sister telling me they had an ice-skating rink at that school too."

"That's true, they do. I was always skating there."

"Well, how about we go ice-skating tomorrow. Ya cool with that?" I ask her. "I know we can't break into your old high school and skate, but I can look up some places that have an ice-skating rink."

Rose excitedly places her hands together and says, "Absolutely! You don't have to look up places either, I know the perfect spot. There's an ice-skating rink in my neighborhood called the Prime Ice Arena. I can meet you there at one in the afternoon if that's a good time for you."

"One p.m. is perfect for me." I step out the car and reach into my pocket, suddenly realizing that the envelope Mr. Cooper gave me is still on me. I pull it out and open it to find that there's a $100 bill inside.

Wow Mr. Cooper, *you really are a generous man! I guess I'll keep this cycle of generosity going and give this money to Rose. She needs it more than I do.*

"Oh wow, look, instead of you earning $350 today, you've now earned $450. That's a good days' work in my eyes," I say as I hand Rose the money.

Rose is startled, and, for a moment, she can barely get any words out. "Wait! What, why?"

"This was in the envelope Mr. Cooper gave me. I want to give it to you. And before you say no, I just need you to understand that I don't want it, and the last thing we need is a $100 bill going in the trash, right?"

Rose looks at the bill that's currently in her hands. "But Eddie—"

I cut her off. "—I don't want or need anything in return. If you don't want it, I'll go throw it away. Hopefully a racoon finds the money and takes it to the grocery store to buy food for its homeboys."

Rose cracks up. "Where do you come up with your jokes, you goofball! And okay, you're right, the last place this money should be is in the trash. I'll keep it . . . thank you."

"Good, well, I'll be at the arena tomorrow on time."

"Awesome, I'll see you then."

Before I can close the door all the way, I hear, "Um, did you forget something?" Rose says.

"What did I forget?"

"You forgot to give me a hug. Can I get a hug before you go?"

"Shoot, you don't have to tell me twice. Here I

come."

Rose steps out the car, grinning from ear to ear as she watches me come around to give her a hug. When we meet face-to-face, I give her a strong warm embrace. We've been hugging long enough to the point where I'm going to miss her when I get home. Having great energy and chemistry with someone isn't something you run into every day. Fuck all the rules I came up with three years ago. I have to keep this connection going to see where it leads.

After we let go of each other, Rose looks at me and says, "I'll see you tomorrow."

"Looking forward to it."

Rose hops back into her car and asks, "Are you sure you're going to be okay driving home?"

"Yeah, I'll be fine...my thigh is practically healed already. I just have to throw these boxer briefs and my jeans in the trash when I get home, since I'm out here looking like a hobo." I tug on my ripped jeans and thermals.

"Alright, goofball, drive safe." Rose starts her car.

"You too." I watch her make her way out of the parking lot safely before I take off.

CHAPTER SIX

December 3rd

The next day, I pull up to the Prime Ice Arena at one o'clock on the dot, but Rose is already here before me. When she spots me parked a few feet away from her, she steps out the car, beaming. We're both excited to see each other, and she's looking fine as hell in her pink beanie hat and pink thermal knitted gloves. Rose should seriously consider modeling, because billboards with her face on it would cause traffic jams.

"Hi, Eddie, are you ready?" She asks me, as I step out the car.

"Oh yeah, I was born ready," I tell her.

As we hug each other, Rose repeatedly sniffs my jacket. "Mmm. You smell really good! This is the third day where you smell amazing. What do you have on?"

Hearing a woman say that I smell good never gets old. That shit gives me the biggest confidence boost.

"You think so?"

"Yes!" Rose leans in towards me once more, sniffing

around my neck.

At this point, it's taking everything in me not to caress her hair, grab her by the waist, and kiss her. I'm trying to maintain my self-control, but it doesn't help that she smells delicious too.

Lord help me!

I resist the urge to randomly kiss her, and force myself to shrug and smile. "It's probably because I recently got out of the shower. I use Dove Men's body wash. But you're probably smelling a combination of that and my Versace cologne."

"Mmm, well it's a perfect combination," Rose assures me.

We finally enter the ice arena, and I'm smacked by the cold air inside.

"Shit, it's freezing in here. I would've thought we were still outside," I murmur, hugging myself to keep warm.

"It's not that bad." She laughs.

"That's because you're used to this."

We make our way to the bleachers to get ourselves ready. "Is this going to be your first time ice-skating?"

"Yeah....well no, I went one time with my family when I was eight years-old. And from what I can remember, I was told to bend my knees, push off my right foot and glide, then push off my left foot and glide. That's all I can remember. I think I did okay, even though that was twenty-one years ago," I explain while performing the motion in front of her.

Rose smirks, fighting back her laughter. "Okay, yeah,

that's basically it. I can't wait to see you in action on the ice."

I watch Rose as she pulls her own ice-skates out of her bag. "For a second there, I forgot you're a vet when it comes to this kind of thing. No wonder you brought your own ice-skates. Where do I go in this arena to rent mine?" I ask her.

Rose looks up after placing on one of her skates. "You can rent a pair right at the front desk over there by the vending machine. I can go with you."

"Nah that's okay, you go ahead and finish putting on your skates, with your pretty ass. I'll be right back," I tell her, causing her to smile.

After going to the front desk and ordering rental skates for the hour, I'm surprised when I see Rose already out on the ice. I rush to put on my ice-skates and wave to her.

"Come on, Mr. Valentine, let's see what you got," she says.

Rose skates like an Olympic pro from the middle of the rink, all the way to the entrance of the rink, and reaches for my hand.

I hope I don't embarrass myself in front of her.

I take her hand and step onto the ice, but out of the blue, my ankles begin to wobble. I eventually get it together and keep my ankles stable before Rose catches me struggling.

"I'm going to guide you around the rink," I say with confidence, holding her hand.

"Ooo look at you being a gentleman."

I attempt to skate, but I forget to do all the basic things I learned from the one time I was on the ice at eight years-old. I go from standing straight up to slipping and falling right on my back.

I look up to see Rose doing her best not to laugh, but eventually she breaks and starts cracking the hell up. She's laughing so hard she can barely breathe. I don't even know what to say, but I'm glad I can easily bring a smile to her face. I lie on the ice, smiling at her, and wonder how I got myself in this position. I thought it would be kind of easy to do this ice-skating thing.

After finally taking a deep breath and getting herself together, Rose asks, "Are you okay? This is our second date and this is the second time you've fallen."

"Yeah, I'm good. I don't know how that happened."

Rose tries to help me up, but she starts uncontrollably laughing again as she watches my legs buckle. I manage to get myself up to a standing position, but I'm not stable at all.

"These fucking ice-skates are broke or something," I tell her as my arms flail around to keep my balance.

Rose wipes tears of laughter from her face. "No, it's not the skates, goofball, it's you. Keep your feet steady, Eddie!"

I'll be damned if these skates are going to control me.

Ultimately, I'm able to get myself together and keep my balance. I reach for Rose's hand again. "Okay, I think I got it this time. We can go ahead and skate now," I tell her, pretending like none of the previous embarrassing actions ever happened. "You want to start with our rhythm going from left to right?"

"Yeah, let's try that. Hopefully you won't fall again." She laughs.

Fortunately for me, I get the hang of it. I take the lead and wrap her arm around mine. Now Rose and I are skating in unison.

"Okay, I see you, you're skating like a pro now," Rose says.

"See, all I needed was a few minutes to get myself together."

While continuing to skate together, whenever Rose and I aren't holding hands, she's showing me tricks she learned in school. She's doing jumps, spins, and skating backwards, all while keeping her balance. As I enjoy what I'm seeing, I keep reminding myself not to fall on my ass again.

≈

After our hour is up in the rink, Rose and I grab two cups of hot cocoa and sit in the middle bleachers.

"Eddie, I honestly have to say it's been really fun hanging out with you. I remember at the mall the other day, I mentioned how we both graduated during the same year. So that means you're currently twenty-nine, right?" Rose asks me.

I'm not sure why Rose is asking about my age, but usually when women ask me about my age it leads to zodiac sign questions. In the past, the zodiac sign questions always ended badly. If I never aligned with their moon or sun or some other planetary system bullshit, then they would stop talking to me. Women overthink too much.

"Yup, I'm twenty-nine, what about you?" I ask her.

"Yeah, me too. I'm twenty-nine. What's your sign?"

Aw damn, here we go with this bullshit. I guess I can kiss Rose goodbye now.

"Why?"

Rose shrugs and smiles. "I'm just curious."

"Rose, I've had a bad experience with this a couple times. To summarize what happened, when I was asked what my sign was, I would give them the answer, and all of a sudden, I would get hit with the *we're not compatible* talk, making me realize I wasted my time. I don't think zodiac signs are that important to the point where you should revolve your life around them," I explain.

Rose tucks in her bottom lip and smirks. "Okay, for one, the way those women handled hearing your zodiac sign is messed up. It says a lot about them, if they just wasted your time like that by running off after thinking you weren't compatible with them. Whatever happened to people trying things and going against the grain. And for two, in my opinion, zodiac signs are important! It's all based in astrology and how the times we're born in play a part in molding our personality traits, behaviors, relationships, and more. If the sun and moon play a part in helping us survive on this Earth, best believe they play a part in your development. And lastly, like I said before, I just wanna know what your sign is. There's no harm in that."

Rose explained so much that I don't even have the

energy to debate her. It's much easier if I tell her my sign and accept my fate. She seems logical when it comes to this thing anyway, so it shouldn't be that bad.

"Okay, you made some good points. Here's your answer: I'm an Aries."

"No freaking way," she gasps. "I'm an Aries too! When's your birthday?" This topic has her super giddy like a child on Christmas day.

"April 4th," I answer.

Rose smacks my arm. "Shut up, Eddie. You shut up right now." She smacks my arm again. "Are you lying? And were you looking at my page to find out when my birthday was, so you could pull this prank on me?"

I let out a slight chuckle. "No, I'm serious, my birthday is on April 4th. Are you trying to say you were born on April 4th too?"

"Yes, Eddie, I am! We were born on the same day."

"Wow! Talk about a coincidence."

"This explains so much," Rose quietly says to herself.

"It explains what?" I ask her.

She ignores my question and asks, "What time were you born?"

"Um, 4:30a.m., my mom never lets me hear the end of it. She always talks about how I kept her up all night just to be born super early in the morning."

"This is unbelievable." Rose is astonished. She grabs her phone and begins scrolling through the pictures.

"What are you looking for?" I ask her.

She smiles and holds up her phone to my face. "This." It's a picture of her birth certificate.

I have no idea why she has a picture of her birth certificate on her phone, but I'll assume most women do. As I look at the picture, I'm able to see that Rose was born on April 4th 1994 at 4:31a.m.

"I was born one-minute after you, Eddie! I have to see your birth certificate when you have the chance. I still can't believe this," she says with excitement.

I have to admit, although I'm not an astrology guy, this is cool to see because of how rare it is to meet someone born on the same exact day and year as you, let alone time.

"I gotcha. I have a copy of mine somewhere in my house. The only problem is that I can't remember where I put it. I know my mom has mine and Emma's original birth certificates at her house. She keeps them stored in her room. If I text her and ask her to send me a picture of it, I'll have it within minutes."

"Oh please do," Rose begs.

After texting my mom if she could send a picture of my birth certificate for passport reasons, she sends it in a hurry. I made up that excuse because I didn't feel like having her asking questions about what girl I'm talking to now.

"Here it is," I say, showing Rose the picture.

"No way! You really were born on April 4th, 1994 at 4:30a.m. Sheesh, I wish I didn't have to work tomorrow. Are you free again next weekend?"

I shake my head. "Not the entire weekend. I'll only be free next Friday and Saturday, because next Sunday, I'll be flying to Seattle for a couple book signings and a documentary I'll be featured in throughout that week," I reveal.

"Oh my god, that sounds amazing! What's the documentary going to be about?"

"If I can remember correctly, my manager was telling me the documentary is going to focus on how creative people find ways to create in a world full of distractions."

Rose looks so intrigued. "Ooo, I'm curious to know how you guys do that too. And did I just hear you say you have a manager?"

I nod. "Yeah, his name is Oscar. He lives in Los Angeles though. He always meets up with me whenever I have big events."

"Mr. Valentine, you're full of surprises. I like it! I wish I had the opportunity to see all of this taking place. Please do me a favor if you can. I would love it if you could send me pictures of the book signing and documentary process when you're out there."

"Yeah, I wish you could see it too, and I'll definitely be sure to do that. But hey, I can take you out next Friday night when you get off work and next Saturday before I leave the following day."

"Aw, are you sure that won't be too much for you? I don't want to have you exhausted before your flight the next day."

"No, it'll be okay. Besides, I'll sleep on the flight there anyway. There's a sip and paint night at the Blue River art gallery on Friday and Saturday night. I can pick you up and take you there on one of those nights."

"A sip and paint night! I love the sound of that!

Saturday night works for me, but on Friday the school I teach at is having a family fun day after school, where we're having a scavenger hunt, a bake sale, and face painting for the kids."

"That sounds fun too."

Rose shakes her head and sighs. "It's fun for them but it's a lot of work for us teachers that have to be there. The scavenger hunts last so long because the kids have a hard time finding everything, even when we make it easy for them. Oh god and don't get me started on the parents not helping with the cleaning up process after the face painting and bake sale is finished."

"Sheesh, well hopefully, it goes smoothly this year."

"Yeah, hopefully." Rose chuckles. "But ya know what? Would you want to come? I invited my sister but she can't make it. And I could use some help with the bake sale."

That's a no-brainer! I'd do anything to spend more time with this woman. Everything just feels right when I'm around her. I still can't explain this shit; even the astrology thing that I oppose, just made me feel more connected to her. How is she doing this?

I shrug and smile. "Sure, why not, I'm all in. Let me pick you up that day too?"

"Sure, I'll text you my address right now so you won't forget about me," she jokes.

Trust me, Rose, that's far from happening.

"Me...forget about you already? Never!"

CHAPTER SEVEN

December 4ᵗʰ

I t's Monday morning and I'm awakened by a text from
Rose.

Seconds later, I receive a call from Xavier.

"Yo, what's up?" I say.

"Yo, bro! I haven't heard from you in a minute. You didn't lose that engagement ring, did you?" Xavier asks.

"Nah, man, it's inside my drawer. I'm gonna throw this shit in the river if you keep asking me about it though."

Xavier is laughing his ass off on the other end of the phone. "I'm just messing with you, man. How did the date go with the girl from the mall the other day?"

"I can't lie to you, it went really good. We went on back-to-back dates Saturday and Sunday and plan on seeing each other again this weekend. I'm glad you convinced me to talk to her."

"Aw shit! Back-to-back dates, see that! Ya boy will never steer you wrong. I told you to go after her. You really like her, don't you?" Xavier sounds more excited about this than I do.

We always talk about girls, but this is the first time in years where I'm talking to him about a girl who isn't a prostitute. No wonder he's this hype.

I shrug. "I mean...she's—"

"—Nah, I don't want to hear this fake hesitation, bro. Come on, admit it. You like this girl, don't you?" Xavier asks again.

Damn, man, give me a break!

"Fine, I'll be direct. Yeah, I like her so far. We're really connecting, we even share the same birthday."

"Oh snap! For real?"

"Yeah, but Xavier, don't start saying that's my wife and everything already. We're both feeling each other out right now, and seeing where this goes," I explain.

"I feel you, bro, just remember that not every girl is Veronica."

Yeah, not every girl is Veronica, but they're all capable of turning into Veronica.

"I gotcha," I reply.

"Listen, Chris and Hannah are watching Monday Night Football at my house tonight. Are you trying to slide through? Jen is making tacos and we'll be ordering pizza too."

I can never resist a football night with tacos and pizza.

"Alright, I'm in, I'll be there."

≈

By nightfall, I arrive at Xavier and Jen's house. As soon as I walk inside, Xavier and Chris greet me by yelling my name.

"EDDIE!" Xavier shouts.

"YO, EDDIE! THE MAN ON THE HUNT," Chris yells. Anyone can hear his deep voice from a mile away, sounding like James Earl Jones.

"Okay, something's up. Why are you two acting suspicious?" I ask.

Jen then comes up to me and tries to give me a hug. "Hi Eddie!"

"Hold on," I tell her. "I'm gonna have to give you a side hug now since your belly is poking out like a fishbowl. I don't wanna smush the baby! What are you, like nine-months pregnant now?"

Jen snickers. "Oh hush, I'm only five-months along. How are you? I heard you probably found love recently," she says.

There it is! Xavier running his big ass mouth. I swear my

friends have been treating me like a sad charity case ever since my breakup.

"I'm doing fine, and what the hell, Xavier. I'm not in love with Rose. We only went on two dates."

Xavier takes a sip of beer and waves me off. "And you're going on another one with her soon, bro, the love is bound to happen for you," he says.

"Relax, we're just joking with you," Jen adds.

Yeah right, they aren't joking!

Chris points at me and says, "Yo, Eddie, in all seriousness, I gotta girl for you. She might be the one. . .her name is Angela."

"Nope," Hannah intervenes. "Chris, we're not hooking Eddie up with anymore of my friends or coworkers. Remember how he played Stephanie and Bianca," she says.

Oh my god, here we go with this shit.

"What! Hannah, are you serious? I didn't play them," I tell her.

"Yes, you did," Hannah repeats with her raspy voice.

Chris squints and looks into the distance. "I don't remember that. Hannah, I don't think Eddie did your friends dirty," he says, trying to defend me.

"Thank you, Chris," I mutter.

Jen wags her finger in my face. "No, Hannah's right, Eddie. I remember what happened because I was doing Stephanie's hair when she asked about you the first time. Stephanie really liked you and asked Hannah and I if we could set you up with her. We wanted to help you get over Veronica so we made it happen. Stephanie said she was really feeling you after your first few dates. She said she told you about her life and that she shared her secrets with you, but all you wanted from her was sex!"

I can't believe Jen and Hannah are calling me out like this. They have everything twisted. "Hold on! I told Stephanie from the jump that all I wanted to do was be friends with benefits. I wasn't ready to be in a relationship at that time because I'd just broken up with Veronica. And you two both knew I wasn't in a space mentally to take someone seriously. It's not my fault that Stephanie kept telling me about her life's problems, I didn't ask her to do that," I clarify to Jen and Hannah.

Hannah scowls at me. "Boy, you know damn well people love venting to you about their problems. I tell you all the time, it's because you're an empath; so people feel comfortable talking to you. Especially women! But when Veronica broke your heart, it was like all your sensitivity went out the door. That was so wrong telling Stephanie that all you wanted was sex."

Xavier stands up off the couch and steps into the middle of the living room to join in on the conversation. "If Eddie told Stephanie that he wanted to be friends with benefits from the jump, then I find that respectful and commendable. Y'all can't be mad because she caught feelings for him. And just because my boy has empath superpowers, that doesn't mean she had to reveal all her secrets to him. It's not like he held a gun to her head or some shit."

"Exactly, bro," I agree.

"Okay, fair enough. Stephanie still thinks you're an

asshole by the way, but she doesn't hate you as much as Bianca does," Hannah reveals to me.

Jen wags her finger in my face again. Jesus Christ! You would've thought I won *asshole of the year* or something. "Yeah, Bianca's still subliminally writing blogs about you till this day. Her name for you on her website is the *Anonymous Man*. There's no excuse for what you did to her," Jen says.

Xavier and Chris have puzzled looks on their faces. They want to jump into this part of the argument, but they have no clue what transpired between me and Bianca. I never told them because I didn't want to make her look crazy, but since I'm just now finding out that she's writing subliminal blogs about me, I might have to air out what she did, just to defend myself.

"What happened with Bianca?" Xavier asks me.

"I'll tell you," Jen says before I can respond to my friend.

Now my head's about to explode because these girls are about to ruin our Monday Night Football based on shit from the past.

"For fuck sakes, Jen, you don't even know what really happened," I spazz.

"I read all about it," Jen says, while pulling out her phone. "Hannah, tell Chris and Xavier what happened while I look for her website," she adds.

Hannah has a proud look on her face like she's about to get a raise on CNN for reporting the biggest news story of all-time. "Well, soon after Eddie's phase with Stephanie ended, he met Bianca at my Halloween party.

She told him, she thought he was cute and he said he felt the same way about her. She ended up inviting him to her apartment on multiple occasions. At first, they got to know each other, with her doing most of the talking of course. She then told him about the state of depression she was going through and how he was helping her get out of it due to his energy. So from a mental health standpoint, Bianca clearly wasn't ready to be with anyone, but she ended up falling head over heels for Eddie. Before you know it, they began sleeping with each other every night! She would tell him how much he meant to her and how he was changing her life for the better, but he never told her that he didn't feel the same way."

Jen holds out her phone and shows everyone Bianca's blog. "Yup, here it is on her website. This is the juicy part. Bianca writes: *One day I asked the Anonymous Man, "Am I the only girl you're seeing right now?"*

The Anonymous Man automatically looked at me with disgust and said, "I'm not seeing you and we're not seeing each other. This is just a sexual thing."

I was so hurt by this because we shared so many parts of our lives together. I was hoping he didn't actually feel this way so I said, "My aunt once told me that a man who only sees you for sex will never want you for love. He's saving the love you want, for someone else."

The Anonymous Man seemed like he didn't care and said, "Your aunt was right. I want nothing to do with you. And after my ex, I no longer trust you bitches, you're all the same. So you can continue to take this dick or leave."

This right here, ladies, showed me that men who are hurt will continue to hurt other women with no remorse, even if their hearts were broken in grade school. Please, look out for yourselves, ladies, and go after men that are healed. That part of her blog has the most views and comments," Jen says.

Hannah snaps her fingers and rolls her eyes at me. "Yeah, you see, that's why I will never hook him up with any girl I know again. I can't have him making our parties awkward by dipping and dodging every chick he meets," Hannah adds.

The puzzled looks on Chris and Xavier's faces are now gone. They're now looking at Hannah and Jen in disbelief. After hearing that bullshit Jen just read, they know something's off.

"Chill, babe, that doesn't even sound like Eddie," Chris says.

Xavier softly fondles Jen's pregnant belly, hoping she doesn't cuss him out after what he has to say next. "Yeah, and Eddie's heart wasn't broken in grade school, it happened while he was a grown man. And shame on you and Hannah. Y'all know damn well he doesn't talk to women like that," he says.

Shit, I could use Chris and Xavier as my future attorneys.

I'm upset with Jen and Hannah at this point. "Xavier and Chris, thanks again! Jen and Hannah, I can't believe you two. What in the actual fuck. How can't you see that Bianca is clearly LYING! Just because she wrote it on a blog doesn't make it factual. That girl obviously has mental health issues, and I found that out the hard way. I told Bianca the same thing I told Stephanie. Once again, I said I only wanted to be friends with benefits from the jump. Where's the harm in that? And guess what? Bianca was completely fine with it for months. But one day after we had sex, she asked me to marry her," I confess.

"She what?" Hannah says, flabbergasted.

"Yeah, you heard me, she asked me to marry her. Out of respect, I never told anyone because I could see that she clearly lost her mind," I explain.

Xavier looks Jen directly in the eyes. "Y'all owe my boy an apology," he says.

"Word. Y'all do," Chris adds.

Jen is too prideful to back down like that. Knowing her she's going to want more details. "Wait, before we apologize, what did you say to her when she asked you that?" she questions me.

"I told her sorry and that I couldn't do that because we didn't know each other on that level. I then reinstated that I had only wanted to be friends with benefits, but now that would have to end because it took a left turn when she asked me to marry her. You wouldn't believe this but she sort of ignored every damn thing I said and asked if I could get her pregnant."

Jen and Hannah are stunned. I bet those blog post look like nothing but tabloid junk compared to the truth I just spit out.

"Yeah, you're speechless, right?" I say to them before continuing. "She said that if I got her pregnant with our baby, it would make me realize we were meant to be. After that I put on my clothes, took the condom I had busted a nut in with me so she wouldn't try to use it to impregnate herself, and did my best to quickly get the fuck out of there. She ended up spazzing out on me and threw a bunch of shit at me while I ran out of her apartment. She's lucky her stories online are fabricated and has me listed as the Anonymous Man, because I would sue her psycho ass."

"Damn, I'm sorry, Eddie. I thought you were the one who drove her crazy. It turns out she was crazy the whole time," Hannah says.

"I'm sorry, too, Eddie. I still do Stephanie and Bianca's hair though, so I hope that doesn't make things awkward," Jen adds.

"Nah, of course not, you have to make your money by any means necessary. I'm just disappointed that you two thought I was an asshole."

"Wait, I didn't say that, Hannah did," Jen says

"No, I wasn't calling you an asshole, Eddie. I was saying that Stephanie still thinks you're one," Hannah says in her defense.

"But you two sort of felt the same way based on the lies," Xavier says, finishing his third beer.

"Hey, at least they know the truth now," Chris says. "Some of these chicks nowadays are crazy, but I can promise you Angela is not like that. You still want me to hook you up with her?"

"Nah I'm good, Chris, thanks for looking out."

"Yeah, let me make it up to you, Eddie, Angela is a good person. We both work at the hospital together. She's a nurse like me and she treats everyone with respect," Hannah says.

"No, thank you, Hannah. I forgive you and I'm all

good," I tell her.

"I can hook him up with Tiana if it doesn't work out with this Rose girl," Jen says.

I place my hands together in a prayer formation. "Oh no, I'm putting an end to this shit right now. Listen, nobody has to hook me up with anyone. I appreciate you guys and I love you all like you're my own family. But I can manage my own dating life. Do you guys understand that?" I ask them.

My friends nod.

"He's only saying that because he found love with Rose already," Xavier utters.

I palm my face in disbelief. "Jesus Christ, I can't with you guys. I'm going into the kitchen to grab some tacos."

Chris laughs and says, "Eddie, real quick, does this Rose girl have an Instagram?"

"Yup," I answer while grabbing three tacos from the kitchen.

"Is it public?" Chris asks.

"I think so. Why?" I ask Chris, making my way back to the living room.

Hannah, claps her hands and says, "Because we want to see what she looks like, duh! Xavier told us she's beautiful."

"Yeah, what's her Instagram name?" Jen adds.

"Fine. It's Rose_94," I tell them. "Just make sure you guys don't accidentally like her pictures. I'm not trying to look like a damn stalker."

Jen hops off Xavier's lap and pulls out her phone. "We won't, we promise," she says.

"Look, look, look, here she is. Wow! Eddie, she's gorgeous," Hannah says, beating Jen to the search.

"Aw, you guys would make a great couple," Jen adds.

I hate all this attention.

"If you're still dating her by the time Christmas Eve comes around, you should bring her over here to the Christmas party," Jen says.

The last thing I want Rose to do is meet you crazy people.

"Oh no, I would rather have somebody throw me off a bridge before she meets you guys," I joke.

Jen deeply exhales while grinning. "Listen, I'm sorry again for judging you due to Bianca's blog. That was wrong of me. I promise Hannah and I will be on our best behavior if you bring Rose to the Christmas party."

"Alright, I'll think about it," I mutter.

"Good, I can see you really like this girl, just remember that not every girl is Veronica," Jen says to me.

"Preach!" Hannah adds. "If you gotta good one, don't mess it up."

My lord, here we go again! What is this, an intervention?

"I know, I know, Xavier said the same thing to me this morning," I inform them.

Xavier grabs a beer and tosses me a soda as he asks, "Yo, who are you betting on tonight?"

Yes, football talk!

"I don't know man, I haven't been keeping up with the season like I did last year, but I guess I'll put $20 on Cincinnati over Jacksonville for this game," I tell him.

"Same here, but I'm putting $500 down on my

ticket," Xavier says.

Jen's eyes widen as she places her hands on her hips and stares directly at Xavier. She can't stand when he wants to bet a bunch of money on football games.

"And no, the fuck you're not, you better put $20 down like Eddie on that damn game, don't waste our money on this football shit like you did at the start of the season. We don't have time to buy new furniture every time you break something when you lose," Jen tells Xavier as she watches him delete the $500 and replaces it with $20 on the sports betting app.

Jen is the only person that can snap on Xavier like that. If it were anyone else, he would be arguing back, saying he's not some little bitch.

Xavier shakes his head and chuckles. "Alright, babe, chill. I deleted it."

"I know that's right, girl," Hannah says as we get ready to watch the kickoff.

here.

CHAPTER EIGHT

December 8th

It's a Friday afternoon, and I'm at my desk brainstorming a new novel I want to create for the upcoming year. I don't know if I want to do a story focused strictly on modern romance or a story that involves dragons in modern times. It all sounds like a bunch of crappy ideas right about now. I've been going through writer's block since Monday night. The conversation I had with Jen and Hannah that night really did a number on me. They made me realize the main reason I started sleeping with hookers was because of Bianca and Stephanie.

Even though I was straightforward with Bianca and Stephanie about being friends with benefits, they didn't handle it well as time went on. They eventually caught feelings which, in return, made me the bad guy by seeming like I was being emotionally manipulative. After those two situations, I no longer wanted to feel like I was hurting women the way Veronica hurt me. That's when I came across brothels during my first book tour in Las Vegas. I finally found women who didn't mind the *no strings attached* type of sex. It just costs money. . . money that I didn't mind spending.

I stumbled upon more brothels when I heard comedians talking about their trips to Brazil on Howard Stern's radio show. After hearing that, I booked my first trip out the country with my manager and his family to Rio de Janeiro, Brazil. While they did family activities during the vacation, I did my own activities and visited brothels. At that moment, I told myself I would visit these places frequently to keep myself sane, and that's exactly what I did.

While outlining and jotting down random notes to help me get out of my writer's block and fucked up thoughts, I get a call from Rose. Whenever I see her name on the Caller ID, it makes my day: either that or seeing her in person does.

"Hey Rose," I answer.

"Hey stranger, I'm on lunch break right now and I was checking in to see if you were still coming tonight. And I don't mean to sound like a burden, but I also wanted to make sure you were alright since I didn't hear from you yesterday. I texted you to see how you were doing," she reveals.

Fuck, that's right, I forgot to text Rose back. That Stephanie and Bianca thing really threw off my game.

I palm my forehead. "Aw shit! I'm sorry, Rose. I've been all out of whack, going through writer's block. My bad for not reaching out to you these past few days. If

I'm being honest, I didn't want to blow up your phone and seem overbearing by contacting you every time I think about you. Because I've been thinking about you a lot." I reveal to her.

"Aw, I've been thinking about you a lot too! And Eddie, you're fine." She laughs. "Even if you decide to start texting or calling me every day, it won't be overbearing to me. I promise. I work with five-year-olds all day so talking to you is like a breath of fresh air."

It's refreshing hearing Rose utter those words; especially since I feel the same way.

"Okay, I'll make sure I remember that. You'll be seeing my name pop up on your phone more often now."

"I'm looking forward to it, Mr. Valentine, as well as you coming to pick me up." I can hear the joy in Rose's voice.

"Before you know it, it'll be six p.m. and I'll be right there opening my car door for you," I tell her before we say our goodbyes and eventually hang up.

≈

That night after picking up Rose, we drive to Maple Elementary. From the outside, the school building looks sort of small but it has a Victorian look to it.

Rose catches me taking a good look at the school. "Have you been here before?" she asks me.

"Nah, this is my first time here. I love the way the building looks. I rarely come across schools that look like this. It reminds me of a school from one of those old black & white films," I explain to her.

"Yeah, the school fits in with the aesthetic of this neighborhood. This Maple County area is a historic location. I learned that when I first started working here. Surprisingly, the inside of the school looks like a circus combined with a daycare. You wouldn't even think you were in the same building."

"No kidding." I step out of the car.

"You'll see." Rose tries to open the car door while holding onto three pans of brownies and chocolate chip cookies she made for the bake sale. They smell so flavorful, it has my entire Chevy Suburban smelling like a bakery.

"You know darn well I'm not going to let you carry all that by yourself," I tell her as I open the passenger side door and grab the pans from her.

"They aren't that heavy for me." She giggles. "But thank you. So before we go inside, do you want the kids to call you Mr. Eddie or Mr. Valentine?"

"Mr. Eddie is fine, because the name Mr. Valentine will have them asking me crazy questions like am I related to the person who invented Valentine's Day or if Valentine's Day is about me."

Rose chuckles. "Ooo, I would love to see that, but I understand where you're coming from. I'll have them call you Mr. Eddie then."

While making our way toward the school, a short elderly Caucasian woman approaches me and Rose. "Hello, Rose, thanks for your help again this year. Who's this young man you're with?"

"You're welcome, Principal Hardwick. This is my friend, Eddie. He'll be one of our helping hands today," Rose tells her.

The principal stares directly at me. "Oh good, thank you for volunteering, Eddie. I'm so grateful to have your help," she says.

"No problem at all, Principal Hardwick. I'm happy to help."

Rose gently touches my back and says, "Principal Hardwick, guess what? Eddie's an author too! He writes all types of books, even children's books."

Principal Hardwick looks amazed. "Really?"

Rose nods. "Yes, he's really good," she adds, promoting my work.

"Wow, that's remarkable! We have to see if we can get some of your books in our school library," Principal Hardwick says.

"Absolutely, we can make that happen!"

"Great, I'll make sure I get your information from you or Rose before the family event is over," the principal tells me.

As we walk into the school, there are parents and kids everywhere. There has to be over fifty conversations happening at once. Rose was right, this place does look like a circus combined with a daycare. The school walls are covered in yellow and blue paint with a ton of colorful stickers covering the classroom doors and school cubbies. I follow Rose down the hall and into her classroom. Her students are inside standing around as their parents stand along the whiteboard, talking.

"Hello everyone," Rose says cheerfully.

Her students' eyes light up when they see her. They immediately run away from their parents to give her a hug as they scream, "MS. MORENO!"

"Hey guys," she says as she hugs them back.

"Who's this?" one of the kids ask her, pointing directly at me.

"CJ, stop doing that, boy," one of the parents orders the kid. I'm assuming it's his father.

Rose crouches down to CJ's level. "CJ, it's not good to point, remember?" she says pleasantly.

"Yes, Ms. Moreno," the boy replies.

Rose then turns to me and says, "Class, this is Mr. Eddie."

"HI MR. EDDIE," the students shout all at once.

"Hey! Are you guys ready for the scavenger hunt today?" I ask them.

"YES," they shout.

Due to their excitement, the students are getting antsy. Rose is trying to get their attention, but a few of them begin chasing each other around the classroom. At this point, I'm thinking the parents are about to get involved to help, but they're all on their phones.

Rose was right about this too. These parents are no help at all.

I guess I shouldn't be surprised since most of the parents in this room are our age or younger.

Out of the blue, Rose does something remarkable to get all of the student's attention. "One, two, three, eyes on me," she says.

"One, two, eyes on you," the students say in unison.

"Great job! Okay class, go ahead and tell your parents you're ready for the scavenger hunt so we can get started," Rose instructs.

As the five-year-olds run to their parents, I turn to Rose and say, "You're an amazing teacher, Ms. Moreno!"

She looks at me and blushes as she removes her coat. "Thank you Mr. Val— I mean Mr. Eddie."

"That was a close one," I laugh.

"I know," Rose confirms.

"And thanks to your students, I know your last name now."

Rose winks. "Well, all you had to do was ask if you wanted to know," she says, making a valid point.

"True. So Ms. Rose Moreno, what's your full name?"

"It's Rosalina Rose Moreno. But I prefer people to call me by my middle name, Rose. And what's your full name? Wait let me guess, is it Edward Valentine the Fourth?"

"Correct, but I prefer people call me Eddie. And how'd you know my full name?"

"I saw it on your website," Rose admits.

I wink at her. "Oh so you're stalking me already, huh?"

She winks back. "Yeah, I figured I should learn more about you, handsome."

Rose walks toward her desk and places her coat on her desk chair. It's at this moment where I'm starting to notice her hourglass figure a little more. Her fitted jeans and thin Christmas sweater is showing me the treat I can eventually receive. I know the dads here probably make passes at her frequently. Since Rose is always wearing a peacoat or a puffer jacket whenever we go out due to the cold weather, I never had the chance to see her full figure. I'm glad it happened that way though because, initially, I was mesmerized by her face and her energy. Her figure is just a plus!

Suddenly my thoughts are interrupted when some of Rose's students come running back into the classroom.

"Ms. Moreno, can Mr. Eddie do the scavenger hunt with us?" one of the little girls ask.

"Of course, Lily, he definitely can," Rose tells her.

Now, I don't mind helping the kids but I'm a little surprised because I was looking forward to chilling with Rose the whole time.

"I thought I was going to help you with the bake sale?" I ask her.

Rose covers her mouth and gasps. "Oh yes, you were and you still can. I'm sorry, I had no idea they were going to ask me if you could do the scavenger hunt with them. They must like you already." She beams, watching one of the kids tug at my sweater.

"Get off of him, CJ, with your silly self," she demands.

"Okay." CJ listens and lets go.

"Yeah, I see they're excited for this. I remember those days," I say.

Rose grins at me. "I don't want you to feel like you're being forced into this. You don't have to do it if you don't want to."

I lift my hands up to assure her that everything is

alright. "It's okay, I'll do it. What will the kids and I be looking for?"

Rose sighs in relief. "Thank you so much, you're the best! The scavenger hunt will go by much faster with your help. Do you know what *Elf on the Shelf* dolls are?"

"Yeah, I've heard of them before."

"Good, you and the kids will have to find ten of them. When you do find all ten, the kids will earn gift bags filled with yo-yo's, Legos, and bouncy balls."

"Cool, I think I can handle this. Are their parents going to help me out too?"

Rose shrugs. "I mean...they can but good luck getting them to try. They usually sit around in the gym and hop on their phones while the scavenger hunt is going on. Every year we try to get them to participate, but only a few accept."

"What the hell," I murmur. "I could never imagine my parents being that occupied with something else when I was little. But I guess this is the new world we're living in," I joke.

"You got that right!"

"Let me see if I can get them to join in." I step into the hallway and approach a group of parents. "Hey, would any of you parents like to join in on the scavenger hunt?"

The parents kindly gesture that they will not participate, and go back to looking at their phones, or talking amongst each other.

One dad even looks at me and says, "Y'all got that one good fella, I'm burned out. I'll be in the school gym getting my grub on."

The rest of the parents who weren't participating laugh at his comment and follow him into the gym to get food.

I look at Rose and shrug. "You were right, I guess I'm on my own."

Rose rubs my back and smiles. Even with that simple action, she's sending chills down my spine. "I truly appreciate you doing this."

"Anytime."

"Hey Myra," Rose calls to one of her students.

A girl with braided pigtails skips across the room, grinning. "Yes, Ms. Moreno?" she says.

Rose crouches down to this student, too, meeting her at eye level. "Can you be one of my big helpers today and make sure everyone is listening to Mr. Eddie during the game?"

Myra nods. "Yes, I can do that."

Paying attention to the way Rose's students interact with her, I can see they have a lot of trust in her, like she's another mother figure.

"Thank you, Myra, and come find me if anything goes wrong." Rose gets the rest of her students' attention again. "Alright, kids, be nice and listen to Mr. Eddie, ok?"

"OK," they reply.

"Good, now go ahead and follow him out the door. Your job is to find ten elves that are hiding in the school."

The kids are excited, antsy, and whispering to each other about where they think the elves could be. I can't think of what to say to them at the moment as they follow me down the hall and into the library. Luckily, during the early part of our search we spot one of the elf dolls sitting on a bookshelf.

"Hey! I see an elf right there," I say to them, picking up the elf.

Myra claps. "One down!"

"And nine more to go," I add.

We then take the stairs searching for more.

"Look, Mr. Eddie, I found five of them," Myra says, grabbing five elves at the top of the stairway behind a door.

"Great job, Myra! We're on a roll," I say to her. "Hey guys, now we have six elves. All we need is four more." The kids are excited to hear that.

Our search continues into the cafeteria when another kid finds three elves in front of a vending machine. We now have nine elves and are searching for one last elf. Rose was correct when she said they do make the scavenger hunts easy for them. On our way out the cafeteria and into the hall, CJ approaches me and says, "Hey. Mr. Eddie, I think I know where one is but I can't reach it on the shelf.

"Okay, cool, show us where it is," I tell him.

CJ directs us to a storage closet right outside the cafeteria, but, when I check inside, I don't see anything. There's nothing but two small boxes filled with pink erasers. Other than that, the shelves are empty and have cobwebs.

"Hey, CJ, I don't see an Elf on the Shelf in here. Are

you sure you saw it in here?" I ask.

CJ smiles and pulls an elf from behind his back. "That's because I have the last one," he laughs and slams the door.

I reach for the doorknob and try twisting it open. After multiple attempts, I realize it's locked. Suddenly, I hear CJ and the rest of the kids running away.

Aw hell nah, this little bad ass kid locked me in here.

"Hey, come on, CJ, unlock the door, lil man," I say, hoping he would come back. I don't hear a response though. There's only one thing to do now. I take a deep breath and lean against the wall. "Holy fuck balls, man, now I have to call Rose. I'm about to look like a complete idiot."

I take my phone out of my pocket, preparing to call Rose. When I press the call button, my call is immediately answered and the door suddenly opens.

"Look who I found stuck in the storage room," Rose answers the phone, simultaneously holding the door wide open. She smiles at me, while her students stand behind her laughing.

"You guys found me," I joyfully say to everyone. "We were goofing around, and I ended up locking myself in here on accident," I add, trying to protect CJ from getting in trouble.

Rose shakes her head and smirks. "Nope, Myra already told me everything that happened."

Wow, Myra really is one of her good students!

Rose motions her hand for one of her students to come to her. "CJ, come here please, what do you have to say to Mr. Eddie?"

CJ walks over to me with his head down and says, "I'm sorry, Mr. Eddie, I shouldn't have locked you in the room, that wasn't nice."

I could go ahead and grill this kid for shits and giggles, but I let it go. He can't help it, he's only in kindergarten. I chuckle a bit and say, "It's all good, CJ, hopefully next time we can complete the scavenger hunt without that happening again. Did you have fun though?" I ask him.

CJ nods and smiles.

"That's good, lil man, now make sure you're always on your best behavior for Ms. Moreno and your classmates, alright?" I tell him giving him a pat on the shoulder.

Once I'm finished speaking, Rose is able to get their attention again saying, "One, two, three, eyes on me!"

"ONE, TWO, EYES ON YOU," the students shout.

It's beautiful to see the way she commands a room and the way these kids respect her.

"Okay, I want you to all head to the gym and wait with your parents. Mr. Eddie and I will be there shortly to hand you your prizes," Rose tells her students.

The kids follow her instructions and begin walking into the hallway and toward the gym.

Before shutting the storage room door all the way, Rose winks at me and asks, "Do you wanna go back in there?"

I point at the door. "Where, in that storage room?" I

ask, winking back at her. "Shoot, only if you come in there with me."

Rose bites her lip and smiles. It looks like she's seriously considering it too. If she is, I will fuck the shit out of her in that room. But who am I kidding, this is an elementary school and her place of work; she wouldn't risk doing that shit with me here.

Unexpectedly, one of the students yells, "STOP, CJ."

Rose and I look down the hall and spot CJ pulling on Myra's shirt.

This little bad ass boy might need some of that 1990s parenting.

Rose grins at me. "Maybe at another place and time," she murmurs. "As of now, I need to keep an eye on my students."

We jog down the hall after the kids. "I gotcha," I utter to Rose. "Hey. CJ, let go of Myra and stand by me. I tried to keep you out of trouble earlier," I command.

CJ puts his head down and let's go of Myra.

"Nope, that sad face isn't going to work with me," Rose tells him. "Now we're going to have a conversation with your parents," she concludes.

≈

By the time the family night is over, I help Rose and the rest of the teachers clean up the school. While folding up tables, I notice a young woman with medium brown skin and short curly black hair tap Rose on the shoulder.

"Excuse me. Rose, is this Eddie?" she asks, glancing

over at me.

"Yeah, this is Eddie, he was volunteering today. I was going to introduce you to him earlier, but you had a long line of students waiting on you while you were face painting," Rose explains to the woman.

The woman walks away from Rose and walks toward me. "That's fine! Hi, I'm Eartha, I'm one of the first-grade teachers here and I'm also Rose's best friend."

I shake Eartha's hand. "Hey Eartha, well as you already know, I'm Eddie. And I hope Rose has been saying good things about me so far."

Eartha grins at me. "Oh yes, darling, she definitely has, believe me!"

I smile and glance at Rose. "I'm glad to hear that because I could say a million good things about her."

Eartha playfully waves her finger at me and says, "My goodness, I can see you have a way with words. See, that's that *writer shit*. All I can say to that is…don't hurt my friend, or you're gonna catch some serious hell." She frowns.

Damn, that took a quick left turn.

Rose laughs and wraps her arm around mine. "Oh god, Eartha, leave the poor guy alone. He's great!"

Eartha immediately turns that frown upside down and starts giggling. "I'm kidding," she says softly.

I smirk. "I know," I say, playing it off as if she didn't have me startled a few seconds ago.

Rose picks up the last piece of trash from the bake sale and says, "Our area is all cleaned up, along with the other teachers. I'm so ready to get out of here, are you?"

she asks me.

"Yeah, I'm ready," I answer.

"Alright then, we're finally out of here," Rose says, hugging Eartha. "I'll see you on Monday."

"Okay girl, you two be safe and hit me up when you make it home," Eartha says.

"I will," Rose replies to her as we place our coats on and exit the school.

≈

After making it to Rose's apartment complex to drop her off, I find myself uncontrollably yawning while parking in the lot.

Her eyes shimmer as she looks up at me. "You had quite the day, huh?" she asks.

I am a bit sluggish. That family fun night event wore me out.

"I sure did. I enjoyed spending time with your students too. They're some pretty cool kids," I respond.

Rose displays a look of sarcasm and pinches her lips. She thinks I'm joking. "You think my students are cool? Even CJ?"

"Yup, even CJ! I've worked with kids like him before. He just wants attention, that's all. His parents should probably put him in basketball or soccer soon to give him something to do. I honestly had a good time though, I'm glad you invited me."

"I'm glad you came." Rose picks up a small container of brownies she has on her lap and places it on the arm rest. "Here are some brownies I have left over for you.

There's only three left."

"Thank you, these were pretty damn good. I tried my best not to eat them all during the bake sale."

"Yeah, I know, you were getting your grub on. I can tell you this, Principal Hardwick definitely appreciated it every time you and the parents bought some baked goods. That was the most money I've ever seen a family fun night make while teaching here."

"Wow! Maybe I'm a good luck charm," I reply jokingly.

Rose snickers and prepares to exit the car.

While witnessing her reach for the door, I stop her. "Hold on, you know darn well I like getting the door for you."

Rose blushes and smirks at me. "Good catch. I was testing you, and wanted to see how you would react."

I hop out and walk around the car to open the passenger side door for her. As I take her hand to help her step out the car, the glow from the moonlight shines on her caramel eyes. And it's truly a sight to see. It feels like I'm staring into her soul.

Kiss her now, kiss her now.

Yeah, that's what I'm telling myself as we gaze into each other's eyes, but I go against my mind and say, "I'll walk you upstairs."

"Okay." Rose playfully shrugs. I guess she wasn't expecting me to say that.

Man, what the fuck am I doing? She clearly wants me to kiss her.

I take her hand and walk her upstairs to the third

floor. As we make it to her apartment door labeled 3D, I'm preparing myself to say goodbye and to redeem myself.

"Thank you for walking me to my door, handsome," Rose says.

"You're welcome."

That's all you have to say, dumbass! I don't know why I'm acting so hesitant like some little fucking boy. I'm a man, I can do this.

Before Rose opens her door, she turns to me and says, "Oh yeah, and Principal Hardwick said she's going to buy a bulk of your children's books online and will put them in the school library. Do you think you can come in one day and sign them?"

I nod. "Absolutely, I can definitely do that."

"Awesome! Well, I know I thanked you a million times already but thanks again for volunteering today at the school. I'm looking forward to painting with you tomorrow too."

Alright make the move.

My nerves are kicking me in the ass. How is she doing this to me? "Oh no worries, I'm glad I could help. And, yeah, so am I. You have a goodnight and get some rest. I'll be here to pick you up tomorrow night." I lean in to Rose and give her a hug.

As I give her a loving embrace, wrapping my arms around her waist, I can feel her soft hands caressing the back of my neck. I attempt to slightly lift my head to look in her eyes, but while slowly pulling away, she kisses me on the cheek. After that innocent kiss from her, I use my opportunity to kiss her on the lips. She continues to caress the back of my neck, as she brings her hips closer to mine. Her lips are soft, smooth, and warm. And I'm careful not to use tongue this first time around, but I'm able to smell and sort of taste the vanilla mint lip balm she's wearing. It's honestly making me want to tongue her down at this point. But I'm able to maintain my self-control and slowly release my arms from around her waist.

Rose looks at me and smiles. "That kiss made my night," she whispers.

"Seeing you again made my night," I tell her.

Rose can't stop grinning. "Eartha was right, you do have a way with words. I already knew that though, but you surprise me with your words every time."

"Well as an author I would hope so," I joke. "I'm going to go ahead and let you rest. You have a good night, *Ms. Moreno.*"

Rose smiles once more. "You have a good night, too, *Mr. Valentine.* I'll see you tomorrow night," she says, heading into her apartment.

I want to make sure I'm moving at a good pace with Rose, she has a special quality and energy about her that I don't want to lose. So every time I see her, I'll make sure the moment is special.

CHAPTER NINE

December 9ᵗʰ

It's the next night, and Rose and I are on our way to the art gallery for the sip & paint night.

"Hey, do you know what tonight's painting theme is going to be?" Rose asks me.

I already knew the answer to that, due to how many times I checked the art gallery's website in the morning.

"Yeah, it's a Winter Wonderland theme. Based on their website, it looks like we're painting a snowy forest," I answer.

"Nice! That should be fun and easy to do."

I laugh. "It'll be fun alright and I'll do my best when it comes to the painting."

Rose notices my sarcasm and smiles. "Wait, you'll do your best? You don't sound too sure about that. So, are you telling me you can't ice-skate or paint?"

"Damn right I can paint," I lie. "It's not that hard. And aw, come on now don't come for my ice-skating skills like that. I was pretty decent."

Rose covers her mouth. trying not to laugh. "You were alright, I guess." She starts to look at the flyer of the paint event I have in my car. "I know there will be wine at this event. I love wine, and, from time to time, I smoke hookah. Do you drink or smoke?"

"Nope, I don't drink or smoke," I admit.

Rose is amazed. "Really? That's good! I have to say I'm a little surprised because you're entertaining. That's one of the reasons I like being around you. There's always something unexpected happening. So the fact you always have a clear state of mind is incredible."

"Hell, I think you're fun to be around too. It's like our energies match each other or something."

"It's an Aries thing." Rose winks.

Here she goes with this astrology thing again.

"Ya think so?" I ask.

"I know so," she answers.

"Oh okay. Well you know that stuff better than I do, so I can't dispute it."

Rose smiles. "Now I'm curious as to why you don't drink. Did something happen?" She wonders.

I shake my head and chuckle. "The reason behind it is kind of embarrassing."

From the corner of my eye, I can see Rose rubbing her hands together. "You already know I want to hear this. I love your stories!"

I keep my eyes on the road and prepare my mind to tell her this story. "It's not as long as the Veronica story, and probably not as entertaining. But one time in the ninth grade, my health teacher brought in the real lungs of a longtime smoker and the liver of a longtime drinker. I damn near had a heart-attack when I saw the tar, pus, scars, and other problems on those organs," I explain.

Rose looks disgusted, even her lips are curling. "Oh god, and did you just say they were real organs?"

"Yeah, they were real alright! Didn't they show you organs in health class from people who donated their bodies to science after they died?"

Rose shakes her head and giggles. "No, not that I know of. The closest thing we did to that was dissecting frogs. And that alone made me want to vomit."

"Oh yeah, we did that too."

"Well dang maybe Bill Pickett High was more advanced than my very own Oakville High," Rose tells me.

"Oh hell nah, trust me, you guys were definitely more advanced. While you guys were working on smartboards and laptops, we still had chalkboards and textbooks. We were ancient as shit."

"Oh jeez!"

"Yeah, so when I came across that, I fainted in class. I recovered a couple minutes after that when my health teacher checked on me, but that impulse to once drink and smoke I had was gone. Those organs scarred me for life."

As soon as I finish telling my story, I pull up near the art gallery and park.

"That makes sense, I probably would've reacted the same way but, hey, I'm glad we're here now. I'm ready to see your painting skills," Rose says.

"Prepare to be amazed," I say, stepping out the car.

I follow my routine of walking around my car and opening the passenger side door. As I take Rose by the hand, she steps out the car and looks at the Christmas lights and decorations on the buildings surrounding us. "I love the downtown area this time of year. It looks like a Hallmark movie."

Before I can respond, I hear a man's voice say, "Hey Rose, long time no see."

I turn around to see a solid built man with a beard and bald head. He looks like he bench presses buildings for a living instead of actual weights. He resembles that famous street fighter I used to watch on YouTube named, Kimbo Slice. There's also a woman with long braids by his side. She's wearing black sunglasses even though it's nighttime and she isn't saying a word. She's just keeping a straight face while her hands clench onto a stroller that has a toddler inside.

"Oh hey, Raymond," Rose mutters, looking away from him and down at the ground. I can feel her hands shivering. It feels like she wants to run away from him.

Whoa! That's her ex-boyfriend, Raymond, the one who cheated on her and had a kid with another woman. Jesus Christ, this is the woman and the kid standing right here. No wonder Rose looks disgruntled.

I can't bear seeing Rose like this. She doesn't have to stand here and feel uncomfortable in front of this motherfucker.

"Hey man, I'm Eddie, I'm Rose's boyfriend." I firmly shake Raymond's hand. "We actually have to cut this short, because we're running late to our meeting to discuss our wedding plans. It was nice meeting you all," I tell him, taking Rose by the hand and walking away.

As Rose and I speed walk down the sidewalk, she holds my hand tight with the biggest smile on her face. "Oh my god, I can't believe you just did that. That was genius. I didn't want to be around that asshole or that snobby bitch for one second."

"Yeah, I could tell, so I thought of something on the fly when I saw your body language."

We bring our speed walking to a halt once we're in front of the art gallery. Rose gazes up at me. "Thank you for saving me, handsome," she says softly.

Light snow begins to fall upon us as we continue to stare into each other's eyes. My adrenaline is rushing, and I know she wants me to kiss her. Maybe I feel that way because I want to kiss her too. I run my hands through her long black hair and go for it, planting my lips onto hers like no one is around.

After our kiss she laughs and wipes my lips. "I'm sorry, I got my red lipstick on you."

"You don't have to apologize; I'll proudly kiss those red lips anytime." I hug her. "I know seeing Raymond again must've been hard. Are you going to be okay?"

Rose nods. "Yeah, because of you I am."

≈

We make our way inside the art gallery and find some available seats in the back row. While sitting next to each other, we notice each canvas has a snowy forest traced on it. I also can't help but notice that me and another guy sitting with his lady friend are the only men in the art gallery. This place is loaded with women. And oddly enough, there's two women who constantly keep looking back at me. They've been doing it ever since Rose and I walked in here. I'm not sure if I know them or not. And I'm starting to wonder if Rose notices their stares. But she seems too distracted by the canvas to care.

Eventually the art instructor walks in and distracts the two women. The instructor gives us directions on how we should paint the snowy forest. It seems like a simple breakdown too. She shows us step by step on how to use the glittery white paint to color the snow. And she shows us how to use the green and brown paint to color parts of the forest that aren't covered in snow. Rose and the rest of the women are doing a great job following along. But while they're on step seven, I'm still on step two, trying to figure out how in the fuck I colored green and brown paint in the spot where the snow is supposed to be. I thought I was on a roll at first, but art has never really been my specialty. As I peek over at the other man's canvas way in the front row, I see he didn't even start his painting. That makes me feel a little better. Maybe it's a guy thing.

After one of the art instructor's assistants passes out wine to us, Rose takes a sip and looks over at my canvas. She snickers when she sees my green paint and white paint sloppily painted and jumbled up. She's trying not to laugh herself to tears again like she did on our previous dates but it happens.

"Quick question," she utters in between her laughter.

"What's up?" I ask, already knowing what she's about to say.

She gulps down some more of her wine. "What in the world is that?"

I point toward the canvas with the paint brush I'm holding. "This painting right here is called, Picasso meets Basquiat."

Rose giggles and smacks my shoulder. "Oh really! Well, I guess we can try selling your painting to a museum then, huh?"

"Yeah, you know we should. This thing is a masterpiece, isn't it?" I pretend.

Rose raises her eyebrows. "I wish I could lie to you and say it's a masterpiece. But before you create a masterpiece, you're gonna have to learn how to paint first."

"Oh yeah?"

"Yeah."

I scoot my chair a little closer to hers, causing her to blush. "Well maybe you can teach me how to paint like you," I mutter near her ear.

Rose crosses her legs and chugs the rest of her wine. "We would have to get a whole new canvas for you, if I were to teach you how to do what I just did."

"Nah, no we don't," I reply, scooting my chair once more, getting as close as possible to her. Our thighs are touching. "I'll just place my hand on top of yours while you paint, and then I'll memorize that motion for the next time we do this again."

Rose blushes and snickers. "Ok," she says softly.

The art instructor's assistant makes her way around the room again, handing out second glasses of wine. "Would you like another glass of wine, miss?" she asks.

Rose nods and says, "Yes, please!"

Damn, she loves her wine.

The assistant places another glass of red wine next to Rose.

Rose wastes no time taking a drink before placing the glass down and whispering, "You're so goofy, but, okay, I'll show you how to paint. Thankfully, I'm already finished with my painting."

I place my hand onto Rose's and pretend to care about the way she's motioning her hand while painting the canvas. She knows what I'm doing, and I can tell she likes it. As I hold her right hand, I place my left arm around her waist. Things are getting hot.

A short period of time passes by when Rose finishes her second glass. She damn near chugged that one down too. Her eyes continue to lurk over towards the glass of wine that's in front of me. It hasn't been touched at all since I forgot to tell the assistant I don't drink.

"Can I have some of your wine, please? We both know you aren't going to touch it." She reaches across me to grab the glass before I can even hand it to her.

Rose is tipsy at this point. Even though I'm still in the mood to get frisky with her tonight, I'd be a liar if I said her actions weren't concerning me. During our small talk, she softly bites her lip from time to time in the middle of telling me how much she enjoys painting. She also continues to turn her face toward mine whenever I make her laugh. At times her face is so close to mine we're nearly inches away from kissing each other again. The blood from my head is running down to my other head right now. If there weren't twenty other people in here, I would just toss her on the canvas so we could make our own painting.

Without notice, Rose stops painting and hands me her paint brush. "Alright let's see if you mastered the motion correctly," she says.

"Yeah, I think I got the hang of it," I tell her, keeping my left arm wrapped around her waist.

Rose then begins to feel my biceps as I paint. "Wow, why am I just noticing how strong you are? Do you like going to the gym or something?"

Now, I'm no fool. I know Rose already noticed my biceps before, but this is her safest way of having some sort of sexual small talk without seeming like she's moving too fast.

"Yeah, I have a weight room and a treadmill at home in my basement. So I usually get a good workout four days a week."

Rose doesn't stop feeling on my arms. She makes her way from rubbing on my biceps to rubbing on my shoulders.

Rose if you keep this up, I might have to take your ass back to my place.

I slowly caress her back and whisper, "You're about to make this more than a sip & paint night if you keep it up."

Rose raises her eyebrows and gives me the most seductive smile I've ever seen. She finishes her third glass of wine and says, "Oh goodness I have to pee." She gets up, stumbling on her feet at first.

"Are you okay?" I ask.

"Yup, I'm fine." She laughs, gathering herself and making her way to the restroom.

That was probably perfect timing, since the paint night is about to be over in a few minutes. I'm going to need my erection to go down a bit before I stand up to get out of here.

"Hey I want to thank everyone for coming to the sip & paint night. I hope you all enjoyed yourselves and I'll be keeping everyone posted on when I'll be hosting my next event. Please don't forget to pack your belongings and take your canvases with you," the art instructor says.

As I feel on our canvases to see if they're dry, the two women who were staring at me earlier, begin staring at me again. They both grab their canvases and leave the front row, making their way toward me. The closer they get to my vicinity, the more I start to recognize one of their faces. It's Bianca! Instead of wearing braids, she now has a curly afro. No wonder I didn't recognize her at first.

I should cuss her out for making blogs about me online.

She throws away paper towels covered in paint in the trash can next to me while staring me down. She doesn't say a word to me though, and I don't say a word to her. After throwing away her trash she says something under her breath that I can't make out. She then laughs with her friend as they exit the art gallery. I mean, come on now, how old are we? I didn't want her; she needs to get over it.

By the time Rose exits the restroom, she looks mildly inebriated. "Are you ready to heaz . . . I mean heaz . . . um I'm sorry, I'm trying to say, are you ready to head out now," she says looking a little droopy eyed.

Aw damn, now she's slurring her words. I think running into Raymond today caused her to want to be in a drunken state. I should've stopped her from drinking earlier. I'm not doing a damn thing with her tonight.

"Yeah, let's get you home," I tell her, grabbing our freshly dried canvases and holding her hand to walk her to the car safely.

After getting Rose into the passenger seat of my car, she falls into a deep sleep. Within twenty-five minutes I finally arrive at her apartment complex. "Hey Rose, you're home now," I say, tapping her shoulder.

Rose doesn't wake up.

"Rose, you're home," I repeat, shaking her shoulder this time.

And still there's no response. As a matter of fact, she's snoring.

"Fuck," I whisper to myself as I rub my temples, trying to figure out what to do.

Suddenly, I come up with an idea to safely get her in her apartment. I reach into her coat pocket and grab her keys. I then exit the car and walk around to the passenger-side door to pick her up. As I carry Rose out the car, I realize carrying her to the third floor won't be so bad. She isn't heavy to me at all. She feels really light in weight. Based on my own estimated guess, Rose has to be five-foot five inches, weighing 120 pounds.

I'm now carrying her like she's a baby with her hair and legs dangling in the air. After carrying her up three flights of stairs, I make it to her apartment door and take her keys out of my pocket. I look down at her keys, and realize my only problem now is I have to figure out which one of these four keys unlocks her door.

Fucking Christ, dude.

I'm able to use my process of elimination tactic by noticing one of her keys has a Toyota logo on it. I then notice two silver keys and one gold key.

"I guess I'll try this gold one first," I say to myself, placing the key in the keyhole while continuing to carry Rose. As I twist the key, the door unlocks.

Yes!

I open the door and step inside, trying to find a light switch to turn on in her apartment. I slide my hand against the walls and can't find a light switch for shit. I'm sure there's one right by me, but the pitch-black darkness has me blind as a bat. It doesn't feel right to attempt walking around in her apartment to find her room, so I reach into my pocket, grab my phone, and turn my phone flashlight on. At that moment, I spot a couch and lay her on it. I then take her shoes off and decide to leave her pea coat on. After spotting a quilt she has on an armchair near the couch, I open up the quilt and lay it on top of her. The flashlight on my phone helps me spot the light switch on the wall.

"Wow! That thing was right next to me when I first

walked in just as I suspected," I say softly. I then turn the light switch on so she can see just in case she wakes up.

After making a swift exit it suddenly dawns on me that I didn't lock Rose's apartment door. As a matter of fact, it's impossible for me to lock her door from outside unless I take her keys with me for the night. And I can't do that since I'm heading to Seattle tomorrow. Hell, I can't even afford to spend the night and miss my flight. I don't want anyone breaking in while she's sleeping, so I have to find a way to wake her up.

I walk back into her apartment and shake her shoulders. "Hey Rose, do me a favor and lock your door, ok?"

Rose doesn't respond to me. All she does is turn her sleeping body over from laying on her left side to laying on her backside.

What am I going to do now?

I take a deep breath knowing I have one more attempt in me. I moderately slap her face. "ROSE!" I holler.

She immediately opens her eyes and then drunkenly smiles at me. "Hey baby, are we going to fuck tonight?" she asks with her breath smelling like wine.

Christ! I wish! Why do you have to be drunk right now?

I shake my head and say, "No, but maybe next time, sweetheart."

"Aw ok," she replies before trying to go back to sleep.

"No, no, no, Rose. I need you to do me a favor and lock the door, okay? I'll see you when I come back from

Seattle," I explain, pulling her off the couch and on to her feet.

"Aw okay, handsome," she answers sluggishly, following me to the door.

Before heading all the way out, I hug Rose and kiss her on the forehead. "Bye, don't forget to lock the door," I instruct her.

"Bye, bye, goodnight," she replies, slowly shutting the door. As I hear the door click and lock, my anxiety goes away and I take a deep sigh of relief.

Thankfully she's safe now.

CHAPTER TEN

December 10th

It's Sunday morning and I wake up to the sound of my phone buzzing on my drawer next to my bed. I pick up the phone to see that it's Rose calling me.

"Good morning, are you feeling alright?" I ask her.

"Oh god, what did I do last night? The last thing I remember doing, is leaving the restroom at the art gallery. After that, everything is a blur," Rose explains to me.

I feel like she remembers more, like the part where she asked me to have sex with her. But I think she's too embarrassed to bring it up. Or maybe that's my ego talking.

"Yeah, you were pretty hammered last night. You were slurring your words and everything, after walking out of the restroom. I made sure I got you home safely though."

I can hear Rose take a deep breath through the phone. "Eddie, I can't thank you enough for looking out for me the way you did. I promise, I normally don't act like that. But when I saw Raymond, all of those scarred memories came back again."

"You're fine. All I cared about was making sure you had a good time and that you were safe. And Rose, if anything is ever bothering you, you can always feel free to talk to me about it."

I hear a few sniffles on her end of the phone. "I appreciate it." Her voice breaks. "Goodness gracious, let me get myself together." There's a brief pause before Rose continues. "Okay I'm good now. Eddie, did I say anything wild or crazy to you while I was drunk? I hope I was on my best behavior."

Oh yeah she knows exactly what she said to me last night. But I'm gonna play it cool and act like I didn't hear shit.

"Nah, I didn't hear you say anything crazy. You were just zoned out for the most part. After carrying you to your apartment, I had to wake you up so you could lock your door."

Rose laughs. "That's so embarrassing! I'm glad you were there to look after me though."

"So am I." While on the phone, I check the clock on the wall and immediately realize that I have to pack the rest of my things and head to the airport so I don't miss my flight. Thank goodness Rose called me because I completely forgot to set my alarm. "Hey, I hate that I have to hang up soon, but I need to get ready for this flight."

"Oh it's okay. Make sure you keep me posted on how everything goes when you're out there in Seattle!"

"I will and I'm going to need you to answer the

phone to keep me company when I'm in my hotel room out there. I hear it can get kind of isolating."

"I promise you I will. Have a safe trip," Rose says with delight.

≈

That afternoon my flight arrives in Seattle. After landing, I make my way through the airport and to the arrival area to meet up with my manager, Oscar.

"Hey brother man, how was your flight?" he asks me.

Every time I hang around Oscar he never addresses me by my name. He calls me *brother man*, *young brother*, and any other type of *brother* that exists.

"Oscar! What's up! My flight was cool, I was asleep the whole time. When I woke up, I noticed there were a bunch of nuns and priests on my flight for some reason. You would've thought they were about to perform an exorcism on the plane or some shit," I tell him.

"Man, I saw the same thing on my flight here last night. They said there's some catholic conference going on this week in the area. But besides all that, I'm glad we're finally here. We have a lot of engagements to take care of this week. You ready?"

Oscar's question goes in one ear and out the other. I'm looking off into the distance staring out the window at the airport. I'm thinking about Rose, hoping she's alright mentally. I know there must be more to the story when it comes to how Raymond treated her. I can't get the memory of how her hands started shaking when she saw him out of my head. Or how she forced herself to drink into an inebriated state after seeing him. I'm not intentionally trying to think about that situation either, but it keeps popping up in my head.

Oscar waves his hands in front of my face to get my attention back. "Are you good, brother man?" he asks with concern.

I snap out of my trance. "Oh yeah, yeah, yeah, I'm good, Oscar. And I'm ready too! This is going to be a great weekend!"

Oscar nods. "Ya damn skippy it is! The amount of money we're about to make is wild! You're going to have a camera crew following you around all week for that documentary you'll be in. On top of that, there are going to be a lot of people at your book signing tomorrow and at the one you'll be having on Saturday!"

I snap my fingers in excitement. "Let's go!" I celebrate. "How's everything going with my pitch for the animation films?" I ask.

Oscar looks as if he's thinking of something creative to say instead of delivering bad news. My frustration is about to kick in because he's taking too long to answer.

"Not good, huh?" I say.

"Look, young brother, I know you want to keep pitching your two children's books as animation films, but the market isn't looking for that kind of thing right now. You should go ahead and allow me to finally call some of those film producers back about your novel, *My Girlfriend's A Vampire*. A lot of producers are interested in talking to us about it. And you know what that means, right?"

"What does it mean?"

"It means they're interested in negotiating a deal with you to turn it into a film. That's the book that got everyone's attention at the moment, and you have to be honest with yourself, too, that's the book that changed your life."

I didn't want to hear that, but Oscar was right. My children's books weren't best-sellers. And no one really cared about my children's books besides a few schools and some children's hospitals. But those same places that have me read to children, invite any children's book author they can find. So I'm not special to them. I guess it's about time I listen to Oscar when it comes to pitching my work.

"Man, this sucks because I really have great animation ideas. I just need these producers to hear me out," I explain.

"I understand that but if you allow me to help pitch your vampire novel then it'll be more of a success when it gets converted into film. From there you'll have the power to make any film you want in any genre. You see where I'm coming from?" Oscar asks.

"Yeah, I see what you mean. Thanks for looking out for me. I guess you can go ahead and give those producers a call."

"Smart move! That's what I'm here for, young brother. I'm glad you're finally agreeing to this, it took me a couple months to convince you, but you finally pulled through," Oscar says.

"My bad, man, I just had my vision set on another path when it came to entering the film industry," I admit.

"That's alright, Things don't always go the way ya planned, but you're on your way to the mountain top. Listen, the promotion staff has all of your books ready for set up tomorrow at the children's hospital and The Hawkins Library. And the promoters put you in a luxury hotel too. You're going to like this place, brother man, it's top-notch."

"I can't wait to see this. As long as they have a pool, I'm cool."

"Absolutely, that's a given. Now I know this place isn't Vegas or Brazil but I know you're about to go crazy with the women out here."

I hold my hands up. "You know what, I'm actually going to try to chill and remain focused from now on. Even when it comes to the Vegas and Brazil thing, I'm officially hanging it up."

Oscar can't believe the words that are coming out of my mouth. "Shiddd, are you crazy? The women out here are freaky . . . in a good way! You can have three girlfriends and three wives out here. They might be even freakier than the hookers you were fucking."

"That may be the case but I'm past that phase in my life. I'm trying to focus on writing more books and learning more about film."

"Shiddd, you can still do that while smashing these chicks. Young brother, you already know I've been married for the past fifteen years with my beautiful wife. We have three amazing kids together. But if I could take a time machine and relive my player days for one day…I would."

I laugh at Oscar's explanation.

"I'm serious," he says. "If I was your age, I would keep moving the way you *were* moving. Have all the fun you can while you can still have it."

I shake my head and say, "Trust me, I'm good man."

Oscar squints at me and asks, "What happened to you?"

"Nothing."

"When you came to Brazil with me and my family, you took off and went to a different brothel every night. We didn't spend time with you until it was time to board the plane again. That's what I call living the life, but now you're telling me you're in a different phase. You in love or something?" He's really intrigued.

I shake my head. "I don't want to say all that, but I met a girl recently who I'm connecting with," I admit.

"Are you married to her?" Oscar jokingly asks me.

I laugh. "Of course not, man, we just met."

"Then you need to take my advice."

I ignore Oscar's persistent bad advice. "Nah, I'm trying to elevate in life."

"Well shit, young brother, I'm your manager, I want you to elevate too. Just like how I want to elevate the rest of the writers I manage. Just remember my saying: enjoy your prime while you still can."

I'll say anything now to get Oscar to shut up about this. "Okay I'll make sure I keep that advice locked in my brain, alright old man?" I point to his gray Rastafarian dreadlocks.

"Shiddd I'm only forty-seven, young buck, nowhere close to old. And my wife loves my gray hair by the way. She says I look like an older version of Bob Marley."

"I can picture her saying that."

Oscar hands me a shiny plastic card, that looks like a credit card. "Here's your hotel key, when the driver drops us off, you'll be in room 311. Get a good rest, too, because tomorrow morning I have to get you up to read to the kids at Seattle Children's Hospital. And right after that, you'll be getting interviewed by those college students for the documentary."

"Gotcha, Oscar, after I hop in the pool and eat, I'll get some rest. And I'll be ready for tomorrow."

CHAPTER ELEVEN

December 11ᵗʰ

It's the next morning and I'm in the middle of a peaceful sleep recovering from jetlag when I hear, "Yo, brother man! Get up!" It's Oscar yelling and banging on my door.

"Damn! I hope I'm not late for the event," I say to myself.

"Are you up, young brother?" Oscar asks.

"I'M UP!" I shout.

"Okay good, we have to be at the children's hospital in one hour." Oscar continues to bang on the door like a cop. He probably thinks I'm going to fall back to sleep like I'm one of his kids.

I sit up and wipe the sleep out my eyes. "Okay, and you can stop banging on the door now. I'm getting myself ready."

"I hear ya! And we ordered some room service for you too. It's Apple juice, pancakes, eggs, and sausages. I hope you can handle all that without having to shit at the hospital while reading to the kids." Oscar laughs.

Way to ruin my appetite.

"Well, now I have to think twice about eating that crap, thanks for the heads up."

"Absolutely, choose wisely, young brother."

I decide to starve myself and place my food in the fridge till I get back. An hour later at Seattle Children's Hospital, I read to the cancer patients in the hospital's playroom. They enjoy both of my children's books to the point where they ask nonstop questions about the characters. I have a good time answering all their questions and handing them coloring sheets of my characters.

As the children and their parents prepare to gather in a line to buy my books, a young boy who looks to be around seven-years-old asks, "Hey, sir, can I have a book?"

He has no hair on his head or on his eyebrows. The chemo must really be taking a toll on this poor kid. I look over to Oscar to see if he's paying attention to me. When I spot him, I see he's setting up a table and a kiosk where people can pay for my books.

"Sure, kid, where are your parents?"

"They went to the store to buy me food."

"Okay, do you know when they'll be back?"

The boy shrugs. "No."

I look at the display copy of *Dreamscape Land* that I'm holding in my hands. "That's fine. Here, you can have my copy." I sign the book and hand it to the boy.

"Thank you, sir. I really liked your story. It's just like

Peter Pan when he goes on adventures with his friends in Neverland."

"You're welcome, kid, and I'm glad it reminds you of that!"

The boy waves and walks away with one of the nurses to his room.

This is my seventh time visiting a children's hospital to read to kids, and it never gets old. My favorite part about it is leaving books for them to have for free. I just got away with giving away my display copy to the little boy. But unfortunately, I'm not able to give away free books anymore because of my contractual agreement. Oscar constantly reminds me that we lose money every time I give my books away for free, and he hates when I do it. With our new contractual agreement, he's looking out for my best interest as he should, but I couldn't care less about trying to get the parents of ill children to buy my books. They have so many other things to worry about like their children dying, and a cluster fuck of hospital bills. Buying my books shouldn't be another concern for them. I guess that's where I fall short in this business though; apparently, I'm too nice.

After signing the books for the families, a nun approaches me. She's a short elderly black woman. And strangely enough, I believe she was with the nuns and priests I saw on the plane on my way here to Seattle.

"Hello, I wanted to come over here and tell you that your book was wonderful. The kids adored the story."

"Thank you. I'm glad I could play a part in making their day better," I tell her.

"Well you surely did make Charlie's day!"

"Who's Charlie?"

"That was the kid you gifted a copy of your book to. That was sweet of you to do. Charlie has leukemia, and we've been told a lot of his days have been hard, but you definitely made him feel better."

It puts a smile on my face to know I made that kid's day. "It's the least I could do. I can't imagine the pain these families have to go through every day."

"Bless you, hon! While you were introducing yourself to the families, I heard you say you were from Delaware. Which area are you from?"

"I'm from Blue River."

The nun gives a slight nod and smiles. "What a coincidence, me too! I'm here with the other sisters and some priests, visiting the hospital for charity work this week."

"That's good. Yeah, I think I saw all of you on the plane on our way here yesterday."

"Yup, that was us. Um, young man, do you mind if I take some time out to pray for you?"

I'm taken aback by her question. Maybe it's because no one has asked if they could pray for me before. She's a nun so I suppose she asks this question to a lot of people she meets. I don't want to offend her by saying *no*. She seems like a nice person anyway, so why not?

"No, I don't mind. You can pray for me."

The nun grins. "Great, let me hold your hands, please."

I place my hands in hers and she begins to pray

silently with her eyes closed and head down. To not feel awkward, I close my eyes and put my head down too. Out of nowhere, the nun touches my forehead while she continues to pray in silence. Instantaneously, I begin to see the faces of all the hookers I slept with. In each scene, I'm positioned on top of them as they lie down on a bed looking up at me. I don't know why I'm having these flashbacks, but I feel like fainting at any moment.

Blessedly, the nun takes her hand off my forehead and the images of the women go away. "Thank you, young man," the nun says after she finishes praying.

Oscar then approaches me. He smiles and waves at the nun out of respect and then looks to me and says, "Hey, young brother, I want you to finally meet Sherry and Ben. These are the college students who are going to feature you in their documentary. They were recording you while you were reading to the kids and they're ready to interview you now."

"Okay, cool, here I come," I tell Oscar before turning my attention back to the nun. "It was nice meeting you Miss—"

I leave my hand out waiting for the nun to say her name.

"—Sister Dolores," she answers.

"Gotcha, well it was nice meeting you, Sister Dolores."

"It was nice meeting you, too, Eddie. Continue to do your best," Sister Dolores says to me.

I appreciate her being kind enough to pray for me, but now I feel off. Almost like I'm in a daze. I'm wondering why the women I've slept with over the past few years entered my head during her prayer. That's never happened to me before.

CHAPTER TWELVE

Before I get around to introducing myself to Sherry and Ben, I get a text from Rose. Seeing a text from her brightens my day, even way out here in Seattle.

> How's Seattle treating you today?

> Great so far! They're about to start filming me soon.

> Yay! Good luck! Let me know how it goes. You got this! 😊

> Will do! I'll call you.

I meet Ben and Sherry in the corner of the lobby. "Hey it's nice to finally meet you guys in person. Thanks for having me take part in your documentary," I tell them.

"Oh, no, thank you, Eddie. We're excited about having you on. Sherry and I love *My Girlfriend's A Vampire*. That novel was incredible," Ben explains.

"Yes, it was so good! It has everything in it! Drama, thriller, comedy, romance, action, and suspense," Sherry adds.

I notice Ben and Sherry have English accents. Their brown hair, pale skin, and Harry Potter demeanor pretty much tells me they're from the UK.

Ben and Sherry have been raving about my book to me through email for months. While reading those emails, I would've never guessed they were from the UK.

"I'm grateful for the compliments about my novel. I had a fun time creating it. And I have to ask, are you two from England?"

Ben laughs. "I see you've noticed our accents. Yes, we're from London, England, and we decided to come here to the U.S. for film school," he reveals.

I envy the people who take a chance to go to film school. I've always wondered what it was like. For me on the other hand, I ended up going to college for Criminal Justice because my parents thought film school was a waste of time and scholarship money. It was either Criminal Justice or the army. I chose Criminal Justice. Eventually after earning my degree, I got a job counseling juveniles and went to school again to study pre-law, but I hated doing both. There was a lot of unwanted stress that came with working at a job I didn't love and at the same time going to school again for a career I didn't care for.

Now I'm in a totally different career field, but that's how life works, I guess.

"That's cool, I love hearing things like that." I then rub my hands together and ask, "So, where would you two like to start."

"We can start the first part of our interview right here in the playroom. It'll be pretty quiet since everyone is leaving now," Sherry says.

"Okay, then I'll leave you both to it," I tell them, sitting down on a chair they have set up for me.

Oscar's phone suddenly rings. "Brother man, I'll be back in a few. I have to take this call," he says, exiting the playroom.

After Sherry and Ben set up their lights and adjust their camera angles, their interview with me begins.

Ben sits down behind the camera and says, "Alright, ladies and gentlemen, we are here with Author Eddie Valentine the Fourth and we'll be hanging out with him for a few days to get the inside scoop on how he creates his stories in a world full of distractions. . . . So, Eddie, first things first. How in the world do you create in a world full of distractions?"

I chuckle and say, "I take a bunch of nature walks, I exercise, and I stay off social media as much as possible unless I have to promote something. All of these things play a role in my creative process. It gives me time to think about new stories and create them."

"Love it, so you do your part in avoiding the things that can distract you?" Ben asks.

"Correct," I answer.

"Great! And based on other interviews and articles we read about you, we found out you were inspired by animation films like Aladdin and Peter Pan when you first started writing your books?"

"That's right, films like those inspired me to write both of my children's books *The Prince and Princess* and *Dreamscape Land.*"

"If I'm not mistaken, those two children's books are stories that you really tried to push on a mainstream level when you published them. Are you still hoping to get them made into animation films one day?"

"Yeah, that's still a goal I have set for myself. It's been a struggle, but my team and I will focus on pitching those stories again after handling the business we have set up for my novel."

"I respect that. I read both stories and to give them a brief summary, *The Prince and Princess* was a fairytale about a young man from NYC who takes a trip to a fictional country in Africa and meets an African princess, who happens to live in a magical kingdom. The fairytale takes off to new heights once they get together, and fight off evil witches and warlocks to save the princess's kingdom. Which leads the princess to falling in love with the young man, eventually making him a prince when they get married. I could truly see the Aladdin inspiration in that book. And with *Dreamscape Land,* you wrote about young orphans dreaming their way out of a terrible orphanage and embarking on a journey to a new world of wonderment. That story displayed how inspired you were by Peter Pan. They were very creative."

"Thanks, man, hopefully I can get film producers to see it that way too one day."

Ben nods and says, "I understand, but, Eddie, I must be honest and say that those two stories don't really stand out when it comes to other children's books that have been made. They kind of get lost in the oversaturated market of children's books that are being published each year. You would have to create a picture book that really stood the test of time."

Hearing Ben explain things the way he did, really hit me in the gut. Maybe this is what Oscar has been trying to explain to me in the most polite way possible without shattering my ego. I might have to come to the realization that my children's books suck balls. They've sucked this whole fucking time! My ego kept getting in the way of me seeing reality. This feels like a shot to the chest.

Ben continues, "Well that leads us to this. After writing your children's books, you randomly took a sharp transition last year when you created an adult novel titled, *My Girlfriend's A Vampire*. This is my favorite book of yours and perhaps one of my favorite books of all-time! Now, this specific story took off to an entirely different stratosphere! In fact, it may be one of the best indie books in the past five years. What made you abandon being a children's book author?"

Ben is asking some really great questions. No wonder he and Sherry are fantastic documentarians. But my newly found imposter syndrome is kicking in extremely bad at the moment. My brain is still stuck on how I've probably made the lamest children's books ever. I feel like nothing but a piece of garbage.

I suddenly feel Ben tap my knee. "Hey, Eddie, are you okay?" he asks me.

I nod. "Oh, yes, I'm fine. Sorry, can you ask me that again?"

"Not a problem at all. What made you abandon being a children's book author?" Ben asks again.

I take a deep breath and prepare to give the most honest answer I can give. "Well, since I published both of my children's books seven years ago after graduating college, I figured I really wasn't making the impact I wanted to make in the industry. In other words, I realized no one gave a fuck about those stories. Well, some schools and hospitals showed love to those stories but not many. My stories didn't have the impact I wanted them to have. Remember the Dr. Seuss books, Ameilia Bedelia books, and Junie B. Jones books? I was looking to create a children's book franchise like those, but none of the stories took off. So I figured the next best thing was to pitch my stories as animation films for people to catch onto my creativity. While waiting on studios to accept or reject my pitches, a few people over the years have asked me if I ever thought about making an adult novel. Writing a novel never crossed my mind, but I'm always up for a challenge. After a bad breakup, I eventually experimented to see what it would be like creating a unique adult novel so I combined magic, action, comedy, and suspense with sex. And that's when I came up with *My Girlfriend's A Vampire*. I thought it would be like the book Twilight initially but it turned out to be nothing like Twilight at all.

I'm glad my story ended up being original."

Ben seems excited by my response. "That's quite fascinating! Yes, there's nothing out there like your novel. It took so many twists and turns with the main characters, Vinnie and Diamond. The only thing I noticed similar to Twilight was that Diamond and her family were vegetarian vampires where they drank cow blood on their farm instead of human blood. But that was it! Other than that, Vinnie and Diamond are college students who keep up this steamy romance while Vinnie's ex-girlfriend, Patricia, becomes jealous and enraged when she sees that he's moved on. Which was crazy since Patricia was the one who cheated on Vinnie with some frat boy in Vinnie's dorm room. That was so absurd! Anyways, I don't want to spoil this for anyone who hasn't read Eddie's book but I have to add that Patricia finds out Diamond is a vampire and tries to harm her. It gets wickedly better from there! This book had a perfect combination of everything," Ben explains.

"Thank you. You did a better job explaining and promoting my book than me," I respond.

"No, thank you for creating this masterpiece. And it all makes sense now, a bad breakup is the thing that caused you to create this magnificent novel. I guess you had a Patricia within your own life," Ben says.

I nod and laugh.

Ben continues, "Your manager told us a lot of film companies are interested in making this into a film. Let me also add that you ended up selling 9,000 copies within the first week, allowing you to enter the New York Times

Best-Seller list. How did that make you feel?" he asks.

"Honestly, it felt alright, I wasn't expecting any of this to happen. I just turned my heartbreak into a creative earthquake. That's the best way I can describe it."

Ben then tells Sherry to stop recording before turning to me and saying, "That was great, Eddie. We're going to ask you more questions at the Hawkins Library downtown. And we're going to record the book signing you have this upcoming Saturday as well. We have a long week ahead of us."

"Awesome, I'm ready for it!"

CHAPTER THIRTEEN

L ater on, I give Rose a call during her lunch break.

"Hey handsome, how did the interview go?" Rose asks me.

I want to tell her about my encounter with that Sister Dolores lady, but she'll never talk to me again if I tell her what I'd seen while Sister Dolores prayed for me. I guess it's best if I don't bring the shit up at all. "It went pretty good," I tell her. "They have a few more interviews for me to do, but I enjoy the direction they're going in so far. The second part of their interview will be inside of Seattle's Space Needle."

"Ooo, I love the sound of that. You're getting all the superstar treatment."

"Nah, I think everyone they're interviewing for this documentary is getting this kind of treatment."

"Well, either way I'm proud of everything you're doing. It really inspires me to make each day count. Oh, and before you go to do the other part of your interview, I wanted to let you know my students have been talking about you all morning. They keep asking about *Mr.*

Eddie," Rose says while laughing.

"You tell your students that Mr. Eddie says hi."

"I will! I went to Barnes & Noble and purchased your novel yesterday too."

"Rose, why did you do that? You could've gotten a copy from me for free," I say, prepared to break my contractual agreement with Oscar once again. But hey, giving a free book to Rose every time I release a new one shouldn't hurt our pockets at all.

"No, that would've felt wrong, like I wasn't compensating you for your work."

I smirk. "You can compensate me in other ways."

"Ooo. That's fine by me," Rose responds with delight.

"The next time I publish a novel, I'll be handing you a free copy."

"Okay, you win, Eddie."

"Good!"

"Ya goofball! Now where was I? Oh yeah, so I started reading *My Girlfriend's A Vampire* last night and, my goodness, no wonder people love it! I'm seven chapters in and the romance between Vinnie and Diamond has me hooked. But I have to ask you something?"

"I already know what it is. Are you about to ask me about the character, Patricia?"

Rose laughs. "Yes, I am! Was Patricia's character inspired by Veronica?"

"Yeah, I have to admit it, she was."

"Oh my god, I knew it! I can't wait to finish this

now. When you come back can you sign the book for me?"

"You got it!"

"Thank you, Eddie! You have fun for me out there today, ok?"

"I'll try, and you enjoy your lunch for me. I'm starving and can't wait till this film day to be wrapped up so I can eat."

"I'll try!" Rose exclaims.

≈

Ben and Sherry shoot the second part of my interview for their documentary inside of Seattle's Space Needle. While looking from the inside out, I notice one of the coolest sights I've ever seen in my lifetime. I can see the entire city from where I'm standing. After Ben and Sherry finish up the second part of my interview about my life and where I come from, they end up introducing me to other creative people who are being featured in their documentary.

The first person they introduce me to is a woman named Cathy. Her talent is outstanding. She creates human sized clay sculptures and mini clay sculptures of people's deceased loved ones. She carves each of these sculptures as angels for people, showing them their loved ones have transitioned to a better place. After meeting Cathy, I'm introduced to a man named Yao who creates AI toy robots for kids. It's cool and also terrifying to see how his robots are able to answer any questions you have about anything the human mind can think of. Yao also mentions that his AI robots may have the ability to babysit kids within the next twenty years. Lastly, I'm introduced to a woman who goes by the name Pixie. She sings, writes, plays the flute, and composes her own music. She calls it ambient music. This is the first time I've heard of that term and genre. When she plays her ambient instrumentals, I realize it's meditation music. Pixie adds a little spice to the ambient music by singing in a slightly lower register than opera singers while the music is playing. Pixie's music is the most soothing music I've heard in my life. I love it so much, I end up adding her songs to my playlist on my phone.

I feel more talentless by the second after meeting Cathy, Yao, and Pixie. "Hey Ben and Sherry, I don't want to tell you how to run your documentary or anything, but why am I on here? These people are way more talented than I am. I'm just a writer. These creators who are featured in your documentary are damn near changing the shape of the world."

Sherry pats my back and says, "And you're changing the shape of the world, too, my friend. We know about the things you do for ill children in hospitals. We also saw you give a free book to the kid with leukemia who didn't have the money or his parents around to buy the book. You didn't do it for the clout, you did it because you're kind. And you're also one of the most brilliant novelists we've come across."

Ben agrees with Sherry. "That's right. Eddie. Dude, you're a genius. We know your career is about to take off.

You're the only person in this documentary who's not from Seattle. We invited you from way across the country for a reason. That's how incredible you are!"

Uh oh, my imposter syndrome is kicking in again. "Whatever you guys see in me is something I surely don't see in myself. But hey, thank you for the positive words and encouragement."

"Absolutely and please never stop writing," Sherry says to me.

"I gotcha, Sherry. I won't."

After speaking with Sherry and Ben, they gather all of us creators around and record us talking and eating with one another as we travel through Downtown Seattle and Seattle's Waterfront. It feels like I'm on an episode of *The Real World*. These types of recordings continue throughout most of the week as Ben and Sherry interview us at many of the landmark spots in Seattle. It's something I'll never forget.

≈

December 16th

It's now Saturday and my book signing event is about to begin. When I arrive at the Hawkins Library, I notice there's a nice size line that starts from the inside of the building and protrudes to the outside of it. I've never had this many people line up to see me before. Wow, I love the people here in Seattle already, this must be a city full of bookworms. It feels incredible seeing this turnout.

After Oscar leads me inside to sit down, talk, and sign copies of my books, I realize the women here are infatuated with my novel. In return, it's making them become infatuated with me. They're asking me questions like, "Do you act like your character, Vinnie, in real life?" or "Are you going to make a sequel?" and lastly "Are you single, because I can see myself with a man like you?" None of this fazes me though, because I'm looking forward to seeing Rose again. We've been talking on the phone every night this week. And she's been excited to hear about everything that's going on, too, literally motivating me each step of the way. Last night on the phone, Rose randomly said to me that I was going to be the next Stephen King and Spike Lee. She has me ready to seal the deal with these film producers as soon as possible.

As the book signing is about to wrap up, I stand up from my seat, looking for Oscar so we could leave. But at that moment, someone speed walks to my table. It's a woman who looks to be at least in her late 30s. She's wearing a tight orange dress and, holy moly, she's sexy as fuck. I can't deny it! The woman holds out my novel in her hand, waiting for me to sign it.

"Hi Eddie Valentine the Fourth, it's nice to meet you in person. I have to tell you that this book right here is my favorite book ever! The chemistry between Vinnie and Diamond is electrifying and sexy. What inspired you to write it?" she asks.

I would answer her right away, but I'm blinded by her sex appeal. My god, this woman looks like a porn star version of Tyra Banks. She has a fat ass, huge titties, and a seductive raspy voice. She's leaning on my table, too, purposely displaying most of her cleavage. Shit, the Easter Bunny, Buddha, Muhammad, and Jesus needs to take the wheel right now before I do something I regret.

Come on, dumbass, focus.

I'm able to force my eyes to look away from her cleavage and stare at her face.

"Thank you! I'm glad you enjoyed the book. And honestly, a lot of life changing events inspired me to write the novel," I tell her.

"Oh okay, I like the range you have in your writing and I get a sense you have an old-school taste with your young self," she says, lightly tapping my hand.

I laugh and playfully wave the woman off. "I can't be any younger than you. You have to be in your early twenties, right?" I ask her, knowing she's older, but I know it will make her feel good.

Oh no, what the hell am I doing?

She blushes. "Boy, I'm fifty-three years-old! You better stop it or I'm going to end up in your bed tonight."

Holy shit, even that caught me off guard. I thought she was at least going to say thirty-eight or thirty-nine years old, but fifty-three? No freaking way. Now I'm even more attracted to her, but I'm trying to keep it together.

Focus. Focus. Focus.

She continues, "Speaking of tonight, what are you doing after this?" she asks me.

At this point, I'm picturing myself talking to Rose on the phone again tonight. I'm visualizing her smile, and

I'm hearing her contagious laugh. I know Rose and I aren't a couple and never verbally said we're serious about each other, but something in my gut is telling me I would feel like shit if I ended up fucking this woman tonight.

I do my best to come up with an escape plan from this woman and our conversation, shrugging and saying, "I don't know, I think my manager said we have something planned."

Luckily Oscar is on his way walking toward me, maybe he can save the day.

"Hey Oscar, what are we doing after this?" I ask him, with my eyes open extremely wide, hoping he understands that I'm trying to find a way out.

Oscar grins as he simultaneously looks at me and the woman. "We're going to Club Hookah around nine p.m.! People are looking forward to seeing you there, young brother! Don't get mad but I told everybody how you usually dance your ass off. Doing all those James Brown and Michael Jackson moves!"

No, Oscar, no! You should've said we were leaving Seattle tonight.

He's laughing and has no clue he completely botched my plan to get away from this woman.

"Oh, okay Eddie, you know how to dance like that? Now I have to find out for myself. My name is Lisa by the way," the woman says, shaking my hand.

"Nah, he's playing around. I can't dance, but I'm glad I was able to meet you, Lisa. Thanks again for showing my novel some love."

"No problem, sweetie. I'll make sure I'm at Club

Hookah tonight. I wanna see what you're all about," Lisa says, winking at me and walking away.

It doesn't help that Oscar and I are staring directly at Lisa's ass while she's leaving. But that ass of hers fits nicely through that tight dress she's wearing. It's jiggling like jello! Fuck, get me the hell out of Seattle! Now!

Oscar takes a deep breath and wipes his forehead. "Man, I know you're gonna fuck her tonight. Ain't no way you're turning that down. You better take that down for every man on the planet," he says, patting me on the shoulder like a proud father. "Dammit, I wish I was you!"

Before I can respond, Oscar's phone begins to ring again.

"Hold on, young brother, I have to get this." He steps away and answers the phone.

CHAPTER FOURTEEN

It's now ten p.m. and Oscar texted me about leaving my hotel room an hour ago. I never bothered replying. I'm really second guessing going to the club. I don't want to put myself in a predicament where Lisa is sucking my dick by the end of the night. If they would've scheduled this documentary and book signing a month prior to December before I met Rose, then I would be fucking Lisa's brains out, and I wouldn't be this conflicted at all. Being able to be vulnerable, compassionate, and feel supported, is something Rose provides me emotionally. This is something I've never experienced before. She reciprocates the same energy I give her. And I don't want to ruin the magnetic chemistry I have with her . . . I can't.

In the process of thinking, I hear a knock at the door.

"Hey, are you ready? You never texted me back," Oscar says.

I open the door to let Oscar in. "Nah man, I don't think I want to go. I have a bad feeling about this," I tell him.

"Come on, you have to go, this is more engagement for you. We need you to get involved with the people who support you. Shiddd man, even Sherry and Ben will be there. And so will the other creators you met being featured in the documentary with you."

I don't respond back to Oscar right away. I just shake my head and think.

Oscar isn't giving up. He's still trying to persuade me the best way he can. "Listen, young brother, nothing bad is going to happen. You don't drink or do drugs, you'll be perfectly fine. And I'll be there, you know I'm not doing a damn thing, but sitting down and having a few beers. I won't let anything happen to you either. I need you to get out on the dance floor, and socialize with people so they can see that their favorite author is a human being just like everyone else."

I nod because Oscar is making a valid point, this will help me connect with my readers on a different level.

"Okay, I understand what you're saying. Seattle is showing a lot of love so I'll do it."

"That's what I'm talking about!"

≈

As we walk into the club, we're greeted by a lot of people who were at the book signing earlier. And lo and behold, Ben and Sherry are here to record us creatives. I thought they were finally going to relax and enjoy themselves. I had no idea they would still be shooting for their documentary tonight. What more could they possibly need? Cathy and Pixie are immersed into the crowd, dancing. Yao is at the bar drinking a beer. He looks like he's nodding off too. Ben and Sherry are getting all of our actions on film, including me walking into the club with Oscar, looking clueless.

"I'm going to be at the bar, young brother. Let me know if you need me," Oscar says to me.

While trying to find a corner to briefly hide in as I shake away my nerves, the DJ suddenly starts blasting Jamaican dancehall music. Everyone on the dance floor is going wild. There are women shaking their asses all over the place. I thought I would be able to hide during one of these songs, but, instantly, some random woman starts throwing her ass on me. And of course, the camera is on me now as people in the club scream, "Go Eddie, go Eddie!"

As the woman shakes her ass on me, I'm now caught up in a situation where I can only react in two ways in front of this camera. I can look like an asshole and walk away from her while she's dancing on me, or I can enjoy myself and dance with her throughout the whole song. It's just innocent fun, right? There's no harm in that.

After the song ends, the woman and I stop dancing with each other and I immediately find a dark corner to sit in. At that moment, the DJ plays another dancehall song and says he's going to play them for the rest of the night. Apparently, he loves the vibe it's giving. From afar I see Lisa strutting to me in a sexy royal blue bodycon dress. It displays all her curves too.

She caresses my chin and says, "Come on, let's dance, baby."

I shake my head. "Aw dang, sorry, Lisa, my legs are killing me already after that first dance."

This cougar is not letting up, she climbs on top of me and sits on my lap. I think she's trying to relive her twenties.

"That's no problem, baby. I'll dance on you then." Lisa starts bouncing her voluptuous ass on my bulge. I know from a distance it probably looks like I'm getting a lap dance from a stripper or even worse, it probably looks like Lisa and I are fucking.

"You sure are enjoying the music," I say to her.

"Yes, honey, this is why dancehall is my favorite," Lisa says, continuing her lap dance on me. Her energy is so overpowering. My dick is getting hard and I know she can feel it, too, because she begins pressing against me even harder. And I don't want to push her off me either, but this has to stop.

Oscar walks up to us, smiling from ear to ear. He's also clapping and pointing at me.

I think his crazy ass is drunk already.

"Shiddd, youngin', I see you," Oscar says, encouraging the madness.

"Chill," I tell him.

"It's okay, honey, I don't care who stares at us," Lisa says, while grinding on me.

"THAT'S MY YOUNG BROTHER, RIGHT HERE," he yells to the crowd.

Just my luck, now everyone's watching. I need to get

my ass back to the hotel.

"Hey Lisa, I'm sorry, I'm not feeling well. I'm going to head back to my hotel. It was nice meeting you again. I gotta go," I explain to her, getting up from the chair.

I wave goodbye to Cathy, Pixie, and Yao even though he's completely hammered and slumped face down on the bar.

I then signal to Oscar, I'm heading out.

"Yo, where ya goin'?" Oscar asks me.

"To bed," I reply.

Back at the hotel it feels like I'm in a sanctuary since I escaped all the chaos at the club. An hour later, I finish showering and call Rose to see how she's doing but I realize it's two a.m. on the East Coast and she must be asleep since she doesn't answer the phone. And once again, I hear a knock on the door. I'm suspecting it's Oscar but, when I open the door, I see Lisa. Her hair is wet and she smells like strawberry body wash from Bath & Body Works. She clearly just got out of the shower from wherever she came from. Lisa invites herself in by stepping inside my room.

"How did you find my hotel room?" I ask.

"Honey, Oscar told me what room you were in," she winks.

Dammit, Oscar! You've been fucking up this whole trip.

Lisa opens up her long black raincoat, revealing the black lingerie she's wearing.

"I wanna fuck," she whispers to me.

Sheesh! This is a situation that every man dreams about, but I don't want anything to do with it. Lisa's desirable and all but I know as soon as I bust a nut, I'll end up feeling like the worst person on the planet. It's not worth it! I need to be stronger than I was at the club and put my foot down. This has already gone too far.

"I'm sorry, Lisa, but I have a girl back home."

Lisa quickly sneaks a kiss on my lips.

I back away and say, "I'm serious, I really can't do this!"

Lisa steps toward me and caresses my chest. "Baby, she'll never know about it. I'll keep this a secret between us. I have a husband at home and I have kids your age, but I still like to have fun."

I shake my head and sigh. The last thing she's gonna do is have me shot by her husband due to jealousy. "Well, how about you have sex with your husband tonight? I think it'll be good for your conscience to know you didn't cheat on him."

"My husband and I have an open relationship. And I don't want him tonight. I want you!"

Shit balls, I swear to god if I hadn't changed my ways, I would be pinning her legs behind her ears right now.

I stand strong and come up with something clever, to make Lisa stand down. "Hey, you said you're a fan of my novel, right?" I ask.

"Yes," she says softly.

"Well please try to understand me when I say this. My girlfriend is like my character, Diamond, and I'm like my other character, Vinnie. You would be highly upset if someone messed that chemistry up, right? Like Patricia tried to do in my book? You don't want to be like Patricia, do you?"

Lisa looks at me and suddenly has a look of grace and empathy. She nods and says, "Oh lord, honey, I couldn't stand Patricia's ass in that book. I was so glad when Diamond got her out the picture. You're right, I do not want to be like Patricia. And I would be highly upset if more characters tried to interrupt Diamond and Vinnie's relationship. I'm sorry, honey, I don't want to get in between what you have going on with your girlfriend. I'm going to get out your way now. Go ahead and give your girl a call. I hope she knows she has a good man."

Lisa smiles at me as I let her out of the room, but as she walks down the hall, I randomly see the nun, Sister Dolores, strolling up the hall. She looks at me but doesn't have a reaction, she just keeps on strolling like nothing happened. It creeps me out a little and now I'm wondering if she's following me. Where are the other nuns and priests? They could've slept at a church or wherever the fuck they sleep. I hope I don't run into her again in Blue River. I don't need this getting back to Rose somehow. My paranoia is kicking in even though I didn't do anything with Lisa.

I walk back into my room and shut the door. "Great job Eddie, you didn't fuck her," I say to myself.

Right after calming myself down, I get a call from Xavier. I pick up the phone. "Hey man what's up, what are you doing up?" I ask.

"Yo, yo, yo, me and Chris are out with Jen and Hannah for a couples' night at the bar. But I had to check on you, bro. How's Seattle going and is my ring still safe?" Xavier wonders.

"Your engagement ring is fine. By the time you give it to Jen, it'll still look like we just got it from the jeweler."

"Psych! I ain't worried about that thing man, I'm just playing."

"No, you're not. Listen I get it. This is an engagement ring you bought for your girl. It's valuable as hell. I would be doing the same thing if I was you."

"I'm glad you understand but, seriously, I was playing. I know you're responsible, that's why I asked you instead of Chris's ass. Besides, you're all the way in Seattle. It's not like you can check on the ring right now. But like I was saying, man, how's Seattle going?"

"It's going alright, the documentary went well. I had a good time traveling around Seattle with the creators of the film too."

"That's good, you're on your celebrity status shit now! They even put you in the Blue River newspaper today, talking about how well your book is doing."

"Oh yeah, I know exactly what you're talking about. The newspaper interviewed me a couple months ago about that and told me it would be released around this week. I already have an early mock copy of the article at my house that they sent to me."

I can hear Xavier breathing heavy on the phone as well as loud music echoing on his end.

"Damn are you good, it sounds like you're out of

breath."

Xavier laughs. "Yeah, bro! My old ass couldn't keep up with Jen while we were dancing in the bar. It's probably from all the beer and vapes I have every day."

"You need to lay off that shit, bro," I tell him.

"Man, I got you. By the end of the year, I'll be done with drinking and smoking," Xavier says, not trying to hear my sound advice. "So was your book signing good too?" he asks.

"Oh yeah, that went good. There was a long line of people there. The people out here in Seattle showed me love. . . but mannn, I met this woman named Lisa at my event today and let me tell you something."

"Uh oh, I gotta hear this shit," Xavier responds.

"She's in her fifties and she's fine as hell, she looks like a rated r version of Tyra Banks. That's the best way I can describe her."

"That's a perfect description!"

"You won't believe this but she wanted to fuck me just now, but I told her no."

Suddenly I hear Chris in the background say, "Wait, what? You told her no? Eddie, you're lying your ass off. We know you fucked her."

"Hey, what's up, Chris! I was waiting on you to join in on the conversation. I knew you were somewhere around. And nah, man, I'm telling the truth!"

"So bro, you're telling me you didn't bang this woman? That doesn't even sound like you, with all the shit you've done," Chris laughs.

"I know, dude, I know! But all I've been thinking

about lately is Rose. I wish I could fully breakdown what's going on in my head. I just enjoy all of her qualities and I enjoy being around her. Rose is the only woman I want. Having sex with her isn't even my first priority; just being in her presence is enough for me," I explain.

Out of nowhere, I hear a woman's voice through the phone say, "Aw, he really likes her."

"I know that was so sweet!"

That sounds like Jen and Hannah.

"When the hell did y'all come out here?" Xavier asks Jen.

"We walked out of the bar to find you guys a couple minutes ago," Jen tells him.

"Yo, Eddie, I didn't know they were behind me," Xavier says.

"I believe you, bro, it's all good. Hey Jen, hey Hannah."

"Hey Eddie," they say in unison.

"Aw, you really like this girl. You need to tell her how you feel. She would really appreciate every word you just said," Jen tells me.

Chris intervenes and says, "Hold on, let's think about this, Eddie passed up on sex with a fine ass cougar, all because he's being loyal to someone he has a crush on. That's dumb because he doesn't know if she's being loyal to him or not. They're not in a relationship."

"It's more than a crush, dummy," Hannah snaps on Chris before continuing, "He clearly understands that Rose is special, and that random sex with random women no longer serves him the way it used to. He's maturing and, to be honest, I think he loves Rose."

I pace around the room holding the phone to my ear. Hearing Hannah use the word *love*, causes me to sweat. She has to be drunk. "Whoa! Whoa! Whoa! Let's not use this love word so fast," I tell Hannah.

"It is love though, whether you like it or not," Hannah adds.

"I still have to get to know her more, I'm not that fucking delusional. I just really like her, that's all."

"No, I don't think that would make you delusional. For Xavier and I, it was love at first sight," Jen says.

"Exactly!" Hannah agrees. "Chris and I said we love each other after the first week of dating. When you know, you just know," she reveals.

"Nah, see. I don't know about that. You guys are my friends and all, but I do think more time has to be developed between two people before saying shit like that. Y'all are crazy for moving that fast. I'm glad it worked out for all of you though, trust me. But the way women move out here nowadays, you'll think you're in love one day, then they'll turn into a completely different person the next day," I explain.

"SHE'S NOT VERONICA!" Jen and Hannah shout simultaneously.

"I KNOW THAT!" I shout back through the phone.

Xavier and Chris are cracking up as I go back and forth with their girls.

"So stop fighting your feelings. Stop being afraid to be hurt. Stop being afraid to be vulnerable again,"

Hannah tells me.

"Oh my god, we have to meet her as soon as possible. Your hardheaded ass better bring her to the Christmas party like I told you to. Do you understand me?" Jen says.

"Jesus Christ! I don't know, Jen. I can't trust you and Hannah's crazy ass friends; especially Bianca. I saw her psychotic ass a week ago giving me the stink eye!"

"Hold on, did you see her at the art gallery?" Jen questions.

"Yeah, how do you know?"

"She wrote another blog about The Anonymous Man taking some girl out painting and how she knows he's going to end up hurting this girl. She said she has a strong feeling he's going to cheat on her and use her like she was used. She finished the blog by saying this is her last post about The Anonymous Man and that she's officially moving on."

What the hell! She thinks I'm going to hurt Rose? She probably wants me to hurt Rose so that she has a chance with me again. This girl is obsessed!

"Yeah. See, she's psychotic, don't invite her, Jen; especially if you want me and Rose to come to your party."

"He's right, after hearing that shit, Bianca is not coming to our party, babe. Neither is Stephanie's ass! I don't care if you're cool with them or not. Eddie doesn't deserve to miss out on our party because of them," Xavier tells Jen.

"Fine, they're not invited," Jen says with a bit of

resistance in her voice.

This is the first time I've heard or seen Jen set her pride to the side and listen to Xavier. It's probably because she knows she owes me one for believing in Bianca's lies. And she knows I wouldn't intentionally step foot in the same vicinity with Bianca and Stephanie; especially if I have Rose with me. That would be a nightmare!

"I appreciate that, Xavier," I say.

Xavier wasn't going to allow anything to mess up his proposal to Jen. "You know I gotchu, bro," he replies.

"So are you going to bring Rose now?" Jen asks.

"Yes, I'll do it," I answer.

"Finally," Jen says, relieved.

CHAPTER FIFTEEN

December 17th

It's four a.m. and I can't sleep. I was able to get a good nap for two hours at the hotel, but my biological clock has been thrown off ever since I've been here in Seattle. I hop off the bed and peek out my window to see the sky is completely dark but the piers on Seattle's Waterfront are still lit up, along with that Ferris wheel they call the Seattle Great Wheel. No one is strolling the boardwalk though. And there's only two security guards standing near the loading docks, smoking cigarettes. Oddly enough, my weird mind finds something peaceful about this sight. Suddenly I'm alerted by the vibration of my phone buzzing in my pocket. It's Rose.

"Hello," I answer, clearing my throat.

"Eddie! I'm sorry I missed your call. I was asleep. How did the rest of your night go after the book signing event?" Rose asks me.

I'm definitely not telling her what went down last night. There's no need to. "That's fine, I completely forgot about the three-hour time zone difference when I called you. Other than that, last night was pretty boring after the event. Oscar and I got some food and eventually called it a night. Since we already explored most of Seattle during the week, there was nothing else left to do," I explain, lying my ass off.

"I understand and oh goodness, I just checked my phone. I forgot about the time-zone difference too. Since it's seven a.m. over here that means it's four a.m. in Seattle. I can let you get more rest."

"Nah, it's all good, how'd your day go yesterday?"

"It was a relaxing day, I hung out with Aida and Eartha at my mom's place. And guess what happened while I was over there?"

"What?"

"Eartha and I saw you on the front page of the Blue River Newspaper! My mom had the newspaper sitting on her kitchen table. Eartha blurted out your name when she saw your face and told my mom that I brought you to my job for the family fun night event. Right after that, we talked about your books, and my mom was so impressed, she ended up buying all three of your books online. So you definitely were a major topic at the dinner table last night."

I smile and say, "Hey, I love the sound of that. When you have a chance, thank her for me. I'm gonna sign those books for her too!"

"Oh yes, she would love that! And speaking of your books, I'm now halfway through your vampire novel, and I can't believe Patricia is trying to figure out a way to kill

Diamond now that she knows she's a vampire. She really thinks if she kills Diamond, she's gonna somehow get back together with Vinnie again? That girl is so delusional."

I love how indulged Rose is in my novel. This is the first time I've felt proud of it. Maybe I really am a good novelist. "You're going to go through an emotional rollercoaster the further you get into the book," I tell Rose.

"Ooo, I can't wait. This story has been so hard to put down. Do you have anything planned today since it's your last day in Seattle?"

"Nah, to be honest I just want to sit in my room and talk to you all day until it's time for me to leave this city."

Rose becomes giddy and giggles. "Aw, well, I'm all in! Can I FaceTime you?"

"Absolutely!"

Our conversation continues throughout the rest of the day as we transition to FaceTime. For a brief moment, it causes me to have a flashback of how frequently Veronica and I would FaceTime each other. And since Rose is currently more than two-thousand miles away from me, it's giving me a PTSD moment of that terrible long-distance relationship. Luckily, that moment passes due to Rose's pleasant energy, helping my mind overcome those unpleasant memories of Veronica.

≈

December 18th

Today is the day I'm finally heading back to Delaware. And boy, am I homesick. I waste no time packing up my luggage and bolting out of my hotel room. As I check out in the lobby, I see Oscar smiling at me.

"Hey man, you didn't come out of your room all day Sunday. So you must've done the deed with that cougar, Lisa, two days in a row," Oscar says.

I don't feel like telling Oscar that I didn't do anything because I cared more about talking to Rose on the phone rather than fucking Lisa. If I tell him that, then he's going to lecture me on how I'm being ridiculous and how I need to take advantage of my youth while I still can. To avoid that, I tell Oscar what he wants to hear.

"Yeah man, thanks for telling her what room I was in. I wore her ass out! She's a pro and a dime-piece," I lie to him.

Oscar shakes my hand, and looks at me like a proud father would his son. "My protégé, I knew you were gonna get some pussy out here. And here you were, talking about you're trying to focus on your work and some girl back home. Man, if you don't go ahead and live your young life," he laughs and pats me on the shoulder before adding, "Come on, let's get out of here."

Jeez! I guess I couldn't avoid a mini lecture from Oscar after all.

≈

After Oscar and I are dropped off at the airport, we

say our goodbyes and part ways as he gets on his flight to Los Angeles and I get on mine to Blue River.

While waiting on my plane, the pilot tells us there will be a delay due to bad weather. He tells us we'll be taking off in forty minutes. In between that time I make a phone call to Rose, knowing she's on her lunch break at the school.

"Hi, Eddie," Rose answers excitedly.

"Uh oh, is that Eddie calling you from Seattle, darling? You two can't go a day without talking to each other on the phone. Rose was just talking about how much she misses you, boy! She's sprung already," I hear Eartha say in the background.

"Oh, shut up, Eartha." Rose chuckles before saying, "Sorry, Eddie, I'm in the staff room with Eartha. Hey, shouldn't you be on your flight right now?" She asks.

"That's alright and yeah, I'm on the plane but there's a delay because of the snow. The plane should be flying out of here within the hour."

"Oh okay, I'm gonna pray that you're safe."

"I'll be fine, you don't have to do all that," I say, thinking about what happened when Sister Dolores prayed for me.

"Why not?" Rose questions with concern. "It's just a prayer."

I sigh. "I know. But I don't think it'll make a difference. If my plane lands *it lands*. And if it crashes *it crashes*."

"Goodness gracious, Eddie, you shouldn't say things like that. Do you happen to be religious by any chance? It sounds like you aren't."

"Nah, I'm not a religious person. I consider myself to be agnostic. What are you . . . a scientologist?" I joke.

Rose laughs. "Oh god no, smart-ass, I'm catholic! Is that a problem?"

"Not at all, I love Catholics; especially the one I'm on the phone with. She's my favorite catholic of all-time."

"Hilarious, now you have me cheesing like a little schoolgirl in the staff room."

"Hey, anything to make you smile. So let me get this straight, you're a catholic who believes in astrology. I'm no religious expert, but I don't think those two things mix."

"What can I say, I like to break the rules a little."

"See, that's why you're my favorite catholic."

"And that's why I'm still going to pray that you have a safe flight."

"Yeah, even though you don't have to. Look, I know I was joking around before with my dark humor. But I'm sure my plane won't crash, okay? There's a high percentage that I'll be landing safely."

"I know you will, ya agnostic meanie. But I'm still gonna pray and hold onto my holy rosary until you make your way back to me."

Damn, I love the way she just said that to me. She won't get a rebuttal from me this time. I'll take a prayer from the fucking Pope if she wanted me too.

"I'll take that. I can't wait to see your pretty ass again. I need something beautiful to see after sitting in that ugly airport."

Rose laughs. "Wow, is their airport that bad?"

"Yeah, Seattle's airport is outdated and musty. The seating at the airport is dirty too, with nothing but old food and gunk in between the seats. I was looking around like where the hell are the janitors in this place. I'm glad I can wait here on the plane now before it takes flight."

"Oh god, I don't know why I was thinking their airport would be much fancier and clean."

"Same here," I reply. "I'm not holding you up from eating your lunch, am I?"

"Oh no, you're good. I finished my salad like ten minutes before you called."

"Okay, well, are you still hungry right now?"

"Well, I do have a sweet tooth for some reason. And why are you asking me if I'm hungry when you're way across the country?" Rose giggles.

In the middle of Rose questioning me, I go online to order her some edible arrangements. While scrolling through the menu I press on two items I hope she will like. I select a Cozy Cinnamon Cheesecake Platter and a fruit bouquet. If she doesn't like them then I'll hold a big fat L for now.

"Because I have a surprise for you," I finally answer.

"Eddie, what do you have up your sleeve now?"

"You'll see."

"Well, I can't wait to see this!"

I suddenly remember how Rose's students were devouring chocolate chip cookies during the family fun night. So I order baked chocolate chip cookies online from one of the local Blue River bakeries and have enough sent for all fifteen of her students.

"I'll have a surprise for your students too. Everything should be there within the hour," I reveal to her.

"Aw, you truly are something special. Thank you in advance for gifting us with whatever the mysterious gift is."

"You're welcome. I'll see you soon."

"Hopefully sooner than later," Rose says before hanging up.

CHAPTER SIXTEEN

I hate the way planes land! It always gives me anxiety because it feels like we're about to crash. Thankfully, my plane just finishes going through its rough landing phase and is now driving through the taxiway to park at the gate.

"Ladies and gentlemen, thank you for flying with Delta Airlines. We are now in Philadelphia, and it is currently six p.m. eastern standard time. Please remain seated with your seat belt fastened and keep the aisle clear until we are parked at the gate," the pilot announces.

Although the Philadelphia International airport is only thirty-minutes away from Blue River, Delaware. It always feels like home when I land here from whatever country or state I'm coming from. While the plane makes its way to a gate, I use that time to take my phone off airplane mode. As soon as I do that, I receive a bunch of notifications. There are text messages from Oscar making sure I landed safe, and messages from my parents, my sister, and my friends. After seeing these notifications pop up, I then notice I received a voicemail from Rose.

I play the voicemail and hear: "Oh my god, Eddie! Thank you so much for the edible arrangements and the kids said thank you for the chocolate chip cookies too! That was really sweet of you, they were so happy! . . . . And ya know what? I was wondering if you could read your book, *Dreamscape Land*, to my students on their last day of school before Christmas break. That's this Thursday the 21st. Let me know, because I would love it if you could read to them, and I know they would too. See you soon!"

After listening to the voicemail, I receive a phone call from my dad.

"Hey Dad," I answer.

"Hey son, how was Seattle?"

"It was fun, I had a great time. I enjoyed being on the documentary I was telling you about too."

"That's good, son, I can't wait to hear all about it. Where are you now?"

"I just landed."

"You just landed? Why didn't you tell us? Me or your mom could've picked you up. Shoot I can be on my way right now, do you need a ride?"

No matter where I go in the world, my parents always expect to pick me up from the airport when I get back. But I hate feeling like a burden, so I usually park my car in the airport's parking garage. It's more satisfying to me, getting off the plane and walking straight to my car without having to rely on an Uber or somebody to come get me.

"Nah, I'm all good. Thanks, Dad, I didn't feel like

bothering anyone, so I parked my car in the parking garage."

"Eddie, you know you wouldn't be bothering us. I would've gladly gone out of my way to come get you."

"It's alright, Dad. I'll see if you or Mom can do it next time."

"Alright, son, are you still going to stop by the house Thursday afternoon to babysit your nephews. Me and your mom still need to go wrap gifts with your sister and her husband that day."

"Yeah, I'll be there!"

"Okay, we'll have dinner ready that day when you get here."

"Perfect."

CHAPTER SEVENTEEN

December 19th

It's a quiet Tuesday afternoon, and, after spending half of the day recovering from jetlag, I'm thinking about how to make my book read-a-long special for Rose's class. I don't want it to be like any of the other book readings I've done in the past. I want her and her students to remember this forever; *especially her.* I'm probably thinking too much about it, but, as I brainstorm, I think about how Mr. and Mrs. Cooper resemble a traditional looking Santa and Mrs. Claus. If I'm able to persuade them to come out and visit Rose's class as those holiday characters, they'll be ecstatic. Luckily, I remember I have Mr. and Mrs. Cooper's number saved from the time Rose used my phone to call them when Sebastian attacked me.

I waste no time giving them a call. "Hey, is this Mr. Cooper?"

"Yes, and who might this be?" Mr. Cooper asks.

"This is Eddie, sir, the guy who was bitten by your dog, Sebastian."

"Oh yes," he says with a resistant giggle. "And sorry about that again. How have you been, young man?"

"It's alright and I've been good. Listen, I know this is a random question, but I was wondering if you and Mrs. Cooper ever dressed up like Santa Claus and Mrs. Claus before for special holiday events?"

"Oh yes, we've done that plenty of times at the mall, back when we lived in Altoona, Pennsylvania. That's how my wife and I know Dr. Lennon. She used to live in that area, too, and she would even bring her kids to see us at the mall around Christmas time each year. My wife and I kept up with that Christmas tradition until we moved here to Delaware ten years ago. We surely do miss it," Mr. Cooper explains, dumping a load of information on me. At least now I know why I was able to get seen by Dr. Lennon so quickly the day I was bitten. And I'm glad he and his wife did the whole Santa thing at the mall back in the day. Now I feel more comfortable asking for their help. "Why'd you ask, do you have something in mind?" he questions.

"Yes, I actually do. My friend, Rose, the girl you met on the day we dropped the DoorDash order off at your house, teaches kindergarten at Maple Elementary and she invited me to read a children's book to her class on Thursday. I was wondering if you and Mrs. Cooper wouldn't mind surprising the kids by being Mr. and Mrs. Claus and asking them what they wanted for Christmas. I can take care of getting you costumes, too, if you're both free to do it."

Based on the brief pause, it seems like Mr. Cooper is

taken aback by everything I just said. I hope I didn't throw too much on him. He just told me he misses it; so hopefully I get a *yes*.

"Wow! Young man, that's the best news Mildred and I have heard in years. We would love to do it. We rarely get out the house and our children and grandchildren come out here to see us when they can but they don't see us often. We would love to do this for you two and the kids. And don't worry about getting us costumes, Mildred and I still have the ones we used to wear."

"Awesome, thank you, Mr. Cooper. You're a lifesaver!"

I give Mr. Cooper more information about Maple Elementary as well as the time I would be reading there so they can arrive shortly after me. I then contact Principal Hardwick and let her know I would be surprising Rose and her students with Santa and Mrs. Claus coming to see the kids. Thankfully, she's all for it!

≈

December 21ˢᵗ

It's the day of the reading and, after executing the first part of my plan by reading *Dreamscape Land* to Rose's kindergarteners, I stall with a Q&A session after the reading to keep the kids busy as I wait for Mr. and Mrs. Cooper. After answering a few questions, Mr. and Mrs. Cooper are led into the classroom by Principal Hardwick.

The students gasp when they see them coming in.

Rose's student, CJ, yells, "IT'S SANTA!"

When Rose sees Mr. and Mrs. Cooper all dressed in their costumes, her mouth drops. She then looks at me and mouths, "Did you do this?"

I nod.

She smiles at me as Principal Hardwick takes over the class.

"Okay, kids, who wants to line-up to tell Santa and Mrs. Claus what they want for Christmas?" Principal Hardwick asks them.

Suddenly we hear a bunch of kids repeatedly scream, "I DO, I DO, I DO."

Students passing by in the hallway are able to hear all the commotion. As they peek into the classroom, they notice Mr. and Mrs. Cooper; who they all think are the Claus's. Now there's a commotion in the hallway, but the Coopers tell Principal Hardwick they are willing to talk to the entire elementary school after speaking with Rose's students. Since this is their last day of school, before preparing for the Christmas break, they don't mind making it a memorable one.

≈

After the school day is over, I thank the Coopers and Principal Hardwick for all their help. Later on, Rose and I are finally able to have a one-on-one conversation as we walk alongside each other in the parking lot. The first thing Rose says to me is, "Wow! I'm impressed. Eddie, you just continue to blow me away." She then grabs my arm and jokingly looks inside my coat sleeve. "Like what else is up your sleeves because you're filled with nonstop surprises," she adds.

I shrug. "Um, I think that was it. I'm all out of surprises now. I'm about to leave and head home. I'll probably see you sometime in February," I joke with her.

As I slightly walk away from Rose, I see the startled look on her face, she's speechless.

I walk back to her and smile. "Nah, I'm just kidding, come on, I wouldn't just ditch you like that."

Rose laughs and repeatedly punches me in the shoulder. "You totally got me. Oh my god, don't do that again, my heart would've shattered into pieces."

I hug Rose as we have a good laugh about it. "I'm not going anywhere. And look, since the school had a half day today, are you free for a while?"

Rose beams. "Yeah, I'm free all day!"

"Good, I'm free till four. I have some family stuff to take care of around that time. But I wanna take you out right now while I still have time."

"Okay, Mr. Valentine, I love the persistence. What do you wanna do?"

"I'm gonna take you sledding. I'll let you go get yourself together and get properly dressed for it, and I'll do the same. I can pick you up in an hour, ok?"

Rose smiles, "Okay! I'll see you then," she says as she kisses me on the cheek.

CHAPTER EIGHTEEN

After picking up Rose from her apartment, we arrive at the Blue River Nature Park. While making our way through the woods, we spot a ton of families lining up to sled down a hill known as the Hill of Death.

Rose looks amazed by the scenery. "Out of all the years I've lived here, I've never seen anything like this. I've never even been to this park before," she admits.

"Wow! You've never been to Blue River Nature Park and slid down the Hill of Death?" I ask for clarity.

"Nope." She shakes her head. "And why do they call it the Hill of Death? Did someone die sledding down that hill before?" she asks me with a look of fright.

"Hell nah." I chuckle. "The hill is so steep that your stomach drops like you're on a rollercoaster. Some people even said it feels like you're plummeting to your death; that's how the hill earned its name."

Rose lies her head on my shoulder and deeply exhales. "Oh, thank goodness, you were scaring me for a second."

I kiss the top of her forehead and laugh. "I thought

everyone in Delaware came here. My parents took me to this park all the time as a kid. So have you ever been sledding?"

"A couple times, my dad would take me and my sister sledding in our backyard. The hill back there was super small compared to the hill here," Rose says, looking at the hill with wide eyes.

"Well, it's going to be alright, I promise. Do you enjoy going through that first big drop when you're on a roller coaster?"

"Yeah, those drops have always been fun to me!"

"Then you're going to like sledding down the Hill of Death. It's one of the steepest hills on the East Coast."

Rose notices park rangers watching people on the hill. "Oh wow, is that why there are a bunch of park rangers around right now?"

"Yeah, they patrol the area a lot around this time of year, just in case people are standing in the middle of the path while people are sledding. They don't want anyone getting hurt or crashing into each other, so they control how many people go sledding on the hill at a time, because that hill can get overpopulated quick."

"Wow, you sure do know a lot about this park," Rose says.

I shrug. "What can I say, I'm a nature lover."

"I see."

As Rose and I wait in line, there are Christmas carolers singing to keep us entertained. After hearing them sing, *White Christmas*, *Silent Night*, and *It's The Most Wonderful Time of The Year*, a park ranger motions to us.

"Hey, you two are up next. Are you ready to speed down this hill?" he asks in a good mood.

"Ya damn right we are," I tell him.

Rose squeezes my biceps as we make our way to the top of the steps. As she stares down at the steep snow hill, she looks petrified. She isn't saying a word. At this point, I know she's only going to sled down this hill because of me. I don't think Rose wants to do this at all.

"Are you sure you want to sled down this hill with me? We don't have to do it if it's too much for you," I tell her.

"Oh yeah, I want to do this. You've done this countless times, so I'm sure I'll be safe," Rose confirms nervously.

I make sure I sit on the sled first. I then look at her and say, "It'll be okay, hop on. Just sit in front of me, in between my legs, and I'll hold you tight, I promise."

"Okay." Rose smirks, tip toeing across the snow. She sits down in between my legs and takes a deep breath, trying to release her nerves.

While my legs hug hers, I wrap both my arms around her waist tight enough for her to feel safe.

And right now, her sweet fragrance has me captivated.

"Everything is going to be fine, alright? Just enjoy the ride," I whisper in her ear.

Rose's nervous mood suddenly goes away. She nods and smiles as she rubs her mitten-covered hands on my forearms.

"Ooo, I really feel safe now," she whispers back.
Oh yeah, it's going down today.

"Okay, are you two ready?" the park ranger asks, as he and the other ranger prepare to push us down the hill.

I literally forgot they were there.

"Yes indeed, we're all good to go, man," I tell the ranger.

"Okay, here we go," one of the rangers say as he and the other ranger proceed to push our sled.

As our sled speeds down the hill like a rocket, Rose laughs and screams the whole way through while we hold each other. The snow from the ground and the freezing wind smacks us right in our faces as we accelerate through each bump.

By the time the sled slows down and stops at the end of the hill, Rose turns to me and kisses me on the cheek. "Your face is cold," she says.

"And so are your lips, but I don't mind kissing them," I say as I plant one on her."

Rose giggles. "Thank you, handsome. I gotta hand it to you, that was fun! And, thanks to you, it wasn't as bad as I thought it would be."

I playfully wave her off. "Hey, that's what I'm here for. Do you want to go again?"

Rose shakes her head and beams at me. "Nah, that's okay," she says as we hop off the sled and allow one of the rangers to pick it up.

Rose wraps her arm around mine and kisses my cheek again.

Okay Rose, you're giving me the signal, I guess it's go time now. Let me test this out.

I look around to see if she wants to get something to

eat or drink out here. "There's some hot chocolate over there, you want some?" I ask her.

She shakes her head again and says, "Nope, I'm good."

Alright, that's signal number two. Now, I'm taking my Michael Jordan shot with three seconds left on the clock. Three...two...one.

"Do you want to come to my place and watch a Christmas movie before I go see my family in a bit?"

Rose grins and blushes. "Yes, I would love to but can we watch the movie at my apartment?"

When I hear Rose say that, she doesn't have to tell me twice. I want to scream FUCK YES, LET'S GO RIGHT NOW. But all I say is, "Yeah, that's fine with me. Come on, let's go."

PART TWO
FIRE & DESIRE

CHAPTER NINETEEN

When I pull into the parking lot at Rose's apartment, she wastes no time grabbing her keys from her purse. She then opens the car door before I can walk around and open it for her.

She's moving fast as hell. I wonder if I'm making her anxious.

Due to the current silence, I'm starting to sense Rose is a little nervous, but I may be wrong. To comfort her, I gently place my hand on her back as we walk to the third floor of her apartment complex. She looks back at me and smiles, tucking her hair behind her ear.

By the time we reach her door that's labeled 3D, she prepares to unlock it, but immediately stops and says, "Hey, I don't normally do this, are you sure you're okay with coming in? I know we're still getting to know each other, and I don't want you to think I'm moving too fast or anything."

She's leaning against her door and we're intensely gazing at each other.

My god, her hair is glimmering, and her aura has me spellbound. I wanna give it to her right now!

"You're fine, I'm okay with coming in there. I've

been inside your place before, remember?" I answer.

Rose snickers. "I know you have...I'm just saying...the vibe is much different this time around, ya know," she says softly.

Rose turns around again to unlock her door all the way, but out of nowhere she turns to me again, and places her back against the door. She looks at me and says, "Eddie, my apartment might be a bit messy, please don't judge m—"

I interrupt Rose's explanation by pulling her into me, lifting her chin to stare me directly in the eyes, and kissing her on the lips. This time around, our passion is at an all-time high. I'm savoring each second. Her lips are soft and warm, and I can taste the sweet vanilla ChapStick she's wearing. Subsequently, we begin to taste each other's tongues. As I press my chest and hips into hers and caress her neck, I hear a faint moan.

When we come up for air, I finally respond to her and say, "I won't judge you, I like when certain things are messy."

Rose smirks at me and I kiss her again, running my hands down her back until it reaches the cusp of her ass. She caresses the back of my head and neck as we begin to take things further. During this hypnotic state, all we can hear is our deep breathing, our lips smacking, and tongues swapping. I place my forearm underneath Rose's backside and lift her off the ground.

She giggles and whispers, "You're so strong."

She then wraps her legs around my waist as I turn the doorknob to enter her apartment. I quickly snatch the key out the keyhole and slam the door.

"Where's your bedroom?" I ask her.

"Down the hall, first door on the right," she whispers.

Rose swiftly takes off her coat and manages to swing off her boots while hanging on to me. I subtly lick and kiss her neck. I'm hard as a rock and I'm ready to enter her. I open the door to her bedroom, and toss her onto her silver queen-sized bed, making her giggle.

"That was hot," she says.

"Oh, it's going to get hotter than that real soon."

After throwing off my shoes, and removing my sweater and jacket, Rose gapes at me.

"Oh my god! Look at those abs! Can you get any sexier?" she says to me.

She climbs to the edge of her bed to meet me where I'm standing, and kisses and licks my abs. I'm ready to remove my sweatpants so her warm lips and tongue can go further, but I want to be the first one to provide oral pleasure.

I surprise her, pulling her hair back and tonguing her down. I then push her back onto the bed, and climb on top of her while parting her legs. But when she looks up and smiles at me, something goes wrong. I'm starting to see flashes of all the hookers I've slept with. I blink multiple times and shake my head to clear my mind.

"Are you okay?" Rose whispers.

"Yeah." I nod. I'll be damned if I allow my mind to ruin this moment.

I close my eyes and thrust my hips into hers. She

moans even though we both have our sweatpants on. I keep my eyes closed as we kiss and are now in a rhythm of massaging each other's tongues.

Rose was already smelling great before, but now she's smelling even better.

I slide my face below her cheek and begin kissing her neck as I reach my hand underneath her sweater, cupping her succulent breast and slowly massaging her nipple. Rose uses both her hands to grab my face and gazes at me. I force myself to open my eyes again. When I look at her, she's biting her lip and staring at me intensely.

Suddenly I see all the hookers again. I shake my head and blink repeatedly. What the fuck is going on?

"Eddie, are you sure you're okay?" Rose asks.

"Yeah, I just had an eyelash in my eye," I lie.

"Okay," she whispers, pecking me on the lips.

I'm noticing that every time I look at Rose while she's laying back on this bed, my mind reverts back to all the beds and women I slept with in brothels. I have to look away from her without displaying that something is obviously wrong with me.

I kiss her neck again and whisper, "Are you wet?" I reach my hand down her pants to receive an answer before she speaks. My middle finger and ring finger are completely drenched inside of her.

"Aw yes," Rose deeply exhales.

I take my time, gently using my fingers to massage her clit. She gasps, and tilts her head back on her pillow while arching her back. I make sure I catch a glimpse of her before my mind plays tricks on me. During that momentary view, I notice Rose is in a trance, closing her eyes, with her mouth wide open as she enjoys the sensation I'm giving her.

"Do you want more?" I tease.

"Fuck yes," she blurts in between moaning.

"Okay." I stop fingering her and grab both her wrists and place her hands behind her head. "Let's see how long you can keep your hands behind your head. Make sure you keep them there."

From the corner of my eye, I can see she's smiling as she eagerly follows my instructions. "My hands will be behind my head the whole time," she says to me.

I chuckle. "Yeah, we'll see."

I sit up, removing her sweatpants and her soaked lace trimmed panties. Her pussy is glistening and she's cleanly shaven. While sitting in between her legs, I bend back down and place my head underneath her sweater to kiss her stomach.

Rose slightly giggles. "That tickles but I like it," she murmurs.

I come out of her sweater and make my way down to licking her right inner thigh and slowly glide my tongue close to her warmth. Rose's breathing gets heavier the closer I get to entering my tongue in her, but I stop and move my mouth over to lick her left inner thigh.

She laughs and whispers, "Ooo, Eddie, you're such a tease!"

I briefly chuckle, taking my time gliding my tongue up her thigh and close to her warmth again. She's wet like a lake, and ready for me to enter her. I finally decide to stop teasing her. I slide down the edge of the bed, pushing her knees back to her chest so I can make my way down to her womanhood. As I dive face first into her wetness, I instantly discover that I love the way she tastes.

She gasps again, removing her hands from behind her head. Now I feel her gripping the back of my head, firmly rubbing her fingers through my waves.

"Oh fuck, Eddie I can't hold my hands back anymore," Rose whispers.

I knew she wouldn't be able to. I smile and proceed to lightly massage the top of her clit with my tongue, studying her reactions with each motion. When I move my tongue in a circular motion, all she does is bite her lip. That reaction is fine but it's not the one I'm looking for. I then motion my tongue from side to side. She moans a bit but I'm still not satisfied. But when I gently push my hand down on her stomach and quickly penetrate my tongue in and out of her, she screams and moans loudly and uncontrollably.

I hit the jackpot!

I dribble my tongue directly underneath her clit like a Jacuzzi jet. Rose clutches the sheets, arches her back, and curls her toes. This is the reaction I was looking for!

I exhale in-between my split-second tongue break, and the warm air from my nose hits her inner lips. The feeling of the air pressure hitting her causes her to shortly convulse. Rose has no idea what to do with her hands. She goes from clawing the sheets, to gripping the shit out of my head again, and now she's attempting to push my head away. But something in her mind must've said *fuck it*, because she pulls my head right back into her opening.

I want to turn this shit up a notch, so I place my arms underneath her backside and wrap her legs around my shoulders as I continue to taste her. During this tasting, I lift her up and press her against the wall, right above her bed frame. Her legs stay wrapped around my shoulders and her hands continue to grip my head.

"AW, FUCK YES, BABY," Rose shouts.

If she's calling me baby already that means she's about to cum.

"SHIT, I'M ABOUT TO CUM, BABY!"

I knew it!

I constantly move my tongue in and out at a rapid pace, aggressively licking underneath her clit until she starts shivering.

"YES," she screams with pleasure, ultimately loosening her grip from my head.

I lay her down on the bed and watch her sit back against her headboard. Right now, I'm not seeing the flashes of the hookers while I stare at her. Rose is smiling at me as she gently bites her index finger. She looks so sexy doing that, I nearly explode on myself.

"Damn, that was so fucking good, you know exactly what you're doing! Do you have a vibrator disguised as your tongue in that mouth or something, jeez," Rose says.

"A vibrator disguised as my tongue. Now that's a compliment I never heard before," I reply with a smile.

Rose laughs. "Well, you deserve it, and for our next round, I want you inside of me."

Even though I'm thrilled to hear Rose say that, I

have to figure out what's bothering me. Why in the world was I seeing the hookers I slept with in Vegas and Brazil? Since Rose and I are going to be taking things a step further soon, I want to make sure I'm able to passionately make love to her. I need to make all our experiences special each time we're together. I clearly know she isn't some random hooker, and, like my friends constantly remind me, she isn't Veronica either. She's a rose that bloomed in Blue River, and I wouldn't want to have it any other way. I have to make this right.

Without warning, my alarm clock goes off on my phone, reminding me it's time for me to babysit my nephews like I promised I would. My sister starts blowing my phone up at the same time too. I decline the call and text her that I'll be on my way. Maybe it's good that I have to leave at this moment, because now I have time to plan things out so I can get my mind straight. And on top of that, I forgot to bring condoms with me. I would've been shit out of luck either way.

"Maybe next time," I reply.

Rose looks astonished. "Aw, is it four p.m. already?"

"Yeah, in about ten minutes. I'm going to be late." I laugh.

"Well, I hope they don't mind because I don't want you to go." Rose crawls to me and kisses my cheek. She then hugs me and squeezes me as tight as she can.

Out of the blue, we hear a knock at the door.

I look at Rose and ask, "You expecting anybody?"

Rose shakes her head. "No, and the only people that show up here unannounced are my mom and my sister.

But they usually call my phone if they're outside the door." Rose checks her phone and sees she didn't receive a call from her mom or sister.

"I'll go check to see who it is for you," I tell her while putting my clothes back on.

"Thanks," she says.

When I look through the peephole, I see a middle-aged woman who looks East Indian.

"Hey, it's a short lady at the door with glasses," I reveal to Rose before opening the door. "Hi, how can I help you?" I ask the lady.

"Hello, you don't have to help me, I just wanted to let you know that the walls in this building are kind of thin. I could hear you and your girlfriend having sex. My place is directly underneath yours. I'm not here to complain or anything, I just recommend that you and your girlfriend play music when you do it again. That way I don't have to hear it, okay sir?"

Whoa!

I'm flustered and don't know how to react. It's quite humorous though. All I can say is, "Okay, thank you for letting me know."

The woman waves and walks away. "No problem, young man."

As I shut the door and turn around, I see Rose standing at the edge of the hall. She's completely red and looks mortified.

"Oh my god, I heard the whole thing," she says.
"You did?"
Rose covers her face. "Yes, I'm so embarrassed. I

can't believe that lady heard me moaning and screaming. I never even met her in person before and she lives right below me. I'm so glad she didn't see my face."

I walk over to Rose, hug her from behind and kiss her on the cheek. "It's alright, I'm sure she won't tell the whole building about it, and she's probably never seen your face before."

"I hope not, and thanks for answering the door," she says to me.

"Anytime," I whisper in her ear.

She starts to laugh. "Why the hell are these walls so thin? How much money did they put into building this place? It's supposed to be a newly refurbished complex."

I laugh and shrug. "How about next time we go to my house? And where's your bathroom?" I ask her.

"I like that idea much better! Yeah, we're going to do it at your house every time from now on. And it's the door right behind you."

"Sounds like a plan to me," I say as I go into the bathroom to clean and rinse my mouth and my face. "Hey, I know I have to leave now, but after Christmas are you free?" I ask her.

"Yeah, why, what else do you have up your magical sleeves?"

"I was thinking we could enjoy each other's company, if you came to stay at my place for a day or two after Christmas. It'll be fun." I dry my face off and prepare to put on my jacket.

Rose smiles and approaches me after I exit the bathroom. "Can I ask you an even better question?"

I nod. "Go ahead, shoot for it."

"Would it be okay if I stayed at your place during the entire winter break . . . starting tonight? Once you're done with your babysitting duties of course?"

Let's fucking go! I wasn't expecting her to ask me that.

I shrug and try to contain my excitement. "Shit, yeah, that's fine by me. If you're cool with it, then I'm cool with it!" I'm going to be ready and I won't allow my mind to get in the way this time.

"Yeah, I mean the only time I would have to go is when I see my mom and sister for Christmas but that's about it."

"Yeah, same here, I have to see my family for Christmas, too, but okay. I'll call you when I leave my parents' house. Go ahead and pack yourself some clothes and I'll come by to pick you up tonight." I prepare to head for the door.

"Okay. But um, Mr. Valentine, can I have a kiss before you go?" Rose asks.

I'm so eager for tonight that I was seriously about to forget to kiss her goodbye.

I turn around and smirk at her. "Damn right you can, Ms. Moreno." I waste no time heading over to her, to squeeze her curvy ass and give her a deep kiss.

She reaches into my sweatpants and caresses my erection. "You're hard again," she whispers.

"And I'm guessing your wet again," I whisper back. "But you know I have to go. My family is going to kill me for being this late. I'll see you later," I add as I peck her on the lips and rush out.

CHAPTER TWENTY

After speeding on the highway and making my way to my parents' home, I rush into the house and say, "Hey, I'm sorry I'm fifteen minutes late everyone. I ran into traffic, I think it was a car accident or something on the road, but it should be getting cleared now."

Hopefully, that lie saves my ass from hearing any complaining. Before I can take my jacket off, I hear my nephews, Jaden and Joshua, sprint to me and shout, "UNCLE EDDIE!"

"Hey, twins! How are you? Are you guys being good?"

"Yes," Joshua says.

"Uncle Eddie, are you ready to make Christmas cookies with us?" Jaden asks me.

"Oh definitely, man," I tell him.

"Are we still gonna watch The Grinch too?" Joshua adds.

"Absolutely! Let me wash my hands first, so I can help you guys out." I take my coat off and hang it on the coatrack. My nephews won't let me leave their sight now.

My mom comes into the foyer with my dad following right behind her. "Hey, son! Your nephews have been asking about you all day. And they're really hyper right now, so good luck," she says. She and my dad are rushing to put their jackets on. I can tell they're ready to leave the house and get this Christmas stuff taken care of.

"Hey, Mom! Hey, Dad! Yeah, I see. They were the first ones to run in here and greet me. And my bad, I don't mean to have you guys running late."

"Too bad, now you're going to be stuck with them all night," my dad says sarcastically.

My mom nudges his side. "Oh shut up, Edward, he is not," she says to him.

My dad laughs. "I'm just teasing, man. You're not the one holding us up, it's your sister."

Abruptly my sister, Emma, and her husband, Brian, walk out of the kitchen and approach us near the front door. I haven't even gotten off the *welcome* mat yet, and I'm getting crowded.

"Sorry, sorry, sorry, I had to make sure the twins had everything they needed," Emma says. "Hey, Eddie, thank you so much for watching them while we go wrap their gifts again this year! We need to get more stuff from the mall, too, so I have their meals in the fridge and their medicine on the kitchen counter for you to give them later," she adds.

"Okay. No problem, sis."

My dad shakes his car keys. "I'm going to be outside warming up the car."

Emma then hands me a list and says, "Don't forget Jaden needs to take his allergy medicine at six p.m. and they both need to take their vitamins around eight before they end up falling asleep. Make sure Joshua eats his sliced apples too. He always tries to eat junk without having his fruit or vegetables."

I've probably watched my nephews a million times, but my sister always gives me directions about what I need to do like it's my first time watching them.

"I got it, Emma."

Brian laughs. "Emma, I'm sure your brother has this down to a T by now."

"I'm just double-checking, that's all," Emma says.

"Well, your brother has proven time and time again there's no need to double check. Now let's get out of here so we can wrap up these gifts," my mom adds.

"Hey, I'm surprised you two don't just wrap their gifts while they're asleep," I tell Brian and Emma.

Brian chuckles and shakes his head. "Man, we really try too, believe me we do, but they wake up so easily. It's impossible to wrap gifts with the twins around. And they're super nosey. Last year, Joshua caught me hiding his Elmo gift in the closet. It's a lose-lose situation we have on our hands," he tells me.

I laugh and say, "Aw damn, I get it now. You and Emma can't catch a break. Well, I'll do my best to keep them occupied this time around."

"Thanks again, bro, we'll see y'all when we get back," Emma says.

My sister and Brian hug the twins before they head

out the door. "Boys, be good, okay? And listen to Uncle Eddie," my sister tells them.

The twins nod, as they patiently wait for me to make the Christmas cookies and watch The Grinch with them.

At that moment it crosses my mind that Emma and Rose went to the same school together. Now I wish Emma didn't have to head out already. I have a lot to ask her. Oh well, I guess I can wait till she comes back. To keep the reminder in my head, I stop my sister at the door and say, "Oh yeah, Emma, I have to ask you something about somebody when you get back. It's about a girl you know."

My sister loves gossip or whatever she thinks is gossip. She cheeses and rocks back and forth on her boots. "Aw snap. I can't wait to hear who this is about."

≈

Later at the house, I help my nephews bake frosted snowman cookies and gingerbread men. After baking fifty cookies, and feeding them the healthy meals Emma prepared for them, I give them their medicine and vitamins, and we end up watching The Grinch twice, until the twins finally fall asleep. While my nephews are sound asleep on the couch, I give Rose a call.

"Hey there," she answers.

It sounds like she just woke up. "Hey, your voice sounds raspy, were you sleeping?" I ask.

Rose clears her throat. "Nah, I was just resting my eyes."

"That means you were sleeping." I snicker. "I can call you back later. Go ahead and get some sleep."

"No, don't hang up and okay yes, I was sleeping, but it's all your fault."

"Ha-ha how is it my fault?"

"You ate me out so good that you put me to sleep. I literally went to bed right after you left."

There goes another ego boost for me. "Well I guess I'm gonna have to put you to sleep every night during this Christmas break then."

"Not if I put you to sleep first," Rose rebuttals.

"Ah, okay, you wanna make this a competition, huh?"

"Nah, I just want to make sure I return the favor."

My god this woman just gets better and better!

"I'm all for that," I assure her.

Rose chuckles. "So, how's the babysitting going?" she asks.

"It's going alright, my nephews are finally sleep after watching The Grinch a million times."

"Aw that's sweet. I used to love that movie as a kid too."

"Which one, the Jim Carrey version or the old cartoon version?" I ask.

"The Jim Carrey version," Rose says.

"Yeah, same here. Now I'm cool with not seeing it for another year."

Rose laughs at my comment. "Oh my god, Eddie! I finished your novel yesterday. I absolutely loved the ending. Diamond was able to kill that evil cunt Patricia along with the other vampire hunters she took out. Her and Vinnie make a great team, not only romantically but on some superhero shit too. I can see it becoming a movie. I meant to tell you earlier but you kept surprising me from left to right with every damn thing you were doing. But anyways, that has to be one of the best novels I've ever read. I'm not saying that just because I like you!"

And once again there's another ego boost she gives me!

"You seriously believe it's one of the best novels you've ever read?" I ask her. "The filmmakers in Seattle felt the same way about it."

"Yes and they're right! Don't you think it's up there with one of the best stories ever written?"

"Nah, I think *To Kill a Mockingbird*, *The Lord of the Rings*, and *Invisible Man* are the greatest stories ever written. My novel doesn't come close to those masterpieces."

"That's because you're not an arrogant narcissist who's full of himself. I can tell that you're critical of your own work and try to perfect it at all costs. But let me tell you this, Mr. Valentine, your novel deserves to be mentioned with the great stories like To Kill a Mockingbird and other books you mentioned."

"Thank you, Ms. Moreno, that's mighty kind of you to say," I add sarcastically.

Rose cracks up and says, "You need to learn how to take compliments."

"That's something I'm working on, trust me," I respond.

"Good. So, what are you doing now?"

"Talking to you on the phone."

"Ha-ha, what are you doing besides that, goofball?"

"Oh nothing much, just walking back and forth from the living room to the kitchen, waiting for my family to get back. They should be here in a few minutes," I reply.

"Oh okay, well I'm going to get all packed up. That way, I'm ready by the time you get here," Rose says.

I love the sound of that!

I suddenly hear my sister and mother's voices coming from outside as the door is being unlocked. They arrive right on time!

"Gotcha, I hear my family coming in the house now. I'll be heading out of here soon and will call you when I'm close to your place."

"Okay, I'll see ya then."

After I get off the phone with Rose. My family comes in kind of noisy, laughing and talking amongst themselves. I politely shush them so they can whisper and talk without waking the kids.

"Oh wow, they're asleep?" my mom asks.

"Yeah, they've been asleep for about thirty-minutes. The Grinch had them calm the whole time."

"Thank you so much, bro. Did they eat their organic chicken and rice I made? And did they have their fruits and vitamins?" My sister questions.

I sigh and say, "Yes, sis, they did."

"Good, and I'm pretty sure they chowed down on those cookies, too, didn't they."

"To be honest, they both had two cookies each with some milk while watching the movie. They dozed off right after that," I explain.

Brian laughs. "That sounds like them. All those boys do is eat and sleep if they aren't running around somewhere."

"Ain't that the truth! I'm about to tear some of these cookies up and watch some tv," my dad says.

"Me too. They smell so good," my mom adds.

My parents grab a handful of cookies and walk out of the kitchen and into the living room where the twins are.

"So Eddie, who's this girl you wanted to ask me about?" Emma asks. Her eyes are filled with curiosity, as she eagerly waits for my answer.

"I wanted to ask you about this girl named Rose. Apparently, you used to cheerlead with her in high school."

My sister raises her eyebrows and smiles. "Oh yeah, I remember Rose! She was the cheerleading captain when I joined the team. I think she's your age."

Yeah no shit, Emma!

"Yup, she's my age. And she's freaking beautiful. How come you never told me about her?"

My sister shrugs and says, "I don't know, I guess I never thought about it."

I shake my head. "Emma! You're supposed to be on the lookout for me at all times! That means, ten plus years ago when you saw her while you were both attending fancy ass Oakville High, you should've been like: *Wow she would be a good look for my brother, Eddie.*"

Brian nods and takes a sip of eggnog that he grabs

from the fridge. "He makes a great point, baby," he says.

Emma grimaces. "Oh god, you guys are so dumb. And you know what, Eddie? Now that I think about it, Rose had a boyfriend when I went to school with her. And you had a girlfriend, ya big dummy! Did you forget you were dating Alauna at the time?"

Aw shit, I did have a girlfriend named Alauna at that time. But that was puppy love, nobody really remembers that shit. Well at least I don't.

"Oh yeah, that's right! My bad." I laugh.

Emma chuckles and shakes her head, pointing at me and Brian. "You two are shit for brains. How did you find out about Rose anyway? Did you find her on Instagram or something?" She wonders.

"Don't worry about it," I say.

Emma grabs Brian's cup of eggnog and drinks the rest of it.

"I was drinking that," Brian tells her with a smirk on his face.

"Oh hush and pour us some more. There's plenty more where that came from," my sister tells him. She can be a handful at times.

"You're lucky I love you," Brian says.

"And I love you, too, baby," Emma says, hugging Brian before he goes back for more eggnog. "Hey Eddie, if you want, I can check-up on Rose if you're interested. I'll message her tomorrow to see how she's been."

That's the Emma I know. Always on the lookout!

"Thanks, sis, but it's actually too late. I have her contact information already because Rose and I have been on a few dates so far," I reveal.

Emma is astonished. "Wow! For real, bro?"

"Yeah, I met her at the mall, and we hit it off from there."

"Aw, I really like her for you. She's always been a sweet and genuine person.... don't end up breaking her heart if she falls for you. There are still some girls out there who still haven't gotten over you randomly ghosting them after a date or two. I had to end up blocking a few of their asses on social media because they kept asking me about you."

"I won't, trust me. I was a different person then and I apologized to some of those girls, and a couple of them were psychopaths anyway," I reply. I head to the front room to grab my coat and put my boots on. "But this situation is different, I promise. I'm gonna head out now, you all have a good one. I'll see you guys on Christmas. I love you all, peace out," I add.

"Love you too," my sister says.

"Love you, broski," Brian says.

"Love you, son," my parents say in unison.

CHAPTER TWENTY-ONE

When I arrive right outside Rose's apartment complex, I give her a call.

"Hey, I'm outside," I tell her.

"Oh good, Eddie, do you think you can help me bring this stuff down to put in your car?"

"Yeah sure, here I come."

I wonder how many things she brought.

When I make it up to Rose's apartment door, she has the door cracked. I step inside to see she has two large pink suitcases lying on the floor.

Oh wow, she's really prepared!

"Eddie, are you sure you don't mind me staying with you through the Christmas break?"

My face must've thrown her off.

"Hell nah, I don't mind, I want you to stay over. We're going to have a great time!"

Rose grins from ear to ear. "Okay great, because I made sure I packed just enough clothes for the twelve days I'll be staying with you."

"That's perfect, are you ready now?"

"Yes." Rose steps toward me and smiles, looking up at me with those gorgeous caramel eyes of hers.

And just like that, my temperature begins to rise. I can't resist her. I give in to my primal urge and lift her off the ground to French kiss her.

"Ooo Eddie, if you kiss me like that again, I don't think we're going to make it out of here," Rose groans.

"I don't mind, I just know your downstairs neighbor is going to hear us again," I remind her while placing her back to her feet.

Rose raises her eyebrows and grabs one of her suitcases. "You're right! Let's get the hell out of here." She giggles as we walk out the door.

≈

As we're pulling up to my development, Rose is fascinated by the homes and the long driveways. "Your development almost looks like the Coopers' development," she says.

"Yeah, it's because whoever developed these homes out here in the woods back in the day made them all look the same," I explain.

"Interesting."

When I finally park in front of my house, Rose gasps. "Wow! So this is it!"

"Yup, this is the home my grandparents passed down to me after they passed on."

"Your grandparents passed down more than a gift. This is a treasure! I love it!"

"Thank you. Yeah, they surely did leave me with a gem. They bought this house in 1970. I'm going to make sure it always stays in my family. Even if I end up purchasing more homes in different states, this home will always belong to a Valentine."

Rose smiles at me. "That's beautiful, and such a rare thing to hear."

"Come on, let's get you all settled in."

After helping Rose out the car and getting her suitcases in the house, she looks around and observes the pictures hanging on the walls. "This is nice, I like all the family pictures. How come you didn't put up any Christmas decorations yet?"

I shrug. "It hasn't been the same putting up Christmas decorations in here ever since my grandparents passed away. Plus, I'm here by myself so I figured there would be no need to do it. But I helped decorate my parent's house and my sister's house with my nephews earlier this year. That was fun."

"Aw . . . . . well I would love to make a memory with you and help you decorate your house, if you don't mind. I'll even help you take everything down after the new year. It looks pretty gloomy and dark in here. It would be cool to brighten it up with some Christmas spirit."

Maybe this place does need a woman's touch. It's been years since it had one.

I nod. "I like the sound of that. And shoot, I should've asked you this before, but are you hungry?"

Rose shakes her head. "No, not right now. Why, are you?"

"Yeah, I'm hungry...hungry for you that is." I smile.

Rose smiles back at me.

"Come here," I tell her.

Rose drops her purse on the ground and rushes into my arms. I grab her backside and gently kiss her.

"I want you," she gasps.

"I want you too." I then pick her up and carry her up two flights of stairs and into my bedroom.

After I lay her down on my pillow, I slowly reach into her sweatpants and underneath her panties; she's soaking wet. I begin kissing and fingering her, trying to give her the best clit massage ever. As she moans and uses one hand to clutch the sheets, she muscles through her pleasure to try and please me by reaching into my sweatpants and stroking me. She can feel me growing.

"Ah, Eddie, I want you inside me," she says in between kisses.

I lay my eyes on her and—aw no, my mind is playing tricks on me again. I no longer see Rose staring at me. I'm now seeing flashes of the different hookers again. They're gazing up at me as they're lying on a pillow. I close my eyes and shake my head to snap out of it. Once I open my eyes again, I see Rose staring up at me while lying on my pillow.

"You did it again," Rose says.

"Did what?" I reply, playing dumb.

"You shook your head and blinked like you have a headache or something. Is there a problem?"

Rose looks devastated as if I'm not attracted to her, and that's far from the case.

"No, I promise there's no problem," I lie.

Maybe it's the beds that are the problem. No matter what Rose does, every time we're about to make love on a bed, my mind takes me to the beds at the brothels I've been to. I need to get her off this bed.

Luckily, I have a back-up plan for me to explore my creative side when it comes to making love to her. I'm gonna make sure I steer clear from this mind-fuck situation for as long as I possibly can. "Hold on," I tell her, while hopping off my bed.

"No, not again Eddie," Rose says playfully. "You have me yearning for you, so stop goofing around!"

I wink at her and say, "Oh trust me, you're gonna get it, I promise. Do me a favor and get undressed. And when you're finished, go into my closet and grab one of the ties I have hanging up?"

Rose is excited and she can't stop cheesing. "Ok," she exclaims.

As Rose undresses herself in my room, I head outside to the backyard patio to turn on two of the gas fire pits. These fire pits are right next to each other so when they're both lit up it almost looks like a walkway of fire. I then shovel the snow off the concrete that's in between the fire pits, and grab three clean thick blankets to lay on the ground.

"This is perfect," I say to myself, enjoying the setup I created.

I make my way back into the house after washing my hands and getting cleaned up.

"I'm ready," Rose exclaims.

As I walk up the stairs, I can hear Rose giggling.

"Are you undressed?" I ask her.

"Yes," she says as her giggles continue.

When I walk into my room, she's lying on my jet-black king-sized bed. Her body looks like the sculpture of a goddess and her beautiful golden tan skin is glowing. My goodness! This is who I'm about to make love to? I'm a lucky man! I notice she picked my red tie and laid it next to her on the bed. I smirk at her and say, "I'm going to blindfold you now."

"Ok," she says softly.

I climb onto the bed and grab my red tie. Once I sit her up to blindfold her, I pick her up off the bed, and carry her into the hallway.

"Wow, I didn't see this coming," she says.

After I carry her downstairs and outside, she sniffs the air. "Why does it smell like someone is about to barbecue, and . . . oh my god Eddie, it's so cold! What are you trying to do, kill me?" She laughs and smacks my chest.

"Of course not." I chuckle while walking in between both fire pits.

I place her down to her feet on top of the blankets.

"Oh good, now it's warm," Rose says, hugging her naked body.

"Here, let me take off your blind fold," I tell her.

When Rose finally sees what's in front of her, she's amazed.

"Get the hell out of here! This is beautiful." She gasps. "The heat from this fire feels so good, you wouldn't even think that we're surrounded by snow right now." She runs her fingers through her hair and says, "I don't know how you do it."

I kiss her on the cheek and stroke her shoulders. "I'm glad you like it, now get on your knees," I command as I slap her on the ass.

"Ooo, yes sir." She smiles and follows my instructions.

"Good, now bend over," I say, slapping her ass once more.

After placing herself in a doggystyle position, Rose looks back at me and says, "I'm ready when you are."

Hearing her say that has me ready to bust in my pants right now.

I pull out a condom I grabbed from my dresser earlier and remove all my clothes. Once my undergarments come off, my erection springs free. While fully exposed, Rose takes a peek.

"Christ!" she says as her eyes widen, followed up with a grin. "Can I feel it again?" she asks softly.

"Go ahead."

Rose gently caresses my length. Her touch feels so good that my eyes roll to the back of my head.

"Am I finally going to feel you inside me now, baby?" she whispers, turning back around in doggystyle position.

"Yes," I whisper, slipping the condom on to my full erection. From there, I lick the rim of her backside, before surprising her by grabbing her ankles, and flipping her upside down; causing us to be in a sixty-nine position while standing up.

Rose anxiously giggles. "Oh shit," she screams. "You almost gave me a heart-attack with your strong ass."

I take my time using my forearms to spread and squeeze her thighs as I lift her womanhood closer to my face. I'm loving every second of this. I dive face first into her warmth, sucking and flicking my tongue directly underneath her clit. *Her favorite spot.* I'm providing her with so much sensation that she wants to return the favor. Hell, she's trying her best to please me orally, but now I'm picking up the pace on my tongue dribble trick, causing her to moan uncontrollably. Luckily, I don't have any close neighbors, and I'm so glad my fence in the backyard is twelve feet high. We really have privacy back here.

While enjoying the passion, Rose is squeezing the fuck out of my legs, "Eddie, I want you inside me... please."

I flip her back around and bring her face to face with me as I carry her. She then wraps her legs around my waist as I finally give her what she wants. I've also been craving her for long time too. At that very moment, I ease my way into her tightness. Her mouth opens wide as we look into each other's eyes. In our trance, we exhale together as she receives all of me. Rose has a tight grasp on my back as I take my time gliding her heat up and down my hardness. While we both do our parts, motioning back and forth, our love making becomes cohesive. To prevent myself from moaning, I begin sucking and licking Rose's neck while she moans in my ear. It feels so good being deep inside her. My heart starts to race when I pick up the pace, bouncing her on me as her wetness streams down my cock.

If she feels this good with the condom on, I wonder how great she feels with it off.

At any moment now I'm going to erupt so I decide to switch positions to keep me lasting a bit longer. I gently lie on my back while still carrying Rose with my arms and my erection. Now she's on top of me.

"Go ahead and ride me, baby," I tell her.

And Rose does just that, while doing that sexy lip bite she likes to do. My god, now I'm the one clawing the blanket while she rides me like a fucking wave. I have no choice but to caress her back and smack her ass from time to time to compete with her pretty ass. On top of that, I can still feel myself about to erupt.

Fuck it. If I'm going to cum soon, then I'll cum with style.

I intense our pleasure by thrusting my hips up into the air, causing her knees and feet to lift off the blankets. She instantly gasps and squeezes my sides. I love it! I repeat this action of thrusting at a faster pace, causing her to moan louder and longer. I damn near have her moving like she's on a seesaw.

"EDDIE," she screams with pleasure, taking all of me. "Fuck, baby, ah, aw, oh my god, I'm about to cum."

I'm right with you, sweetheart.

I'm seconds away from cumming, too, but I can't even speak. My mouth is wide open and I'm admiring her beauty as the fluid within me rises. Rose continues to ride me and our pace accelerates.

Yup here it comes.

I can no longer hold back as I ejaculate. My eyes roll back as Rose and I clutch each other's hands.

"YES BABY! HOLD IT RIGHT THERE!" Rose hollers as she suddenly chokes me with both hands, and rides me back and forth with her mouth open wider than I've ever seen it.

Oh yeah, she's cumming.

I hold my position with my hips thrusted into the air. I stay that way until Rose's grinding comes to an end.

"Fuck! That felt so good, baby," she exhales.

The glow from the fire pits reveals Rose's sweat pouring down from her forehead to her navel. Our bodies are completely soaked.

"It sure did, woman, you're incredible," I admit.

"And you're even better," she says softly, laying her head on my chest.

CHAPTER TWENTY-TWO

Damn, I enjoyed the love making so much that I end up carrying Rose into the house and up the stairs like she's royalty. Well, she's royalty in my eyes at least. While carrying her through the hallway, Rose notices that I walk past my bedroom.

"Where are you taking me now?" she asks.

"To the shower," I answer.

She smiles. "Are you going to get in with me?"

"Hell yeah!"

She snickers.

As I walk into my bathroom, I place Rose into the shower, standing her on her feet. "Let me make sure this is warm for you." I turn on the rain shower head I have.

I delicately grab her hand and pull it into the water for her to feel. "Is that warm enough for you?"

Rose gives me a fifty-fifty signal with her hands. "It's alright, I guess, but I like my showers a little hot."

"Hot...no problem." I turn the temperature up a notch until I think it's hot enough for her. "Try it now," I tell her.

Rose walks in and lets the water run over her face and her breast. Now I'm getting hard again. Rose sees my hard-on and motions for me to come into the shower with her. "Alright, now I'm waiting on you to get in here with me, Mr. Valentine," she says seductively.

As I hop in the shower with her, I tilt her head back and kiss her. I attempt to grab the wash rag and soap to wash her up, but Rose gently stops my hand from reaching the soap.

"What's wrong?" I ask.

"Nothing, I just want you to let me bathe you," she tells me.

"I guess we're on the same page then, because I was going to wash you up too."

"Look at you, always trying to take care of me. I want to take care of you now."

I laugh because I think Rose is joking around.

"What's so funny, goofball, I'm serious. You've been spoiling me a lot lately. Gifting me with things, providing me with a good time, and giving me pleasure. I just want to return the favor."

Wow! Veronica should take notes from you.

Rose is putting her hair in a ponytail and I'm not sure why she's doing that.

"Listen Rose, you'll have plenty of time to return the favor I promise, but let me—"

Rose puts an end to my babbling by stroking my erection and instantly getting on her knees.

Oh shit! She's about too.....oh—my—god that feels so fucking good.

Rose is on her knees pleasing me with her mouth. Her tongue is swirling all over the tip of my cock. She's also taking the time to lick my jewels. I almost fall back against the glass shower wall. She deepthroats my semi-erection until she no longer can once I'm completely aroused. At this point, I'm so stiff, my dick is slightly curving to the left. Rose clutches me with her hands, and bobs up and down my manhood. How the hell is she doing this, I don't feel any of her teeth. Due to the suction and moistness coming from her mouth it feels like I'm being fucked by a vacuum pussy. That's the best way I can describe what I'm feeling.

Rose comes up for air and says, "I'm not stopping until you cum."

"Well go right ahead then, baby," I respond.

The water from the shower head hits my shoulders and my back as I hold onto both sides of the glass shower doors. The more I feel and hear the sounds of her slurping all over my rod, the closer I get to pouring into her throat.

"Aw shit, it's about to happen," I moan in between my quick breaths.

When Rose hears me say that, she begins slurping me even faster. Suddenly my cheeks squeeze together and my legs stiffen as Rose takes my fucking soul. And I mean that! It literally feels like I flew out of my body and flew back into it.

Rose swallows every last drop of me too. She then uses the water from the shower to wash her face and mouth before getting up and saying, "That was for the amazing head you gave me today at my apartment, Mr. Valentine. It's going to get better from here."

"Oh okay, I see you, Ms. Moreno. This is going to get better for you too. And listen, since you're going to bathe me, I'm going to bathe you, too, when you're finished. I don't want to hear a rebuttal either."

"Alright. You win!"

After we wash each other up and put our robes on, I carry Rose from the bathroom into the bedroom. As we cuddle with each other in the dark, she whispers, "I really like you, Eddie."

"I like you, too, and I love our chemistry. I have to be honest with you, I can't see myself with any other woman besides you." I kiss her.

She kisses me back. "I feel the same way. You're the only man I want to be with. I don't want anyone else."

"Well, I want to make this connection official between us, and I promise I won't do anything to hurt or mislead you."

"I know you won't, handsome, you've already shown me through your actions how great you are."

Minutes later, we're both yawning, lying in darkness. The moment is filled with peace and tranquility as we continue to cuddle each other until we fall asleep.

CHAPTER TWENTY-THREE

December 22nd

It's the next morning, and I awake to the sunlight shining into my room. What makes this morning even better is seeing the sun rays shining through my half opened black curtains and beaming onto Rose's face. She's sound asleep, looking like an angel. It feels good waking up next to a woman I have feelings for.

As I sit up, I'm a little thrown off because I know I turned the heat on last night, but I can feel a cool breeze coming from downstairs and through the door sill. I open the bedroom door and head downstairs to investigate. Without notice, I catch a whiff of weird odor.

"Ew, am I smelling shit or some type of funky mildew?" I mumble to myself.

I finally make my way into the living room and into the kitchen. The smell of the weird odor has gotten stronger. It almost smells like rotten fruit. And to make matters worse, I see my side door is wide open, answering my question as to why the house is freezing cold.

Aw shit, I must've left the door open when I was carrying Rose in last night. But where the hell is that rotten smell coming from?

Out of the blue, Rose comes downstairs. "Good morning, handsome, what's that smell?" she asks.

"Hey, good morning," I reply, walking toward the side door to shut it. I then shrug and say, "I have no clue, that's what I'm trying to figure out now."

I suddenly see a big piece of poop on the kitchen floor behind the counter.

"WHAT THE FUCK," I snap.

Unexpectedly a large black bear trots out of the dining room and into the kitchen where I am. Rose screams hysterically when she sees it coming toward me.

"OH SHIT! ROSE, GRAB MY GUN! IT'S ON THE SHELF IN MY CLOSET."

Rose stops screaming and runs upstairs. I hope she grabs my gun for me. To keep her safe, I don't want this thing following me up the stairs, so I'm trying to figure out a way to get it out of here while I wait for the gun. The bear stares at me across the kitchen counter, as I back away into the living room. While calming myself down, I have a flashback in my mind about a video I saw on YouTube. From what I can remember, the man on the video got a bear to leave his house when it was chasing his dog and scaring his wife. He protected his wife and dog by beating on his chest like a gorilla and hollering the entire time to intimidate the bear. These actions caused the bear to run away.

I make sure I repeat the same actions of the man from the video I'd seen. While the bear is on the opposite side of the counter away from the side door, I sprint into the kitchen and open the door.

I then speed walk around the counter, beating my chest like a gorilla and hollering, "GO! GO! GO!" I look like a stupid caveman, but, lo and behold, this method is working.

The bear is scared and it trots away from me, making its way around the other side of my kitchen counter. I chase the bear toward the side door and it eventually bolts out of my house. I quickly slam the door shut after it runs into my backyard and through the cracked open door on my fence.

"Thank heavens that bear is out of here now," I say in relief.

When I turn around, I see Rose standing at the bottom of the stairs, holding her phone and my Beretta pistol in her other hand. I know I just chased a bear off, but she looks sexy as hell in her red satin robe and lingerie while holding that gun.

When she hangs up the phone, she looks to me and says, "I was on the phone with animal services. I just told them you were able to scare the bear out of the house. And Eddie, you wouldn't believe this." Her face lights up.

"What?"

Rose begins to gradually walk down the stairs. "Apparently, they've been hearing about this bear for the past twenty-four hours. Some guy who had it as a pet in his house lost it. He was arrested yesterday for having illegal exotic animals in his house too."

"Well damn, I hope nothing else broke out of his

house. And I was about to say, I've never seen a bear in Delaware before. All I usually see in the woods are squirrels, deer, rabbits, and foxes."

"Same here! They said not to worry though, they have wildlife officials patrolling our area now and they'll let us know when the bear is caught and taken to its proper habitat," Rose tells me.

"Okay good! And shit, my bad, Rose. That's my fault. I forgot to close the door all the way, when I brought you in last night," I admit.

Rose places my pistol on the coffee table as she steps into the living room and rushes toward me. She wraps her arms around my neck and gives me a peck on the lips. "It's fine, I'm just glad you're okay. Lord knows what could've happened if you didn't scare it off," she says before kissing my lips again.

"Well I guess that situation already makes this day a memorable one, doesn't it," I add sarcastically.

Rose nods and laughs. "Yes, it does."

"Let me check these rooms for a second to make sure nothing else got in here." I step back from Rose and look around the kitchen, living room, and dining room.

After searching the entire inside of the house, every area was clean besides the shit on the kitchen floor. The bear left snow tracks and damp footprints behind too. Luckily there was nothing else the bear touched. I must've caught it at the right time.

"The crazy part is that I was coming down here to make you breakfast, but now I have to clean this bear shit off the ground, spray the house with Febreze, and wipe down the floor with Pine-Sol before I do that. Thankfully, that bear didn't tear anything up. It must've just used this place as a bathroom," I explain.

Rose blushes and twiddles her fingers. "Aw, you were going to make breakfast for me?"

"Damn right! And I still am."

"You're the best! How about we do it together? I'll help you clean the house and I'll cook with you."

I shake my head. "Rose, I can't have you do any of that. I got it. My goal wasn't to have you come over and do chores."

Rose holds her hands together and says, "Please, I don't wanna just sit here and do nothing. And it'll be good if we do things like cook and clean together. It helps develop trust."

I nod. "I see what you mean. We both have trust issues from our last relationships, don't we?"

Rose nods. "But I do trust you."

"And I trust you too."

"So we should make this trust stronger; starting with you allowing me to help you."

"Okay how about this, you can spray the house with Febreze, and you can cook with me. I'm going to get a shovel from the garage to scoop this bear poop out of the house, and I'll scrub this floor down with Pine-Sol. Do we have a deal?" I hold my hand out for her to shake.

Rose shakes my hand and says, "Deal!"

I pull her into me and kiss her one more time, before we begin our tasks.

CHAPTER TWENTY-FOUR

Rose and I finish cleaning the house when she receives a call from animal control.

"Hello," she says, answering the phone.

I'm watching her nod her head repeatedly as animal control talks to her. She suddenly smiles and says, "Okay, thank you so much for letting us know."

After she hangs up, I ask, "What happened?"

"Thanks to you, they caught the bear! They were able to track him down about a mile away from here!"

"Good! Now we can go outside stress free, but we aren't going to fuck outside again. I can't risk something like another bear popping out on us."

Rose laughs. "I'm with you on that!"

I clap and rub my hands together. "Alright, are you ready to cook with me now?"

Rose smiles. "Yes, I'm starving! What did you plan on making?"

After her question, I reach into the pantry and pull out a loaf of bread. I then grab an egg carton and a pack of turkey bacon from the fridge. "We're gonna make some French toast with eggs and bacon. Sounds good, right?"

Rose beams at me. "That sounds really good."

"Perfect," I reply while turning the stove on.

As I start making the Cinnamon egg dip for the French toast, I notice an awkward silence.

Before I can ask Rose what's wrong, she says, "Hey, Eddie, I have to tell you something."

Aw shit, based on Rose's tone it doesn't sound too good. I hope this isn't bad news. Why do women always have to deliver bad news when things are going so good?

"What's up?"

She drops slabs of bacon in the sizzling pan and sighs. "So yesterday when you told me to grab one of your ties out your closet to use a blindfold, there were a couple of papers sitting on top of your ties. One was a medical report from your doctor. It showed you tested negative for STDs recently. I'm sorry for reading your results but is there something you need to tell me?"

My heart starts beating twenty times faster than it usually does. That STD test was to make sure I didn't catch anything from the hookers I'd been sleeping with while I was away in November. Even though I used condoms, I always take more precautions.

"Oh nah, I get a routine checkup from my physician once a year, where they test me for everything. After the death of my grandparents, I always request to get tested for everything just to be on the safe side," I lie to Rose, while placing slices of toast in the Cinnamon egg dip and tossing them in a heated skillet. I hope she buys it.

"Oh okay, I understand. So here's my next question;

when was the last time you had sex?" she asks me, placing the cooked slabs of bacon on an empty plate before she starts working on scrambled eggs.

"Last night," I answer without hesitation, knowing that's not the answer Rose wants to hear.

Rose giggles and smacks my shoulder. "No, goofball, I'm talking about before me. When was the last time you had sex? For me it was three years ago with my ex."

I shake my head as I picture Raymond's husky ass busting a nut in Rose. It causes me to become a bit jealous. "I didn't need to know that," I tell her, feeling bad about being the whore I was previous to meeting her.

"I know, but now you do. Now I want to know about your last time," she says.

"Well, let me think. My ex and I broke up three years ago, too, and then I had a random one-night stand two years ago. That was the last time I had sex because I was dealing with a lot mentally," I lie to Rose again.

The truth is that after the two failed situationships with Stephanie and Bianca, I ended up having sex on multiple occasions with at least twenty-two different hookers within the past three years. And of course, all of those actions stemmed from my breakup with Veronica. Unfortunately, or fortunately in my case, right before I met Rose this month, I had sex at a brothel in Vegas a week before Thanksgiving. But I can't tell Rose that. She'll be devastated and I already feel dirty and like a piece of shit for going through that phase in my life anyway. Being with Rose changed my mind set and it makes me regret the way I was moving before I met her.

"Are you lying to me, just to make me feel better? You don't have to lie to me, Eddie. It won't make me change the way I feel about you," she says, pouring the pan of finished scrambled eggs into a clear glass dish on the counter.

"No, trust me, I'm telling you the truth, I promise."

I feel like shit now. I'm a horrible human being.

Rose hugs me, displaying her innocent grin. "Okay, I believe you."

After making sure all the French toast is cooked and comes out with a golden-brown color, I place them on an empty plate next to the crisp bacon and scrambled eggs. "Alright, it looks like we're all set. Let's eat!" I'm hoping Rose doesn't have any more difficult questions for me to answer.

"There was a ring box in your closet too," she says.

Oh for fuck's sake! I can't win.

"I saw you placed a sticky note on it that said *Xavier's engagement ring for Jen*. That's sweet! Are you hiding it for him or something?"

That sticky note saved me from what would have been the longest interrogation ever.

"Yeah, since this proposal is going to be a surprise, Xavier wanted me to hold it for him until it's time for him to propose to Jen."

"I love that!" Rose is looking suspicious.

"You peeked at the ring, didn't you?" I smirk.

Rose grins. "No."

"I wasn't born yesterday."

"Okay, fine, I peeked at the ring. It's freaking

gorgeous! And that diamond is huge!"

"Yeah, Jen means the world to him. They've been together since our college years. Now, do you have any more questions or are you ready to eat now?"

Rose approaches me and puts her hands underneath my shirt to rub my abs. "I'm ready to eat."

"It seems like you're ready for more than just food," I tell her, causing her to smile.

I pick her up and sit her on the counter.

"I'm ready for a quickie before we eat," she says, pulling a condom wrapper out of her pocket. "I took this from your room," she adds.

"That was sexy as shit." I kiss her.

She snickers. "After last night, I've been impatiently waiting to feel you inside me again."

"Say no more," I utter, snatching off her robe and pulling off her thong.

I glide my hands up her thighs and slide my fingertips into her essence as I passionately kiss her. She then reaches into my pajama pants and gently strokes my manhood, causing me to get hard immediately. As things continue to get heated, I slightly pull my pants down while Rose rips the condom wrapper open. She then slides the condom onto me and guides me inside her. At that moment, I waste no time thrusting into her repeatedly as she wraps her legs around my waist. In the process of my motion, she moans in my ear, causing my adrenaline to rush. My urge to pick her up off the kitchen counter takes over and I begin pumping faster.

Watching her ass jiggle as I look down behind her

back, has me flexing my hips like I'm the greatest male stripper to ever hit the stage. While enjoying this passionate lovemaking, we switch positions as I turn her around, causing her to grip the counter as I hit it from the back. I take my hand and grip her neck, choking her a bit as I continue to pump myself into her. The sound of her ass smacking against my pelvis and her wet pussy slurping my dick is echoing throughout the house. Eventually I cum, but I still have a hard-on and I want to keep going until I know Rose cums too. And just like that, Rose throws her back against my chest and holds on to my neck for dear life. She tells me to hold still as her legs shake until her orgasm is complete.

My god, I love it when she does that.

CHAPTER TWENTY-FIVE

W hen Rose and I finish eating, I catch her staring at me while I'm watching the sports channel. She's staring but she isn't saying anything. She has a look of suspicion written all over her face. Maybe she's still wondering about the last time I slept with someone. Or I wonder if she thinks we're moving too fast.

Dammit it's so hard to understand what's going on inside a woman's mind.

"Is everything okay?" I ask.

She grins. "Yup, everything's fine. I'm just wondering if you're still up for putting up your Christmas decorations," she says.

My eyes widen. "Oh, you still wanna do that?"

Rose stands up from her seat and smiles at me. "Absolutely, it'll be fun, let's do it today" she exclaims.

I'm kind of dreading this, because seeing those decorations will bring up all of the childhood memories I have, celebrating the holidays with my grandparents. But life goes on I guess, and Rose must've entered my life for a reason. Maybe it's time for me to start making new holiday memories, and doing that with her will be a perfect start.

"Alright, let's start with you first," I joke around while getting up from my seat.

Rose grins again and says, "What!"

I rush around the table and pick her up, tossing her over my shoulder.

"Ah!" She laughs as I playfully tap her ass, and carry her to the basement.

≈

Moments later, Rose and I bring up five boxes from the basement. Four of them contain a ton of Christmas lights and ornaments that are wrapped in newspaper. And the last box contains an old seven-foot plastic Christmas tree inside.

Rose's face lights up. "Now, this is more like it! Where do you wanna start first?"

"I'm going to start with hanging the outdoor Christmas lights on the roof. There're still outdoor clamps hooked onto the house so it'll be easy to hang up. While I'm doing that, you can wrap the pre-lit garlands on the bannisters around the house," I explain.

Rose doesn't say a word, all she does is give me her precious wide-eyed look.

"What's wrong now?" I ask.

"I thought we were going to do each task together, remember?" Rose sighs.

"Look, I just don't want you getting sick out there,

it's fucking freezing outside."

"Eddie, I want to do this with you. Let me hold onto the ladder or something while you're on the roof. What if you fall off and get hurt?"

I chuckle. "I'm not going to fall off and get hurt. I've done this a million times before."

Rose folds her arms. "You don't know that! It's a possibility you might."

I know I'll be perfectly fine hanging up the lights outside by myself, but I don't want to turn this into an argument. The poor girl just wants to help me and spend as much time with me as possible. And to be fair, I did agree to start doing tasks together as a team. Let me stop being a dumb fuck and give in already.

I smile at her and shrug. "I'm just kidding with you, come on let's put our jackets on, and get these lights up."

She smiles back at me. "You better stop playing with me like that. And okay, make sure you get bundled up good, too, because I don't need my superman catching a cold."

I shouldn't even be thinking like this or about Veronica but it blows me away to see how I went from a cold-hearted woman like Veronica to a woman who actually cares about me.

≈

After an hour goes by, I'm almost finished hanging all the Christmas lights on the roof. While standing on top of the roof, an idea strikes my mind. I think about the first conversation Rose and I had at the mall, and how she misses eating lemon risotto with shrimp and asparagus. It was her favorite dish at Oakville High.

"Eddie, is everything cool, what's wrong?" she asks me, while I stand on the roof in a daze.

"Oh yeah, I'm fine. I just have to check a string of lights by the chimney area, I'll be right back," I lie to her and walk away toward the chimney so she no longer has a view of me.

I use this time to quickly do an internet search on my phone to find a restaurant that makes risotto. The nearest restaurant I find is called Giovanna's Cucina. It's in Yorkville, about an hour away from Blue River. On their menu the only risotto they have is parmesan risotto. Since I can't find another restaurant that makes the specific dish I'm looking for, I decide to give Giovanna's Cucina a call.

"Hello, this is Giovanna's Cucina. Are you calling for pickup or to make a reservation?" The woman who answers has a piercing voice.

"I'm calling to make a reservation, and, if it's not any trouble . . . I was wondering if you guys could make lemon risotto with shrimp and asparagus. On the menu I saw you only had parmesan risotto. I think a lemon flavored one will go great for my date tonight, she loves that flavor," I explain.

"Aw, how sweet! So you want lemon risotto with shrimp and asparagus?" the woman asks.

"Yes. Would you be able to do that?"

"We can absolutely do that for you, sir. What's your name and what time will you and your date arrive?"

"My name is Eddie Valentine and we'll arrive at

seven p.m."

"Eddie Valentine, oh my, that's a lovely name. And okay, great, I'll have a booth reserved for you at seven p.m."

"Okay, thank you!"

"You're welcome. I'll see you then."

As I hang up the phone, I hear Rose say, "Were you able to fix the lights?"

I walk across the roof and wave to her so she can see me. "Yup, I fixed it. Now I'm just gonna plug these two cords together and the entire roof should light up."

I take one big step off the roof and onto the top of the ladder. I then attempt to plug in the lights while standing on the ladder.

"Okay, be careful. And I don't mean to sound like I'm nagging you, but it looks like you're struggling to get those cords to connect," Rose says. "Are you good?"

"Yup, everything's all good," I tell her.

The only problem is, things weren't *good*. While leaning half my body on the roof with my forearms, I realize I'm stuck, trying to plug the last two cords together. I think the wires have reached their stretch limit because they won't plug into each other, unless I pull them with all my might. This didn't happen to me when I hung up the lights for my grandparents. Hopefully, the wires are just tangled and won't snap apart.

"Are you sure you're good, Eddie?" Rose asks me, as she holds the ladder and watches me.

I give Rose a thumbs up and a smile. "Yes indeed," I reply, even though I'm still struggling.

Fuck it, I'm going to quickly press these two cords together as fast and hard as I can. Whatever happens, happens! I waste no time snatching both cords and plugging them into each other, but, as soon as I do that, I lose my balance on the ladder. While trying to regain my balance, I attempt to grab hold of the gutters attached to the roof, but my hands slip and I fall off the side of the ladder and land on my back. Thankfully, the pile of snow breaks my fall so it feels like I landed on a pillow. And once again, my clumsiness causes Rose to crack the hell up.

"I'm sorry for laughing. Are you alright?" she asks in between her laughs.

"Yeah, I'm straight, I can't believe that happened. It felt like I had it all under control."

Without notice, Rose lays directly on top of me in the snow. "See, I knew you needed me out here with you."

"Yeah, maybe I did *or* maybe I fell on purpose," I tell her right before kissing her.

She giggles. "No, you didn't."

I stand up and bring us both to our feet. "Okay, I didn't but look, we're finally finished," I say as I step back to see how the lights look on the roof. "It's not too bad, they'll look much better during the nighttime." I add.

"Yeah, it's not bad at all. I like it," Rose exclaims.

$$\approx$$

After helping Rose hang up the garlands, put up the

Christmas tree, and hang the ornaments, we sit on the couch together and take a good look at our decorative work. I'm satisfied with it, and I'm pretty sure she is too.

"Now this place looks like the holiday homes I see on HGTV," Rose says to me.

"Good, if you're rocking with it, then I'm rocking with it," I tell her. I then look at her and say, "Thank you for bringing some life back into this house again. You're truly a gift in your own right."

"Aw, no problem, handsome. I'm just returning all the good energy you've been giving me. The positivity you bring to so many people shouldn't be one-sided, you need some love and care too."

Oh yeah, this woman is from Jupiter or something because you won't find anyone more perfect than her on this planet.

"I'm taking you out tonight," I utter.

Rose beams at me and asks, "Really? Where?"

"To an Italian restaurant called Giovanna's Cucina. It's in Yorkville, about an hour away from Blue River. Have you ever been there?" I ask her.

Rose shakes her head and says, "Nah, I've never been to Yorkville or that restaurant before. It sounds amazing, but I wouldn't want you to have to drive us an hour away just to take me out to dinner. We can go to a restaurant nearby."

I shake my head. "It's fine, really! And besides, I already made reservations."

"When did you do that?" she asks in astonishment.

"I made sure I did it when you weren't able to see me for a couple minutes while I was hanging up the lights on the roof."

Rose smacks my shoulder. "You are so damn sneaky…in a good way."

I wink at her. "I know I am! And I'm glad you've never been to this place before because this dinner will be a special one."

Rose chuckles and asks, "Why is that, Mr. Valentine?"

"Because they'll be serving lemon risotto with asparagus and shrimp," I answer.

Rose grins from ear to ear. She tries to contain her excitement, but her joy takes over. "Oh my god, Eddie, you remember me telling you about that? I damn near forgot that I mentioned that to you!"

"Yeah, I remember. You said that was your favorite meal when you were in high school. So I searched some restaurants who serve that specific meal in the area, and Giovanna's is the only place that makes that dish."

Rose sits on my lap and gives me a kiss. "Thank you, thank you, thank you!"

"Anytime," I reply.

CHAPTER TWENTY-SIX

We arrive at Giovanna's Cucina and I already love the aesthetic this restaurant has. The first thing I notice is a shoveled walkway that reveals a mini cobblestone road leading to the front door. On our way to the door, we can hear the restaurant's outdoor speakers blasting the song, *Beyond the Sea*, by Bobby Darin.

Rose taps her foot on the cobblestones to the beat of the song. "I love it here already! It makes me want to visit Italy."

"I can see why this place has nothing but five-star reviews," I reply, while opening up the entrance door for Rose.

As we walk inside, we're initially hit with a whiff of garlic, tomatoes, fresh bread, and wood-fired pizza. It's an elegant and welcoming place. The chandelier lights inside are dim, and candles are lit on every table.

"It smells great in here," Rose says.

I nod as we approach the host in the lobby. "It sure does! Now I'm starving."

Suddenly the host politely intervenes by saying,

"Excuse me, Mister and Missus, name please."

"The name is Eddie Valentine and I booked a party for two at seven p.m."

The host looks through his guest book and says, "Oh yes, I see you here. Follow me, please."

We follow the host to the back left corner of the restaurant where there are glistening burgundy booths placed against polished brick walls. "Mister and Missus, you'll be sitting here at this lovely booth."

"Thank you, sir. I appreciate it," I reply.

"You're welcome. Your waiter will be with you shortly," the host says as he walks away.

After Rose unties her peacoat, I look to her and say, "Let me help you with that."

She smiles and turns her back to me as I remove her coat. She looks stunning in her purple sequined bodycon dress. It looks perfect on her, shit, even one of my hoodies would look perfect on her.

When we take our seats, a waiter approaches our table. "Hello, my name is Dante. I'll be serving you two tonight. This is Eddie Valentine's table, right?" he asks.

"Yes," I answer.

"Great! The kitchen already knows what entrées you'll be having," Dante says, handing us menus. "Here are the menus for you to have a look at our appetizers while you wait on your entrée." He then places a warm breadbasket on the table and fills our glasses with water.

"Can I start you off with drinks?" he asks.

I look at Rose and gesture for her to go first.

"I'll have the red wine you guys have listed here on

the menu," she tells him.

"Red wine it is, and what about you, sir?" Dante asks.

"I'll have a lemonade, and I'll go ahead and get that lobster soup appetizer too," I tell him.

"Awesome and have you decided on an appetizer, Miss? It's no rush if you haven't."

"Yes, I'll take the crunchy vegetable salad with ricotta crostini," Rose says.

I can tell Oakville High gave Rose high quality taste buds because I never even heard of ricotta crostini. What in the world is that?

"Great, thank you, I'll be right back out with your appetizers," the waiter says, before walking away.

Rose places the menu down and gazes at me. Suddenly her long gaze turns into a bright smile. "Eddie, I didn't see lemon risotto anywhere on that menu. I only saw parmesan risotto. . . .what did you do?" she asks delightfully.

It was time to give up my little secret. I shrug and say, "Well, I may have asked the person on the phone if they could make the lemon risotto for us. They had no issue with it and said they would gladly do it."

"Ooo, so this part was planned too? No wonder the waiter said they would have our dinner out shortly. I was so confused, thinking to myself like this isn't normal." Rose shakes her head at me while smiling in disbelief.

"Yeah, you caught me."

At that moment, our waiter comes back and brings my soup and Rose's salad along with our drinks.

"Thanks, Dante," I say to him.

"My pleasure and if you guys don't mind, the chef wants to come out here and meet you," Dante says right before he looks at Rose and adds, "She said she thinks she knows you."

"Me?" Rose replies while pointing to herself.

"Yeah."

"What's her name?"

"Marisa Lucci," he says.

Rose's face lights up. "Oh my god! Chef Marisa works here now!"

Our waiter, Dante, nods. "She actually owns it."

"Wow! Yes, I know her, she can come out here asap!" Rose exclaims.

"Okay, I'll get her," Dante says as he walks toward the back and into the kitchen.

Rose crumbles up one of the napkins near the bread basket and throws it at my face. "Eddie!" she laughs.

"What?" I ask.

"Did you plan this too?"

I shake my head. "Nope, I honestly had nothing to do with this part. I wish I could lie and say I did, but this right here is truly a coincidence. Delaware is so freaking small. Who would've known your former high school chef owned this place?"

"This is so crazy and I'm so happy right now! Chef Marisa would always hook me up when I was in school. I need to come here more often!"

Moments later, a middle-aged Italian woman with dark brown hair comes to our table wearing her chef's uniform.

Rose stands up and cheerfully greets the chef. "Chef Marisa!"

"Hey, Rose," Chef Marisa says.

"I miss you so much!"

"I miss you too! And your sister, how is she doing by the way?"

"Aida's doing good, she's a computer software engineer now and she does website designing too."

"That's incredible. You girls were always so smart, and I heard through the grapevine that you're a teacher now," Chef Marisa says.

"Yup, that's true! I teach kindergarten at Maple Elementary and I love it there. But that's enough about me and Aida, I'm so happy for you! This restaurant is amazing! So you're not cooking at Oakville at all anymore?" Rose asks her.

"No, I left in 2015, and opened up this place a year later. I named it after my grandmother. Her name was Giovanna."

"That's beautiful. I love the name, and, wow, so you left the school a year after Aida graduated," Rose mentions. She then looks at me and says, "Oh sorry, Ms. Marisa, I forgot to introduce you to my boyfriend, Eddie."

"Hi Eddie, I remember talking with you on the phone this morning. As soon as you mentioned wanting the lemon risotto dish, I was like this must be a former Oakville student! Did you eat my food in high school too?" Chef Marisa asks as she shakes my hand.

"Oh no, I wish I did, but I went to Bill Pickett High," I answer.

Chef Marisa snickers. "Okay, so you went to the school that served McDonald's for lunch. I heard other things about that school, too, but I don't want it to seem like I'm being rude."

"You're fine. Bill Pickett High was a little unusual," I say, embarrassed.

"His sister, Emma, went to Oakville too. Remember her from Aida's class? Emma Valentine," Rose intervenes.

"Wow! Emma's your sister! No wonder your last name started to ring a bell with me when you talked with me on the phone. It's all starting to click now. Your sister really made a name for herself at Oakville. She helped start a fashion program at the school. How is she doing?" Chef Marisa asks me.

"Emma's doing good, she goes by Emma Johnson now since she's married. She also has twin boys," I disclose to the chef.

"What! Shut the front door! Is she still into fashion?" she asks.

"Yeah, she currently designs outfits for musicians and athletes whenever they do award shows or walk the red carpet."

"Wow, that's fascinating! I'm so happy for her! And what do you do?"

"Oh nothing special. My sister is doing things light years ahead of me." I then point to Rose. "They all are." I really don't feel like talking about myself.

Rose rubs my back and says, "Aw don't say that,

Eddie. You're both doing incredible things." She continues to rub my back and adds, "He's an author and he's written three books so far. And that includes the greatest novel I've ever read. You have to check out his book called *My Girlfriend's A Vampire*. I think it'll be made into a movie one day."

Rose, you're the incredible one.

Chef Marisa pulls out her phone. "Interesting, so it's *My Girlfriend's A Vampire*, ya say?"

Rose nods.

"I love it, I absolutely love seeing you young people do great things. Eddie, I'm purchasing your book right now online. It says it'll arrive at my house in two days. I can't wait to read it."

"Thank you, Chef!"

"No, thank you for being you, and for supporting my restaurant," Chef Marisa says jokingly. "You sure do have a supportive girlfriend in Rose."

"Don't I know it," I agree.

"Alright now, you two relax and enjoy yourselves. I'm going to head back to the kitchen to check on your food. I'm also going to make sure this dinner is a special one," the chef tells us.

Moments later, Chef Marisa brings out her famous lemon risotto that Rose loved so much. And I have to say, my god, it's delicious. I can see what all the fuss is about.

"I still can't believe you found this place! I haven't had this meal in eleven years," Rose says, savoring every spoonful she has. "It tastes just as good as I remember."

While finishing up our meals, we see an elderly couple slow dancing to the song *Unforgettable* by Nat King Cole.

Rose looks at them and beams. "Aw, they're so cute. I love that."

I never turn down an opportunity when it comes knocking at my door. After gazing at the elderly couple, I stand and hold my hand out toward Rose. "May I have this dance?" I ask her.

She raises her eyebrows and smiles. "For real?"

"Yeah, I'm serious. May I have this dance?" I smile.

"Yes, you may," Rose says as she takes my hand.

We then step out on the small dance floor and begin to slow dance. The elderly couple smile as they catch a glimpse of us dancing just like them. The sight of seeing two couples dancing causes more couples to step out on the dance floor until the song ends.

After enjoying an ice cream sundae for dessert, providing a nice tip to the waiter, and saying our goodbyes to the chef, we grab our belongings and prepare to leave.

CHAPTER TWENTY-SEVEN

We're on our way out of Yorkville and I'm driving down a shopping district that'll eventually lead us to the highway. While my eyes are on the road, Rose leans across the armrest and fondles my crotch.

She then whispers, "Thank you again for the dinner tonight. You made my night. As a matter of fact, the night isn't over yet." Followed by a kiss and a moan directly in my ear.

Immediately, I begin to rise and push on the gas a little more as I bite my lip. "Whoa, don't cause me to crash now, baby."

She laughs. "I'm sorry," she says, kissing my neck. "You just make it hard for me to keep my hands off you. Especially when you go out of your way to make my day a memorable one."

I chuckle again. "How so?"

Now, I already knew how I made her days memorable, but hearing it from her would definitely be a confidence booster. Or maybe an ego booster.

"Because you're so thoughtful," she says before

kissing me on the cheek. "You're full of surprises," she adds, followed by another kiss. "And you're sexy," she finishes, putting her hand in my pants and gripping me.

"Baby if you keep this up, we're not going to make it to my house. We might start fucking in my car since we're still an hour away from Blue River," I explain.

"That sounds like a good idea. I'll do it with you anywhere," Rose responds.

Bloody fucking hell! This woman just gets better and better!

To make the night even greater, I suddenly spot a couple's boutique near some fast-food places and a barbershop. The closer my car gets to passing this boutique, the more I tell myself I should stop there and go inside. Besides, I like the feeling of surprising Rose, and always making unexpected moves.

"You see that store over there," I say, pointing to the boutique.

Rose smiles. "Yep! The sign says they have some kinky toys inside for couples." She then turns to me and asks, "Why, what are you thinking about?"

I immediately make a sharp turn and pull into the small shopping center. "I'm thinking it's time for more surprises," I answer, while parking in front of the boutique.

Rose smirks. "Are you serious, Eddie?" She releases her grip and takes her hand out of my pants.

"Damn right I am," I answer. "Come on, I'm going to pick out some things for you."

"Oh my god, I've never done anything like this before," she exclaims.

"Neither have I, but, hey, there's a first time for everything, right?"

Rose grins and nods.

As we walk inside the couple's boutique the very first thing we see are role-play costumes and porn DVDs. It looks like an old Blockbuster store but with all X-rated videos inside. The further we walk toward the back, the darker it gets. The lights change from a bright yellow to a dark red tint as we go through these red satin curtains that lead us to where all the sex toys are in the store.

Rose laughs as she points to a dildo on one of the shelves. "Are we getting that?"

"Hell no, I'll throw that shit in a volcano," I reply, making her laugh even more.

"Goodness gracious, Eddie, you're going to have me randomly laughing at that for about a week. Now I'm picturing you throwing a dildo in a volcano."

After her comment, I notice a clit vibrating sex toy sitting in the glass display case at the counter where the cashier is. As I observe the toy through the glass, I see that it's called a rose vibrator.

This toy is shaped like a rose and it matches Rose's name. It's perfect!

Next to the rose vibrator are remote-controlled vibrating panties. "Here we go," I say, tapping the glass.

"Let me get the vibrating panties and the rose," I tell the cashier.

"Shush, not too loud, babe. I'm embarrassed," Rose whispers while hiding behind me.

"Oh trust me, hon, there is nothing to be

embarrassed about. What you and your man are buying is completely normal, compared to what I see on a daily basis. And none of the customers in here will judge you," the cashier says as she grabs the items and rings them up. She looks like a cool hippie who most likely knows every detail about the sex toys in this store.

"I guess you see a ton of crazy things in here each day, huh?" I ask the cashier lady.

"You got that right. People have the most bizarre kinks. But hey, whatever floats their boats pays my bills."

"I know that's right," Rose adds.

I grab a box of condoms to throw into the order since I only have a few left at the house.

Rose clutches my arm and whispers, "I like this freaky side of you too. So that's another quality I must add to my list. You're thoughtful, surprising, sexy, and . . . freaky."

After Rose's comment, she grabs flavored lubricant and hands it to the cashier. It's a pink lemonade flavored lubricant for women. "We'll be getting this too," she adds.

"Alrighty then, lucky you," the cashier says joyfully.

"I can't wait till we get home," I whisper back.

"I don't know if I can wait that long," Rose teases.

"We'll see," I say.

By the time we leave the store and get back in the car, I realize Rose was right! She couldn't wait long. As soon as I begin driving, she leans over to my seat and puts her hand in my pants again and starts licking my neck. She's softly stroking my tip, and I'm fully aroused. Rose knows I have tinted windows and I can tell she's ready to go all out right now in this car.

"Baby, you're going to have me explode all over myself if you keep this up. We're still an hour away from Blue River, and we haven't even tested out our new toys yet," I explain.

Rose doesn't respond, she just continues to rub and stroke me.

I guess we can use the toys another day.

I match her energy, unbuckling my belt, and unzipping my pants. I pull my pants down just enough for my manhood to be exposed. "Get on top of me," I command.

"What?" Rose makes sure she responds to that.

I hit the electronic seat adjustment button to push my seat back as far as I can with just enough distance for my foot to still reach the gas and brakes. "Grab a condom out the box and get on top of—"

Rose doesn't waste a second stripping from her panties, ripping open a condom, and climbing on top of me, while I drive the car on the highway. I know what we're doing is dangerous and we've probably reached an all-time high of stupidity, but our adrenaline rush has taken over.

"Can you see the road fine?" she asks softly.

"Yes," I mutter as she caresses me.

"Good." Rose gently grabs my erection, places the condom on me, and eases my erection inside of her.

The moan she lets out near my ear sends chills down my spine. She thrusts her hips back and forth while slowly riding up and down on me. At this very moment,

I'm driving the car like I'm ninety-years-old and my knees are feeling weak. If I keep this up, we're going to get pulled over. I do a combination of squeezing and slapping her ass until I come up upon a sign on the highway. It reveals that there's a nearby rest stop and campsite in Yorkville at Exit Four. I remember that exact campsite too. I used to work at Camp Yorkville Lake during the summers when I was in high school. There are so many hidden and private areas to park in those woods, I'm sure Rose and I won't get caught by the police if we decide to fuck in the car while I'm parked out there. I've made my decision! As Rose continues to ride me, I grip the steering wheel tight with my left hand and instantly take Exit Four. After passing the rest stop and heading toward the entrance of Camp Yorkville Lake, I find an empty parking lot near an empty campground.

Yes! There are no humans in sight!

I park the car and position it with a perfect view of the semi-frozen lake shining from the moon's reflection.

"Hey, babe, hop up real quick," I tell Rose, helping her glide off me as she makes her way back onto the passenger seat again.

"What's wrong? Did I not do something right?"

My jaw drops. "What! Of course not, babe," I kiss her lips. "You did everything right. I just wanted to take us here so we wouldn't get pulled over by the police. I was driving slow as shit."

She giggles. "Where are we anyway?"

"We're at Camp Yorkville Lake. I used to work here in the summer as a teen. Hopefully, it's a ghost town right now during the winter." I take off the condom and pull up my pants before hopping out the car. "Stay right there for me, please," I add, while walking to the back of my Chevy Suburban to open the trunk.

I push all four seats down in the back, giving us some more room to make love there. I then take a warm quilt I have in the car and lay it on the folded back seats. After finishing my setup, I climb through the trunk and shut the trunk door. When I look toward the front seat, I catch Rose squinting at me. I can tell she has a question.

"Why are you staring at me like that?" I ask her with a smirk.

"Have you ever fucked somebody in these woods before?" she asks me.

I laugh and shake my head. "No, the only thing I ever did at Camp Yorkville Lake was kiss another camp counselor. Her name was Cindy, we were coworkers, and we were both sixteen at the time. That only happened because we were all playing truth or dare late at night while the campers were asleep, and Cindy dared me to kiss her. But other than that, I never did anything wild here. I can promise you that."

Rose's straight face slowly turns into a grin. "Oh okay, that's innocent, I believe you."

"Thank you! Now bring your sexy ass to the back seat and come sit on my tongue." I tell her while removing my clothes.

After undressing, Rose reaches into the shopping bag from the couple's boutique to put on that pink lemonade flavored lubricant. I'm aroused again and my mouth is watering. She climbs to the back of the Suburban and takes her time climbing on top of me. She licks my abs, saying, "One, two, three, four, five, six, seven, eight. You have a delicious eight-pack."

When she finishes licking my abs, she moves up my body to finally sit on my face. My tongue eases into her wetness, penetrating her special place. I love the way she tastes. I would lick and suck her clit all night if I could. The tingling sensation she's feeling is causing her to squeeze my head in between her thighs. She's loving it and I'm loving the pleasure I'm giving her. Rose presses her hands against the roof of the car and moans breathlessly. She's flexing her hips back and forth, enjoying the repeated motion coming from my tongue. I'm ready to pleasure her to the max. I lift Rose off my face and flip her into a doggystyle position. After I open up a new condom and place it on, I grab Rose by her hips, easing my way into her. She feels like heaven as she throws herself back repeatedly up and down my length. Once again, we're in unison, and, as always, I want to crank it up a notch. I grab her forearms and pull back on them with the right amount of pressure, like I'm holding onto two leashes. Now her backside is clapping on to my hips with each thrust.

"Oh my god—yes baby, I—I—fuck!" Rose incoherently says in between deep breaths, as she suddenly mashes her face into the quilt and bites it.

She's groaning and moaning as we pick up the pace. The ass claps are getting louder, the car is shaking harder, and her pussy is getting wetter. The windows are completely fogged up now. I can no longer see the moonshine reflecting off the lake. Rose was so horny that she reaches her climax before me, she eventually slows down her rhythm and stops. Her beautiful ass is completely drenched in sweat.

"Gawd damn, my legs are so weak now, baby." Rose says as I lie down next to her and kiss her. "Did you cum?" she randomly asks.

Why do women ask this whenever we don't cum?

"Yeah," I lie.

Rose looks at my dick with the condom still on and doesn't see any semen. She smacks my shoulder and looks disappointed. "No, you didn't."

"Look, it's all good. It was still amazing like always."

"No, I'm not pleased with that, you got me off, so I need to get you off too," Rose says.

"You don't have to. We can do it next time."

"No, I wanna do it now," Rose insists, climbing on top of me while I'm semi-hard with the condom still on.

I guess her legs aren't feeling so weak anymore.

She glides me inside of her and starts riding me like a rollercoaster. "Cum for me, baby," she gasps, gently caressing my jewels while continuing to pelvic thrust up and down my manhood.

Rose has me completely stimulated. With the combination of her fondling my love sack and feeling the motion of her warmth, before I know it, I'm cumming. And my god, each climax we have together gets sexier.

CHAPTER TWENTY-EIGHT

R ose sleeps on our hour ride back to Blue River. Well, it actually took an hour and thirty minutes due to an accident that caused a traffic jam. But after finally arriving home, I was able to wake her up since she wasn't in a drunken sleep like she was during the paint night. After showering, Rose and I cuddle together. I love spending time with this amazing woman. She's beautiful inside and out and I can't see myself ever getting tired of her. I know most people would call this the honeymoon phase but, when it comes to us, I don't think a phase exists.

We're currently scrolling through channels and clicking in and out of streaming apps. We're having a hard time picking a holiday movie we want to watch.

"You wanna watch It's a Wonderful Life or Miracle on 34th Street?" Rose asks me.

I think about it for a moment. I've seen those films so many times throughout the years, and it starts to get redundant after a while. "Yeah, we can but, after leaving that restaurant, I'm in the mood to watch some Italian-

American films like The Godfather or Rocky," I reply with a chuckle.

"Oh god no, not the Godfather, that'll put me to sleep. I can never get through the whole thing, but I never watched Rocky before. What's that?"

I'm flabbergasted by what I just heard from Rose. "What? You've never seen Rocky before?"

Rose shakes her head and gazes at me with her beautiful eyes. "No," she answers with a smile.

"Aw, man, well we have to watch it then. It's the greatest boxing movie ever. It's a classic! There's like six of them and then the Creed films follow up after the Rocky films."

Rose snaps her fingers and says, "Oh, I've seen Creed before!"

I palm my face and shake my head. "So you watched Creed but not Rocky? I swear this new generation is something else."

Rose sits up and hits me with a pillow. "We're the same age and part of the same generation, big head, and besides, after seeing Michael B. Jordan in that trailer with his shirt off, I had to see it," she says, smirking at me.

I laugh. "Oh so that's your celebrity crush huh?"

Rose nods. "Yeah, I have a celebrity crush on him and Bad Bunny," she admits.

"Wow! So I have to compete with Michael B. Jordan and Bad Bunny."

"Yup." She giggles.

I slowly nod. "It's all good. I feel the same way about Halle Berry."

Rose lays back down and snuggles up against me. "Well, me and Halle Berry are going to have some problems. I'm gonna have to fight her."

"You're something else! Are you ready to relax and enjoy this movie, Ms. Moreno?"

"Yes, Mr. Valentine!"

≈

Surprisingly to me, Rose enjoys the first Rocky film, and wants to watch the second one right away. It brings me joy knowing how much she likes the same film as I do. Moments later, as we're watching Rocky II, we're on the scene where Rocky and Adrian are walking around at the zoo and he's preparing to propose to her. And at that moment, Rocky says to Adrian, "I was wondering if uh, you wouldn't mind marrying me very much."

Rose's jaw drops. "Wait . . . wait . . . pause that really quick, what did he just say?"

I laugh. "He said, I was wondering if you wouldn't mind marrying me very much."

"What in the world! Put some more effort into it Rocky, jeez," Rose shouts to the tv.

I laugh and resume the movie. We're now engulfed in the scene again. After Adrian asks, "What did you say?" Rocky then pulls up one of her ear muffs and answers, "If you wouldn't mind marrying me too much."

Rose gasps and shakes her head. "What kind of proposal is that? And Adrian's crazy ass said yes."

I rub her shoulder and say, "What's wrong? You

don't find that romantic?" I joke.

"Hell no." Rose laughs followed by a yawn.

"When we finish watching the rest of Rocky II, we'll catch up on the rest of them tomorrow, okay? I can tell you're getting sleepy," I mention to her as I kiss her forehead.

Rose nods and falls asleep with her head lying on my chest.

CHAPTER TWENTY-NINE

December 23rd

The next day, Rose and I try to spend most of our day watching all the Rocky and Creed films while chowing down throughout breakfast and lunch. Luckily, we finish watching all the Rocky films, but our watch session of Creed is interrupted by the doorbell. I sit up, wondering who that can be. Subsequently, I get a text from my sister, Emma, telling me she's outside with her husband, Brian, and their kids, Joshua and Jaden.

"Who is it?" Rose asks me, as we both climb out of the bed.

"It's my sister, Emma. She's here with her husband and my nephews. I forgot to tell you they pop up unannounced sometimes to check up on me," I explain.

"Aw, that's sweet of them," Rose says before asking me a multitude of questions anxiously. "Should I come down with you . . . or would that be too awkward for you? Or would it be too soon? What should I do?"

I wrap my arms around her waist and pull her into

me to hug her. I then kiss her forehead, reassuring her that I'll be comfortable with her around me in any setting. "Baby. relax, of course you can come down with me. I want them to see you, and I want you and Emma to get reacquainted again. I know she'll be happy to see you," I tell her.

A joyous smile grows upon Rose's face. "Okay, I'm going to get changed," she says as she kisses me and walks into the bathroom.

I place my slippers on and head downstairs to open the front door.

"Hey Eddie, Joshua and Jaden wanted to come by to see you today so we could drop off a gift for you to have on Christmas," Emma explains to me.

"Emma, you guys didn't have to do that. I'll be at Mom and Dad's house on Christmas. I can open my gift there," I reply as I let them all in.

"We know, but we honestly wanted to check on you so you wouldn't be lonely," Emma says as she observes the house.

My sister has been treating me like a child or an abandoned puppy ever since I've been living here alone. Her and my mom act like I'm going to have a mental breakdown or some shit. I constantly have to remind them I'm fine.

"Wow, so you decorated, I see. This looks nice, the outside looks great too! Did you have help?" Emma adds.

"Yeah, Rose helped me. She's actually here right now," I reveal.

Emma raises her eyebrows. "No way, big bro! Really?

Eddie, are you playing around?" she asks, looking like a proud parent.

I shake my head. "No, I'm not playing around. I'm serious, Rose is here! So your big bro is no longer lonely anymore either," I say sarcastically.

Brian chuckles and says, "That's right, tell her, man. I try to tell your sister all the time that you're enjoying your life."

"Oh shut up, Brian. And gosh, Eddie, I didn't mean to sound harsh when I said that," Emma says.

My nephews catch her off guard when she hears them getting comfortable in my living room, throwing their shoes and jackets off.

"Um, no boys, keep your jackets on," she repeatedly claps at them to get their attention.

"Aw man," Joshua says.

"Why do we have to keep our jackets on, Mom?" Jaden asks.

"Because we're about to leave," Emma tells them.

"But we just got here," Joshua adds.

"Hey, you two heard what your mom said. That's final. No more complaining, ya hear?" Brian tells the twins.

I feel sort of bad, because the twins love hanging out with me and chilling at my house. They never have to leave early when they come here.

"You guys can stay if you want," I tell Emma and Brian.

"No, that's not fair to you, big bro, you have company. And it's good that you finally have a girl over here," Emma tells me.

"Holy shit balls, Emma, well damn, I guess you didn't mean for that to come out harsh either, huh?" I say.

Brian laughs. "Word, babe, can your brother catch a break? That came out like you were trying to play him, like he doesn't get girls or something."

"Oh goodness, here we go again! I'm not saying it like that. I'm just happy for him, that's all. Can't I be happy for you, Eddie? You can finally start popping out more grandkids for Mom and Dad and finally some nieces and nephews for me," Emma adds.

I shake my head. "I appreciate you being happy for me. Now as far as making a family, I'm not thinking that far ahead," I tell her, even though in reality, having kids with Rose has randomly crossed my mind a few times. But I don't want to say it out loud at the moment and jinx it. Rose will probably feel like it's way too soon to talk like that.

Rose suddenly trots down the stairs. "Oh my god! Hey Emma, long time no see."

"Hi Rose!" My sister shouts as they hug each other.

Rose looks amazing too! Wearing a red blouse, black jeans, and a gold necklace. Even her hair is flowing like she just left the beauty salon. You would've never guessed she was lying in bed with me all day.

"This is my husband, Brian," Emma says, making her introductions.

"Hey, Brian," Rose says.

Brian waves. "Hey, nice to meet you, Rose."

"So, how are you doing, girl? Eddie told me you two have been dating. I love that," Emma mentions.

Emma you didn't have to say all that. Sheesh!

"Yes, we've been dating and he's wonderful. Your brother is the best! And other than that, I'm doing good! Still teaching kindergarten and getting through life," Rose responds.

"That's good, girl! My two boys are in preschool now. I'll have to send them to your school next year so they can be in your class. What school do you teach at again?" Emma asks Rose.

"Yes, please do! I would love to have them in my class! I teach at Maple Elementary," Rose says.

"Oh okay, that's the private school in Maple County, right? I've heard wonderful things about that place. Jaden and Joshua might love it there. I need to introduce you to them. Boys! Where did you two go? I want you both to meet Ms. Moreno, she's going to be your teacher next school year," Emma says, looking for my nephews.

As Rose and Emma walk into the kitchen to find the twins, Brian nudges me and says, "Yo, Eddie, she's beautiful, where did you two meet?"

"We met at the mall at the beginning of this month. I handed her the gifts she dropped on the ground and a conversation started from there. I haven't looked back since," I explain.

"Oh wow, man, that sounds like a movie. Talk about perfect timing. And you seem happy too. You started blushing as soon as she came downstairs," Brian tells me.

"I didn't do all that," I say, chuckling.

Brian laughs. "You sure did. And man, listen, whenever a man has the look that you just had on your face, that means he's in love."

Now Brian is right, I believe I'm falling in love with Rose, or I'm probably already in love with her. I'm just afraid to admit it to myself at the moment.

I end up waving Brian off. "Nah, get outta here with that kind of talk, man. What's up with everybody and this love talk lately?" I say in fun.

"Alright man, you can't hide how you actually feel about her for too long though, or it'll come back to bite you."

Suddenly Emma and Rose make their way back to the front room with my nephews.

"Okay boys, say bye to your Uncle Eddie. We'll see him on Christmas," Emma says.

"Alright man, I'll see you soon. Let me go start this car up to keep it warm," Brian says to me.

"Alright, take it easy, Brian," I reply as he heads out the door.

Joshua and Jaden place their coats on and give me a hug. "Bye, Uncle Eddie," they both say at once.

"Bye guys, love you. I'll see you in two more days, okay?"

"See ya, bro! And see you, Rose. I'll make sure I text you soon, we'll be in touch," Emma tells Rose.

"We sure will and bye, Joshua and Jaden. It was nice meeting you," Rose says, waving to them.

After I shut the door, a notification pops up on my phone. It's my calendar reminding me that Xavier is throwing a Christmas Eve party tomorrow and will be proposing to Jen. I palm my forehead because I nearly forgot all about that, and the engagement ring I have to bring to the party tomorrow. Thank God for technology! I need to ask Rose if she would be comfortable with going to that party tomorrow. I just hope Stephanie and Bianca don't show up like Xavier promised me they wouldn't. If they do, all hell will break loose.

"What's the matter?" Rose asks me, noticing some concern on my face.

"I forgot to ask you if you wanted to come to this Christmas Eve party with me tomorrow. Remember that engagement ring I'm holding onto for my friend, Xavier, upstairs?"

"Yeah."

"Well he's throwing a surprise baby shower, which is pretty much a party for Jen; since they're party animals. And he'll be proposing to her tomorrow too. So I have to make sure I get that ring over to him. I almost forgot about it. Anyways, I say all that to ask, do you want to come with me to the party tomorrow?"

"Yes, of course! I probably won't know anyone there, but as long as you don't abandon me at the party, I should be fine, right?"

"Of course, you're going to be fine. And I could never abandon you," I tell Rose as I kiss her.

"Will there be a lot of people there?"

"Yeah, there's gonna be a ton of people in that house."

"Are you allowed to invite more people?" Rose

wonders.

"Absolutely, Xavier wouldn't mind. I'm his best friend. Why...is there someone else you want to invite?"

Rose nods. "Yeah, I want my sister, Aida, to come. She needs to get out more and I want to introduce you to her. So can she come? Ooo and my friend, Eartha! Can she come too?"

"Yeah, that's no problem. The more the merrier. I'll let Xavier know!"

CHAPTER THIRTY

December 24th

By the time the evening gets here the following day, I go online to order Rose a bouquet of roses and a special glass-dome rose from the floral shop for Christmas. I understand my order is a little late when it comes to trying to receive a gift by Christmas day; so hopefully the flowers arrive by the 26th.

After placing that online order, Rose and I are on our way to her mother's house to pick up her sister. She told me Eartha is going to meet us there, too, so we can all carpool to the party tonight. I must admit, I'm a bit nervous about meeting her mother and sister. I've seen pictures she's posted of them on Instagram and Facebook. And I must say, all the Moreno women look alike, sharing the same jet-black hair and caramel eyes. Even Rose's mother looks like she could be her sister. I haven't seen her post about her father though. I don't even know if he's in the picture or not. Now that I think about it, she hasn't talked about him either. I wonder if she'll ever tell me about him. While I'm in deep thought, I notice Rose has been awfully quiet during this car ride, staring at her phone and rapidly texting somebody.

"Is there a problem?" I ask her, taking my eyes off the road briefly.

Rose instinctively lifts her head and puts her phone in her pocket. "Um yeah, I'm just a little nervous about my mom meeting you. I don't want her to embarrass me. As a matter of fact, I just texted her and told her not to *embarrass me.*"

I chuckle and say, "I'm sure it'll be fine."

Rose sighs. "My god, I hope so."

Later on, we arrive at her mother's house. From the outside it already looks welcoming. It's a sky-blue two-story home with a small front yard. Rose takes her time getting out the car and walking up to the porch.

"Remember, everything's gonna be okay," I remind her.

She grins and takes out a key she has to her mother's house and unlocks the door.

"Here we go," Rose says nervously as we step inside.

I'm immediately greeted with smiles from Eartha and Rose's mother once we're completely inside the house. Rose's sister isn't smiling at me though, all she gives me is a death stare, so I instantly look away.

"Hello again, Eddie," Eartha exclaims.

"Hey, Eartha, how are you?"

"Good, I'm just excited to witness this meeting happen between you all," Eartha adds as she lays back against an armchair.

"Oh hush, Eartha," Rose laughs.

Mrs. Moreno gets up from her couch and approaches me. "Oh my lord, is this the famous author? Hi, Eddie! I've been hearing about you nonstop," she says, hugging me like she's known me forever. "Rose and the girls talk about you all the time."

"Mom, please don't! You haven't been hearing about him nonstop. That's an exaggeration, we've only talked about Eddie a few times," Rose says.

I snicker. "Hi, Mrs. Moreno, happy holidays to you! How's your day going so far?"

"Thank you, it's going good, how has—"

"—Excuse me we need to talk." Rose's sister, Aida, intervenes as she grabs my wrist and walks me out the front door.

Aida may be short and thin, but she's awfully strong.

"Whoa, I wonder what that's all about." Eartha laughs, in between munching on barbeque chips.

"Yeah, what the hell, Aida? I told mom not to embarrass me but now you're doing it. You don't even know him. Why are you taking him out here?" Rose adds, following us out the front door.

Aida turns to her with a straight face. "I know he's Emma's brother."

Rose shakes her head. "That doesn't count. You still don't know him personally. Where's your manners? Act like a human being for Christ's sake."

Aida rolls her eyes and puffs at her sister. "Jeez! Don't worry, Rose, I'm just going to interrogate him for five minutes and then he's all yours. So please allow me to talk to him privately for just a sec. Thank you," she says, pushing Rose back in the house.

Rose throws her head back. "Okay you have three minutes though, not five."

"Fine," Aida replies, shutting the front door.

This entire situation is awkward for me. I don't even know what's going on. All I can say is, "Well, it's nice to meet you, Aida."

She gives me the death stare again. "What are your intentions with my sister?" she asks.

Her question catches me off guard, but thankfully I do know what my true intentions are with Rose. "Um, I intend to be a person who she can always trust. I intend to be there for her, protect her, and to always show her a great time."

Aida squints at me. She squints just like her sister. "Mhm, so you don't have some ulterior motive, where you're putting on this nice guy act just to get in her pants and dump her when you get tired of her?" she asks me.

I clasp my hands over my head. "No way! Rose means a lot to me, and I really love the connection we have. The last thing I would ever want to do is destroy that connection," I explain.

"Okay, Eddie Valentine." Aida pats me on my shoulder. "I think I like you so far. You still have a long way to go so don't think you're off the hook just yet. I don't want my big sister encountering an abusive fuckboy like the last guy she had."

"Wait, Raymond was abusive to Rose? Do you mean like mentally abusive?" I ask Aida, curious to know the answer.

"Both! He tortured her mentally and physically. Beat her up whenever he didn't have his way with her," Aida reveals to me.

Yikes, hearing that shocks the fuck out of me. Rose never said anything about Raymond abusing her. It all makes sense now why she looked down at the ground that night we saw him near the art gallery. No wonder Rose got so drunk that night, she was trying to forget about him and what he did to her.

It's good to see how protective Aida is when it comes to Rose. I want to make it clear to her that I'm nothing like Raymond was and I'll never be like him. "I understand. And Aida, I want you to know that you can always trust me. I'll never do anything to hurt or harm your sister. With the way things are going with me and Rose, I hope you can eventually become like a sister to me one day."

Aida smiles and says, "I hope so too."

Rose suddenly opens the door and says, "Okay, Aida, your time is up now!"

Aida waves her off. "Oh hush, Rose. I'm all done with your boyfriend now."

Rose shakes her head and hugs me. "I'm sorry about that. She can be mean sometimes." She giggles, watching her sister walk past her and into the house.

I laugh. "It's all good, your sister was cool. She's just looking out for you, that's all."

I make my way back into the house as Rose closes the door behind me.

"Well I'm glad you're a level-headed individual

because that girl can bring the crazy out of people," Rose says. "Now, can my boyfriend finally get comfortable in this house?" she adds while rubbing my shoulders and attempting to take off my jacket.

"I can get his jacket, Rose," Mrs. Moreno insists.

"No thank you, I got it, Mom!"

After Rose takes off my jacket, Eartha comes up to me and says, "Well you've made quite the entrance, sir! And I'm excited to check out this party tonight. Are any of your guy friends single?"

I shake my head. "Nah, my friends, Chris and Xavier, aren't but I'm sure there'll be some single guys there we used to play college football with."

Eartha enthusiastically claps her hands. "YES, HONEY," she shouts. "I'm ready to mingle with them. What about you, Aida?"

Aida looks like she couldn't care less about the party tonight. She gives Eartha a quick glance and shrugs. "We'll see…. If there's a guy there that looks like a rockstar then he'll have my full attention. Other than that, I might be cool with just being distant." She ends her explanation with an unexpected grin.

I'm suddenly pulled by Rose's mother.

The women in this family sure do love pulling on people.

"Here, come sit down, baby boy. Are you hungry?" she asks me, sitting me down with her on a cream-colored couch.

It's mighty comfy too! I'm currently not that hungry but something in the house smells amazing. There's sizzling ground beef, tomato sauce, and adobo seasoning seeping right into my nostrils.

Shit now my mouth is watering.

I guess there's no harm in getting a bite to eat, besides I don't want to be disrespectful and say no. She obviously cooked for a reason.

Rose abruptly comes rushing around the couch and sits next to me. Now I'm sandwiched between her and her mother. "Mom, we're going to be leaving for the party in an hour. You don't have to stuff the poor guy's face before we get there."

Mrs. Moreno looks directly at me and says, "I'm sure Eddie can speak for himself. I made empanadas and he might like them."

Eartha repeatedly nods while displaying a bright smile. "It's so good, Eddie! Mrs. Moreno puts her foot down on those empanadas!"

After hearing that, I turn to Rose and say, "It sure does smell good. I'd love to have some!"

"Are you sure?" Rose asks.

"Yeah," I confirm.

Mrs. Moreno smiles and stands up. "Great! I'll go get you some from the kitchen."

"Now Mom is going to cook for him every time she finds out he's coming over here," Aida states.

"Yup, you know it. I'll just let Mom chat with him for a few while he eats, then we can head out," Rose adds.

Seconds later, Mrs. Moreno comes back with a plate of four empanadas and yellow rice. "So, Eddie, are you working on more books?"

"Yes, I'm at the brainstorming phase of another

story I'm developing," I reveal.

"Ooo. I love it, would you mind signing the copies of your books I have when you have the chance? I saw that article about you in the newspaper. You're doing big things, young man. I love how goal-oriented and intelligent you are," Mrs. Moreno says, patting my thigh.

Rose snaps her fingers to get her mother's attention. "Alright, that's enough flirting, Mom," She takes an empanada off the plate and feeds me with it. "This is my man," she adds.

Mrs. Moreno giggles at her daughter. "And I want it to stay that way. You better not drop the ball with him, *Rosalina*. He's a good man."

As I bite into the buttery flaky crust filled with seasoned ground beef, tomato sauce, onions, and green peppers, I savor each ingredient. It's so delicious I almost melt.

"Eddie, are you gonna stop by here for Christmas tomorrow?" Mrs. Moreno asks me.

I initially look at Rose for a response because I wasn't sure how to exactly answer that question, but Rose looks at me with a glimmer of hope. I assume she's hoping that I say yes to spending time with her and her family during Christmas tomorrow.

"Sure, I can come over after spending some time with my family. That's no problem," I answer.

I'm already finishing my third empanada too. My

god, these are delicious!

Mrs. Moreno twiddles her thumbs. "Yay! And I have to say you and Rose would make some cute ass babies. Please give me four grandkids at least!"

Rose gasps as she sits up and says, "Alright, we're getting out of here. Eddie, you can finish your last empanada in the car."

Aida agrees with her sister. "Yup, you're moving the needle way too fast, Mom."

"Aw, Mrs. Moreno is so precious," Eartha adds.

"Hold on Rosalina, he still has to sign the books," Mrs. Moreno utters, rushing into the kitchen to grab the books I've written.

"Okay make it quick," Rose tells her.

After I sign the books and stuff my face, I thank Mrs. Moreno for the support. Rose doesn't allow another second to go by before handing me my jacket. She wants to get out fast before her mother says another embarrassing thing. I'm glad she sees me as the man Rose needs to be with. It just shows me I'm on the right path.

"It was lovely meeting you, Mrs. Moreno. I'll be here tomorrow," I tell her, giving her a hug.

She takes my empty plate and says, "Okay, handsome, I'll see you then."

Wow, that's why Rose calls me handsome, she gets her charming vocabulary from her mother.

CHAPTER THIRTY-ONE

When we arrive at Xavier and Jen's house with pampers and baby toys, we're instantly aware that this party is packed. I already knew there were going to be a ton of people here. Based on all the cars parked outside, you would've thought we were at a music festival. I can't even find Xavier and Chris anywhere, but I do notice some people from Bill Pickett High and Blue River University.

Out of the blue, Hannah bursts out of the crowd and hugs me. "Hey, Eddie!" she shouts over the music and million conversations taking place.

"Hey, Hannah. Where should we put these gifts?" I ask her.

"Here, you can just place them on the table by the door," she says, taking the gifts from us and doing it herself.

She then notices Rose holding my hand. "And you must be Rose," she adds, giving her a hug too. "I'm Hannah, and, sorry, you have to forgive me, I'm a hugger."

Hannah's talking so fast I don't even have the chance to introduce her to Aida and Eartha. But somehow Rose finds a way to intervene. "That's alright, it's nice meeting you, Hannah. This is my sister, Aida, and my best friend, Eartha."

And unsurprisingly Hannah greets Aida and Eartha with a hug. "Hi, girls," Hannah exclaims while mushing my shoulder. "Eddie, you're so rude, why didn't you introduce me to everyone first?"

I shake my head. "Well dang, Hannah, I tried but you talk too damn fast!"

Hannah waves me off. "Oh whatever, do you all want something to drink?" she asks us.

The girls tell her no, but I was thirsty as hell after having those empanadas from Rose's mom. "I'll take any soda you can find," I tell Hannah.

"Okay, I'll get you one," Hannah replies.

Rose snaps her fingers, like she just had an idea. "You know what? I'll take a soda, too, but let me help you with that," she says to Hannah.

After Rose and Hannah walk into the kitchen together, Aida taps me on my shoulder.

"What's up?" I ask.

"That's hilarious, Rose is acting like she's being helpful but in actuality, she doesn't want that girl pouring a drink for you," Aida reveals to me.

I'm quite surprised. "Really? Rose has nothing to worry about though. Hannah is like a sister to me and she's married to my boy, Chris. I told Rose that already."

Aida shakes her head. "Well, let me tell you this.

That doesn't mean shit to her. Rose came here to check out your so-called gal friends, Jen and Hannah, to make sure none of them want you."

Eartha steps right next to Aida to add her *two cents*. "Yup, I know that's right. We're her eyes and ears to make sure you're really a good man and so far, you've proven yourself. I'm so glad you're nothing like Raymond."

Aida looks to Eartha and says, "Eddie still has to prove himself to me when it comes to being nothing like that asshole, Raymond, before I fully accept him. So far, he's earned twenty points out of one-hundred. He still has eighty more points to earn."

I shake my head while Aida and Eartha laugh about how low my boyfriend approval score is, before turning my attention to the kitchen. While Hannah and Rose are in the kitchen, I notice there's a tall dude with locs, looking Rose up and down. He's doing it so much, it's starting to piss me the fuck off. As I get a better look at him, I'm able to tell exactly who it is. It's Chris's cousin, Shawn. Sometimes I can't stand Shawn, he's always doing some dickhead shit. And that dickhead shit follows him everywhere he goes. He's been like that since we were teenagers. He better not try shit with Rose. I don't know if he even knows she's with me, but he knows not to fuck with me. I might have to make it known that she's with me. I'm hoping we can maintain the peace though if he keeps his mouth shut, but my senses are telling me something is about to go down.

And lo and behold Shawn approaches Rose. I'm so

focused on what he's saying that I'm able to read his lips. It's almost like I can hear him over the music and the crowd noise. "Hey what's ya name, shawty? Let me have your number," he says.

"No thank you. I'm here with someone," Rose tells him politely.

I'm glad she said that but I'm already making my way through the crowd to get into the kitchen.

"Yeah, Shawn, leave her alone, go find some other girl to holler at. Just because you're six-foot-five with dreads doesn't mean every girl is going to want you. I keep telling your ass that," Hannah explains to him.

Shawn shrugs and frowns. "So, what does her being here with someone else mean to me? That shit don't matter to me."

Rose and Hannah ignore him and attempt to walk away, but Shawn disrespectfully grabs Rose's arm and says, "Hold up, cutie."

I finally barge my way through the last few people in my way and step in between Rose and Shawn. "She told you no thanks and that she's here with someone. So abide by that shit, before you get fucked up," I snap on him, slamming him against the refrigerator.

The entire party freezes; even the DJ turns the music down to look at what's going on.

Fuck! I didn't mean to cause a scene.

Hannah grips the top of her head. "Shawn, you idiot! She came here with Eddie! That's Eddie's girlfriend."

Shawn's jaw drops as I have him pressed against the wall, grabbing him by the collar. "Yo, my bad, Eddie. I didn't know she was with you, man. I'm sorry, bro."

Xavier and Chris race into the kitchen. Jen follows after them, waddling with her pregnant belly sticking out.

This place is turning into a circus.

"What the hell?" Jen mutters.

"Yo, Eddie, what happened?" Xavier asks.

Chris follows that up with another question. "Shawn, what did you do?"

I release my grip from Shawn. "Nothing, we're all good now. Right, Shawn?"

Shawn nods and fixes his shirt. "Yeah, that's right. We're all good."

Jen slowly backs out of the kitchen and makes a hand signal to the DJ to turn up the music. "Okay, good. Let's get this party started again," she says.

I embrace Rose to see how she's doing. "Are you okay?" I ask her.

"Yeah, I'm good, thank you," she replies, giving me a quick kiss on the lips. "Here's your soda," she adds, handing me a cup of ginger ale.

"Yikes, Eddie you had his big ass lifted off his feet when you pressed him against the fridge. Are you on steroids or some shit?" Eartha says to me.

I laugh at her. "Steroids? Get out of here!"

Eartha cracks up. "I'm just playing, but look, I see a guy over there with an afro. You see him? He's tatted up, tall, and he has a beard too! Do you know who that is?" she asks me. Eartha is crushing on him hard.

As I look across the room to where she's pointing, I see she's talking about an old friend I played football with named Jaleel. "Oh yeah, I know him. That's my boy, Jaleel."

I think Jaleel realizes we're talking about him, so I wave to him, signaling him to come over and talk to Eartha.

"Oh my god, I love his name already with his chocolate ass. He's my type, can you introduce me to him?" Eartha insists.

"Yeah, it looks like he's making his way over here already," I tell her.

Jaleel approaches Eartha and says, "Hey, beautiful, anybody ever tell you that you look like Nia Long?"

Eartha snickers like a schoolgirl. "Yes, people have told me that from time to time."

"Well, Ms....?" He reaches out for her hand.

"Eartha?"

"Well, Ms. Eartha, you wanna dance with me and talk afterwards?"

Eartha puckers her lips and becomes giddy. "Yes!"

As Eartha and Jaleel walk away and dance together, Rose kisses me on the cheek. "You wanna dance, handsome?" she asks me.

I take Rose by the hand. "Yes, I do, beautiful, come on." I gently grab her by the hips as she sways back and forth dancing with me.

Aida walks away from us and sits on the couch.

After a few dances, Xavier approaches me and Rose, saying, "Hey Eddie, do you have the engagement ring on you?"

I nod, reach into my pocket and hand Xavier the ring

box. "Here you go, bro. And I didn't have a chance to introduce you to Rose yet," I tell him. "Rose, this is my friend, Xavier."

"Hey, Xavier, congratulations on the baby coming soon, and Eddie told me you'll be proposing to Jen today. That's amazing, I'm happy for you both," Rose says.

"Thanks, Rose, I'm glad you connected with my boy, Eddie, you definitely brighten his world. I can't wait to talk to you more and introduce you to Jen after we get this proposal finished with," Xavier says.

"I'm looking forward to it," Rose tells him.

"Yeah, me too, bro. Good luck," I add.

Xavier signals to the DJ to cut the music and says, "Okay y'all, I'm sorry I had to cut the music off. I just need everyone's attention and for y'all to quiet down real quick."

The crowd of people in the house quiet down and focus solely on Xavier.

"Hey, Jen, where you at, babe? Come here, please," Xavier says.

Jen pops out of the crowd and takes his hand. he says, "Hey, what's going on, honey?" She truly doesn't have a clue.

"Baby, I have something life-changing to ask you," Xavier says.

"Yes," Jen replies.

Xavier then gets down on one knee. Jen gasps, covering her mouth and instantly crying. I can even hear Hannah crying somewhere within the crowd.

Xavier pulls the ring box from his pocket and opens

it, displaying the beautiful diamond ring. "Will you marry me?"

Jen cries and nods her head. "Yes," she responds, struggling to get any words out as Xavier places the engagement ring on her finger.

"Congratulations to the lovely couple. Let's toast it up," Chris says.

The DJ then turns the music back on as everyone congratulates them and talks each other's heads off.

CHAPTER THIRTY-TWO

After leaving the party, I stop at Mrs. Moreno's place to drop Eartha and Aida off since their cars are still parked at the house.

"That was more like a college party with a proposal and baby gifts lying in the corner," Aida utters.

"Yeah, Xavier and Jen are something else. I guess that's how they wanted to celebrate their baby shower," I respond.

"When is their baby due?" Eartha asks.

"Sometime in April, I believe," I tell Eartha.

"Wow, so there's a chance their baby might be an Aries like us," Rose exclaims.

"Yeah, that's crazy, right?" I reply.

"Who in the world has a baby shower four months before their due date?" Aida questions with a frown.

"Lots of people probably do. Why do you always have to be a Debbie-downer," Rose says to Aida.

Eartha and I sit awkwardly in the car. We can tell there's some tension there.

"Um, let me help you ladies out the car," I add, to

break the tension.

As I help the women out of the car, Eartha takes my hand and bows. "Why, thank you, good sir," she says sarcastically.

"My god, Eartha, you're such a goofball," Rose says.

"Oh girl, trust me I know," Eartha replies.

"Do you have all of your stuff with you?" Rose asks her.

Eartha nods and gives Rose a hug. "Yes, darling," she says. "Now I'm about to head home and give Jaleel a call before I freeze to death out here," she adds, zipping up her jacket and running to her car.

"Alright, girl, text me when you get home, and drive safe, please," Rose tells her.

"I'll make sure I do that, Rose! And see you later Aida and Eddie!"

Rose turns to Aida and hugs her. "You know I love you right, sis?"

"Yeah, I know, and I love you too," Aida says.

"Good, are you going into the house to check on Mom or are you going straight home?"

"I'm going home," Aida replies, giving Rose the peace sign.

"Okay. Well, I'm going to go inside and head to the bathroom real quick while I check on Mom. I'll be right back," Rose tells us as she makes her way into her mother's house.

Aida randomly calls out to me. "Hey, you!"

"Yes."

"You're not one of those possessive or abusive types,

are you? I saw how you lifted that guy off the ground and pressed him against the wall when he approached my sister. I hope you don't think you own her," Aida explains to me.

I shake my head and raise both my hands to my chest to display my innocence. "Oh no, of course not. Shawn was being disrespectful to Rose, so I had to defend her, that's all. Aida, I'm nothing like Rose's ex. I would never hit a woman, and, like I told you before, I would never harm your sister. I'll make sure I prove that to you a million times if I have to."

Aida slowly nods and analyzes me. "Oh, okay. Well, he's significantly bigger than you and he looked scared when you jumped in his face. Why didn't he hit you or try to fight back? Are you dangerous or in a gang or something?"

I laugh. "Not at all. Look, Shawn and I went to Blue River University together. And one time there was a big fight that happened on the football field where everyone saw me fight this guy twice my size. I knocked him out. From then on, people found out I used to box and do martial arts. So no one fucked with me after that....Shawn and a lot of my old classmates remember that day. That's probably why you didn't see him retaliate," I reveal to Aida.

Aida smiles at me, looking relieved. "Oh okay, Eddie. I'm starting to figure you out more and more. Well, you passed another test... for now. You've earned thirty more points; which gives you fifty out of one-hundred so far."

I rub my hands together to keep myself warm. "Thank you for the new score, Aida, I appreciate it!"

"I'll catch you and Rose later. Have a good night and thanks for the invite," Aida says as she walks to her car.

"Good night, Aida," I respond.

After Rose walks out of her mother's house she smiles at me and says, "I hope my sister didn't bother you while I was in there."

I shake my head and smile. "Oh nah, she was cool," I tell Rose.

"Good."

≈

When we arrive at my house, we see a red and white striped giftbox on my porch.

Wow, the floral shop dropped off the gift I ordered for her. That was fast! Talk about one-day shipping.

"What's this? Did one of your family members buy you a gift?" Rose asks me as she looks down at the box.

I shake my head and pick it up. "Nah, it doesn't look like anyone dropped this off for me because it has your name on it," I say nonchalantly, as I hand her the box and unlock the door.

Rose tries to hold in her smile but she can't fight it. She's grinning from ear to ear. "Eddie!" she exclaims, punching me in the shoulder. "You got a Christmas gift for me?"

I raise my eyebrows and smile. "Yeah."

"I've been around you pretty much every day, when

did you find the time to do that? And now I feel bad because I wasn't able to get a gift for you."

By the look on Rose's face, she's having an inner battle with herself, trying to figure out if she wants to open the gift or not.

I shrug. "Don't worry about it. It's alright. Go ahead and open it," I tell her as we both make our way into the house.

Rose opens the gift and sees a bouquet of roses in one section of the box, and a preserved rose in a glass dome in another section of the box.

"I told myself Rose deserves roses for Christmas," I disclose to her.

After opening the gifts, she remains silent for some time. During her brief moment of silence, I don't know what to think. But suddenly she begins to cry. And I don't mean sniffle cries either, I'm talking about boo-hoo crying. I'm a little startled now. Did I fuck up and buy her the wrong gifts that remind her of something bad? Or is she overwhelmingly happy? Either way, I guess I'll find out soon. At that moment, I embrace Rose and let her cry in my arms. "What's the matter?" I ask.

"Did Aida or my Mom tell you about my Dad?"

"No."

She lowers her voice and says, "Really? You aren't lying, are you?"

I lift her chin so I can look her deep in the eyes and tell her the truth. "Rose, I promise you I'm not lying. They didn't tell me anything about your father. Is he okay?"

Rose takes a deep breath before telling me about her father. "My Dad used to give me a bouquet of roses every Christmas Eve. He would always pick out a rose from the bouquet he bought me and say, *Here's a rose for Rose*. And you kind of just did the same thing he did."

"Ah, man, I honestly had no idea. I'm sorry if it just brought back painful memories," I mutter.

I still have no idea where Rose's father is or what happened to him. I want to ask her more about him, but I know she has to do that whenever she's ready. All I can do is comfort her.

"It's okay, it brought up a beautiful memory. My dad died three years ago in a motorcycle accident. He was hit by a drunk driver," Rose finally reveals to me.

I shake my head at the situation and hug her tighter. "I'm sorry to hear that."

It's so hard talking to someone grieving because I never really know what to say or do. I wish I had the perfect thing to say, rather than *I'm sorry to hear that.*

"You remind me of him." Rose surprises me with that comment.

"How so?" I ask her.

"It's the way you treat me and care for me. Growing up, I watched my dad do the same thing for my mom," Rose states.

"Well that's good news, right?" I say cheerfully, trying to cheer her up.

"Yeah, it is. But the worst part about his death is that we found out he was headed to another woman's house when the police recovered his phone and gave it to us.

My dad had a mistress he was sleeping with for several years," she explains.

Now I'm really speechless. All I can utter is this stupid comment. "Damn, I'm sorry."

Rose lets go of me and takes a step back. "No, I'm sorry for dumping all this on you." She wipes the tears from her face.

"You're fine. I wish I had the right words to say and I wish I could make you feel better. But all I know is that time is the only thing that can heal the hurt you've been through."

Rose looks directly into my eyes and beams at me. "Baby, you do make me feel better."

Her intense stare shows me she wants my love right away. She leans into me, and lifts herself up onto her toes to kiss me. It's a deep kiss too. "I actually wanna feel better right now," Rose whispers.

"I can take care of that," I whisper in her ear, wiping the last bit of her tears.

I take both of our coats and hang them on the coat rack. I then wrap my arms around her waist and pick her up as we begin to gently kiss.

"Are we going to finally make love on your bed?" she asks softly.

Shit! Not again. I can't have flashes of those hookers cross my mind if I take her to my bed again. I have to find somewhere else for us to make love. Come on... think!

"If you can make it there," I whisper.

"Ooo, what does that mean?"

Yeah, what did I mean by that?

I look at the stairs and think of something clever.

"It means I'm going to fuck you on the way upstairs and into my room. I want to see if you can last through each step and each stroke before cumming. If you cum before we make it to my room....then you lose."

Rose smiles at me and says, "I'm up for this stair challenge."

"Okay let me go grab——."

"——I don't want you to grab a condom this time…I want to feel all of you," Rose intervenes.

"Are you sure, baby?"

"Yes, I'm sure."

"Hell, that's fine by me!"

I lay Rose on the couch and rapidly throw off her jeans and toss her panties on the floor. When I lick her thighs, she stops me from traveling up to her warmth.

"What are you doing?" I question, curious by her actions.

She looks at me and giggles. "As much as I want you to eat me out right now. That'll be cheating. By the way you lick on my pussy, I'll cum in no time and will fail the challenge. You know that, too, you sneaky devil!"

I giggle at her comment. "Okay, you got me! I'll make sure my mouth behaves tonight."

I quickly toss off all my clothes before picking Rose up again. As I carry her and make my way onto the first step, I squeeze her ass and ease myself inside of her, causing her to slowly gasp. Now that I'm not wearing a condom, I can feel all of her wetness. She feels much warmer and it feels like our souls are intertwining. Rose clenches the back of my neck and moans in my ear; allowing me to feel every breath she takes.

"Each step equals a stroke," I whisper, being careful not to speak too much so I don't ruin the moment.

I take my second step up the stairs and stroke inside of her twice this time. She moans even louder and starts sucking on my neck. I don't know how this is possible, but I'm turned on even more. I want to master her body and satisfy her every need in every way. I'm hoping I can get out of my own mind when it comes to making love to her on my bed one day. But in the meantime, I need to focus on making her cum. I take a third step and give her three thrusts. Now I just have twenty-one more steps to go, and by the way she's clutching my back, she's not going to make it to my bedroom. I change up my pace for the fourth step and slowly glide myself inside of her four times. I do this slow thrusting method until I reach the eighth step. Delivering eight slow strokes. By the ninth step I pick up the pace again, stroking my cock back and forth inside of her nine times.

"YES, BABY," she shouts.

I think Rose is starting to make my back bleed as I force myself not to take a break between each step. By step seventeen it sounds like Rose is speaking in tongues.

I'm able to hear this part clearly though: "FUCK, I CAME," she yells.

We didn't even make it to the eighteenth step, let alone step twenty-four. I walk up the stairs and lie her gently onto the bed.

"Eddie, you lucky bastard. Why do you have to be so

good at everything?"

"I'm not, I can't ice-skate or paint, remember?" I say causing Rose to laugh as I lie down next to her and stare at the ceiling.

"I can't with you!"

"After our shower, I wanna sleep in front of the fireplace tonight, okay? It's Christmas Eve, and I want to wake up next to the tree staring at my gift; which is you."

Rose gets teary-eyed and gives me a peck on the lips. We then do our normal routine of cleaning up and lying down together. But tonight's sleep was more special than the others since we're sleeping on the couch in front of the fireplace. The sight of the multi-color Christmas tree in the corner makes it even better. Rose insists we fall asleep listening to Nat King Cole's Christmas album. She loves listening to him whenever we go to sleep together now ever since we slow danced to his song at Giovanna's Cucina. I must admit, I love listening to his songs now too.

CHAPTER THIRTY-THREE

December 25ᵗʰ

The next morning, I wake up to the smell of food. The fireplace is off and the daylight is shining through the open blinds. "Merry Christmas and good morning, sleepy head," Rose says from the kitchen.

Whatever she's cooking smells good as hell.

"Well, Merry Christmas to you too, beautiful," I say.

She opens the fridge and pours a glass of orange juice. "I want to thank you for yesterday," she says, approaching me with the drink in her hand.

I shrug and wink at her. "Shoot, I want to thank you for yesterday too," I respond, taking the glass she hands me.

Rose knows I'm talking about the sex we had last night based on me winking at her. She laughs and shakes her head. "No, not that...even though it was every bit of amazing! But I wanted to thank you for putting that guy, Shawn, in his place yesterday. I seriously thought you were going to take his head off."

"Yeah, I was going to fuck him up, but I was able to calm myself down. The last thing I wanted to do was ruin the night."

"I'm glad you were able to calm yourself down, because I would never want you to be put in a situation where you have to fight somebody over me," Rose says.

"Rose, I'll be damned if I sit back and let somebody disrespect you."

"I understand, and, again, thank you. I just want you to be safe at the same time. You never know how some immature guy might take being embarrassed or man handled publicly. I know you know how to fight and all, but a lot of guys would rather shoot first nowadays," Rose elaborates.

"I gotcha. Look, I'll try to be more aware of that next time." Out of the blue, I started to feel a sharp pain in my upper back. "Hey can you check my back for me? It feels like something is stinging me," I tell Rose as I take my shirt off.

"Sure," Rose says as she sits behind me and takes a look at my back.

Suddenly she's snickering.

"What, what is it?"

"Aw, Eddie, I'm sorry. I did this to you. You have scratches on your back from last night. I didn't realize I scratched you that hard. I'm gonna go get some peroxide and ointment from upstairs."

I laugh and say, "Hey, those are the best battle wounds a man can ask for."

"It definitely is! The peroxide and ointment is in your

drawer, right, or your medicine cabinet?"

"It should be in my medicine cabinet, but you can check my drawer just in case I used it and put it there after getting bit by that dog."

"Ha-ha, okay."

Seconds later, Rose comes back downstairs with the peroxide and ointment. "Lay on your stomach for me, please," she says.

As I lay on my stomach, I can hear Rose opening up the peroxide bottle. "Alright, handsome, this is going to sting a little bit. I'm going to pour the peroxide on your back first."

I chuckle. "I know how peroxide feels, it's not that b— OUCH!"

Rose snickers. "I told you it was going to sting."

"A warning or a countdown would be nice next time," I tell her.

"I'll make sure I do that next time, now I'm about to apply the ointment on your back. You aren't going to cry about that are you, ya big baby?" Rose jokes as she rubs my back with antibiotic ointment cream.

"Nah, I can take the ointment," I say sarcastically.

"Mhm…So Eddie, when I was looking through your drawer to find the peroxide and ointment, I came across some older flight tickets you have. You sure did go to Brazil and Vegas a lot. What was that all about?" Rose questions as she rubs my back.

Oh god no! Why didn't I throw that shit away?

"Yeah, I don't think I flew out to those places that much. Um, my manager, Oscar…remember I told you about him?"

"Yes."

"His wife works at Delta Airlines, so she always gets us free flights to anywhere we want to go in the world."

"So out of all the places to go, you just go to Vegas and Brazil?"

Aw damn, I'm panicking! I don't know what to say. Oscar's wife does work at Delta Airlines and I do get hooked up with free flight tickets all the time. But I can't tell Rose the real reason I was always in Vegas and Brazil.

"Oh no, I've been to plenty of places like Seattle of course, and Dallas, Chicago, Orlando, Mexico, and I even lived in Los Angeles for a while to have a peace of mind some years back," I explain to her.

"Aw. That was good for you to do that, but what were you going to Vegas and Brazil for? It feels like you're avoiding the question," Rose interrogates me. Right now, her voice is still at a pleasant tone, and she's curious. All I have to do is come up with a good lie and not panic.

"Oh no, I'm not avoiding the question, ha-ha. Um, I would go to Brazil to read to a lot of the homeless children out there. I would also help feed the homeless families out there with the World Food Program," I lie.

Although I did read to a group of kids out there once while I was walking around with one of the prostitutes. Her name was Paulina, and I needed her help to translate what I was reading to the kids.

"Aw, that's beautiful, Eddie. Why are you such a saint."

No, Rose, I'm not a saint, I'm a horrible human being. And I don't deserve you.

"Thank you. Now when it comes to Vegas, that's a completely different situation. Oscar's wife always asks me to go out there with him to chaperone him, and make sure he isn't drinking or gambling too much," I lie again. Oscar does drink but he's not a gambler. And his wife trusts him because they have an incredible marriage.

"Thank God for you, she needs to make sure he doesn't go out there anymore," Rose says.

"Yeah, I think Oscar's done with Vegas for good now." Which actually means, I'm done with Vegas for good too.

"That's great, good for him!"

While Rose continues to rub my back, I think about changing subjects. My nerves are skyrocketing right now and I can no longer lie or talk about Brazil and Vegas. My mind suddenly jumps back to the conversation Rose and I had about protecting her and protecting myself from knuckleheads with guns.

"And hey, I don't mean to bring this up again, but I want you to know you don't have to be afraid for me when it comes to immature knuckleheads. I have a gun too. I probably need to start bringing it around with me since I have a license to carry. It'll be good to have on me just in case I find myself in a situation with a trigger-happy maniac."

"Uh yeah, I don't want you to think like that, Eddie. Let's think positive, please," Rose says.

And she's right. I don't talk like that. Talking gun talk isn't me at all.

"My bad, I just want you to know I'll always be there for you. But hey, it's me, Eddie, back to being the average guy I am," I joke.

Rose snickers. "Baby don't downplay yourself like that, you're truly special."

I joke again and say, "Nope, I'm average."

Shit, I know I'm not average. I know I'm a hardworking and caring man. But I'm also a liar and I never want Rose to find out about my freaky past. So I feel much better downplaying myself rather than saying things that uplift me. I'm psychologically conflicted right now.

Rose sucks her teeth. "Well, I never met an average guy who would fight off a bear with his bare hands to protect me. Only Eddie Valentine would do that," she says after she finishes applying the ointment and rubbing my back. "There, now you should be all better. You want something to eat?"

I had panicked so much that I forgot about Rose cooking food for me. "Well, you have the house smelling good." I tell her.

She smiles and says, "Thank you. Right before you woke up, I finished making you some pancakes and omelets."

"Well thanks for hooking me up, sexy. I'm ready to dig in."

"You're welcome. And I know you probably have to rush since you have to head to your parents' house soon," she says in a curious tone.

I'm assuming she wants me to invite her to meet my

parents since I met her mother yesterday. I was already going to ask her anyway. "I want you to meet my parents, you don't mind coming over for a bit, do you?" I ask her.

A big smile grows upon Rose's face. "No, not at all. I would love to come." She places omelets and pancakes on a plate for me as she turns red. She looks like a joyous kid on Christmas day.

CHAPTER THIRTY-FOUR

I pull into the driveway at my parents' house when Rose clutches my forearm. "I'm so nervous," she says with a smile.

"Trust me, there's nothing to be nervous about. My parents are going to make you feel right at home," I inform her.

Rose follows behind me as we walk into the house. Inside, we see gift wrapping paper all over the place.

"Jesus Christ, this place looks like a hurricane hit it. The twins must've gone crazy opening gifts this morning," I say out loud, looking for my family.

"I hear more tearing. I guess they're still opening gifts," Rose says.

"Hey, people, I'm here!" I announce to my family.

"Boys, go thank your Uncle Eddie for all the toys he bought you," Emma says. I can hear her voice travel from the living room to the front room.

"THANK YOU," my nephews shout from the living room, but they are so occupied with their Christmas presents, they don't even bother approaching me in the front room. I don't mind it though. I remember how excited I used to be at that age during Christmas.

Eventually, my parents and my sister meet me and Rose in the front room.

Here we go! I have to make sure there's no awkward silence.

"Hey, Mom and Dad, I want you to meet my girlfriend, Rose."

My mom instantly embraces Rose with open arms.

"Hey, sweetheart, I'm so happy I get to finally meet you," my mom says as she hugs Rose.

"I'm happy I finally got the chance to meet you, too, Mrs. Valentine."

"Oh you can call me Grace, honey. And this is Eddie's father, Edward."

My dad then follows after my mom and hugs Rose. "How ya doing, sweetie pie? I'm glad you're here. It's about time Little Edward brought a girlfriend to the house. He hasn't done that in like ten years."

I can see Rose trying to hold in her laugh after my dad just called me Little Edward. My god, he's embarrassing at times.

My mom then looks at my dad and says, "Edward leave that boy alone. Obviously, Rose is special. That's why she's here."

My dad shrugs and laughs. "Either way, it's been a long time coming," he says.

Emma agrees and says, "True. I'm happy you're finally in a relationship again."

"Wow, Emma! You and Dad are just playing me like I'm not standing right here," I tell them.

Brian walks into the room, giggling. "Sheesh, first it was your sister and now it's your dad playing you."

"Exactly, man," I chuckle.

"Yeah, you two leave my oldest child alone and let's go enjoy the rest of this holiday with the twins," my mom demands.

Eventually, Rose and I enjoy our time with my family; eating snacks, playing board games, and singing karaoke. She fits right in and I love every bit of it.

≈

Later on, we head out with the few gifts of cologne and sweaters my parents and sister got me. After going to Rose's apartment to get the gifts for her family, we head to her mom's house. We walk to the porch while holding their gifts in my hands. As we are about to walk inside, I can see Aida and Mrs. Moreno through the open curtains in the window. I feel bad because it looks like there's nothing but sorrow and gloom there. Aida is sitting in an armchair with dark circles around her eyes and she's hypnotized by her phone. Since her hair isn't done and she's in baggy sweats, I'm assuming she might have come back late last night after we all left and ended up spending the night here at their mother's house. Mrs. Moreno is watching Hallmark Christmas movies on the tv but her eyes look a bit gloomy too. When Rose opens the door, her mother smiles brightly. It smells like coffee inside, but that's it. I don't smell food at all.

Mrs. Moreno cheerfully approaches us and gives me

and Rose a hug. "Hey you two, come sit down." We listen to her mother and sit on the couch. Aida takes her eyes off the phone and says, "How's your Christmas going?" I wasn't sure if she was talking to me or Rose.

"I think she's talking to you," Rose says.

Suddenly there's some awkward tension between them. Everything seemed fine with them yesterday, besides their little argument in the car.

"It's been good, I'm enjoying the day so far. How about you?"

"It's been so-so."

I'm not sure what's going on, but Rose doesn't look happy.

"I wish we could've stayed at your house," she mutters.

I gently place my hand onto Rose's hand. "What's going on?"

"I'll tell you later," Rose says softly.

I nod and turn to Mrs. Moreno and ask, "Hey, do you and Aida want to open up your gifts?"

"Sure," Aida says as she walks toward the couch and grabs her gift from Rose. She then hands Rose a gift and sits back on her seat. Something is off about Aida today. I can't really tell what it is, but it's like her mind is in another dimension.

Mrs. Moreno then hands Rose a gift bag full of new clothes and perfumes. They all say thank you to each other after opening their gifts. But without notice, Aida sits up and grabs her keys and her jacket. "Okay, Merry Christmas everyone. I'm going home."

"Okay, honey, make sure you drive safely. And get some rest," Mrs. Moreno says, hugging her with a gloomy look on her face.

Rose stands and quietly says, "I'll be right back." She then follows Aida outside.

While they're out there, it looks like their conversation is getting pretty intense. There's no physical fighting taking place, but I can see the emotion in their eyes. Mrs. Moreno is too busy in the kitchen to see them arguing.

I unexpectedly get a call from Oscar. "Hey what's up, Oscar."

"Hey, young brother, Merry Christmas. I have good news. I have a couple producers who want to meet you and talk about your novel. They said they have a strong feeling they can negotiate a deal where your story can be made into a movie on Warner Brothers or a TV series on HBO Max. They're excited to get this done, that means this is a solid deal, my guy. You have to come down here to LA the day before New Year's Eve so we can be ready to speak with them at their New Year's Eve meeting the following day."

No way. I can't believe it. I'm literally one step closer to making my film dreams happen. I want to shout from the roof top and go crazy, but I manage to contain myself.

"Merry Christmas to you, too, man, and that's great news! Can I bring my girlfriend, Rose, with me?"

"Oh shit, I knew you had a girlfriend that you were serious about! No wonder you were acting all weird in

Seattle."

"When I was in Seattle, Rose and I didn't make it official yet. Not until I got back."

"That's cool, young brother, but let me ask you something. Did you really have sex with the cougar, Lisa?"

"Nope. I lied to you because I didn't feel like hearing you lecture me about how young I am, and how I need to experience life and not be tied down. I really like Rose and I can see this working out."

"Hey, I understand. Who am I to shit on true love? I can't wait to meet this lovely young lady."

"You're going to love her, she's amazing."

"Alrighty brother man, I'll have my wife email you the access to two free first-class tickets for Delta by tomorrow."

"Okay cool. Thanks, Oscar."

"No problem, young brother, enjoy the rest of your holiday."

After hanging up with Oscar, Mrs. Moreno steps out of the kitchen and approaches me. "So, Eddie, did you enjoy it, at your family's house?" she asks.

"Oh yes, it was great, we played board games and sang karaoke after opening gifts," I tell her.

"Aw, that's such a blessing and it sounds like you all had a fantastic time. Always appreciate your family, okay? Never take them for granted." Mrs. Moreno's voice breaks and she starts to cry.

Aw, shoot, I don't know what to do. But I can't just leave her standing there, crying. I stand up and give Mrs.

Moreno a hug. "I'm sorry," she says. "It's a sad day for us right now. The girls lost their father three years ago today. He died on a Christmas night, so this is an unusual time for them," she reveals to me.

I remember yesterday, Rose told me her father died, but the fact that I just learned he died on Christmas day from her mother makes this even sadder. Now all I want to do is be Rose's peace and joy at all times, and a bright light to her family.

"It's okay, I can't imagine what you all have been through," I tell Mrs. Moreno.

Suddenly Rose walks back in the house, and sees me hugging her mother. "Oh no, did she see me and Aida arguing?" she asks, rushing to her crying mother. Rose wraps her arms around both of us. Now Rose and Mrs. Moreno are both crying. I bring her into the group more to comfort both of them at the same time. Once again, I don't have the right words.

"Can you two stay awhile longer and watch Hallmark movies with me?" Mrs. Moreno asks, wiping her tears with her sweater.

"Absolutely, Mom! I'll do anything for you," Rose says.

"I have more empanadas I can reheat if you two want some," Mrs. Moreno tells us.

"Sure, that's fine with me," I answer.

Rose sniffles. "That's fine with me too."

≈

After eating and watching a few movies. Mrs. Moreno thanks us and tells us she's going upstairs to go to bed. Rose and I leave her mother's house and sit in my car as it warms up.

In the car, she looks at me and says, "Thank you for being here. Believe it or not, this Christmas was better than the last one for us because of you."

Hearing her say that made me feel like I was her Superman and she was my Lois Lane.

"Well you know what. I hope I can make the holidays memorable for you and your family each year," I tell her.

"You always know what to do and say. I wish I knew what to say to my sister, Aida." Rose deeply exhales before continuing. "I think she's on drugs again. She's either taking Oxy or Vicodin. And it's so heartbreaking because I thought she stopped last year."

I can't believe what I'm hearing. I would've never suspected Aida was on drugs. "Aw, damn, no wonder you two were having a heated argument. Is there anything we can do to help her?"

Rose shakes her head. "I have no clue. She's a grown woman, making these decisions on her own. She was popping pills for years and would tell me she wouldn't overdose and that she knows how to take the right amount to relax her body. But my mom and I pleaded with her every day to get her to stop."

I intervene. "And like you said, she eventually stopped at one point, right?"

Rose runs her hands through her hair saying, "Yeah,

last year she finally listened and put an end to it. It was like she had some sort of awakening. I didn't think the anniversary of our dad's death would make her start again. Sometimes I feel like there's no hope when it comes to helping her."

"Shit, Rose, that's a scary feeling knowing she's relying on these drugs to ease her trauma."

Rose blinks away the tears that flood her eyes. "I know. I'll figure something out."

There's no way I'm going to let her go through this alone.

I touch her hand and say, "*We'll* figure something out."

Rose smiles at me. "Thank you. I really just need a day out of Blue River," Rose mumbles under her breath.

This would be the perfect time to tell her that Oscar needs me to come to LA for a meeting on New Year's Eve. "Hey. Rose, my manager called me earlier about coming to LA and spending a couple days out there up till New Year's. I have a meeting with a couple film producers. I would love it if you flew out there with me. I can make sure you're back by the time it's January 3rd. Just in time for you to go back to work."

Rose is ecstatic, she smiles bigger than ever and hugs me. "Oh my god, yes! I would love to go!"

PART THREE
LOVE

CHAPTER THIRTY-FIVE

December 30th

While boarding the flight on Delta, Rose can't stop smiling at me and hugging my arm. "I'm so excited to see LA for the first time."

I nod. "Yeah, I'm going to make sure you have a good time out there."

She smiles once more and leans on my shoulder.

I've been flying so much over the last three years that every time I hop on a plane, I get sleepy within seconds. I made sure I told Rose this just in case she needed me up or anything but fortunately for me, she falls asleep before I do. And before I know it, we're both napping on the plane while it's in flight.

When we land, Oscar meets us outside of the L.A.X. airport. As he steps out of the car, he prepares to help me put the luggage in his Chrysler 300. By the look on his face, I assume he has a lot to say. He has a smirk that won't go away. I hope he doesn't say anything dumb, and I really hope he doesn't talk about what happened at the club in Seattle either.

"Hey, Oscar, this is Rose," I say.

"Hey, young sister, it's nice to meet you. Brother man over here told me he couldn't wait to show you around this weekend."

Good job Oscar!

"It's nice to meet you, too, Oscar. And I'm glad, I think I'll really like it out here," Rose tells him.

"Oh you definitely will," Oscar says.

I open the backseat door for Rose. When I shut the door, I turn to Oscar and say, "Thanks again for picking us up."

"Man, you know it's no problem for me. Shiddd, it's my job to make sure you're taken care of. You're going to make sure I can retire soon," Oscar jokes. He then says, "Your girlfriend is a fox, too, man! I mean an absolute fox! You better put a ring on her. Trust me."

I shake my head and laugh. "Oh, now you want me to tie the knot in my young life."

"With her…absolutely. She's not going to be a waste of time for you."

"You're right about that. I can't wait to show her around. We're going to visit a lot of places in the city today."

"Oh okay, good. How are you two going to get around LA?" Oscar asks me.

I shrug and say, "I was thinking about taking an Uber

around the city, to be honest."

Oscar nods. "Well, you already know I can't allow you to do that young brother. And plus, I also know you might end up showing her your favorite places on the outskirts of LA too. So you can borrow my Chrysler for the weekend, alright?"

I raise my eyebrows. "Seriously!"

"Yeah, of course, I'm serious. You're like a son to me. And I already have the hotel parking pass for you guys and everything. I'll drive y'all to the hotel and I'll catch an Uber back home," Oscar says. "You know I have like three cars back at home in the garage anyway."

I hug Oscar and say, "Thanks, Oscar, you're the best."

≈

After Oscar drives us to a luxurious hotel in downtown LA, he gives me his keys. "Have fun you two," he says, before leaving in an Uber.

Rose and I check ourselves into the hotel. As we walk inside, we see a gold chandelier glimmering as it hangs from the ceiling right above a glowing sculptured water fountain. After getting our room key, we take a clear-glass elevator to the top floor, and head inside our royal suite.

"This place is remarkable," Rose says with a grin as she opens up the curtains to view the city.

Our room is *remarkable* like she said. There's a living room, a kitchen, three flat screen TVs, four navy blue couches, a luxurious bathroom, a master bedroom with a king-sized bed, and a beautiful view of the city. When it comes to having a hotel suite, it doesn't get any better than this!

"I'm glad you like it. Do you want to get in the pool or jacuzzi first? Or are you ready for me to take you out around the city?" I ask her.

Rose runs up to me and kisses me. "I'm ready to see the city," she exclaims.

"Gotcha, go ahead and get yourself ready."

After getting cleaned up, Rose throws on denim jeans, walking shoes, and an orange blouse. And all I throw on is a white t-shirt, a silver necklace, black jeans, and black and white Jordans. Rose is so excited to experience LA, she almost beats me to the parking garage.

Moments later, I drive us to the Santa Monica pier first and it's crowded as hell. "My goodness, is it always this crowded?" Rose asks, as we enter the pier.

"Yeah, unfortunately it is. It's a never-ending crowd over here."

The Santa Monica pier is a wonderful tourist attraction, but I forgot how annoying it is getting bumped by random people on the boardwalk. I swear if I didn't have patience, I would fight the next person that bumps into me or Rose.

"Alright, so the first thing we're going to do is get on the West Coaster rollercoaster ride, then we're going to get some boardwalk fries and Bubba Gump shrimp, and lastly, we'll get on the Pacific Wheel before we get out of here. You like the sound of that?"

Rose smiles. "I love it. And I'm glad you brought up food, because I'm starving. As soon as we get off that ride, I can't wait to eat."

Abruptly a couple of kids throw fries on the boardwalk, right in front of me and Rose. And at that very moment, a bunch of seagulls come swooping down to eat them.

"Damn, those bad ass kids," I snap while covering Rose in my arms so the birds don't touch her or shit in her hair.

She laughs. "It's alright." Luckily, she takes it like a champ.

"Are you sure?" I ask.

"Yes, handsome, I'm sure."

"Okay, get ready to jog with me to this ride, okay? We're about to storm through these people," I tell Rose while rushing us through the crowd to get on the West Coaster ride.

After that ride on West Coaster, eating some boardwalk food, and getting an incredible view of the ocean on the Pacific Wheel, the rest of our adventure in the city of LA happens like a big blur. We head to the Hollywood Walk of Fame, taking pictures of some of the celebrity names Rose wanted to capture on her phone. She snaps photos of Marilyn Monroe, Michael Jackson, and Jennifer Lopez's Hollywood stars. After getting pictures of the names she loves, Rose and I head to the Madame Tussauds Wax Museum. In here, I end up taking more pictures of the celebrities she loves, now that she's standing by their life-sized wax figures. After taking a million pictures of Rose standing next to The Rock, Marilyn Monroe and many more celebrity wax figures, we leave Hollywood Boulevard and drive to Rodeo Drive in Beverly Hills. While we're there we stop at the Louis Vuitton store, and I intend to buy Rose a purse. But when she sees the prices, she shakes her head and tells me she doesn't want me spending that much. I insist and tell her it's fine, letting her know she can get whatever she wants. Rose walks away from the $5,000 purses and picks out a skirt and a top she likes that ends up being cheaper than the purses. Following those purchases, she hugs me with love and genuinely lets me know she doesn't want any more material things out here in LA; and that she just wants to spend time with me. A man's life is truly fulfilled when he has a woman like this by his side. I place her shopping bag in the trunk and drive us to Venice Beach to close out our day.

"Is Venice Beach populated like Santa Monica?" Rose asks me with curiosity.

"Yeah, but they have a ton of electric scooters out here in Venice Beach. You're going to love it," I tell Rose, after parking the car.

While walking up to the boardwalk, we spot some electric scooters lying on the ground.

Rose can't believe it. "This is so bizarre because we don't have anything like that in Blue River."

"I know, right? It's kind of a culture shock coming out here," I say as I use my app to get myself a scooter and help Rose get the app to rent another one.

We then ride around on scooters, making our way

past bikers and skateboarders.

"I'm having the time of my life right now," Rose says to me.

"Wait till we have ice cream while watching the sunset, the homeless people who live on the beach always put on a show," I surprise her.

"Are you serious?"

"Yes, I have to show you what I'm talking about."

As the sun begins to set, Rose and I go to a place on the boardwalk called Turn Dough ice cream. After we both order chocolate sundaes and rent a beach chair, we sit on the chair together while rubbing our feet against the sand. In the midst of watching the sunset, I drop fifty-dollars into a homeless man's ukulele case as he prepares to play us a song. He tunes up his ukulele and then begins to play it while singing *Somewhere Over the Rainbow/What a Wonderful World* by Israel Kamakawiwo'ole. The man has a great voice and sounds just like the singer who sang the song. His voice is so angelic, it matches the serenity of the orange sky and the sun setting past the ocean. I hear a sniffle from Rose as she lays her head back against my chest. I was going to do my usual routine of asking: *Are you okay,* but, this time around, I already know most of the things that are bothering her, and I also know she's just happy to be in a peaceful setting with me, where she doesn't have to worry about anyone but herself just for a moment. Even if it is *just for a moment,* this moment means everything to her. I wipe her tears and kiss the top of her head as she watches the sunset and listens to the man sing. We conclude our adventurous day perfectly.

≈

After making it back to the hotel and showering, Rose says, "Ugh, my feet are so sore after walking around all day. Do you think they have icy-hot in here?"

I shrug. "I don't know if they do, but I can fix your foot problem, don't worry about it. Go ahead and lay down on the bed."

Rose smirks at me. "What are you thinking about doing?"

"Nothing, I'm just going to massage your feet, that's all. Your feet are sore, aren't they?" I smirk back.

"Yes." She lies on the bed with her robe on while exposing her feet.

"Okay, I gotcha then," I tell her as I grab some lotion to rub on her feet and massage them. "I also brought the kinky toys with me," I add.

Rose gasps then laughs. "Shut up, you really brought them?"

I hop off the bed and reach into my suitcase grabbing the rose vibrator and the vibrating panties. "See, they're right here. I know you wanna try them."

Rose smirks again. She can't believe it. "You're so crazy. Listen, I don't know which one I want to try first."

I drop the rose vibrator on the bed and hold up the vibrating panties. "Try this one first, it came with a remote. I'll massage your feet, but every time you move your feet interrupting my massage, I'm going to raise the vibration up on those panties. If you last with that, we'll play with the rose."

Rose cheeses. "Gawd dammit, handsome, I'm getting wet already. Alright, hand me the panties."

She takes the panties from me and puts them on, adjusting them so the vibration part sits close to her clit. While she does that, I reach into my suitcase to grab my tie and my belt.

"What are you doing?" Rose asks me, after placing the panties fully on.

"I'm going to make sure you don't cheat, by using your hands to remove the panties or the toy when I use them," I tell her, taking her right arm to tie her wrist to the wooden headboard with my leather belt.

She nods when she hears my answer and licks her lips while winking at me. After seeing her tongue graze across her lips, I bend down to kiss her before tying her left wrist to the headboard with my black tie. I then stand at the edge of the bed and begin to massage her feet.

As I firmly use my thumbs to stroke the back of her feet, she starts to laugh. "That tickles," she utters, jolting her feet back.

"Uh oh, you moved," I tell her, while using the remote to turn the vibrator to level one. It has nine levels.

Rose giggles. "That level is light work. I barely feel anything."

I lightly caress the back of Rose's right foot, causing her to jump again. "Hey, you did that on purpose. You knew that would tickle me!"

I giggle and say, "No I didn't, but, oh well, it's time to move this up another level." I hit the level two button.

Rose feels something but she's trying to play it cool. "I guess this vibrator must be a weak one," she says.

"Oh really?"

"Yes . . . really," she snickers. "You probably need to get your money back."

"Hm, that's odd, I wonder if you can handle level seven," I say, pressing the level seven button.

Rose instantly moans and tilts her hips up. "Aw, fuck, that feels way better. You don't have to get your money back."

I then skip level eight and press on level nine. Rose closes her eyes and grits her teeth. For a second, she forgets her wrists are tied to the headboard when she tries moving her hands below her shoulders. The only thing she has success doing while feeling this vibrating sensation is kicking the blankets off the bed.

At that moment I turn off the remote, causing the vibration on the panties to stop. "Don't cum yet, I still want to try the other toy," I tell Rose as I grab the rose toy and climb on top of her kissing her lips.

"Forget that rose toy and fuck me right now, baby," Rose whispers, after kissing me.

Hey, I'm ready baby! I'M READY!

As I slide my pants off and look at Rose lying on the pillow, the flashes of the hookers come back. Shit, I should've known this was going to happen again.

I come up with an excuse and say, "I want to try this rose out on you first and then we'll go further after that, okay, babe?"

"Okay," Rose says, puckering her lips to kiss me

again.

I give her a peck. "Spread your legs," I command.

Rose smiles and spreads her legs apart.

I then place the rose toy against her clit and press the bottom of it. As soon as it vibrates, Rose knees me in my thighs. I wince because that shit kind of hurt, but when I see the look on her face, I'm able to see that she's feeling nothing but maximum pleasure. The more I click on the button and change the settings on this toy, the more Rose flinches and rocks the headboard with her tied up wrists.

"Ah, I'm sorry for kicking you, ooo, ah, I can't talk, ah!" She's literally shivering and curling the hell out of her toes.

And my damn, did she just squirt....what the hell, she squirted.

This rose toy is sucking the life out of her clit. The tone of the vibration is competing with Rose's moaning. Out of the blue she frightens me with a scream, but her gaping mouth quickly turns into a smile, calming me down.

"Aw fuck, baby, get it off me, I just came."

Damn that was only like one-minute and thirty seconds.

"I can't believe I'm about to say this, but I think I'm jealous of this little piece-of-shit," I tell Rose, as I throw the rose sex toy across the room.

Rose begins to uncontrollably laugh. "Aw, why babe, don't be jealous."

"That piece-of-shit just made you squirt. I never made you squirt before." I untie both her wrists from the headboard.

Rose sits up, rubbing her wrists. "Um, newsflash, Eddie, you've made me squirt before. I've literally watched it happen a few times. It even happened the first time I rode on top of you. Why do you think your balls are always soaking wet when I get off of you? And why do you think we have to clean up so much. You're usually so busy looking at my face or my breast when we fuck, you don't notice," she reveals.

I sigh in relief. "Oh damn. I had no idea, and I wasn't really jealous of that toy, I was just kidding around."

Rose kisses my cheek. "Yeah, right." She kisses my lips this time and says, "That thing drained me, can I take care of you first thing in the morning?"

I'll do anything to avoid sex on the bed at this time. I need a freaking witch doctor or something.

"Yup, that's fine by me. We have a busy day tomorrow, but I'm looking forward to celebrating the New Year with you."

"Me, too, handsome."

CHAPTER THIRTY-SIX

December 31ˢᵗ

No matter where I've been in the world, every hotel has had generic TV channels, including this luxury one Rose and I are staying in. And their Wi-Fi is pretty pathetic too. I can't even access my Netflix or Hulu here, due to how bad the signal is. The only good part about being awake right now is having this angel sleeping peacefully with her head on my chest. After going through a cycle of all the TV channels a dozen times, I land back on the news station where the anchors are talking about how excited they are for the New Year.

"I guess I'll just keep it on here," I say.

Rose must've heard me because she begins to rub on my stomach.

"My bad, I didn't mean to wake you up," I tell her.

She doesn't answer though, I'm assuming she's half asleep since she still has her sleep mask on; but she knows what she's doing. I start to fill up in my pajama pants, when she reaches inside and strokes my boner. She then finds my face and starts kissing my cheek.

"Alright, now you have me all worked up," I chuckle. I catch her off guard when I sneak underneath the blankets and unbutton her silk pajama top. At that moment, I squeeze and suck on her succulent breast.

"Eddie, I'm supposed to be the one pleasuring you this morning," she groans.

Yeah, she says that but there's no resistance. She has no problem with currently caressing my head as I subtly kiss her belly button, and make my way down to her lower lips. She gasps and takes a deep breath as my tongue does circles around her clitoris. "Ah yes," Rose mutters.

Without warning, I hear a few hard knocks at the door.

"Shit," I snap, popping out of the blankets, and hopping off the bed. I know exactly who it is.

Rose sits up and takes off her red sleep mask. "Who is that?" She asks me.

"It's Oscar's crazy ass. He always does this to wake me up for something important, whenever I'm at a hotel. And don't worry, I'm not gonna let him in. I'll just meet him at the front door," I answer while flipping my boner into my waistband.

Oscar continues to bang on the door like a mad man. "Dammit, Oscar, I'm up, so you can stop banging on the door now," I snap, opening the door and meeting him outside the hotel room.

"Good, I'm sorry about that, young brother, but there's been a change of plans," Oscar says.

"Like what?" I wonder.

"The New Year's Eve meeting with the producers is about to happen in one hour," he reveals.

"What? I thought the New Year's Eve party was tonight?"

"Oh, the party is still on tonight, but the producers wanted to meet with you today because they want to talk about your book right away!"

I prevent myself from smiling. "No way! Can I take Rose with me?"

Oscar shakes his head. "Nah, I wish you could, but the only thing she can do is wait outside the conference room in the waiting room if you do bring her," he reveals.

"Okay, I understand."

"I'll be downstairs in the lobby waiting for you. Try to get yourself together and down there within the next thirty-minutes."

"Gotcha man, I'll be down soon."

Rose smiles at me when I walk back in the room. "You guys sounded pretty excited out there."

I nod. "Yeah, we were. We just found out the producers want to meet with us right away. I have to be downstairs in thirty-minutes since the meeting is in one-hour."

"That's incredible, I wish they could've given you a heads up when it came to rescheduling a meeting out of nowhere like this," Rose says with a sense of logic.

I quickly go into the closet where I left my suit hanging up and throw on my black blazer, white collared shirt, and black slacks. "Unfortunately, in Hollywood this is a heads up." Before I can put on my suit, I realize that my tie isn't in the closet. I then check my suitcase and see nothing but socks, boxer briefs, and a bunch of sweats. "Damn, where's my tie?" I ask myself, looking around in my suitcase.

Rose chuckles, reaching underneath the sheets. "It's right here, you forgot to put it back after tying me up last night. Oh, and here's your belt too," she says, handing me my belongings.

I laugh. "Thanks. And come on, you can come with me, but you'll have to wait in the waiting room while the meeting is going on."

Rose pulls back the blanket and lies back onto her pillow. "Aw, that's okay, Eddie, I can stay here and catch up on some sleep while you do that. It'll take me forever to get myself together anyway."

I nod and grab one of the hotel pamphlets in the room. I'm glad Rose doesn't have a problem with me going to this business meeting without her. She's way more understanding and mature than women I've dealt with in the past. On the pamphlet it shows a menu of the hotel's room service. "Okay cool. Well, before I go, check this out. They have a good breakfast menu. Do you want strawberries with buttermilk waffles and bacon? Or would you like the maple pancakes with Greek yogurt and blueberries?" I ask Rose as I hand her the menu. "I can call room service right now and have them deliver that to you right away."

"Why are you so good to me?" she asks with a grin. "And you know what? The strawberries with the buttermilk waffles and bacon sounds excellent. I'll have that."

"Good! When I come back, I'll take you to my favorite place to go hiking in Monrovia. And hey, to answer your question, I'm good to you because I'm lucky to have you," I say before ordering room service and kissing Rose goodbye.

After meeting Oscar downstairs, we drive to a building near the Crypto.com Arena. In this building, Oscar and I meet two short middle-aged Caucasian men. They both have brown hair with shades of gray and still look a bit young in the face. Surprisingly, one guy is wearing a brown flannel and the other is wearing an orange floral print shirt. I came in thinking the men would've been dressed in suits. Now I feel like a fool, wearing a suit just like Oscar. We look like the Men in Black.

"Eddie, I want you to meet Charles and Troy," Oscar says as I shake their hands.

This is the first time Oscar has called me Eddie in years. That alone solidifies that this is the most important meeting of my life.

"Hey, how ya doing, bud?" Charles asks.

"I'm fine, just happy to be here," I reply.

"Great, we're happy to finally get the chance to talk with you," Troy says. He then pulls papers out of a yellow backpack. "I'm going to cut straight to it. We can truly develop *My Girlfriend's A Vampire* into a streaming series. You did a great job writing a classic American story about two college kids who are madly in love with each other.

We've really been missing great film ideas such as this since the 90s."

Charles puts in his two cents. "That's right. Your story isn't focused on dividing an audience, it's just a couple trying to live their love life peacefully without getting tracked down by vampire hunters. The gore is great, the sex is great, and the comedy is even better. I'm telling you, this can be as big as Stranger Things."

My eyes widen. "Hold on, did you just say that a show based on my book can be as big as Stranger Things?" I ask, doing my best to contain excitement.

Troy shakes his head. "No, I think we're doing you a disservice when we say that. It actually can be as big as Stranger Things, Game of Thrones, and Euphoria combined. We can probably dish out two seasons from your one book alone, but we think with some rewrites from you to extend the story or even possibly publishing more books as a series for us to go off of will truly help."

That's it! During the entire year I was brainstorming on a new origin story to come up with when I could've been focused on making a sequel to my vampire novel. I feel so stupid. I'm going to start working on that sequel ASAP when I get back to Blue River.

"Get the fuck out of here, that's fantastic," I say. I then cough and add, "Sorry for cursing in your office."

Charles laughs. "No problem, man, we cuss in this shitty place all the time too."

"Our partners at Warner Brothers will be back from their long vacations in February. You and Oscar will be hearing from us then! If you would like to work with us, please let us know," Troy says, handing Oscar the papers he took out of his yellow backpack.

I've never seen Oscar this quiet before. Maybe he wanted me to do all the talking in this meeting since he's been talking on the phone with these guys frequently.

"Awesome, thanks again for having me and I really appreciate you guys reading and enjoying the story."

"Of course! And you two will be at the New Year's Eve party tonight, right?"

"Yes, we will," Oscar says.

"Alright, you guys have a great one," Charles says, as we shake their hands and exit the office.

"Great job, brother man! Did you hear that? They said it has the potential to be as big as Stranger Things, Game of Thrones, and Euphoria. That's some life changing shit right there."

"My god, it is! Thank you so much, Oscar! Why the heck didn't you say anything in there?"

"Because, young brother, they already know me and talked to me before, but they wanted to meet you to see if you were the kind of person they could have a good working relationship with."

"Oh okay, well thanks again. You're the best manager ever, man!"

"No problem! You just keep pushing out your imagination and I'll make sure you financially benefit from it."

After coming back to the hotel. I head up the elevator and enter my room. But Rose isn't on the bed anymore and she has an empty plate with just a bit of syrup on it and a half empty glass of orange juice.

Suddenly I hear, "Hey Eddie! How did your meeting go?"

I find her in the bathroom with the bathroom door open. She's combing her hair. And my god, she looks sexy as ever wearing black leggings and a thin white hoodie. But who am I kidding, I think she looks sexy in anything. She's clearly ready for the hiking trip today.

I walk into the bathroom, picking her up and spinning her around. "It was incredible. I might end up striking a deal with Warner Brothers! But we don't know for sure yet. We have to make sure they are all in and that they don't rip us off on a future contract."

Rose smiles at me. "Oh my god, that's amazing! It's all going to work out the way it's supposed to, I know it will! I'm so proud of you!"

"Thanks baby." I place Rose back on her feet and hold her hand, observing her outfit. "Well, my oh my," I say, holding on to her hand. 'Spin around slowly for me."

Rose giggles and spins around slowly. I then smack her ass to make it jiggle.

"You look so fine," I tell her.

"I don't know how; it's just hiking clothes."

"Yeah, hiking clothes that look good on you."

"Well, I appreciate it, now I'm ready to see your favorite hiking spots."

I kiss her. "Okay, let me throw off this suit and put on some comfortable clothes."

$\approx$

Afterwards, we take an hour ride from Los Angeles to Monrovia. Without the horrific LA traffic, the ride would've been thirty-minutes. That's one of the things I don't miss about this place.

As we prepare to enter Monrovia Canyon Park, Rose taps my side and says, "Eddie, look!" She points to a caution sign the park has. It's displaying how we should be cautious of wild animals.

I slightly chuckle. "It'll be fine, Rose, there's no need to be scared. I walked this park countless times and I've never encountered any of these animals."

"Are you reading the sign, it says: Attention, you are entering BEAR HABITAT. Please adhere to the following rules and regulations. Keep picnic areas clean. Do not leave food unattended. Store leftover food in vehicle. Deposit trash in BEAR PROOF trash receptacles. Avoid contact with BEARS AND ALL WILDLIFE. Make noise while hiking to ward off BEARS. And do not feed BEARS or any other WILD ANIMALS. Be cautious of RATTLESNAKES, MOUNTAIN LIONS, and BEARS. My god, Eddie, did you have a death wish when you walked around this area?"

I rub my chin while reading the sign and giggle. "No, trust me, you won't see any of the animals out here. Look at all the reviews online and look at the people walking into the park right now. I'm sure they have wildlife officials patrolling the area to keep us safe. And I'll keep you safe, okay? I've protected you from a bear before."

"Alright! But I swear to god, if a bear pops out and

kills us then I'm going to kill you," Rose nervously giggles.

In the midst of our hike, Rose's nerves settle and she begins to enjoy the walk.

"When you came out to LA a few years back, how long were you out here?" Rose asks me, as we walk through the rough trails and gaze at the beauty of the mountains and the cloudy sky.

"I was here in LA for about six months. And I chose to only be out here for that amount of time so I could clear my head from a lot that happened back home in Blue River."

"Like what?"

I shake my head. "It was just a lot of things that I really don't know how to put into words," I say, doing my best to avoid a pity party conversation about myself.

"Oh…so where were you staying?"

"I lived in an apartment complex in the downtown area, but I hated it. It was too busy for me, so I would leave LA every day and go to Monrovia. I was able to take nature walks out here without all the noise and combustion, and I loved every bit of it."

"You're the first person to introduce me to going out to nature parks and realizing how peaceful it is. My Dad's version of nature walks was taking us out into the backyard to play tag."

I laugh. "Well hey, that sounds like a good exercise."

"It was, and sometimes he and my mom would set up a camping tent outside in the back yard for us. We would all sleep out there some nights during the summer after roasting marshmallows and making s'mores. Aida and I didn't like scary ghost stories so my dad would always tell us the same cute love story about how he met our mom and how it led to us being born. He would set it up like a fairy-tale. It never got old to us."

"I like that, I'm glad you still have that core memory. Those are the ones that last forever. You should keep replaying those moments he had with you and the family. When you do that, the memories play in your dreams almost every night," I explain, reaching out to hold Rose's hand.

"Is that what you do when it comes to your grandparents?" Rose wonders.

I nod. "Yeah."

"You never really told me about what happened to them, did they pass away in the same year?"

I never told Rose what happened to my grandparents because the story is hard to talk about. Talking about them is one of the few topics I get emotional about. And I don't like getting emotional, especially in front of a woman I like. To me it's a sign of weakness. "Mhm, they died eight months apart from each other," I answer.

"Aw, was it a sickness or something?"

"Yeah, they both got really sick," I answer quickly.

I believe Rose senses that I don't want to talk about it, because she kisses my cheek and hugs my forearm. She then comes to a stop and you can no longer hear our boots crashing against rocks and branches.

"Why'd you stop?" I ask her.

"I want you to know you can always vent to me, and

tell me about your feelings. You don't have to be a brick wall. Remember when you told me about your situation with Veronica during our first date? I love when you show your vulnerable side like that because you're releasing so much built-up frustration. And I don't mean to ramble I just want you to know, I'm here for you, and I won't use your vulnerability against you ever," Rose wholeheartedly explains.

I appreciate how much she cares about me. At the same time, I still don't want to open up and display my emotions too much. But I decide to tell her just enough for her to feel like we're at a nice start.

"My grandfather died from cancer . . . and my grandmother died from heart failure," I admit. "I feel closer to them when I'm surrounded by nature, rather than a church or a graveyard. And that's pretty much all I can say right now."

"That was more than enough." She kisses me on the cheek again. "Just remember what you told me, play all the great memories you have with them in your head. I'm assuming you do that already which is why you told me in the first place."

We both laugh.

"Yeah, I do it all the time. And that's right, I think if you think about the fairy tale your dad would tell you and your sister while having your backdoor camping trip, it'll really resolve the disdain you have for him. That's if you wanna get rid of that disdain of course."

"I mean, I like what you're saying, but I'm kind of thinking I don't need to remember the fairytales he told me when I'm already living in a fairytale right now. And besides, you're the one who gives me peaceful dreams," Rose says as she blushes.

"Oh really," I say, kissing her neck and hugging her from behind as we look at the mountains.

"Yes," she giggles before pausing for a moment and saying, "Ya know, with all those great qualities my dad had as a father, I still can't believe he came out to be such a disappointing husband for my mom."

"Have you ever talked to your mom about his infidelity?"

"Not really. Aida and I were the ones who discovered the text messages between him and that woman after he died. When we brought it up to my mom a week after his funeral, she looked at us as if she already knew he was sleeping with other women. She told us she would always love him and that we just need to focus on how amazing of a father he was to us."

"I think if you talk to her one more time, she'll most likely provide the closure you and your sister are looking for."

"I hope you're right," Rose sighs. "I can see why you loved coming out here. It's peaceful and soothing."

"You want to know what else is peaceful?" I ask her.

"What?"

"Malibu Lagoon State Beach. It's not as populated as Venice Beach is. Let's go now."

"But, Eddie, it's only 68 degrees and it's cloudy out. It looks like it's going to rain soon."

"So, that's even better, come on."

"You're crazy," Rose smiles as she takes my hand and we jog to the car.

≈

I drive us to the parking lot at Malibu Lagoon State Beach.

"Take off your boots, so I can carry you to the beach. I don't want to track sand in Oscar's car."

"Okay but how are we going to clean our feet?" Rose asks as she takes her hiking boots off.

I reach into the bag I brought with us and pull out a hand towel. "We can use this hand towel I brought."

"Ooo, I think I brought a washcloth from the hotel too," Rose says as she reaches into her purse.

"Perfect," I say, throwing my boots off and running around the car to carry Rose out.

She laughs and screams as I position her for me to carry her on my back. By the time we make it to the sand, I begin sprinting to the water.

Rose nervously laughs, "Eddie, I'm not trying to get soaked. You aren't going to run into the ocean, are you?"

"Why? Do you not know how to swim?"

"Yes, I can! Can you?" Rose asks me.

"Yes, I'm an excellent swimmer. I'm a greater swimmer than I am a skater or painter. So we should have no problem taking a nice deep dive."

Rose laughs. "Eddie, we don't have any change of clothes, you're going to regret jumping all the way in there."

"I'm just messing around, we're not gonna jump all the way in," I answer, continuing to sprint toward the ocean while tightly holding onto her.

Rose squeezes my neck with both her arms and buries her face in the back of my shoulder. "I hope you're telling the truth."

I rush into the ocean and stop when the depths of the water begins to get a bit higher than my ankles. "I'm not going to throw you, baby. Look, the water is only up to my ankles."

Rose lifts her head and sighs in relief. "Thank God!"

I place her down and help her stand in the water.

"Oh okay! The water isn't too bad, it feels good," she says.

"See, I wouldn't do you wrong like that," I say while looking around the beach. There's barely anyone around, besides a few people walking along the shore and it looks kind of dull right now. "I do wish the scenery looked a little better like how I remember it. The clouds are kind of messing it up."

"That's alright, I like it. It's still calming," Rose admits.

Right after Rose says that, we hear thunder and it begins to rain. In a short period of time the rain pours down even harder. We're getting swamped by nature's tears.

"I guess it's not calming anymore," I joke.

Rose stomps her foot in the water, unintentionally splashing me. "Wow! Of course it would rain after I said that."

"Since we're all wet now, I guess you wouldn't mind if I did this," I say as I splash ocean water on to Rose.

She splashes me back. "Yes, I would mind."

I then race after her, causing her to laugh and scream as she sprints out of the ocean. I catch up to her and pick her up.

"Don't throw me in there, Eddie, don't you do it," she says, staring me down as I hold her up.

Her hair is completely drenched, and the rain is splashing against our faces, but I can still see her angelic face clearly. For a moment we aren't saying anything at all. We're just staring into each other's eyes. The only thing we can hear are the waves and rain splashing into the ocean and the sand. I've been feeling someway about Rose for a longtime, but I haven't been able to work up the courage to say it until now.

"I love your eyes, Rose," I tell her, trying to work my way up to what I really want to say.

She giggles because I've probably told her I loved her eyes before. "Thank you, handsome," she says softly.

I take a deep breath and finally build up the courage to say how I feel. "And I love you...I'll always love you," I finally admit.

Rose smiles at me. A combination of rainwater and tears stream down her face. She kisses me and says, "I love you, too, Eddie. I always will."

≈

Nighttime arrives and the roads are almost dried up

since it stopped raining minutes after we left the beach. Rose and I are all freshened up, wearing our formal attire for the New Year's Eve party. I'm wearing the same black suit I had on this morning at the business meeting, and Rose is wearing a sequined black dress. At the party I quickly realize this is all about networking and introducing myself to people. Charles and Troy introduce me to a handful of directors and screenwriters. It felt like I met a million of them. I got a bunch of, "*Hi, it's great to meet you, hopefully we'll work together one day*" type of greetings. Other than that, I receive a bunch of business cards, and hand out some of my own with Oscar. I hate business cards because nowadays people just throw them in the trash and forget about contacting you. I'd much rather give my social media accounts or phone number to people during these types of events.

After all the greetings and fake conversations, people begin to leave. It's odd, seeing so many people leave at the same time when no one even made an announcement. Even the producers, Charles and Troy left.

"Oscar, why are people leaving?" I ask him.

"A lot of them are going to some after party. But don't worry about that, I would never have you go with them there. It gets crazy as shit, like some freak shit. I never go! But this right here was a get together for you to get familiar with the faces in the industry. And for them to get familiar with you. You and Rose are free to go and do whatever you want now," Oscar explains.

"Alright man, you have a Happy New Year. Tell your wife and kids I said hey," I say.

"Will do, young brother, you did great today! We're about to shake the film world. I'll make sure I drop you two off at the airport tomorrow afternoon. You have a good one and you, too, Rose. Enjoy yourselves tonight, and Happy New Year!" Oscar replies.

"Happy New Year to you, too, Oscar," Rose answers.

≈

"We're finally back inside," Rose says with relief as we enter our hotel room.

"Yeah, now it's time to celebrate," I reply, picking up the phone near the hotel lamp. I then dial room service and say, "Hello…yes, this is Mr. Valentine again. Can you bring us some champagne please, with two glasses?....Yes, thank you and Happy New Year to you too!" When I hang up the phone, I see Rose staring at me with her mouth wide open in shock. "What?" I ask.

"Are you about to drink?" She wonders.

I nod. "Yes, for the last night of the year and for us pledging our love to each other, I will."

Rose approaches me and kisses me on the lips. "Aw, you don't have to."

"I want to," I answer.

She beams at me. "Okay." She then touches the digital clock near the hotel phone and lamp in the room. It looks like she's searching through apps on the clock.

"Wait is that clock touchscreen?" I ask her.

"Yeah, duh." She giggles.

"That clock is touchscreen and has had apps on it this whole time? I had no clue. I thought all they had were horrible channel choices on the TV and terrible Wi-Fi."

"When you were at your meeting this morning with Oscar, I figured out how to work some things in this room. And the Wi-Fi is much better now. They were able to fix the signal in our room," Rose says, still tinkering with the clock.

"Oh okay, well, what are you trying to do now?"

"I want to play some music, they have the iHeartRadio app on here," Rose reveals.

Abruptly there's a knock at the door. "Room service," a voice says.

I open the door and let a man in. They've had so many different people come to our room that I don't bother asking for names anymore. The man rolls in some champagne and pours us two glasses while leaving the bottle with us, after I give him a twenty-dollar tip.

Out of the blue, I hear music coming from the clock.

"I love this song, I just had to play it," Rose says, as the song *Cupid* by 112 plays on the clock.

"You can never go wrong with 90s R&B." I take a glass and hand Rose one. I then hold it up and say, "Here's to the last day of the year."

"Cheers," Rose says tapping her glass against mine.

We both chug down our champagne, and, of course, Rose takes it like a champ. I damn near want to fall out and die from the terrible taste. I seriously can't stand the taste of alcohol, but I want to look like I'm the shit in front of Rose right now.

After we put our glasses down, I take Rose's hand. "I love this song too. Come here and dance with me." I pull her into me and place my right hand on her waist as I keep my left hand clasped with her right hand.

She then lays her head on my chest as we slow dance and asks, "Did you enjoy the party?"

"Nah, that party was boring as hell."

She snickers. "I knew you were gonna say that. Yeah, the party sucked but it was necessary, right?"

I shrug. "I guess so but I'm not a fan of the Hollywood *in-crowd*, most of them are fake. Charles and Troy seemed like the realest people there, but that's probably because they know I can make them money."

Rose nods. "Yeah. I see what you mean. There were a lot of fake smiles and people pretending to act like they cared about what you were telling them. I sensed it."

"Exactly. I wish we could've walked in then walked right on out. But other than that, I hope you enjoyed LA. Did you like it out here?"

"Absolutely, it was fun! I wouldn't want to live here though."

"Same here, it's a lot more chaotic than Blue River, isn't it?"

"Yes! And I didn't like seeing all the homeless people sleeping on the sidewalks or sleeping in tents on the boardwalk when we were at Venice beach. It's crazy! The homelessness is even worse right outside our hotel here in Downtown. I feel sad seeing all these people live like this. I'm glad we rarely see any of that at home."

"That was my main dislike during my temporary stay out here too."

"But don't get me wrong, I'm glad you flew us out here. There were a lot of things I enjoyed like the Hollywood Walk of Fame and the Wax Museum. You didn't have to take me shopping on Rodeo Drive, but you did anyway," Rose laughs.

I laugh with her and say, "Sorry, I couldn't help myself."

"Ha-ha it's okay. Thank you for spoiling me even when I don't want to be, Mr. Valentine. You made me feel like I was Paris Hilton when we were in the Louis Vuitton store. And I loved our nature walk through the mountains, but one of my favorite parts about this trip was when the homeless man sang to us at Venice Beach. That was special!" Rose lifts her head and stares deep into my eyes. "You want to know what I enjoyed most of all though?" She asks while proceeding to unbutton my suit jacket.

"And what was that?" I ask her, as she removes my suit jacket and tosses it on the floor.

"When we were hit with the surprising rain at Malibu beach, and you told me you loved me."

More R&B slow jams play through the iHeartRadio app on the clock, matching the vibe perfectly.

I place Rose's hands to the side and kiss her shoulder. I then slowly slide off her dress and un-snap her bra. "That was my favorite part too," I whisper, taking my time to remove her panties. When she attempts to take off her heels, I stop her. "Uh uh, keep those on, baby."

I then take off my clothes, turn all the lights off, and open up the curtains since we're on the top floor. The city lights delicately peek into our room, and we're seconds away from the clock striking midnight into the new year. I then place my back against the glass window and carry her on my rod so she can see the fireworks while I make love to her. I do a countdown waiting for the fireworks to go off while watching the clock. With each count there was a thrust, "Seven" thrust, "Six" thrust. Rose's left-hand presses against the window while her right-hand stays wrapped around my neck. Five, four, three, two, one. The fireworks go off and explode in the night sky. I slow down my pace to catch the reflection of the fireworks in her eyes. While staring out the window, Rose tells me this is the greatest display of fireworks she's ever seen. Eventually, after reworking my rhythm, Rose closes her eyes and wraps her arms around my neck as I rock her up and down. When we finally reach a climax, I lay her down and kiss her as we continue to watch the fireworks. This is a perfect way to bring in the New Year!

CHAPTER THIRTY-SEVEN

January 24th

A few weeks go by since that passionate New Year's Eve night. Rose and I haven't missed a step since then. Although she's back in her apartment since the Christmas break is over, she stays over my house during the weekends when she's off work. And I don't know how the hell I'm getting away with this, but I still haven't made love to her on a bed yet. I've recycled my creativity with the stair sex game, sex in the shower, sex in the kitchen, sex in my car, and we've also been having sex in my living room by the fireplace frequently. Thankfully, she hasn't asked me about making love on my bed in a while. I hope I can figure out how to get rid of this mental block by the time she does ask me again.

It's now an early Wednesday morning and I'm currently leaving the gas station. I left my house earlier to fill up the tank in my car and grab some coffee from Dunkin' Donuts. I usually do this when I'm home alone and have a serious need to brainstorm for the next scene in a story I'm writing. While driving out of Dunkin' Donuts, I see a woman slowly walking on the sidewalk. It looks like she's struggling to take each step too. Her long black curly hair looks familiar, but I haven't gotten around to passing her yet to see her face. Out of the blue, the woman passes out and falls flat onto the snow.

I instantly slam the brakes on my car and yell, "ARE YOU OKAY, MA'AM?"

Subsequently I get out of the car and come to the woman's aid. When I turn her to her side, I see that it's Aida. And just my luck, no one is around since it's still super early in the morning.

"AIDA, ARE YOU OKAY?" I shout. She doesn't answer me and her eyes are closed.

I don't want to assume the worst but I think she had a drug overdose. There's a glimpse of hope when I feel her beating pulse. Thankfully, I realize the hospital is only five minutes away. If I call 911 right now and wait, it'll probably be too late. I immediately pick Aida up and put her in my car, speeding to the emergency room.

"Everything's going to be okay. I gotcha, Aida," I tell her, hoping she can hear me.

After rushing to the hospital and slamming the brakes in front of the emergency room, I hop out the car and carry Aida inside.

"Hey, I need a doctor, I think my friend had an overdose," I tell the staff members at the hospital.

A nurse unlocks the side door for me to exit the lobby and enter the hallway. "Come on, follow me," she says. I follow through one of the many hallways that leads to an unoccupied room with an empty bed. "Are you her husband, relative, or have any type of immediate relation?" the nurse asks.

"I'm like a brother to her. I'm her sister's boyfriend," I answer.

"Alright. Well, sir, please wait in the waiting room, one of the doctors is on their way to help the patient."

"Her name is Aida! Can I stay in here until her family gets here?"

"No, I can't allow that. However, after the doctor helps her recover, I'll come and get you from the waiting room. You can come back inside then and just remember, she's only allowed to have two visitors at a time in this room," the nurse says as she begins to do her physical examination on Aida.

I listen to the nurse's orders and step out into the hall. I then walk into a restroom for privacy as I make a call to Rose.

"Hello, Rose, are you there?"

"Hey, handsome, what are you doing calling me at 4:44 in the morning? Are you trying to make a wish?"

"I'm sorry, Rose, but your sister's here at Blue River Hospital. I saw her pass out in front of the Dunkin' Donuts not too long ago. I immediately drove her to the hospital. She's in the emergency room in room thirty-eight."

"WHAT?" Rose panics. "Is she...is she okay?"

"Yes, she's breathing and has a pulse. She just isn't responsive at the moment."

I hear tussling in the background of Rose's phone,

and keys jingling. "I'm on my way," she says frantically.

Moments later, the nurse comes into the waiting room and tells me Aida's awake and that I can see her now. The sound of that brings me relief. When I walk into the hospital room, I see Dr. Lennon helping one of the nurses place an extra blanket on Aida.

I knock on the door to get their attention and not startle them. Dr. Lennon turns to me and smiles. "Oh hey, I remember you. Mr. and Mrs. Cooper brought you here when you were bitten by their dog. You're Eddie, right?"

I nod. "Yup, that's me. Hi, Dr. Lennon."

"Hey, so is this your friend?"

"Yes, do you remember the woman I came here with the last time I was here? Her name is Rose, she's on her way here now. This is her sister, Aida....thank you for saving her life."

Dr. Lennon tucks her clipboard into her arms and walks toward me, patting me on the shoulder. "No, you're the one who's the lifesaver. Without you, she wouldn't have made it," she says quietly.

"I don't know about all that. Aida's a tough person, I think she can survive anything," I say.

"No, she's right, you're a lifesaver," Aida intervenes with a smile.

"Hey, how are you?" I ask her.

"Well, I can officially say I'm done with oxy. And I'm also alive, thanks to you. Now you have my full approval for being my sister's boyfriend. You earned it," Aida jokes.

I laugh. "Thank you, I'm glad you approve of me now."

Dr. Lennon approaches Aida's hospital bed. "I'll be back in a few. I have some forms and programs I believe can help you," she says.

Aida nods.

After Dr. Lennon exits the office, Aida turns to me and says, "Eddie, I seriously want to thank you though. I would've been dead today if you hadn't found me." She has tears in her eyes.

I hate being thanked or praised for anything; especially when I think I don't deserve it. "I'm just glad you're safe now. And I want you to know, if you ever need someone to talk to, I'm always here. Since I have your full approval of being Rose's boyfriend, I hope I can have your full approval of being a big brother to you too."

Aida chuckles and says, "Yes, I'll hold you to that. You're officially my big brother."

Suddenly Rose and her mother come storming into the room.

"Oh my god, Aida!" Rose says, sprinting past me to hug her sister.

Mrs. Moreno follows right behind her and hugs them. "Don't scare me like that ever again, you understand me? I love you, baby girl."

"Please talk to us, tell us everything that's going on with you. I'm not leaving your side," Rose demands as she sits on the bed. Tears are continuously rolling down her face and her emotions are going through the roof.

"We could've lost you today," Mrs. Moreno adds.

I decide to step out of the room to give them their privacy. While sitting on a random chair in the hallway, I notice that a good thirty-minutes goes by before Rose suddenly comes out to see me.

"Hey, how are you holding up?" I ask. As I stand, she hugs me and cries.

"Thank you for being here and thank you for saving Aida. I don't know what I would do without you," Rose mutters.

Dr. Lennon makes her way back to the hall and approaches us. "Hey, Rose, Eddie told me Aida is your sister."

"Hi, Dr. Lennon. Yes, she's my sister and my mother is here too. She's inside the room with her."

"Okay good, well I have some good news that can help Aida when it comes to drug rehab programs. Would she be fine with having you and your mother both in the room while we talk?" Dr. Lennon asks Rose.

"Yeah, she should be," Rose says.

Dr. Lennon nods and heads into the room. Rose follows behind her. Before the door shuts, Rose stops it from closing and asks, "Are you coming in?"

I shake my head. "Nah, I think that discussion you guys are about to have is more of a family matter."

Rose smiles. "Eddie, you are family."

It felt good hearing that, but I think Rose and her mother deserve this personal moment with Aida.

"Thank you, I just… I don't want to make things more awkward for her. So, I'll just wait out here."

Rose nods then kisses me. "I understand. I'll be back out in a few."

After Dr. Lennon talks to Aida, I learn from Rose that Aida will be checking into the Paradise Treatment Center to overcome her drug addiction. What happened this morning was a miracle.

CHAPTER THIRTY-EIGHT

February 14th

To celebrate our love and the holiday, Rose and I spend Valentine's Day, at Giovanna's Cucina. I knew she was dying to go back there again. Chef Marisa even hooked us up with the lemon risotto again. The night went perfect, we ate and slow danced, but, once we enter my house and start kissing, I hear that question I haven't heard in a long time.

"Can we make love on your bed?" Rose asks me.

In fear, my heart begins to pound rapidly like the Earth is about to explode. The entire first half of the day was perfect, but now it's about to be ruined. I can feel it. For the past two months I've been able to avoid this by being creative with our sex, but there's no way for me to avoid making love on the bed now.

Come on Eddie you can do this.

"Damn right, baby," I courageously say, overcoming my fear and carrying Rose up the stairs.

When I lay her on my bed, I hope to God I don't see

or have any visions of the hookers I've slept with. I briefly close my eyes while taking her pants off and kissing her from her neck down to her navel.

As I begin to remove her panties and meet her lips down there, Rose stops me. "No foreplay tonight, please. Can you look me in the eyes tonight while I lay back as we make love? I feel like we've done every position in the world besides missionary."

I climb on top of her and nod. "No problem, baby."

Yeah, I say there's *no problem* but of course there's a problem. My dick isn't getting hard and Rose's face is now morphing into all the hookers I've slept with.

The visions are back! This is not good.

I blink a few times and quickly shake my head. I'm at a standstill and Rose can see it written all over my face.

She taps my chest and says, "Eddie…again? What's wrong with you, why can't we ever do it on a bed?"

"We can, baby, let me just…." I shake my head again, so I can see Rose's face. I'm still seeing the hookers. What the fuck!

"You did it again," Rose utters.

The hookers disappear and Rose's face appears clearly to me. "I did what?" I ask.

"You blinked and shook your head. You do that every time we're about to make love on any bed. Then we end up not doing it."

"I'm sorry." That's the only answer I can give.

Rose sighs. "I'm asking you this with all love. Did something traumatic happen to you when you were a child that happened to take place on a bed?"

I grimace, realizing what she was insinuating. "Oh god, no. Nothing like that ever happened to me."

"Well, is there a psychological issue when it comes to other women you may have dealt with in the past when it comes to being in a setting like this?" She asks me like a therapist.

I have to give it up to her though, because she hit the nail on the head.

It's finally time for me to come clean. I sigh. "Yeah, you may be right. I'm sorry, after my trip to Seattle, I've been having bad memories," I tell her as I lay on my back and look at the ceiling, disappointed in myself.

"Did something happen out there that I should know about?"

"No nothing happened. The book signing took place, and I was interviewed like I told you. That was it…. maybe it was the plane ride or something that brought up bad memories. I just can't seem to shake it off."

Rose lays her head on my chest, kisses me there and says, "It's okay, baby, we can just cuddle tonight. And I also think you should talk to my spiritual counselor. I'm not gonna try to pry these bad memories out of you by myself. We need an expert."

I shrug. "I don't know about all that."

"Come on, please, she's great and I guarantee she'll fix this problem you have," Rose says, giving me the puppy dog look.

I haven't seen that look in a while, but it works. As I let Rose's words sink in, I become more grateful for her. I should know by now that she's an understanding partner, and that she's trying to help me.

"Alright, I'll go," I answer, kissing her forehead.

"Thank you, handsome."

CHAPTER THIRTY-NINE

February 17th

That Saturday afternoon, Rose and I are on our way to meet with her spiritual counselor. While listening to her directions as she tells me which turns to make, my nerves are running through the roof. The steering wheel is getting a little damp due to how sweaty my palms are. Eventually, Rose's directions lead me to a cathedral called Holy Trinity Cathedral. "Sheesh, your spiritual counselor works at a church?" I ask her.

Rose laughs at me. "She does work all over the world, but she's normally working here at this church if she's not doing some type of mission work or prayer work somewhere. She's a Sister."

"Oh damn, she's a nun."

"No, a Sister," Rose retorts.

"Well shit, what's the difference?" I laugh.

"A nun pretty much works in the church and a school all day. The Sisters do more travel work."

"Are the titles that big of a deal?"

"Yes, Mr. Agnostic," Rose jokes.

After I park, we make our way out the car and walk through the cathedral doors, into the church. As I look around, I see empty pews.

Great, no one's here!

"Aw dang, it looks like nobody's here, you wanna come back another time?" I ask Rose, gently pulling her back to the exit.

She chuckles. "No, goofball, I know she's here, she just texted me. She said she'll be right out."

"Sisters have phones?"

"Ha-ha. Yes, this isn't the 1800s."

"It looks more like the 1400s in here," I tease.

When we walk past the oak carved church pews, I see a short lady dressed like a nun. At this point, I'm not sure if I should call her a nun or Sister, thanks to Rose, who has me all confused with the terms. The lady opens a door that's a few feet behind the pulpit and begins to walk toward us. After taking one look at this lady, I'm hoping my eyes are deceiving me. But as she comes closer and closer to us, I realize my eyes aren't deceiving me at all.

Rose clutches my biceps and smiles. "Hello, Sister Dolores, this is my boyfriend, Eddie....Eddie, I want you to meet my spiritual counselor, Sister Dolores," she says.

My heart skips a beat and my eyes widen. This is the same exact nun I saw in Seattle. The same one who may have caused the memories of my whore-mongering days to resurface in my brain when I'm about to be intimate with Rose. And the same one who saw Lisa come out of my bedroom. I hope she pretends not to know me, and doesn't mention anything about Lisa leaving my hotel room that night she saw me. If Rose hears about that, I'm done for.

"Hey, Eddie! I'm glad you're here. It's wonderful to see you once again," Sister Dolores says.

Dammit. Sister Dolores, do you understand anything about no snitching!

I keep my face looking joyous to hide my anxiety from Rose. "It's good to see you too, Sister Dolores."

Rose is bewildered. "You two met before?" she asks.

Sister Dolores excitedly nods. "Yes, I saw him reading to the children at the children's hospital in Seattle while I was there for a Catholic Conference."

"Oh wow! I had no idea," Rose says, hugging me tighter. "Well, I'm glad you two met already."

"Me too," Sister Dolores says, grinning at us. "Eddie is a good person. I can see it in his spirit," she tells Rose.

Aw damn, why did she say that.

I look away from Sister Dolores's eyes and stare at the ground. "I appreciate that, Sister Dolores." I then look to Rose and say, "Oh, look at that, Rose, I think I'm healed now." I slowly turn around and attempt to walk away toward the exit.

Rose and Sister Dolores crack the hell up.

In a jiffy, Rose hunts me down. "Not so fast, Mr. Valentine." She hugs me so I won't go anywhere.

"Ha-ha, I was just messing around, I wasn't really going to leave," I lie.

"It's alright, Eddie, I wish healing the soul, body, and

mind was that easy too. Rose contacted me a couple days ago because she said you both need to go through a spiritual healing journey," Sister Dolores says.

Rose nods. "Yes, Sister Dolores, I remember after you helped me fight my battle with grief, you told me to reach out to you whenever I needed you or when I found love again," she adds, laying her head on my shoulder.

Sister Dolores grins and points to me. "And Eddie is the man you fell in love with! That's wonderful! So that means you two should be ready for a couples counseling session to help maintain this love," she explains.

I shake my head. "Couples counseling? Oh nah, we don't need couples counseling. Everything's fine between us," I assure her.

"Which is why this one counseling session should show you how fine things are. If anything, you two will come out appreciating each other more after the session. I've known Rose since she was a baby, and this is the happiest I've seen her in a long time. So clearly, you're doing something right," Sister Dolores says.

Rose taps my shoulder and whispers in my ear. "Let's just give this a try. You promised me you would. This is something I wish my mom and dad would've done. It would've probably prevented a lot of bad things from happening," she says.

Christ! I just had to make that promise and Rose just had to mention her parents' relationship. I know that's a sensitive topic for her. Shit, now I have no choice but to do this session. Hopefully, it isn't too bad.

"Okay, you're right. I'm going to keep my promise,

we can do it," I reply.

Rose beams. "Thank you, thank you, thank you!"

"Alright now, step into my office," Sister Dolores demands, as we follow her to the back of the church and into an office room.

CHAPTER FORTY

Minutes later, we're sitting in Sister Dolores's office, watching her pull out a couple bibles and a notepad she places on her desk. She has life-size statues in here of Mary and Jesus that look like they're about to move. It's kind of frightening. Even the stained-glass window painting of Jesus holding a bible looks like it's staring directly at me.

"Now, I want you two to be completely honest with each other," Sister Dolores insists as she smiles at us.

Rose and I are holding hands and calmly sitting down, but my heart is racing faster than the speed of light. "Okay, honest about what?" I ask, already feeling guilty about everything.

"I'm getting to it now," Sister Dolores replies politely before continuing. "So, Eddie, here's my first question."

I slowly gulp my saliva down as I anticipate the worst.

"Is Rose someone you look forward to marrying and having kids with?" Sister Dolores asks.

That's not a bad question at all. I can give an easy

answer to that, because I already know the answer.

I gently grip Rose's hand and smile. "Absolutely, there's no other woman I would want to spend the rest of my life with. Rose means the world to me," I respond.

Loving my response, Rose grips my hand a little tighter and caresses it.

Sister Dolores nods and jots down some notes. She then looks at Rose and asks, "What about you, Rose?"

Rose exhales and says, "Oh my god, yes! Eddie has all the qualities I look for in a husband. He cares, he listens to me, he's full of surprises, he's also a protector, and a provider. And he loves to go on adventures too! I love everything about him."

Sister Dolores goes back to jotting down notes again before looking up at me asking, "Eddie, which religion do you practice?"

I shrug and say, "Um, my family is Christian, but I'm more of an agnostic."

"Are you sure about that?" Sister Dolores questions.

"Yeah, I was never really into all the church stuff. I mean, my parents are. They go to church every Sunday. I pretty much stopped going once I was allowed to say I wanted to stay home on Sundays around twelve-years-old."

Sister Dolores nods her head. "Okay, well that's alright. Do you have any belief in God or a higher power?" she asks me.

I nod. "Absolutely, something had to create the trillions of galaxies and planets out there, right? And nature looks like artwork to me. So, I definitely believe there's a creator. I just don't think this creator intervenes in the good or evil that happens in this world."

Sister Dolores looks at me and smiles. "Oh, I see. Well, you definitely aren't agnostic, my dear. You probably got your terms mixed up. You're a deist, which is basically the polar opposite of an atheist." Sister Dolores then looks to Rose and asks, "Would you prefer him to be catholic like you?"

Rose shakes her head. "No, it doesn't matter to me," she says, smiling at me. "I've been around Eddie long enough to know he genuinely has a good spirit."

"That's good, this is going great so far. Now let's keep up with the positives, before I switch to harder questions. So Rose, when did you first fall in love with Eddie?"

Rose blushes and covers her face. "Okay, so I hope this doesn't sound crazy, but I fell in love with you after our first date," she reveals.

"The DoorDash date?" I ask her, just to be sure.

"Yes," she replies.

"So did I. Shoot, I wanna say it was nearly love at first sight for me at the mall. But there was a spark during that first date that I could never forget."

"Yes, something about it just felt right, from the conversations we had in the car up to the point where I had to take you to the hospital for the dog bite. It was like we'd known each other for years." Rose says.

Sister Dolores nods and starts writing again, before looking up and saying, "Rose, is Eddie able to trust you?"

"Yes," she answers.

"What about you, Eddie, is Rose able to trust you?"

"Yes," I answer.

"That's excellent. Now here's where we test that trust," Sister Dolores says.

She then points to Rose. "Is there something you want to tell Eddie, but never told him because you thought it would upset him?"

Rose nods and turns her chair to me. She then rubs my hand hoping that it eases the blow from whatever she's about to let out. "Please don't get mad, but a couple weeks ago after work, my ex reached out to me from a new phone. He invited me out for coffee so he could apologize about everything he did to me. I wanted to see if I had the strength to face him again. And during our talk, I accepted his apology and we left it at that. Nothing happened after I left the coffee shop. And Raymond and I haven't talked since. I'm sorry I never told you. But I swear on everything, nothing happened."

I'm fucking pissed.

"Why would you go alone?" I ask her.

"Because like I said, I wanted to see if I had the strength to face him."

"You should've called me."

"It's fine, Eddie!"

"No, it's not," I snap back, standing to my feet. "I know what he did to you, Rose! Aida told me that Raymond used to physically abuse you. What if he would've hurt you again, and I wasn't there to protect you?"

Rose is already crying. "We were in a public area, I

made sure of that."

Sister Dolores gets up and hands Rose a box of tissues. "Eddie, try to relax, please. Let's appreciate her honesty and courage to share that with you just now. I know you clearly care about her, but it seems like nothing happened and she's safe. Raymond didn't hurt her."

I listen to Sister Dolores and sit back down on the chair. I hold Rose's hand and say, "I'm sorry, baby, I just wish you would've told me about what Raymond did to you."

"It wouldn't have made a difference, you can't hurt him now. That was three years ago, when you and I weren't together."

"Rose, after I saw how you reacted toward him when we saw him during that sip and paint night, I knew something was off. You mean everything to—"

"—She means the world to you, so you want to be the one that protects her, right?" Sister Dolores interrupts me.

"Yes, she means the world to me. I really can't explain what she truly means to me. It's like Rose is my angel. She's an angel that brought light into my life and freed me from darkness."

Sister Dolores smiles. "Well, that was a perfect explanation."

Rose sniffles and giggles while wiping her nose with the tissues. "Yeah, Eddie has a way with words."

"He sure does," Sister Dolores adds.

"Eddie, I love what you said and I know you mean it, but here's my problem. What darkness did I free you from? Why can't you tell me that because clearly that dark cloud is still hovering over you?" Rose asks.

"Great question," Sister Dolores says, jotting down more notes. "Rose, give me an example of what you perceive as a dark cloud hovering above him."

"Okay, for example, whenever we're about to make love on any bed—"

"—Whoa that's private," I interrupt.

"It's alright, Eddie, whatever you guys talk about here during your counseling session will remain between us and the Lord."

"Well maybe the Lord doesn't need to hear this either," I reply looking at the stained-glass painting of Jesus.

"You'll be fine, go ahead, Rose, finish what you were saying," Sister Dolores says.

"Every time we're about to make love on a bed, he freezes up. It's like he's seeing things. So we always end up making love in other places," Rose admits.

Sister Dolores goes back to writing again. I'm kind of getting tired of her pen and notepad.

"I see, so that brings us here. Eddie, is there something you need to tell Rose, but never told her because you thought it could possibly upset her?" Sister Dolores asks.

I shake my head. "Nope."

Sister Dolores raises her eyebrows and writes down some more shit. "So there's nothing in your past or present that you've done that will upset Rose?"

Jesus Christ, lady, keep your mouth shut! Rose and I are

doing good. I don't need you to fuck it up.

Rose turns to me and says, "Don't worry, Eddie, we're here for a reason. This will be a good start for us. I promise I won't be mad."

I clench my teeth. "I understand what you're saying but there's nothing for me to add or say about the past and I can't think of what would make you upset. And to be honest, why would I want to find something to make you upset? That sounds pretty dumb. I think we're all good, we should honestly just finish up here."

And with that comment I can tell I'm starting to piss Rose off. The last thing I want to do was make this conversation worse. Now I'm getting antsy and sweat beads are starting to form at the top of my forehead.

"So you've been completely honest with me ever since we started dating?" Rose asks with a frown.

"Yes," I lie.

"Really, Eddie?" Sister Dolores adds. "Does she know about what happened in Seattle?" she asks me unexpectedly.

Aw, no the hell you didn't, Sister Dolores. That's a low blow!

"What is she talking about, what happened in Seattle?" Rose asks me.

"Listen, Sister Dolores, can we talk in private real quick?"

"Nope, whatever you have to say to Sister Dolores you should be able to say to me," Rose says. She pulls more tissues out the box and begins to cry again.

"Baby, it's really not that big of a deal, trust me," I say.

"No don't *baby* me now. How can I trust you if you won't tell me what happened? Clearly something happened in Seattle or Sister Dolores wouldn't have brought it up," she says.

Jeez! This is going to suck.

I take a deep breath. "Alright, here's what happened. There was some woman who I met during my book signing. She was flirting with me the whole time and she was all over me at some club Oscar and I went to," I reveal.

Rose has an intense look on her face. "I thought you went straight back to the hotel after your book signing and interview. You never told me you went out to a club."

"I know, I'm sorry but I lied to you," I admit, feeling ashamed of myself, knowing this was only the beginning of the bad news.

Rose frowns. "You could've told me the truth about that. Like why lie about it?" She scrolls through Instagram on her phone. "What was the name of those two directors that directed that documentary again? They follow you on Instagram, right?"

"Yeah, their names are Sherry and Ben, why?" I ask.

Rose doesn't respond to me. She ends up finding their profiles and clicks on them. She eventually goes to Sherry's Instagram story highlights.

"And what else happened, Eddie?" Sister Dolores asks me while I feel like shitting myself as Rose continues her investigation.

I frown at her and clench my jaw. I can't believe I'm

being held under interrogation like this when I did nothing wrong. *Besides all the lying.*

Rose suddenly holds her phone to my face and says, "Yeah, so what the hell happened after this? I see this woman here gave you a lap dance. Is this the same one that was flirting with you? It looks like you enjoyed every second of it. There's clearly some chemistry here." Her voice is breaking and I can see the anger on her face. She's probably comparing me to her dad in a bad way now.

"Nothing happened," I answer.

"Eddie," Sister Dolores utters with her holier than thou look.

My god, I want to get the hell out of this place.

"She tried to come into my hotel room and sleep with me after that, but I told her to leave because I had a girlfriend back home who I was in love with. When she realized I wouldn't sleep with her, she left my room, and then I saw Sister Dolores in the hallway when I let the woman out. But I'm telling you both the truth. I did nothing, absolutely nothing," I explain.

Once again, Sister Dolores writes some more shit down. "I'm glad you finally spoke your truth, Eddie. And Rose, I did see a woman leave his room with a look of unpleasantness. Her hair was still neat and Eddie was fully clothed so I do believe no physical interaction happened. My only wish is that he would've told you when it initially happened," Sister Dolores says.

Rose nods and agrees with the Sister. "I wish he did too. What else have you been lying to me about?"

"Nothing, I swear that's it," I lie again.

Sister Dolores taps her desk and says, "Are you sure about that?"

"Yes, I'm sure about that, Sister Dolores. I'm not hiding anything from her. She knows everything about me," I say frantically.

"I'm sorry, Eddie, but you know everything about Rose but she doesn't know everything about you. This is supposed to work both ways," Sister Dolores reveals.

"Eddie, I love you, but if you don't come clean about what's been affecting our intimacy, then you don't have to worry about seeing me ever again," Rose says to me.

This is a lose-lose situation.

Sister Dolores and Rose are now staring at me in silence, waiting for me to spill the beans about everything. I know Rose is going to want to run away from me when I tell her the truth about why I'm the way I am. But fuck it, here goes nothing.

CHAPTER FORTY-ONE

I sigh, preparing myself to give a full confession to Rose. "After my breakup with Veronica and a couple situationships that some girls wanted to turn into relationships, I got tired of being emotionally tied to the women here. So I ended up frequently flying to Vegas and Brazil to go to brothels. I wasn't looking for relationships at all anymore, I just wanted pleasure with no strings attached. I guess you can say I was a whoremonger for three years straight," I explain.

Rose is balling her eyes out, and I feel pitiful.

Sister Dolores gets up to console her. "Go on, please continue," the Sister insists.

"I lied to you when I told you I was flying to Vegas to look over Oscar because his wife needed me to. I lied to you when I said I fed poor children in Brazil. I read to a group of kids out there once but the majority of my time was spent sleeping with hookers at these brothels. And lastly, I lied to you when I told you I didn't have sex for the past two years before I met you. I actually had sex with a hooker in Vegas a month before we met at the mall. I used protection with all those women but I always took extra precaution by getting STD tests and I never tested positive for anything. But here's the answer to what you're looking for. The reason we're struggling with making love on the bed is because I keep seeing your face morph into the different hookers. And I think it's because all the brothels had beds."

"Are you finished?" Sister Dolores asks me.

I really don't appreciate her tone and I feel like she has something against me. Wait! Now that I think about it, the visions started happening right after Sister Dolores touched my forehead and prayed for me.

"You did this," I snap, while pointing at the Sister.

"What are you referring?" Sister Dolores asks.

"That day you prayed for me in Seattle, after you saw me give the free book to the little boy with leukemia. You asked to pray for me and you touched my forehead. The moment you touched my forehead, I began to have sudden memories of the hookers I slept with. This is your fault," I say.

Rose stands up and throws the tissue box at my chest. "Are you really going to sit here and blame Sister Dolores for your freak shit? Are you that delusional?"

"It's true though, Rose, she made the strange visions happen," I admit.

"Unbelievable! I assume she made you sleep with prostitutes too, you lowlife!"

"The prostitution stuff happened before I met you, I'm a changed man now."

"Oh my god, you're disgusting. I damn near want to

throw up. You weren't honest about shit," Rose insinuates.

"I was honest with you about a lot of things but I couldn't tell you about the prostitutes. You would've never talked to me if I had told you."

"Exactly. I would've dodged a bullet and you would've saved me from wasting my time with you. And you know what? You're just like every other guy out here. You're all liars, you all cheat, and all you care about is sex."

I stand up to plead my case. "I swear I never cheated on you and you know sex isn't always on my mind. We do everything together," I say, reaching for her hand but she quickly snatches it away.

Rose then grabs her purse. "I'll be reaching out to you a little later, Sister Dolores. Thank you for everything you do for me and my family," she says as she quickly exits the office.

"Rose, wait up. Just hear me out some more," I plead.

"Let her be, Eddie, allow the time to pass by so she can heal. In the meantime, you and I have a lot of work to do," Sister Dolores says to me.

I turn my attention to the Sister with a frown on my face. "Excuse me. Did you just say we have work to do? What the hell are you talking about, lady, you just ruined the best thing that ever happened to me."

I sprint out of Sister Dolores's office and catch up to Rose, grabbing her by the arm as cold rain falls upon us.

"Babe, let's talk about this in the car. I'll be honest

about everything. A lot happened in my life that led me to those moments, but, like I said before, I'm a changed man," I explain.

Rose yanks her arm away from me. "A lot happened in my life, too, Eddie, and I was completely vulnerable and honest with you about everything. I even revealed things in Sister Dolores's office to you with no hesitation. But after watching how you handled yourself in there, I can see this isn't meant to be."

My heart was shattering with each second. This is the worst type of pain. I don't think I know how to handle loving someone when they no longer love me back. Or trying to make a relationship work when the other person feels it's over.

"No, no, don't say that, Rose. We can work this out," I plead again.

"Eddie, when you lied to me, you completely diminished the respect I had for you."

I look down at the ground because I can no longer look at the disappointment on Rose's face. "I'm sorry."

Rose doesn't respond to me, she just storms away and places her jacket above her head to prevent the rain from hitting her hair and face.

"Where are you going? I still have to give you a ride home, at least," I tell her.

"I'm catching an Uber, it's right here. I'm heading to your house to get my things. If you have any real ounce of love for me left, please allow me to grab my things in peace. I'll leave your spare keys in the mailbox when I leave," Rose says as she gets in her Uber and drives off.

As I watch the car drive away, the rain comes down even harder. All I can hear is the rain splashing against anything in its way. Right now, it's the most peaceful sound I've heard in my life, while I sit here wishing I could rewind the time to when Rose was happy with me again.

Sister Dolores opens the church doors and says, "You still love her, right?"

It takes a lot in me not to cuss this old lady out and throw a rock at the cathedral windows. After taking a few deep breaths, I finally answer her. "Yes, I still love her."

"Then I can help you because she still loves you too. She's going to restart her counseling sessions with me alone once a week. All you have to do now is start your counseling with me too. We can do it once a week, but are you willing to listen?" Sister Dolores says.

I have no choice at this point.

"Yes, I'm willing to listen."

CHAPTER FORTY-TWO

I take a seat in Sister Dolores's office and prepare to listen to whatever she has to say to repair my relationship with Rose.

"Alright, come sit down now and let's try this again," she says.

"May I ask you something?"

"Go ahead."

"Did you do some type of magic that prevented me from making love to Rose on a bed? Please just keep it real with me."

Sister Dolores chuckles. "No. All I did was ask God to allow you to face your shadows before you face the next chapter in your life. That way you'll know how to overcome any darkness that comes your way."

"Well, that prayer has magic in it or something because I'm facing some damn shadows alright. Are you sure you're able to get Rose and me back together?" I ask her.

"Trust me, I can definitely do that if you choose to work with me. You must learn how to open up again. I can tell you're a closed off individual."

I'm shocked she just said that, even though I shouldn't be. "I'm closed off," I say, pointing to myself.

"Yes," Sister Dolores confirms.

"But I spilled my guts out to you and Rose just now."

"You and I know that wasn't everything."

"How so?" I question, now I'm curious to know what the hell she's talking about.

"Well, you know when I saw you in Seattle, that was the second time I met you," Sister Dolores admits.

"No way."

"Yes way."

"I don't remember meeting you prior to Seattle," I tell her.

"That's probably because all you did was wave to me and the other Sisters. I saw you in Rio de Janeiro last summer. You were reading one of your children's books to the kids on a street corner. You had Paulina translating the words you were saying to the kids in Portuguese so that they could understand you. It was an innocent moment, but I knew you were with Paulina. She had her arm around you, and she was a known prostitute in Brazil. You two frequented the brothel she lived in many times, and she grew accustomed to you. In fact, you two became so close she imagined that you were going to marry her one day and bring her to the US. Her dream died shortly after you wrote her a letter telling her that you felt bad for leading her on and that you were never coming back to Brazil again. I also know you sent her enough money for her to move out of that brothel and live on her own. Even though she was heartbroken, she was grateful for what you did," Sister Dolores reveals.

I've been sitting here stunned by everything Sister Dolores dropped on me. "I have so many questions, but I have no clue where to start. I'm honestly speechless. All I can say is that I was in a dark place at that time in my life," I confess.

"I know you were. I'm not here to judge you, Eddie."

"How do you know about the things that transpired between me and Paulina? And it just dawned on me that you were talking about her in past tense. Did something happen to her?"

"One day she came to me and a few other Sisters and told us she wanted to change her life. She pretty much told us her life story after that, and we ended up taking her in. Paulina is no longer selling her body and she's currently going through the process of becoming a nun in Piauí, Brazil."

"Wow, that's amazing. I'm happy for her. Why didn't you tell me you'd seen me in Brazil when we met in Seattle?"

"Because I felt like I didn't need to. I had no clue you were with Rose until today. She's been telling me about some boy she likes and how much he means to her for the past two months," Sister Dolores explains.

I smile when I hear that because it makes me feel like there's hope for me and Rose.

"But do you know what her main concern was

whenever she talked about you?"

"What?"

"You weren't open and you didn't allow yourself to be vulnerable with her. She doesn't know about your hardships and sorrows but you know all about hers," Sister Dolores tells me.

"Wrong. I didn't know about the physical abuse with Raymond, remember? I had to find out from her sister, Aida."

"Come on, Eddie, you're better than that. Do you think Rose would've hidden that from you forever? Ask yourself that," Sister Dolores says.

I shake my head. "No."

"And would you have hidden your promiscuous past from her forever, if this day never happened? . . . And you don't have to answer that question because I already know the answer."

She got me there.

"My whole thing is this, why would I talk about all the bad things that happened in my life? All it does is bring me down and it isn't productive. The last time I spilled my emotions to a woman I loved is the last time I got my heartbroken."

Sister Dolores snaps her fingers and says, "Ah! That's it!" She starts to write down notes again. "We're going to cover everything that happened to you during the time frame of when you were with your ex to the time you broke up. We're going to talk about your jobs, family life, friendships, and your relationship with her during that time period. This will count as your first week. We'll keep

going each week until I feel like you're where you need to
be…. So, are you ready?"

I nod. "Yeah, I guess."

CHAPTER FORTY-THREE

That evening after an emotional counseling session with Sister Dolores, I head to my house and see that Rose left the spare key in my mailbox. I'm absolutely crushed. When I open the door and search all around the house, I see all of Rose's belongings are gone. Her jacket, her blow dryer, her nail polish, and her perfume. She took all her things with her! I could just stand here and die. I know Sister Dolores told me to take my time and let Rose have time to herself, but I feel like I need to do something about this. There must be a way I can save this relationship now. All the love Rose and I have can't go down the drain like this. I try calling her and texting her but I quickly realize that I'm blocked. I hop in my car and race to her place. After parking my car like a maniac, I rush up to her apartment and bang on her door.

"Hey, Rose, it's me, Eddie. Please talk to me. I can explain everything."

"Eddie, go away," Rose snaps.

"I'm going to stay here until you hear me out," I tell her.

"I don't want to have to file a restraining order against you," Rose replies.

After hearing that, my soul melts.

"Really?...You would seriously do that to me?" I ask.

I don't get an answer. I then lean my head against the door and say,

"Okay, I'll go, but I want you to remember this. All I ever wanted to do was bring you peace, not problems. I wanted to take part in being your joy, not your misery. And if you think you truly aren't going to be happy with me then I'll let you go. I hope someone out there is able to light up your world the way you light up mine. I hear everything has an expiration date, but I wish our love didn't have to expire...... Goodbye, Rose. I'm sorry for hurting you."

Now I have to take this pain like a fucking man and drive home, while listening to Usher's song *Throwback* on repeat. "THE LOVE OF MY LIFE, BUT I WASN'T LOVING YOU RIGHT, BABY," I sing at the top of my lungs while losing my mind.

CHAPTER FORTY-FOUR

March 16th

Over the past month my counseling sessions with Sister Dolores have been going great. I've been healing, opening up about shit I never talked about with anyone and even crying. And I hate crying but this old lady finds a way to get it out of me every time we talk. Unfortunately, Rose still hasn't talked to me and still has me blocked on everything. Not communicating with her has been hard on me. Some nights I can barely sleep. All I do is wonder what she's doing, and how I fucked up. The only thing that helps me take my mind off of her is when I write, or when Oscar calls me about the progress being made when it comes to my future deal with Warner Brothers.

But today while leaving Sister Dolores's office I spot Aida coming into the church.

She smiles at me and gives me a big hug. "Oh my god, Eddie! Hi!" She looks much better than the last time I saw her. She no longer has dark circles under her eyes and she's glowing. I can tell she's been taking care of herself.

"Hey, Aida, how are you holding up?"

"I'm feeling much better. I left the Paradise Treatment Center a couple days ago and now I'll be meeting with Sister Dolores once a week," Aida explains.

"Oh, wow, I see Sister Dolores once a week too. She's been helping me a lot," I reveal.

"That's good, did Rose introduce you to her—" She cuts herself off from talking then smacks my shoulder. "Aw no, that's right. Shit, Eddie, what happened between you and Rose?"

I shake my head. "It's a long story and you'll be just as upset as she was with me if I told you what happened.

"Come on, shoot it at me. I can't be that mad and it can't be that bad. You saved my life, remember? I owe you one by at least hearing you out and forgiving you up front. So come on, spill it. What happened?" Aida asks eagerly.

"We had a couple's counseling session with Sister Dolores, and, during that session, she found out about my past."

Once again, I find myself embarrassed to talk about it, but I'm not going to allow it to make me lie again.

"What happened in your past?"

"Due to a failed relationship that ended horribly, I ended up spending my time sleeping with women in brothels in Las Vegas and in Brazil."

Aida starts laughing. "Oh damn, so you were sleeping with prostitutes? Not the ones you pick up on the street but the ones who live in the elegant whore houses? Ooo, Eddie, you were a freaky man."

I put my head down. "Yeah, I get it."

"Look, I'm fucking with you. You aren't or weren't the only man who fucks women in brothels. It's been happening since the beginning of time and will continue to happen in the future. It's not the worst thing I've heard."

"I'm not the same way anymore, though" I say.

"I know you're not. Your actions truly showed me you care about my sister. But not only her, you care about my family as a whole. So with that being said, I want you to know that Rose misses you. She's probably acting stubborn right now but she wants you back."

"For real?"

"Yes! I want you two to get back together sooner than later. I'm so tired of her stupid ass ex-boyfriend, Raymond, trying to pursue her now that they're both single again," Aida reveals.

"Raymond's single? I thought he was married with a kid?" I should've known Raymond would try to step back into Rose's life some way or another. The way he kept staring at her outside of the art gallery that night seemed like he wasn't over her.

Aida must see the bewildered look on my face.

"They're separated and his wife took the baby with her. But don't worry, Rose doesn't want him. The only problem is that she thinks he's changed for the better. He cried to her, telling her how much he regrets hurting her and how he goes to therapy and church now. He even offered to go to church with her. Luckily, she turned down his offer, and doesn't respond to his messages anymore. She told me she heard him out a couple times so she could overcome her fear of being scared of him and that she felt like he was honestly being apologetic. But I need you to get her back, Eddie, and make sure this Raymond dickhead never finds his way back in the picture. I don't care how much counseling he gets."

"I can't do anything about that, Aida. Rose threatened to file a restraining order against me if I ever tried to see her again."

Aida waves me off and giggles. "She doesn't mean it. That's just her pride talking. She even threatened Raymond the same way when they broke up, but she should've really put a restraining order on his woman-beating ass. But look at him now, he had a chance to have coffee with her. When she told me about that I spazzed out. You had every right to be upset about it. She should've never gone out to get coffee with that man last month. Now he probably feels like he can access her anytime he wants even though she doesn't respond to him anymore."

I feel sick to my stomach because all my jealous mind can picture is Raymond's hulk looking ass fucking my beautiful Rose on a bed now that we're no longer together.

"If I just stay on the course Sister Dolores has for me, I think Rose and I will be together again just like that," I snap my fingers.

"Okay, well I'll put my faith in that too. I'm glad I ran into you today. You'll forever be like a brother to me."

CHAPTER FORTY-FIVE

March 30th

I t's a warm Sunday afternoon, and another one of my sessions with Sister Dolores is minutes away from wrapping up. "Your progress has gotten way better. I'm so proud of you. "

"Thank you. It's probably because you're great at your job."

Sister Dolores smiles.

"I know you can't tell me what you and Rose talk about during your sessions, but have you told her I've been coming to see you consistently?" I ask her.

Sister Dolores cheeses at me and says, "All you need to know is that her progress has been going well too. Just continue to be patient, Eddie. I know you both share a quality of both being an Aries and being born at the same exact time." She winks.

"Oh wow, she told you that?"

Sister Dolores doesn't respond to my question. "I know I'm a catholic but sometimes *the creator,* as you kindly put it, has a way of linking soul mates through elements beyond the church."

I'm exhilarated and feel like jumping through the ceiling. "I understand, Sister," I answer, preparing to make my way out the door.

"Okay good and Eddie?" Sister Dolores says, causing me to stop in my tracks.

"Yes, Sister."

"Make sure you're doing these sessions for *you*...not for Rose," she says.

I smirk and nod as I walk out of her office.

≈

April 4th

Today is my birthday....and it's Rose's birthday too. We still haven't talked, but a day hasn't gone by where I haven't thought about her. I haven't even told my friends or family that Rose broke up with me. I want to do something crazy like drop off a gift at her place, but that'll go against everything Sister Dolores and I have been talking about.

Yeah, fuck it, I'm gonna do it. I'm crazy about Rose.

I end up driving to a floral shop to buy thirty red roses. While I'm in line, I randomly come across Raymond. He's picking out flowers too. He has a bouquet of daisies in his hands, and, without notice, he catches me staring at him while I'm in line. I look away and do my best not to be bothered by his presence. After making my purchase through the cashier, I take my roses and attempt to leave the shop.

"YO, WHERE ARE YOU GOING AT?" Raymond yells randomly.

Did this motherfucker just yell at me? What in the world is going on?

I wanna snap, but I keep my composure and say, "Don't worry about it."

Raymond puts the flowers back on the shelf and follows me as I exit the store.

"Are you going to see Rose? I've been trying to find her new address since she doesn't live with her mom like she used to. Where does she live?" he asks me. He looks psychotic, and like he hasn't shaved or bathed in days.

I clench my fists. "I'm going to tell you this one more time. Don't worry about it. Mind your business, playboy, it's about to get dangerous for you in a minute."

Raymond just stands there and doesn't say a thing. He's probably shocked by how I'm not afraid of him. He must think I'm the crazy one now. I get in my car and begin to drive away. As I drive off, I notice Raymond quickly hops into his car and follows behind me like a mad man. There's no way this dickhead is going to follow me all the way to Rose's apartment. But what if he does? I don't want that type of energy following me to her place. I take a detour by making a sharp turn down the street, knowing Xavier's barbershop is minutes away. If shit is about to go down, I'm going to need him to be a witness. After I pull up to the barbershop and step inside, I'm immediately greeted by Xavier.

"Yo! My boy, Eddie, happy birthday, man. Jen is going to be due any day now, I can't wait. We were hoping the baby came today so he can share it with his Uncle Eddie, you feel me?" Xavier says.

"I know that's right, it's all good though, I'm just excited he's going to be an April baby," I say, greeting him, while constantly checking behind me to see if Raymond's coming.

"You alright?" Xavier questions, realizing something's off.

I nod. "Yeah, man, I'm cool."

Xavier has a young man sitting in his barber chair waiting to get a haircut. It looks like he's probably in his teens. "Okay. Are you trying to get a haircut real quick, bro?"

I shake my head. "Nah, man, I can wait till the young guy gets his cut first."

"Nope, he can get his ass up and wait," Xavier says.

The young man frowns. "Yo, what!"

"You heard me, you can wait and sit ya ass down. It's my boy's birthday today. Go ahead and sit down with ya friends while y'all wait on this cut," Xavier commands.

"Man, shit, I hate coming here sometimes," the young man says, taking off the barber cloth and hopping off the barber seat. He sits down with two other teens who look like they're waiting for a haircut too.

"Shit, well you know I'm the best barber in Delaware. You better slide your ass to Philly if you want to find the next barber that's just as good as me."

I end up sitting in the barber chair. "You didn't have

to do that to the kid, Xavier."

Xavier shakes his head and laughs. "He'll forget about it in no time. Look he's already on his phone like the rest of his friends. That's all they do is look at that TikTok shit all day anyway."

While sitting in the barber chair, I hear the door open and heavy footsteps coming my way."

"Yo, if you're here to get a cut, you're gonna have to wait in line," Xavier says, to whoever just walked inside. He places the barber cloth on me and turns on the clippers.

"Man, shut the hell up." I suddenly feel wind brush past me as Xavier gets shoved into a mirror. The mirror shatters and now there's glass everywhere.

"OH SHIT!" One of the teens sitting down shouts. All three teens are now holding up their phones and recording what's going on.

I immediately rip off the barber cloth and hop to my feet to help Xavier. And who do I see? Fucking Raymond's crazy ass. He's standing there giving me this psycho look again. This man really has mental health issues.

"WHAT THE FUCK IS WRONG WITH YOU? I hardly even know you. Are you on drugs?" I ask him.

"Rose is all mine, don't try to get her back. She's going to be my wife. Stay away from her, Eddie."

"Yo Eddie who the fuck is this?" Xavier asks, holding his clippers tightly, preparing to use them as a weapon.

Before I can answer Xavier, Raymond charges at me.

I instantly step to the side and trip him, causing him to fall onto his head.

The teens laugh at him while they continue to record everything taking place.

"Raymond, get the fuck out of here. I'm not trying to hurt you," I inform him.

Raymond stands to his feet and charges at me again but, this time, he slows down when he's inches away so he doesn't get tripped again. As he tries to grab me, I punch him directly on his throat. He wheezes and holds his neck. I then take him by the head and pull him down to knee him directly on his forehead, causing him to fall on the ground again. I drag Raymond by his collar and push him out of the barbershop. "Take your ass home or somewhere far from here, man," I tell him.

He continues to lie flat on the concrete sidewalk. I hope I didn't accidentally kill this bastard.

"Damn, he knocked his big ass out," I hear one of the teens mention as I shut the door, making my way back inside.

Xavier turns off his clippers and smacks his barber chair in excitement. "That's right, that's my fucking dawg right there! I be trying to tell people they can't fight Eddie, that's Bruce Lee right there! You see that, young boys? And don't go around posting that video. Just delete and keep that shit in the barbershop between us."

The teens become wide eyed like they've done something wrong.

"Man, what y'all do?" Xavier asks them. He picks up a broom and begins to sweep the glass on the floor.

"We recorded the fight as a live feed. People already seen it and it's already out there," one of the teens reveal.

Xavier's sucks his teeth. "Man, you young boys always have to record shit and show it to the world. I hope my son never turns out like y'all."

I laugh while helping Xavier clean the shattered glass up. "It's cool, don't worry about it. Look, bro, I'll be back, I'm about to go check on Rose because he's probably about to try to see her. He clearly needs to be in an institution or something."

"Alright, bro, let me know if you need me," Xavier says.

"Can I get back in the barber chair now?" I hear the young man ask as I leave the barbershop.

When I step outside, I see that Raymond and his car are now gone. I attempt to give Rose a call, but I realize I'm still blocked.

Dammit Rose!

I hop in my car and quickly get on the highway. But lo and behold, as soon as I enter the highway, I see that Raymond hasn't made it to Rose's place yet. He's actually still stalking me down. I see him directly in my rearview. He's tailing me like crazy, and randomly starts honking his horn. *What the fuck?*

Suddenly he rear-ends my car while we're still driving.

"Oh, this motherfucker is trying to kill me."

People on the highway are honking their horns at Raymond to try and get him to stop, but there's no stopping this mad man. I take the nearest exit I can find, so he doesn't put any innocent lives at risk by trying to hurt me. And it doesn't help that a lot of cars see what's going on. Some of the nosey fools follow us down the exit. But maybe they're looking out for me and have called the police. I don't need law enforcement helping me. I can handle Raymond on my own. It's gonna be a nice old-fashioned ass kicking. After parking, I step out the car and say, "You want me to kick your ass again, Raymond? I kind of gave you a pass the last time."

"Rose is for me, Eddie. I'm going to do right by her this time around. I'm going to do this family thing right too. Let me start this family thing over, but with her this time. I don't need you in the way," Raymond says.

The closer he walks toward me and my car, I notice he's crying, but he maintains a frown.

"Well, go ahead and find a way to get your wife and kid back."

"Hey, guys, is everything okay?" A random woman asks that followed us off the highway.

I turn away from Raymond to answer her. "I'm okay. But something is mentally wrong with this guy."

Suddenly I hear, "Hey, Eddie."

As I turn around, I see Raymond holding a handgun. He's pointing it directly at me.

Shit! I should've brought my gun from home with me.

Before I can take off running, Raymond shoots me on the right side of my chest. I don't feel a thing at first. All I hear are screams and I notice that, instead of standing, I'm now staring at the blue sky while lying on my back. When I hear police sirens, I start to feel an excruciating pain in my chest. It feels like a bee-sting made of lava. I think I'm smelling smoke, too, or is it my burning flesh? Raymond approaches my body and stands over top of me with the gun pointed at my face.

"DROP YOUR WEAPON AND PLACE YOUR HANDS ABOVE YOUR HEAD," a police officer orders.

Raymond pulls the trigger, but thank heavens, this maniac's gun jams. Another police officer who crashes into the back of Raymond's car wastes no time shooting Raymond directly in the head. It's the scariest thing I've ever seen. Half of his face is gone and he slams to the ground.

Yup! I'm probably gonna have to seek counseling from Sister Dolores for the rest of my life now.

After seeing Raymond's half shot off face lying next to me, the burning sensation in my chest finally stops as everything goes black.

CHAPTER FORTY-SIX

I open my eyes and see I'm lying down on a hospital bed. My hands are hooked to IV's and I see Dr. Lennon and some nurses checking on me.

"We have to stop meeting like this, cutie pie. If you want to go on a date all you have to do is say so," Dr. Lennon jokes. I'm assuming she revived me or something but I still feel drowsy. I can't even talk, all I want to do is sleep.

"Aw, that morphine must still be hitting you hard. We had to give you emergency surgery to get that bullet out. Go ahead and get your rest, okay, Eddie? Everything will be okay," she says to me.

I can't respond but I want to thank her. All these thoughts are running through my head right now. Oh my god, there's something in my nose and wrapped around my mouth! Am I on a ventilator? Am I going to die? I start to panic but drift back into sleep.

≈

I don't know if it's days, hours, or minutes later, but

I'm in and out of sleep; closing my eyes and opening them again. My head is heavy and I can't move my neck from side to side. It feels like my neck is numb. As I stare at the ceiling, since that's all I can do, the only thing I'm aware of is multiple conversations taking place. Well at least what I think are multiple conversations taking place, but I'm probably hallucinating.

The entire time I'm in and out of sleep, and looking at the ceiling or closing my eyes, I feel someone holding my hand. They aren't saying anything but they're comforting me. It's probably a nurse, but whoever it is smells like Rose's vanilla flower bomb fragrance.

"He's going to be alright, we were able to save him. He suffered a gunshot wound to the chest and severely sprained his neck. Thankfully we were able to get the bullet and bullet fragments out," I hear Dr. Lennon tell someone.

During my lost track of time, my eyes are heavier than ever. There's no way I'm opening my eyelids now. My brain is up and I'm aware of the sounds around me, but the rest of my body has completely taken over as far as resting is concerned.

At one point, I hear cries coming from my mom, I can recognize her cries anywhere. "My baby, you're gonna pull through, I've been praying all day for you," my mom says.

"Your son is going to be fine. Some good civilians provided us with a video of the entire situation. The suspect was the aggressor and was on Xanax. He's been on the run from us for physically abusing his wife.

Unfortunately, he killed her and had her stuffed in his trunk. Their baby was found safe alone in their house. Although the suspect is now dead, we would like to talk to your son whenever he wakes up about this situation. Here's my card. Please give me a call when he wakes up." I'm assuming that was a voice of a detective. And shit, man, Raymond killed his wife, that poor woman. I feel bad for the baby too. Now the baby has to grow up without their parents.

Time briefly goes by before I hear more voices.

"Aw, damn. Eddie, if I would've known that bitch ass dude had a gun, I wouldn't have let you leave the shop. I should've stabbed him with my clippers. I swear on my momma I should've stabbed his big ass yo! Man, you wouldn't believe this, but Jen is in labor right now, upstairs. You can't die on me, man. Your nephew is gonna be born soon." Xavier is crying. "Please don't die on us, man."

"Eddie, you better wake up. I still need to apologize a million more times to you for thinking Bianca was telling the truth about you on her blog, okay?" Hannah cries. "And besides, Jen and I can't deal with these knuckleheads, Chris and Xavier, alone. We need you here with us, you're the levelheaded one. And we need you here to see the baby being born." That's all Hannah can let out, before she completely breaks down. I can hear Chris crying in the background, too, while trying to console Hannah.

Chris and Hannah suddenly fade away, now I hear Aida's voice. "Hey I saw that video online. You kicked

Raymond's ass. And I'm glad that bastard got what he deserved, he's finally gone," her voice breaks. "But now I need you to stay, we don't need you to be gone too." I can hear Aida blowing her nose. "You better fight for your life, Eddie, so you can wake up and marry my sister. I need you as a brother, don't forget about that part."

If Dr. Lennon told everyone I'm going to be fine, then what's with all the emotional shit? And when are my eyes going to stop being so heavy.

Moments after that, I hear my sister sprinting through the hall crying, "Eddie!" I then hear her footsteps coming into the room.

"Hey, Rose, I'm so glad you're here with him, holding onto him. How has he been?"

My god, it's been Rose holding my hand the whole time? No wonder I could smell her fragrance.

"Hey. Emma, I think he's doing better." Rose instantly breaks down into tears after saying that. "I can't lose him. I love him so much," she sobs to my sister.

I can hear Emma speedwalk to her and hug her. "You're not gonna lose him. One thing I know about my brother is that he's a fighter. He'll fight anything; even death."

I hear Rose sniffle and say, "I'm sorry, I'm a mess. Here I am telling his own sister that I don't want to lose him. And you're handling this better than I am."

"Girl, you don't have to apologize," Emma says. "It makes me happy seeing you love him the way you do. Have you heard any updates from the doctors?"

"The doctor said he's gonna be in and out of sleep

for a while. Your mom and dad will be right back up too. They went to the cafeteria to get food for us," Rose says. My god I miss the sound of her pleasant and soothing voice.

I feel a hand clench my wrist. "Damn, Eddie." Yup that's my sister Emma. Always cursing like me. "You can't catch a break," she adds.

"Have you talked to him recently?" Rose asks my sister.

I think Rose is wondering if I told Emma about our breakup. Don't worry, Rose, I didn't say a thing. Emma still thinks we're together.

"Not since Brian and I left for our cruise. He told us to enjoy ourselves and that he would check in on Jaden and Joshua at our parents' house while we were away. I haven't had the chance to talk to him since we've been back though," Emma answers.

"Oh, okay. I hope you and Brian enjoyed your cruise. How was it?"

"We sure did, girl. It was fun, I loved everything about Hawaii, we were able to visit all four islands. But after a while, I started missing my babies and couldn't wait to come back home."

Rose laughs. "I understand, I can only imagine how I'll be with my kids one day."

"Mhm, you'll be just like me." Emma chuckles.

"Hey, so I overheard you say that Eddie can't catch a break. He hasn't been shot before, has he? I'm not trying to be nosey or anything, I'm just wondering that's all," Rose says innocently.

"Oh no, you're all good girl. So I don't know if Eddie ever talked to you about this or not but three years ago was the most depressing time for him."

"Because of that Veronica girl, right?"

"Oh, not just because of that bitch! She was just the icing on the *shit cake* for my brother. It was a hard year for the entire family but he got hit the worst."

Come on now, Emma, don't tell her about everything I went through. I don't feel like reliving that crap and crying in my sleep.

"So when our grandpop was dying of colon cancer, Eddie was doing everything in his power to try to cure him. The doctors told us that our grandfather was already at the stage four symptom of his cancer but Eddie felt like the doctors weren't trying hard enough to treat him."

Suddenly the memories strike my mind of me and my grandmom taking care of my grandpop while he was sick. I'm doing everything in my power not to relive it and get it out of my mind, but my sister telling Rose this story isn't helping.

"Eddie was online contacting naturalists and health gurus who told him he could cure our grandpop with certain foods and herbal teas. So he went ahead and bought organic fruits and vegetables and made all the teas you could think of. My grandpop ate and drank whatever Eddie made for him but he also insisted on continuing to go to the doctor to get his chemotherapy too. It wasn't too long after that when our grandpop could no longer walk and his body began to deteriorate. Eddie couldn't believe that none of the health remedies worked. When our grandpop eventually died, it tore him apart."

Yup here we go, I think I'm crying. I can't feel anything on the outside, but the inside of me is really crying right now.

"Aw, I know that had to be a hard thing to process,"

"And, girl, that's just the beginning. Eight months later he found our grandmom passed out on the dining room floor," Emma says as her voice breaks from the sorrow she's currently feeling.

"Aw, no," Rose replies.

It sounds like she just gave my sister a hug.

"When he took her to the hospital, they told him she had suffered a heart-attack. She was conscious for a while at the hospital, we were able to talk to her and hug her but she eventually passed away while she was sleeping from heart failure. I think she must've really missed my grandpop," Emma explains.

"That's so sad," Rose says. Now she's crying. I can't take this!

"Eddie stayed at our grandparents house since they left it to him in their will. During that time, he was teaching writing classes to the youth. One of his students was a fourteen-year-old boy named Shawn. He was in a juvenile detention center but Eddie saw the potential Shawn had when it came to being an author. Unfortunately, when Shawn finished his time at the juvenile facility and was sent back home, he was shot in the head by a rival gang member," Emma explains.

Man, I remember Shawn was so excited about the plans we had to create his first book one day. He couldn't wait to get out of juvenile hall and get back into regular school. He was like a little brother to me. That poor kid, he had an entire life ahead of him.

"And lastly that year, another student of his who took part in his writing classes was an eighth grader named Tonya. Eddie said she enjoyed writing fairy tales and he was impressed with her publishing ideas. Unfortunately, he didn't know she was being bullied at school as well as cyberbullied. I guess one day Tonya couldn't take the bullying anymore and took her own life by overdosing on sleeping pills. She wrote a suicide note thanking her parents and Eddie for being her only true friends and named the people who bullied her in school. That was the straw that broke the camel's back right there. Eddie eventually ended his writing classes after that. His heart couldn't take it anymore," Emma explains.

"He never told me about any of that. I wish he would've," Rose says, continuing to cry with my sister.

"He's probably still being secluded when it comes to his vulnerable emotions with you because of Veronica. Can you believe that while he was going through *everything* I just told you about, she had the nerve to treat him like shit and never came to visit him here or see the family?"

"Goodness gracious, I know you wanted to strangle her," Rose says.

"I wanted to do more than that to her for hurting my brother," Emma replies.

"This has been on my mind a lot lately, because I remember he specifically told me what happened between them. But what made him think she was the one for him even though she was treating him like shit?" Rose questions.

"Girl, I think it was because Veronica snatched him up at a time when he wasn't mentally strong. I guess during their messages, she was telling him everything he wanted to hear. He was already going through a depression while our grandpop's health was declining. When he lost all hope, he ended up going to a fortune teller. Apparently, she didn't give him good news when it came to our grandpop either, but she did tell him he would find love soon, and I guess he thought Veronica was it, but clearly it wasn't her. I think the love she was telling him he was going to find was referring to you."

≈

While Rose and Emma stay in the hospital room, I suddenly hear another voice.

"Hello, hello, thanks for contacting me, Rose. Has Eddie spoken or moved around yet?" the voice asks. By now I recognize that voice too.

"You're welcome, Sister Dolores. This is Emma, Eddie's sister. And Emma this is Sister Dolores, she—"

"—I'm just an old lady that works for the Lord and likes to pray for people," she interrupts Rose. "Do you mind if I pray for your brother? It'll be quick." Sister Dolores says.

"Sure, that's fine by me," Emma says.

"Um, sorry only two people should be in here at a time unless you're family, ma'am," a nurse says.

"Oh hush, child, I'll be quick." Sister Dolores places her cold palm on my forehead and prays for me.

As she leaves her palm on my forehead, I feel like I was shot with adrenaline. My eyes are no longer heavy, I can feel my body, and fuck, . . . my chest hurts! I knew this lady had powers. She's hiding that shit from the world!

"Alright, thank you, it was nice meeting you, Emma! And Rose, I'll be doing some work in Thailand for three weeks. Keep me updated on everything while I'm gone, okay," Sister Dolores says, as I hear her little footsteps scurry out the room.

Suddenly that adrenaline goes away and I can feel the morphine all over again. Well damn, what did you give me, Sister Dolores, a tiny whiff of cocaine? And, just like that, I feel myself shutting down into a deep sleep again.

CHAPTER FORTY-SEVEN

April 11ᵗʰ

I wake up to Rose lying in the hospital bed with me. Clearly a day or two has passed. At least that's what I think.

"Rose," I croak.

She lifts her head, smiles, and kisses me on the cheek. "You're awake," she rejoices. She taps me gently on my nose. "Happy belated birthday and don't scare me like that again," she adds with tears in her eyes.

"Happy belated birthday to you, too, and I won't. And whatever happens from here on out, please don't ghost me like that again," I say to her.

"I won't, I promise I won't," Rose informs me.

"I miss you," I tell her.

"I miss you too," Rose replies. "You really couldn't wait more than an entire month and a half without us communicating, could you?"

"Nope, I couldn't. I just knew I was gonna die if I had to wait any longer," I joke.

Rose smiles and cries. "I'm so sorry, Eddie, I'll never do something that childish again. I don't wanna block you from my life."

"Don't apologize, let's wipe the slate clean, okay? Hi, I'm Edward Valentine the Fourth but I prefer people to call me Eddie. What's your name?"

Rose wipes her tears and giggles. "Hi Eddie, I'm Rosalina Moreno, but I prefer people call me Rose."

"Well Rose, now that I just met you, I have to tell you something."

"And what's that?"

"I love you."

"I love you too."

We kiss each other. "I hope I don't stink too bad," I tell her.

Rose sniffs my neck. "You smell good. You smell like hospital soap," she giggles. "I helped the nurse give you sponge baths," she adds.

"Thank you for taking care of me and being here with me the whole time. I couldn't speak but I felt your hand holding mine the entire time."

"Of course, I'll never leave your side again."

I notice a bunch of balloons and cards in the room. "What happened in here? Did Chuck E. Cheese stop by?"

Rose laughs. "There's that sense of humor I miss. And no, goofball, the Coopers, Principal Hardwick, Eartha, my mom, and plenty other people dropped off get well cards and gifts for you. Even Oscar and his wife flew out here to see you. His wife was really sweet."

"Oh yeah, Ms. Irie is a sweetheart. I should've made

time for Oscar to introduce you to her when we were in LA."

"It's fine, you can't do everything for me, Superman! And Eddie, you were right!"

I raise my eyebrows. "Right about what?" I ask with confusion.

"About me going to my mom to finally get the answers I needed about what went wrong between her and my dad. She told me they both were going through a rough patch, and that they both could've been better partners to each other. But they always kept me and Aida out of it. So we would've never known about my dad going to see another woman if we hadn't looked through his phone after his accident. My mom told me they were separated during that time and would've been filing for a divorce the following month if my dad hadn't died that Christmas. This provided so much clarity for me and Aida," Rose explains to me.

I kiss Rose on her forehead. "I'm glad that conversation helped. That probably helped your mom just as much as it helped you."

Rose nods. "It did. And just so you know, that fight between you and Raymond surfaced all around the internet. I know he's dead now but I'm glad I saw footage of you kicking his ass. It felt good seeing him take a beating for once. It's so sad what he did to his wife. After seeing her wear those sunglasses the night we saw her by the art gallery, I had a feeling he was beating on her. But I didn't want to jump to any conclusions and figured he was a changed man. And I know I didn't get along with her but I wouldn't wish death on my worst enemy."

I shake my head. "I can't believe he did that shit. That was nothing but evil."

Rose almost cries but she stops herself. "That could've been me."

"But it wasn't, babe. You're here and you're safe."

Our conversation is interrupted when Xavier and Jen come into my room holding their newborn son.

"Hey, everybody," Jen says, walking in her hospital gown. "Meet Xavier Jr."

"Aw, he's so cute," Rose says.

"No way. was the baby born on our birthday?" I ask.

"No, he was born yesterday on the tenth."

"We thought he was going to be born on your birthday but she was just experiencing contractions, that's all."

"Wait, what's today?" I ask.

"The eleventh, babe," Rose informs me.

"I've been in this hospital for seven days?" I say in shock.

"Yes," Rose says.

I sit up, feeling a sharp pain in my chest. It's not as bad as it was seven days ago, but I'm ready to go.

"Take your time, bro, don't rush it," Xavier says.

"Man, I'm ready to get the fuck out of here," I tell him.

The next day, Dr. Lennon examines me one last time and finally gives me permission to be released from the hospital. I'm grateful as hell and happy I can see the real world again. I don't know if I could've lasted sitting in that hospital for another week.

CHAPTER FORTY-EIGHT

*April 27*th

After thanking Sister Dolores a million times for healing me spiritually and thanking Dr. Lennon a million times for saving my life, I find myself waiting in the house for my body to come back to full health. My wounds do feel much better and I'm almost completely healed. Other than this big white bandage wrapped around my entire chest like a mummy, there's nothing to complain about, and I'm happy to be alive. And I'm glad I have another day with this beauty. This is the first time Rose has spent a day with me in my house since February. I'm currently staring at her as she lies on my bed staring back at me. The rays from the sun peek through the curtains and shine on her golden tan face as if she's an angel. My goodness, I miss her physical love, her seducing touch, and I miss making her climax.

"I wanna make love to you, right here and now," I randomly tell her as we lie down, staring at each other.

Rose smiles and says, "On the bed?"

I nod.

"Are you sure?" Rose asks me.

I nod again. "Take your clothes off and lie on your back," I tell her.

Rose bites her lip, taking the baggy white t-shirt off, exposing her exquisite breasts. She lies back onto my pillow as I help her remove her sweats and panties. My shirt is already off since I'm wearing this chest bandage, but Rose helps remove my sweats and my boxers, allowing my erection to spring free.

"I miss this," she whispers.

I don't say a word. I climb on top of her and slowly kiss her, allowing our tongues to dance together. As we kiss, I place both my index and middle finger inside her and moderately massage her clit in circles. I can feel her mouth open wider as her tongue stops dancing with mine. She gasps and moans while arching her back. I continue massaging her clit in a circular motion, but at a quicker pace. I'm enjoying this moment. I love making her feel good.

Rose whispers, "I want it, baby. Let me have you again."

After hearing those words and feeling her amazing hands, my erection grows harder and up to its fullest length. I slide my way in between her thighs, spreading them apart so I can ease into her wetness. For the first time, I'm able to look her directly in her eyes as she lies on the bed and stares back at me. Her face doesn't change into the women I've slept with in my past. Rose is still Rose. I smoothly rock my hips back and forth into her warmth while sliding my hands underneath her ass and squeezing it. Rose wraps her legs around my waist and clenches the back of my neck. We begin kissing again, tonguing each other down. We're savoring each moment, and her heat is hugging my member. I want to give her a baby right now. I pick up the pace to keep her stimulating.

"Aw, fuck," Rose moans.

My abs rub against her flat belly as I continue to pump harder and breathe heavier while gazing into her eyes.

"I'll never stop loving you," I say in between my heavy breathing and the bed rocking.

My headboard is knocking up against the wall. And the entire bed is vibrating. "AH, ME TOO BABY," she squeezes me tighter as her toes are curling.

I thrust faster, suddenly she's squirting all over my rod. I take my eyes off of her for a moment just to witness what I'm feeling. The sight of her enjoying pure pleasure has me cumming at this very moment.

"GAWD DAMN," I shout as I pour all my life into her.

It was the best lovemaking session we've ever had, because our love means so much more now.

CHAPTER FORTY-NINE

April 4ᵗʰ (the following year)

A year goes by and Rose and I are still together, and our relationship is stronger than ever. Today is our thirty-first birthday and oddly enough, this has been the best weather we've had all year. It feels like the beginning of summer! Everyday Rose never forgets to remind me of how our year has been filled with blessings so far. Sister Dolores says the same thing to me on occasion. I'm still not a religious guy but I can't say they're lying. We've been having a great year. In January, I was able to strike a partnership deal with Warner Brothers and I have creative control of the upcoming streaming series based on my vampire novel. *My Girlfriend's A Vampire 2* has been written as well. Even though the film series and the novel's sequel won't come out for another year, these Warner Brothers checks are the highest checks I've ever received in my life. In February I was able to be the best man at Xavier's wedding. I'd never seen him cry that much the day he saw Jen walking down the aisle. I hope I can keep it together when it's my turn to get married. That night we partied at the wedding reception like there was no tomorrow. By the way the couple was drinking I think they almost forgot they had a son to take care of. But hey, that's wild ass Xavier and Jen for you. During the month of March, Aida earned a job as a substance abuse counselor. Life really came full circle for her. She's helping a good amount of people overcome drug addiction. We're all proud of her.

Now everything leads me back here to this beautiful Friday. It's a school day so I couldn't plan anything extravagant for our birthdays since Rose has work. I wanted to fly out to Hawaii on Monday so we could celebrate a whole week out there. I've been dying to go to Hawaii ever since Emma and Brian told me how amazing their cruise trip was when they went to visit the islands. Instead of leaving on a Monday, Rose said she would rather start our birthday celebration when she gets off. And that we could fly out there this Saturday. I tell her all the time that she can leave Maple Elementary after my nephews graduate from kindergarten. With the money I make, Rose doesn't have to work at all. But she constantly reminds me that she loves her job and doesn't want to be at the house, bored and doing nothing. I understand her love and passion for teaching, but I'll be damned if I don't make our birthday a memorable one.

I pull up to Maple Elementary to pick up Rose and my nephews from school. Rose steps outside walking down the school steps, while holding my nephews' hands. My nephews have nothing but smiles on their faces as

Rose walks with them. It looks like her cream-colored blouse and her sky-blue jeans are glowing, and that's all because of her angelic essence.

Damn she would make an amazing mother.

"Were you guys good for Auntie Rose today?" I ask my nephews as I step out and help them get in the car.

"Yes, Uncle Eddie," my nephews say at once.

"They're always good," Rose says as she caresses my goatee and hugs me. Of course she adds a smile too. Even a year later, her smile still gives me butterflies.

"Don't forget to tell Principal Hardwick that you'll be going to Hawaii this weekend with me and we'll be gone all week. I hope they find a substitute because I'm not losing this argument again. We're going to celebrate your birthday right."

Rose snickers. "Yes, I already told her, and don't forget this is *our* birthday. I have a lot of gifts for you, and I have a special surprise for you in Hawaii."

"Oh okay, I can't wait to see this." I wink at Rose.

"Why are you and Auntie Rose talking about Hawaii? I thought we were going to the zoo today." My nephew, Joshua, says.

"We are, Joshua, I promise. We're going to the zoo."

"What about Hawaii?" Jaden asks.

I laugh. "Hawaii is for me and Auntie Rose when we go on a trip."

"Oh ok," Jaden replies.

At the zoo, we're watching rescued tigers and rescued gorillas enjoy the habitats the zoo created for them. As the animals run around and entertain themselves, my nephews are being entertained by watching their every move.

As we continue to walk through the zoo past Polar Bears, giraffes, and penguins, I stop and take a look at Rose's beautiful face.

She smiles at me, running her hands through her hair. "Hey, why did you stop walking, goofball?"

I ignore her question and ask, "What are you doing forever?"

Rose twiddles her fingers while cheesing. "That's a unique and silly question. Why did you ask me that?" She squints at me, growing mysterious.

"Because I want to know what you have planned forever?"

Rose twiddles her fingers again and smiles. "Hopefully, being somewhere by your side, why?"

I smile. "Well, I was wondering if you wouldn't mind marrying me too much."

Rose throws her head back and laughs, remembering the marriage proposal scene we watched from Rocky. But then it hits her when she sees me get on one knee and pull out a ring box. She suddenly gasps and waves her hands in front of her face to prevent herself from crying. But the tears fall anyway. Suddenly, Mrs. Moreno, Aida, Sister Dolores, my friends and family, Rose's friends and coworkers surround us at the zoo.

Rose smiles brighter than ever as she notices everyone around us and suddenly whispers, "Yes," then adds "YES! I'll marry you. This ring is huge! It looks like a glowing star."

I put the shimmering diamond ring on her finger and stand up to embrace her as we kiss. And at that point we hear a round of applause.

I then pick Rose up and kiss her while spinning her around. As I look up at the sky behind her face, I can see she truly was my angel who brightened up my world that was full of darkness.

"This is the greatest gift ever! I guess I can't wait to surprise you in Hawaii now since all of this is happening. I have a gift for you too Eddie," Rose says to me, while pointing to her belly.

My eyes widen. "No fucking way." I smile. "We're having a baby!"

Rose nods. "Yes."

I kiss her and smile. "That ring isn't the greatest gift ever, you're the greatest gift ever," I tell her.

Within our first decade of marriage together, and three kids later, Rose and I continue to find new ways to fall in love over and over again. I wouldn't trade my wife for the world. We're committed to each other, committed to communication, and committed to embracing our strengths and flaws each day. She's the love of my life.

I guess true love does exist and it wasn't a crock of shit after all.

-Eddie Valentine

ACKNOWLEDGEMENTS

I want to thank legendary creators and comedians for inspiring me to write this novel. Here's a special thanks to comedians, Patrice O'Neal and Jim Norton, for talking about their wild trips to Brazil on the radio years ago. Thanks, Seth Rogen and Evan Goldberg for creating the film, *Superbad*. Thank you, Richard Pryor, for creating the film, *Jo Jo Dancer, Your Life Is Calling*. Nicholas Sparks, I can't thank you enough for writing the novel, *The Notebook*. Lastly, I would like to thank E. L. James for writing the *Fifty Shades of Grey* novel. These specific films, novels, and people inspired me to combine comedy, action, life, romance, and eroticism to ultimately create my novel, *A Rose for Rose*.

ABOUT THE AUTHOR

Author Lenny Williams has been writing for ten years. As a creator, he believes nature, the night sky, and dreams inspire most of his work. His past published works consist of four children's picture books, a fairy tale, a horror screenplay, and a paranormal romance novel. When it comes to Lenny's adult writing, he's inspired by many authors, screenwriters, and creators to provide unique aspects of storytelling. These inspirations include Richard Pryor, Seth Rogen, Donald Glover, Lil Dicky, Nicholas Sparks, and E. L. James. Williams credits them for bringing life into their art.